P9-DGP-955

Sinister Shorts

ALSO BY PERRI O'SHAUGHNESSY

Sinister
Shorts

Perri O'Shaughnessy

DELACORTE PRESS

SINISTER SHORTS
A Delacorte Book

Published by
Bantam Dell
A Division of Random House, Inc.
New York, New York

This is a work of fiction. Names, characters, places, and incidents either are the
product of the author's imagination or are used fictitiously. Any resemblance to actual
persons, living or dead, events, or locales is entirely coincidental.

Book design by Glen Edelstein

Delacorte Press is a registered trademark of Random House, Inc.,
and the colophon is a trademark of Random House, Inc.

ISBN-10: 0-385-33797-3

Printed in the United States of America

"The heart has its reasons which reason does not know."
—Blaise Pascal

Contents

Introduction

MY SISTER MARY AND I BEGAN collaborating on writing legal suspense novels twelve years ago, using the pen name of "Perri." From the first book, we found that Perri had a distinct style: optimistic, fast-paced, no-nonsense, and seldom given to fanciful literary gestures. However, we both knew that Perri had another side: a darker, more divided self aching to appear.

In fact, just before our first novel was published, Perri had published her first short story, "The Long Walk," a paranoid tale about a murder investigation that takes place on a hike in the Berkeley Hills, in *Ellery Queen's Mystery Magazine.* This first outing earned Perri an encouraging award from the Mystery Writers of America and begins this collection.

Many short stories followed over the years. Like Perri's novels, they were always about crime, but we experimented with many different writing styles and explored the grotesque, the hidden, and the frightening rather than the legal landscape of our Nina Reilly novels. We published some of them in *Ellery Queen,* online, and in literary journals, but others lay moldering in a box in my humid Hawaiian garage, or stashed in the back of Mary's file cabinet in California. The stories often seemed to write themselves or fall from dreams.

With our short stories, we each felt free to imprint an individual style. When Mary presented me with a new story, like "The Furnace Man," about a housewife whose obsession with keeping her husband's love leads to bizarre consequences, I gave it a light once-over, but knew better than to touch the style. The same went for my story about a man in a wet suit going over a waterfall, "Dead Money." I dreamed the whole story one night, plot point after plot point, and Mary checked it over and let it go.

Only one story in this book was a fifty-fifty collaboration like our novels: "Juggernaut," maybe because Nina Reilly, the lawyer in our legal novels, makes an appearance. We'll let you guess which one of us was the main writer of "Tiny Angels," "The Second Head," "To Still the Beating of Her Heart," "The Couple Behind the Curtain," and "The Young Lady." Then see if you can guess which one of us wrote "Sandstorm," "Chocolate Milkshake," "A Grandmother's Tale," and "Lemons."

Two of the stories are stylistic homages to far better writers. "His Master's Hand," in which Peter the Gravedigger goes looking for Mozart's grave in Vienna, bears more than a passing resemblance to the style of Dostoyevsky's *Notes from Underground.* "Gertrude Stein Solves a Mystery" is a mostly true recounting of a strange incident in the great writer's life, written in my personal version of Steinese.

Other figures important to us blew into stories like "Success Without College," in which Paul van Wagoner, the investigator in our series, helps a victim in a shooting come out ahead, and "O'Shay's Special Case," inspired by the stories our late brother, Patrick O'Shaughnessy, a lawyer who represented injured workers in Salinas, California, used to tell us.

In all, these stories represent a different kind of collaboration between Mary and me. We egged each other on, helped each other, and played around. We hope you enjoy the result as much as we enjoyed writing them.

Oh, and Perri, who of course will get all the credit, thanks you for reading, from the bottom of her black little heart.

Best,
Pam and Mary O'Shaughnessy for "Perri"

Sinister
Shorts

The Long Walk

A t eleven the phone buzzed. Fleck had been dreaming, gazing out the window at the busy Atlanta street scene four floors below. He punched the conference button and heard the loud tinny voice of Franklin Bell calling from California. "Hey, John," Bell said. "You are a hard man to track down."

"You found me now," Fleck said. He had been relaxed; now he was uneasy. He straightened his back and the action down there snapped into sharp focus.

A woman pushing a stroller paused to extricate an angry child while Bell talked through the speakerphone.

"I got a job for you," he was saying. "The firm has a problem."

"I'm listening." His eyes stayed with the mother on the sidewalk. The child struggled out of her arms, made a break for the street.

"Just how tied up are you in Atlanta?"

"Depends," Fleck said. "What have you got?" By now he was standing, watching the woman tear after her kid.

A roaring semi blasted through Fleck's sight line. The woman launched herself into a tackle, arms out. When the truck had passed, his eyes searched for her again and found her dragging her child across the sidewalk. She picked him up, smacked his butt, and tethered him back into the stroller, tears streaming down her cheeks. Fleck sat down, turning to face the wall.

Bell said, "Pete was talking about you the other day. He liked your work on the Ibanez fraud case. I told him you were in Atlanta. He said call you. Confidentially, of course."

Law firms were like that. Discretion was the big virtue, even bigger than turning misery into money. Fleck didn't like Franklin Bell, but he liked Pete Altschuler, Bell's boss, a senior partner at Stevenson Safik & Morris, Berkeley's best-known law firm. Pete had represented him in the divorce and taken his middle-of-the-night calls, calls he was ashamed of now.

So he waited while Bell moseyed through the Berkeley weather report—hot and sunny—and talked about the fraud case, and Pete's mild heart attack, and the latest craziness on Telegraph Avenue, a shoot-out at one of the college bars, until he got back around to the reason for his call, which was to ask Fleck to catch the Delta red-eye Sunday night and meet him and Pete Monday morning to look into something important.

"I've got four more weeks on contract here," Fleck said.

He was working a temporary security job at one of the Peachtree Plaza skyscrapers. He had been in Atlanta for several months, and he liked it, the jazz, the bars, the style. In fact, he was thinking about moving here. In Atlanta, people of color could feel comfortable, could forget the race issue much of the time. In Berkeley, his hometown in California, it would always be black folks in the flats and white folks in the hills, white guilt and condescension, black rage. His ex-wife had been white. She still lived in their house on the old Grove Street, on the borderline.

"Interrupt it for a couple weeks," Bell said. He kept talking, wheedling, persuading.

Fleck let him talk. His mind returned to the memory he had been caressing. Last night in the candlelight, and Charisse in his bed.

In his small apartment for the first time, shy with each other, they had moved together to a slow song, bodies slick with heat where they touched. Charisse had started it, dancing him toward a blowing curtain and then past it, to the door of his bedroom. He had forced himself to follow her, lighting the candles by the bed, lifting her onto the pillows. He meant to hold back his emotion, but he couldn't help himself. Groaning, he had buried himself in her soft flickers.

Toward morning, brief thunder and lightning filled the sky off his balcony. Fleck admired Charisse's body with his hands. She stirred, mumbling something. Thick drops splashed against the glass. She sat up in bed, reached over to the bedside table for her glasses, wrapped her arms around her knees, and peered out, unself-conscious.

"You ain't goin' nowhere." He had reached up to tug gently at her.

"Fleck fits you," she murmured, looking down at him. "Yellow flecks in green eyes...where'd those light eyes come from, your mama or your daddy? Hey, now...hey."

Later, he had rolled his fullback's body out of bed, embarrassed because he knew Charisse was watching him. She got up too, classic as a temple goddess wrapped in the yellow sheet, stretching her brown arms above her head and yawning. They showered and dressed, then walked together across the concrete plaza toward the concrete tower they both worked in, avoiding the puddles, not hurrying.

Charisse had said, "Having second thoughts?"

"No, ma'am. Never. Just scared of my luck," he'd answered.

"Not luck," she said. "Don't you believe in destiny? Paths always cross for a reason." They walked into the building, got into the same elevator they had met in.

"Paths cross by chance," he said. "You never know."

Charisse laughed, said, "All those chance events, all those co-incidences for the last ten thousand years, all those ancestors, all those travels, all those births and deaths and tragedies and come-dies, all that led to you and me meeting right here, going up. Honey, that is destiny."

He had looked at her, so small and sure and important-sounding, having to tilt her head up even in her high heels. He loved how she thought, big thoughts. He had wanted to hiss something sweet into her ear. Instead, as he stepped out, he touched her cheek, saying, "Doesn't matter why. Here we are."

Fleck wondered how long his silence had lasted. "No. I'll have to pass," he told Bell.

Now Bell paused. "We'll give you a five-thousand-dollar bonus for the rush."

"Now you have my attention. But get specific, okay?"

"Julie Mattei, remember her? Pete's legal secretary, pretty, ah, black girl, her desk right in front of Pete's door?"

He remembered Julie. He felt the familiar chilly liquid rush up his spine. "Yeah."

"She's dead," Bell said. "Beaten to death, awful thing, on a trail up behind the UC campus, up in the hills. Just before Easter. It's one of those random killings, some joker freaked on the latest street drug."

"She had a nice smile."

"Among other things," Bell said. "Three months now, and your former colleagues at the Berkeley PD still can't find the guy. They had to reopen the trail to the public. They're interviewing all the partners and staff again. They act like they suspect one of us. We're talking major PR problems. The Berkeley press is frothing at the mouth."

"Bring in a few clients," Fleck said.

Bell took him seriously. "This kind of coverage doesn't bring in the right kind of clients. Pete's upset. He got the okay to hire you to look into the murder at the last partners' meeting."

"I'm sorry to hear all this. But I don't want to come back right now, Frank."

"I'm authorized to offer a further bonus of ten grand if you locate the killer," Bell said, squeezing each word out as if it hurt him.

"Unless it's somebody at the firm," Fleck said.

"Would we be bringing you in if we thought that? Look, you know us; you know Berkeley." Another pause. Bell couldn't resist. "Come on, John, what's the big deal? You need the money, I happen to know."

"I'll call you back," Fleck said. The money, he needed. The job . . . it was wrong to go back there. Stupid, even. He hung up, thought a minute, then called Charisse, waiting impatiently for her line to clear. Finally she said, "Hello?" with that breathy Southern voice she had, and he said, "How about you fly to California with me?" She surprised the hell out of him when she said yes.

They flew out Sunday at midnight, first class. Charisse slept the whole way with her head against his shoulder. He froze his arm, not wanting to wake her up. While he sat there, he memorized her, her dark springy hair brushing his face, her full lips parted like a child's, her smooth broad forehead, her long eyelashes resting peacefully on her cheeks. The emptiness in him receded, to be replaced by something he was afraid to name.

He left her in the hotel room in San Francisco, driving his rental car against the traffic over the Bay Bridge the next day, morning sun assaulting his eyes the whole way. Atlanta had been warm and humid, but above downtown Berkeley, the East Bay hills shimmered dry yellow, the brush desiccating in the August heat. Sun baking him through the driver's window sucked the moisture out of him.

Stevenson Safik & Morris occupied the third floor of a downtown office building on Shattuck, half a mile from the UC campus. Inside, it felt too cold, too dark.

Franklin Bell hadn't changed. The smooth pasty face was crowned with a short TV-interview haircut and the muddy eyes appraised Fleck coolly. He didn't offer to shake hands. He'd done the job, brought Fleck in. There was no need to make nice anymore. He motioned at the secretary to bring some coffee, and strode off to find Pete Altschuler.

The two white lawyers came into Bell's office together a few minutes later. Pete Altschuler pumped his hand, saying how glad he was to see him. Altschuler had lost weight since the heart attack. When he smiled, the folds in his cheeks made deep parentheses; his lips had turned purplish. He sat down carefully in the other client chair. Bell frowned at both of them, then slid a heavy brown accordion folder stuffed with papers across his wide desk toward Fleck.

"The police reports. Autopsy. Photos. Lab stuff. It's all there. Take it with you," Altschuler said.

"We want you to clear the firm's name," added Bell. "Tamp the rumors. So she worked here; it's not like she got killed at her desk. No, she had to go marching around by herself out there in the hills until a crazy got at her. So much for the feminists."

A note of triumph sounded in his voice. Fleck thought, His wife's left him.

"Are the police focusing on anybody in particular here?" he asked Altschuler.

Altschuler seemed to have used up all his energy shaking hands. "Pete was just about to let her go," Bell interposed. "Her work performance wasn't up to par. She had told some of the other secretaries. She threatened to sue."

"So?" Fleck said.

"She was a flake. She told stories," Bell went on. "Never considered the consequences of her mouth."

"Ah, let's get it over with," Altschuler said in a weary voice. "You might as well hear it from me, John. We were having an affair. She wanted to break it off with me and I wanted to keep her. There were scenes. Everyone here knew about it."

"Why was she breaking it up?" Fleck said.

Altschuler shrugged. "Who knows? They never tell you the truth when they want to dump you." His voice was light, but his hands patted his thighs as if he needed comforting.

"Did you kill her?"

Altschuler's smile had turned into a grimace. "No. Guilty? Hell, yes. But not of murder."

"What about your wife?"

"You've got to be kidding. Anne never knew."

Franklin Bell's expression said, Yeah, sure. "Who else might have done it?" Fleck asked Bell. "Any ideas, Frank? Not that you knew her well, right?"

"It's no use looking for a motive," Bell said smoothly, leaning back in his swivel chair, clasping his hands behind his head, elaborately casual. "You of all people know this town, John. Every misfit with a grudge comes to Berkeley. Nobody follows the rules. Nobody leashes 'em. It was somebody she didn't even know. She met him on the trail, he had it in his head to kill somebody that morning, and there she was."

"She lived alone," Altschuler said. "Her mother lives in the city, teaches anthro at San Francisco State. She played piano, liked Japanese food, worried about her weight, decorated her desk with bottlebrush in a vase. This was a good, decent, fine girl, John."

"Have there been any other killings, attacks, anything like that, on that trail?"

"Not this one," Bell said. "But all those hill trails, bad things happen now and then. Berkeley's no exception. There was the

Hillside Strangler in Santa Cruz. The Tamalpais trails are really dangerous. Hikers find bodies there every year."

"What about this trail—what is it called?"

"The college kids call it The Long Walk," Bell said. "It's about five miles, winding up from the UC stadium behind Strawberry Canyon. It's popular with the students, of course, and the hikers and the runners. At the top there's a stretch of flat granite and a rocky place they call The Cave, with a spring. They sunbathe there, rest up before going back down. It happened on a side path near The Cave."

"No witnesses."

"No witnesses, no weapon, no evidence. Somebody just grabbed her and bashed her brains in," Altschuler said. "It's not just for the firm, John. It's for her."

"She was a flake," Bell repeated, "and we really don't need this kind of attention."

"Why did you call me?" Fleck said. "Why do you think I can step in, when the Berkeley PD can't close it?"

"You worked there all those years. You know how it is," Altschuler said. "Other priorities. Drugs, runaways, domestic violence, foreign students getting robbed and killed, political demonstrations, the annual riots on Telegraph, the big murders, the orders to keep a low profile..."

Bell looked bored. He hauled himself out of the chair, said, "It's in the reports," looked at his watch. On cue, his phone buzzed. "Take care," he said. The meeting was over.

"Call me in a day or two, John," Altschuler said at the door into the hall. "Where are you going to start?"

"The Long Walk," Fleck said. He hefted the file under his arm. "You ever been there, Pete?"

"Not me," Altschuler said. His mouth opened in his long mournful face like he was about to say more, but the door closed, and Fleck was shut out.

★　　★　　★

Charisse had never been to the huge amusement park of San Francisco. That night they climbed the Coit Tower hill in a balmy sunset and ate at an Italian restaurant in North Beach. Then they drove across the Golden Gate Bridge to Sausalito and had a few drinks on the outside deck at the Reef, looking back over the dark brilliant water toward the glowing city.

Some kids leaned too far over the railing, tossing bits of sourdough. A sea lion barked itself hoarse in the shallows below the deck and Charisse ran over to look. Pelicans and gulls circled and dove. Fleck sat there, too big for the flimsy wicker chair, finishing his drink, the sharp aromatic fumes of the brandy blending with the salt tang of the air. He had read the reports. He should not be on this case.

"So beautiful," she said, pulling her chair out. Her thin dress with its full skirt poufed around her as she sat down and he caught her perfume. "John—"

"Um-hmm." He tossed off the last of his drink.

"Why'd you leave California?"

"Because it smells like death to me," he said. He hadn't meant to say it that way. He didn't want her to be afraid of him. But he wanted her to understand him. She deserved to know what she was getting. It smells like fifteen years of crime scenes, corpses, court, he said to himself, swirling the ice in his glass. Finding the victims in bed, in old abandoned buildings, in the ashes of their homes, in the gutters, on the playgrounds, under the dirt. Always too late to save them. Trying to be satisfied locking up the pathetic killers.

"Working homicide, every day was the same," he went on. "Somebody killed somebody. I found out who was dead, and who did the killing. I found out why they did the killing. More and more, there was no reason. You know, some kid would say, he got in my face, he looked at my girl. Or, I needed a few bucks to buy crack. Or, I just exploded, I can't explain why. Everybody dying, and I couldn't stop it. I come back here and it's just the same."

Charisse covered his hand with hers, shivering. "You're only here for a little bit, and you and me, we're apart from all that."

"Atlanta's still got some of that...innocence," he said. "Like you. Not spoiled."

"Maybe you shouldn't have come back so soon, feeling like you do." She turned his hand over, kissed the palm, her lips a bird's wing brushing his skin.

"I came back for the money. There's so much money here. Maybe when I go back to Atlanta, I can buy a little house. Get over it."

"You wouldn't be leaving...family here?"

"No. No family. Not anymore. And you? Who do you come with?"

"Aunts, uncles, nieces, nephews, dozens of cousins. You should see the party on the Fourth of July."

"If I'm in Atlanta," Fleck said.

"I hope you will be." She was bold, but her voice was so gentle it sent a root down into his soul. "Listen, John. Let's fly back right now," Charisse went on, her voice half-playful, half-serious. "I feel like—this isn't good for you. Our business is in Atlanta."

"I'll be fine," he said. Fifteen, eighteen thousand, he said to himself. Make me worth knowing, maybe. "Tomorrow I have to get up early. I'll be back to take you to dinner."

"Are you going to take The Long Walk?"

"Yeah. I have to leave San Francisco before dawn and get over to Berkeley. The girl was killed in the morning. I want to check it out at about the same time of day." He stood up abruptly. "Let's get out of here."

While they drove back to the hotel, Charisse rested her hand on his leg. They lay down on the bed as soon as the hotel door closed and kissed for a long time.

Once more he didn't sleep well. He wasn't used to having a warm solid woman pressed against him.

He shifted and her arm swept across his bare chest. Damn her. The only sane thing was not to care.

★   ★   ★

In the predawn he heard Charisse rustling around, running water in the bathroom, opening the curtains. He had been deeply asleep for the past hour. He felt like he'd just had his bell rung by Mean Joe Green. He pulled on his khaki pants and T-shirt.

"You didn't have to get up," he told her.

"Do you always bark like that in the morning?"

"I'm working, that's all. I shouldn't have dragged you here. This is a bad place for me."

"I'd like to come with you," Charisse said. "I could use the exercise."

"What? Go on The Walk? Don't be ridiculous," he said coldly. "I'm not putting you in any danger."

"Danger? What danger? It's just a hike."

"I can't be responsible," he said.

"That all happened months ago. Anyway, baby, don't you know me well enough by now to know that this is exactly the way to make me do what you don't want me to do?"

The sentence made them laugh, and cleared the air for breakfast at a greasy spoon on the corner. Fleck ate the dripping special, Charisse refused. She would go hungry and she would go with him. So be it.

By six they were driving the rental car up University Avenue toward the campus. Nobody was around, unless you counted the heaps in the doorways. The sun cast low warm rays down the long street, its asphalt already storing up heat.

They turned right on Oxford Street and then left on Haste, cruising up the south side of the campus. As they waited for the light at Telegraph, a sharp pain lanced Fleck's stomach. His heart pounded, and his eyes blurred. He said nothing to Charisse, who watched with pity as a ragged human shape slowly pushed a shopping cart across the intersection.

Fleck had seen the early-morning scene before too many times. Dizzy and angry to be back, somehow he kept driving, parking on Durant near the Greek Theatre two blocks from the stadium. "Just give me a minute," he said, angling his head back. In a moment he was half-asleep.

"John?"

"Yeah." He roused himself with difficulty. They got out and he locked up.

Charisse leaned down, tightened her laces, said, "We should have brought a water bottle."

"There's safe water at the top. A spring."

"Okay. You're not going to bring that thing, are you?"

He was strapping on his shoulder holster. He looked at it, and at her. A couple of girls bounced past them, jogging toward the trail, chattering. An old man threw a soggy-looking tennis ball across the tall dewy grass by the fence. His dog sniffed around eagerly, nose down in the wetness.

"I mean, it'll show, and scare people. And you said the trail's been open a month, with no problems."

"A precaution," he mumbled. His eyes had blurred momentarily. He wondered what was wrong with him.

"Put it away, please, John."

Reluctantly, he took the gun and holster and opened the car door, reaching for the glove compartment. Charisse started up the trail, and he followed a moment later, slinging the big telephoto-lens camera case around his neck.

The Long Walk, a dirt trail about five feet wide, wound along the side of the stadium. A jogger pounded past them on the trail, his ponytail flying. They fell in behind a middle-aged couple leaning on walking sticks, arguing in German.

"Just a hike," Charisse said again, squeezing his hand. Now that he was moving, Fleck felt better. The temperature must already be over eighty degrees. In March, when Julie Mattei died, it must have been much cooler.

The trail began to climb and they left the athletic field behind. They passed a few people, and more passed them. Some of them said hi; most ignored them. Representatives of the Berkeley social hodgepodge, graybeards, couples with dogs, and loners hiked the path. Fleck didn't need to read minds to picture the broad fields they ranged: the sane, the crazy, the mild, the wild.

They all thought they were safe, but they were all walking the death beat every minute of their lives, and he'd given up trying to save them.

Julie, just like these young women looking so arrogant and confident this morning, had walked past this clump of manzanita three months ago, directly into the path of a truck. No. He shook his head to clear it. That was the kid in Atlanta, the one with a loving mom standing by to change his history.

Charisse looked out of place in tailored shorts and pristine white shoes rising above the dust. He must, too. These hills attracted white, except for a group of Asian boys they passed, sitting on rocks loading their cameras, and one other black girl who passed them with a wave, tall and broad-shouldered as a basketball player. They watched the girl's muscular calves disappear around the curve.

The walkers thinned out after the first mile. Fleck and Charisse walked along a ridge, the golden underbrush on their left climbing the hillside, poison oak the only green, fresh and glistening everywhere. They passed more stands of sharp-branched manzanita. Now and then they got into culverts and flats where looming eucalyptus trees cast shapes across the path, their acorns littering the ground, releasing a dry pungency that made his stomach churn.

He was sweating. The sun reflected off the ground and

speared his eyes under the sunglasses. So Altschuler and Julie had an affair. Fleck wondered if that started before or after she helped break up his own marriage.

Charisse stopped and reached out to pick a solitary purple flower on the slope. Fleck pulled her back, said, "Drop it."

"Why?" She held on stubbornly.

"The whole hillside's infested. Poison oak. Don't touch any of the plants."

"Hoo, boy." She withdrew her hand, rubbing it on her pants. "Do you think the senior partner killed her?"

"Altschuler? No." She didn't ask why, just sat down on a rock and looked at him with interest.

"How about the guy who called you? Bell."

He said nothing.

"You said the firm was small. Bell had to know her."

"I walked into his office one night after hours. Just opened the door. It was like a TV comedy skit. He had her over the desk. She pulled her skirt down and turned her back to me. He never mentioned it after that. He never mentioned it to the police, either." Fleck had sat down beside her. "Damn, I am thirsty."

Charisse said, "It was one of them."

Fleck said, "No," again.

"How can you be so sure?" She looked exasperated.

He turned away. "I've done it for so many years. Pete Altschuler, he's a city boy. He wouldn't climb up here to do it. Too worried about his health."

"He could have hired a hit man. A hit man in hiking boots." She smiled, inviting him to join her, but he wasn't in the mood.

"He's not that ruthless," Fleck said as she got up, smoothing her shorts. "He cared for her."

They wound around another corner, through another dry canyon. The sun blazed down. Fleck stumbled and would have fallen if she had not caught hold of his arm.

"John, you're sick. Shouldn't we go down?" Charisse said.

"I'll take a rest on top. You were right about the water bottle."

She let go of him, gave him a playful shove. "Okay, Macho Man," she said. "Why not Bell?"

"He might get her fired. He might poison her. He might even shoot her," Fleck said. "But he'd never get actual blood on his hands."

"But he was hiding the fact he was seeing her!"

"They all hide everything. It's second nature for lawyers."

"Then who did it?"

Voices carried down the hillside. Three kids, two girls and a boy, descended around the switchback ahead. They were all dressed alike, in jeans torn out at the knees and tank tops, hair tied back with bandannas. "Hot today," the boy offered as he walked by. His nose was peeling under his enigmatic shades. A buck knife sheathed in leather looped through his belt. The girls passed by without a word.

"Nobody murders another person for no reason," Charisse went on. "It's just that the reason isn't obvious—like if it's not money, or power, or revenge—everything else gets lumped under general craziness."

He trudged forward, irritated, watching his big feet move up a steep place, step by step.

"For instance, a woman kills her child for what seems like no reason. She's been neglected her whole life, and this is the only way anybody will pay her any attention. So they say she's nuts. They put her in an asylum, but she had her reasons, didn't she?"

"I'm talking about a random crime, not somebody's baby," Fleck said.

"Or think about it. A man goes into his old office with an assault rifle and starts shooting. It's terrible. He didn't even know some of the people he killed. But he could explain it, John. He'd call it a payback. The people represented something to him, something he had to kill."

"Some reasons can't be called reasons." His tongue felt thick in his mouth, and he wasn't even sure she'd heard him. He didn't want to talk anymore. He just wanted to get up the hill.

They had been climbing hard. After a long time, long enough for Fleck to remember everything about his life in California, his wife's face, Julie's, all the dead faces he had looked into all those years, wanting to say I'm sorry, I'm so sorry I failed you, they came to an area where the Oakland fire had passed through. The dirt turned black, and all around them stood skinned-looking fire-seared trees. Across the canyon, on top of the next hill over, distant but clear, they saw bare burned land, a stone chimney still standing guard in the middle of nothing at all.

Fleck said, "Suppose a man's wife leaves him. He blames the woman he was sleeping with . . . is that a reason to kill her? Shouldn't that man have blamed himself?"

Charisse didn't answer. She was watching a tarantula skitter across the path, hairy legs moving much faster than they should. She pointed, excited, her hand with the long nails and sparkling rings incongruous in the dirt and heat and stillness. Fleck kicked dirt after the spider. "This is what I think," he went on, repressing the moan the pain in his stomach had started. "Julie Mattei hiked up into someone's hate zone. If she hadn't shown up, the next walker would have been killed. Simple as that."

"I don't believe it," Charisse said. "They have their reasons." She left it at that.

Another rest. The pain had settled in his gut, cramping him, making him stop and bend over now and then till the worst of it passed. Charisse was tired, too; she had slowed down and she walked with a slight limp. No one had passed them for some time. He was burning with thirst.

This walk was acting on him, replacing the forgetting with awful, fresh memory. Why had he returned?

"John, did your work make you start to think that life is senseless, too? Random and meaningless like you keep talking about?" She went on without waiting for an answer. "Because if it is, then you could do anything to another human being. I mean, what kind of morality would be left?"

"There you go," he said quietly, so quietly she didn't even hear him.

"Just think of her up here, on an overcast day. A spring day, everything blooming . . . she was thinking about making love the night before, maybe. Or about chicken tarragon for dinner. Then, like this"—she snapped her fingers—"she's gone."

He had stopped to catch his breath and wipe the sweat off his face. Gnats floated around their heads. "If they get too bad, walk with your hands raised above your head for a while," he said. "They circle the highest point."

"Did you ever meet her?" When he didn't answer, she wiped her forehead and repeated the question.

"We went out a few times," Fleck said. The trail had narrowed between two boulders. They were hidden there. You could bury something here easily, he thought. An earthquake right now would bury them together.

If his words had surprised her, she didn't show it. "When did you move to Atlanta?"

Fleck ignored the question. "Doesn't this place scare you, Charisse? A woman died here and all."

Now it was her turn to remain silent.

"I wish you hadn't come today," he said. She stepped back, her spine pressing against the rock.

"You moved to Atlanta at the end of March. Right after Julie Mattei was killed," she said, her voice low.

"That's right. And you've only known me for two weeks, that's right, too." His head swam; he licked his dry lips. The camera case banging against his chest had been beating him up rhythmically with each step. "You look a little like Julie," he said to her. "She was a glamorpuss like you."

He was leaning over her, both hands against the rock above her head. Charisse said levelly, "You're trying to scare me. Why?"

Some tension in him went back into hiding at her words. He moved back from her and said, "You're too trusting."

"Don't play games like that, John. I'm not like you. I'm not afraid of the world like you."

"You should be," he said. They went on, back into another patch of blinding sun.

"We're almost there," he said. "Up another quarter mile, past that stand of pine."

Charisse had stopped again. "What?" he said, then remembered he'd told her that morning he'd never been on The Long Walk. "I forgot," he said. "That's all. I did hike this trail once, a long time ago. Come on, Charisse, don't look at me like that."

"I'm going—back down the trail."

"No," Fleck said. "It's dangerous." He grabbed her arm, as much to support himself as to restrain her. They stood there on the dusty path in the hard sun. "C'mon. We'll get some water, then we'll go straight down."

She tried to shake him off. He held on.

"Let go of me, John."

She started back down the trail. He took her arm again and turned her around. "No, I'm not letting you go," he said. "We're going to get some water, then we can go back. I'm sorry if I scared you," he was saying to her as he half-pushed her ahead of him up the trail. Silent, tearful, and exhausted, Charisse went along, which was fortunate since the immense pain that had lodged in his gut had fragmented and he could barely control his legs. Into a buzzing black shade they climbed, unable to see ahead through the psychedelic play of light and shadows beneath the canopy of leaves.

One more steep incline. The hillside turned rocky. Off to the right, beyond the scarred hillsides, he could now see the whole bay, a vast glittering silver lagoon dotted with boats, ringed by sunlit cities, the four great bridges connecting the peninsula and the headlands of Marin and the East Bay, San Francisco on the horizon partially veiled in its mountain range of white fog, the city of Oakland spread along the water, just below their feet. It all looked so pretty from far away.

One more thick stand of eucalyptus, and the trail abruptly delivered them out onto a flat sweep of granite. On the other side, about a hundred yards ahead, Fleck made out a rock wall, what looked like a depression. The Cave. Where the spring would be, inside and out of sight. On the right, another cliff fell away into miles of air.

"That's it," he said, pointing. "Water." Just saying the word made him feel better. He must have heatstroke, plus whatever else was gnawing away inside him.

Ducking down to enter, he nudged Charisse ahead. The dark blinded him; the coolness immediately started him shaking.

The Cave was a small rock room, lit only by the blazing open arch where they had entered. As his eyes adjusted, he saw Charisse in the corner, her whole head under the spring, her hands splashing up clear water, drinking greedily while it flowed over her head and neck.

Another shadow in the dark, an older man, drank water out of a tin cup, watching Charisse. Fleck put his hand against the wall and blinked several times. Some of the faintness went away. The man was a white biker type, tall and brawny, with a heavy gnarled walking stick. He stepped aside into indistinct shadows when he saw Fleck. Charisse came up for air, saw Fleck, and moved back.

Heedless, Fleck dove for the spring.

Freezing! It hurt, burning his head. His neck muscles spasmed. Red waves crashed inside his eyelids—

He slid down on the hard cold floor, his back propped against the wall, choking and sputtering. "Charisse," he gasped as soon as he could speak. "Wait a minute. I'm sick."

Charisse didn't answer. With a sound like a sob she turned and, lowering her head at the arch, ran outside. Fleck was gripped by sick dread. He scrabbled to get up, but he fell into a cramp.

He had to be with her. He got to his knees, shaking his head like a bull, droplets flying off his hair. Suddenly he felt the man behind him, wrapping long arms around his chest, pinning his arms.

His dread degenerated into physical panic and he struggled. So it was this stranger, the one he had forgotten to watch. A snap of the fingers—

Fleck was hauled to his feet. The man stepped back, saying, "You okay, buddy?" Fleck pushed him off, walking unsteadily to the mouth of The Cave.

His hand shading his forehead, he saw Charisse out in the glare, crossing the flat, looking so small. The sight of him made her rush off the main path, off to a narrow shaded walkway fringed by exotic red plumes of bottlebrush...

She ran up the path where Julie died.

Blind again, each breath a scorching effort, Fleck loped out of The Cave after her, hunched over, but she ran hard until she disappeared. It wasn't until he reached the far end of the flat and made his way to the brush that he saw the sister, the black girl who had waved at them earlier, way up the path beyond him, rising out of the eucalyptus forest behind Charisse. She had to be almost six feet tall, her hair in a natural like pictures he'd seen of Angela Davis in the sixties.

Stepping behind Charisse, the girl wrapped her arms around her neck in a choke hold. They struggled and Charisse fell. The girl went down with her and began methodically beating Charisse's head against the rock—

He tore up the path, his pain forgotten, the biker hollering and waving his stick, following, both trying to scare her off. The girl jumped up alertly. Charisse wasn't moving at all. Then the girl lifted a heavy stone, grunting a little, and raised it above her head, the muscles on her arms as strong and defined as the forelegs of a tiger above its kill—

They heard her say, angrily, almost petulantly, "Renee, you stay dead this time—"

—and Fleck shot her, from fifteen yards away. She fell slowly, as if she had all the time in the world, still holding the stone, eyes wide and startled. Her big handsome body twitched, would never move again—

—and he was holding Charisse, crying out her name. Her eyes were closed and her hair in back was matted with blood.

"Can you make it, pal?" the old biker said. He scooped Charisse up, and they ran down the trail, taking turns with her. Halfway down she roused and said she wanted to walk, so they supported her the rest of the way.

ER at Alta Bates Hospital admitted her. When Fleck passed out in the waiting room, they admitted him, too, and pumped the rotten food from his stomach. "Health department closed that place down where you ate today. You're our fourth customer," the nurse told him.

He slept then, and a few hours later two officers he knew came to talk to him.

Through the window in her door, on the outside looking in, he could see only the bottom part of her body on the bed, the sheets lifting and falling with her breath, one elegant hand at rest.

She sat up, saw his face in the window, and wiggled a finger at him. "Aren't we a fine pair?" she asked when he came in, adjusting the white gauze bandages in back where hair used to be.

He gathered her up. Neither of them talked for a long time, until she said, "You were right to bring the gun. In the camera case, wasn't it?"

"Ex-cop, ever vigilant. I was afraid—"

"Of me. You think everyone around you dies—"

"You almost did. You walked into her zone."

"You didn't let her take me. You saved me, John."

Snatched her off the dangerous street, and loved her.

"It wasn't random," Charisse said. "She had her reasons." She held him even tighter.

Charisse and her big thoughts—

Fleck wondered where she was—Renee, the woman who looked like Julie, who looked like Charisse. Out there, everywhere, women who wouldn't stay dead.

Success Without College

Paul van Wagoner swiveled in his desk chair, observing the bustle at the Hog's Breath Inn below, indulging himself in a pat on the back. You couldn't pick a more beautiful place on earth than Carmel, California. He'd seen the world, and remained unimpressed. What did Italy have that California didn't have? Ruins? California had missions. London? San Francisco had sexier water. Well, okay, there was no Himalaya to climb. But from his front door, it was five hours to the Sierras, max. Here he could enjoy a sea as blue as the Mediterranean and beaches lounged upon by people as cosmopolitan as any in Nice.

He had started his morning with a steaming espresso at a sunlit café for breakfast, and finished it up with a few phone calls to organize his subcontractors for the next day. He would leave about four, he decided, and take a long fast walk up the beach, get his feet wet, let the waves bury his feet and the sandcrabs tickle his toes. In the late afternoon on a glorious blue-on-blue day like today, all the pretty women would still be out baring their midriffs to the air and his gaze. He didn't want to miss that. And now that he had his own business, he could do as he pleased on any fine afternoon.

After spending years getting educated on the East Coast, he loved everything about California. Even crime paid here, for him as it did in Hollywood. California could transform the most venal crime into a song and dance and success for somebody.

He liked his work. He dealt in issues of life and death. What could be more important? And if lately the rest of his life seemed less vital than usual, well, that was subject to change. That could be remedied instantly, with a certain sway of the right someone's hip.

Today, he had new clients coming in at two o'clock, the Maldonados, Victor and Delilah. They were parents whose son had been shot four times, allegedly by a drive-by shooter. In the hospital now, in intensive care, the teenager was just barely alive. When Paul spoke on the phone to the parents right after the incident, their son had not been expected to live.

Matter-of-fact people who never expected a tragedy to blow their simple dreams for their son and themselves sky-high, he could tell the Maldonados had gone through several phases by the time they called him, using voices calm and hopeful. They had entered the denial phase, one that Paul recognized all too well. Years ago in Nepal, Paul had seen a woman hang a strip of cotton with inked messages on it onto a line, next to a dozen others, multicolored, at various stages of fading. She hung it there as a message to a presumably benevolent god. As the flag faded, her god absorbed the message. The Maldonados had been hanging out their prayer flag, not giving up. He didn't know what to expect from them.

He poured himself another jolt of coffee for fortification. This part of his job could get him down.

Victor Maldonado entered the room first. His wife trailed in behind. They sat side by side in his client chairs, not touching, but bouncing thoughts off each other the way married people did, flinging questions and arguments his way. He imagined they'd been married for a very long time. The wife's whole milk–colored face seemed to be a frame for a generous mouth with perfectly straight white teeth. Her skin had lost its youthful flush, and lines ran along the edges of her lips, but the lines told Paul about a life full of laughter and smiles.

She didn't smile now; the face that was made to smile looked painfully tense. Her husband sat close by, tall and dark and round around the middle, his voice booming, and his body movements closely aligned to hers, responsive to her nuances, physical and verbal. They were close; Paul could see that. Good. They needed each other now. Roman, the shooting victim, nineteen years old, was their only son.

"How's Roman?" Paul asked.

"We called this morning," said Victor. "They took him out of intensive care. The doctor said he was 'cautiously optimistic.'"

"Great," Paul said, surprised. He had steeled himself for bad news, he realized now, as the tension in his neck relaxed, and he felt the ache of holding it stiff for the past few minutes. How amazing to be shot four times and hang in there anyway. Good for Roman. He asked them to fill him in on the events surrounding Roman's shooting.

They explained that he had been working for two months at Taylor's Corner Store, north, up near Gilroy, being paid under the table, in cash.

"We can't afford college, even though he really wants to go." Roman's mother spoke in a voice loaded with regret and guilt. "We have just enough on paper so nobody would give him the financial aid he needed, and his test scores were okay but not great. He was sick the day of the test, and too demoralized to try again. He's actually a smart kid. Always got real good grades. I worry about what's going to happen to him. You can't get any-where today without a college education."

"Don't beat yourself up about that anymore, Delly. He'll get there. Have a little faith."

Delilah adjusted her purse on her knees. "Victor buys twenty bucks' worth of faith every week. Thanks to the lottery, he dreams away our bills, our bad health..."

"Our mortgage," teased her husband, shrugging, looking okay with the characterization.

"Lord," she said to Paul, "if dreams were real."

"So your son went to work to save money for college?" Paul prompted.

"So he got this dumb job that hardly kept him in black T-shirts. He never meant to stay long, just until he could get something that paid better and had some benefits," said Victor.

"He should've been looking for a better job then, shouldn't he have?" his wife said. "None of this would have happened if he had a decent job. Roman's so young. He thinks he can play around, and everything will turn out right anyway."

"Nothing wrong with being young and expecting a lot of the world, Delly," her husband said. "Keeps the spirit happy and engaged."

"His boss, Bert Taylor, has owned that store for twenty years. Now he claims Roman never worked there, that he's always run the place on his own," Delilah went on. "But why in the world would Roman make up a job?"

Paul could think of a few reasons. Maybe Roman had another way of making money that he felt shy talking about, or maybe he just wanted out from under his mother's eagle eye for a few minutes every day.

"I can't see why it makes a difference," Victor said with exasperation. "They found Roman lying out front, didn't they? It's nothing to do with his job."

"He's not out of the woods yet, the doctors say," said Delilah, reality breaking through as her flag faded but her wishes remained undone. "He could still take a turn... I can't stand to think..."

"Did you talk with Roman's boss, with Taylor, after the accident?" Paul asked.

"Went over to the store when Roman got shot, on Sunday," Delilah said. "The ambulance had just gone. We were going to hustle over to the hospital. But they said he wasn't expected to make it. We needed a minute . . . our son's blood was on the sidewalk and Taylor was inside, doing all the normal end-of-the-day stuff. Wiping counters, tidying. You know. It seemed so strange to me."

"You shouldn't have yelled at him, Delly," her husband said, looking softly at his wife.

"No, I guess not. But my son nearly died in front of his store and he's so concerned about all that blood on his precious sidewalk."

"People don't know what to say," said Victor. "Keeping busy helps. You know that."

"But Roman wouldn't lie to me," Mrs. Maldonado said, getting a little weepy.

Putting an arm around his wife, Victor gave Paul a look. The brown depths of his eyes told Paul he knew their son better than his wife did. All sons lied to their mothers.

"Have you talked to Roman since he was shot? Is he conscious?"

Victor Maldonado picked up the thread while his wife sniffed into a tissue. "He is. He's foggy about what happened. They say it's a miracle he's survived. Nobody expected it. The police said they'd send someone over to see him today, see if he remembered anything helpful about the car."

"We're going over there to see our boy right now," piped Delilah, obviously relieved by her tears, more relaxed, ready to reenter the fray.

Paul decided to tag along. He could walk down to the water tomorrow.

He followed the Maldonados in his car to the hospital in

Monterey, met them in front, and walked with them up slippery floors to Roman Maldonado's room. The boy's parents kissed him gently. His mother smoothed the hair off his broad, wet forehead. A mouth as wide as his mother's, but wrecked and torn, was patched together with neat black rows of stitches ending in small knots. The couple introduced Paul, and left their son with promises to return shortly. Until Paul knew if the kid was lying, the parents were better occupied elsewhere.

Roman lay on the bed, his muscular body so long his feet hung off the end. Thick white bandages broke the dark expansive skin of his chest, a sheet furled down around his waist, and his eyes remained closed.

"Roman, I just want to ask you a couple of questions about what happened, okay?"

Roman nodded slightly, opening his eyes.

"You know you've been shot?"

He nodded.

"Were you clerking at Taylor's store yesterday?"

He nodded again.

"He paid you in cash?"

"Yes." He groaned. The puffy red lips strained against their stitches.

"We'd like to find out if you saw the person in the car. Do you remember anything about that person? Or the car? What color was it?"

The boy's face, splotched white and red, screwed up. "What car?" he asked.

"You remember going outside right before you got shot?"

He shook his head, eyes wide-open now, looking perplexed.

"You don't remember going outside?"

"No."

The word came out simple and clear. Dang, no memory of the incident. Well, these things sometimes came back with time.

"I never went outside. There was no car."

Paul looked at him for a moment, hands in his pockets, pondering the many lies he had told his mother and other inquisitive adults while he was growing up. Then he said, "You know you're in the hospital, Roman? You know how badly hurt you are?" He didn't add, They took four bullets out of you yesterday and you could die any minute.

From Roman's face, his father's clear brown eyes told Paul Roman knew he could die.

"Who shot you?"

"I never saw him before."

"Okay. Then what happened in the store that day?"

But Roman had closed his eyes again and sunk back into his pain. He stiffened his body in the bed as if preparing for some private ordeal.

Paul pushed a button to call the nurse, who took the time to frown at him on the way to her patient.

Well, thought Paul, a mystery. He trotted off to bribe a talkative cop.

He invited Armano Hernandez out for a beer after his shift.

They met at five that evening at the Pine Inn, a few blocks from Paul's office. A decade younger than Paul, around thirty, Hernandez had worked under Paul when he had managed a special homicide task force a few years before. Small and agile, with fine features, he was a handsome and funny guy who loved being a cop; when Paul left his job in minor disgrace, Hernandez took his place. Hernandez seemed to feel he owed Paul something, and although Paul couldn't agree, he found Armano's loyalty both touching and useful.

Hernandez needed two beers and several long minutes to vent his misgivings about sharing cop business with Paul, the latest fracas between him and Chief Carsey and a brief update on the ongoing soap opera starring his younger sister Lena before settling into a conversation.

"There's two things you got to remember, Paulo," he started out. He never intended to patronize Paul, but to him and to all of his friends on the police force, Paul fell into that category of pitiable creatures, cops without a badge. Once an ex-cop, always a disreputable failure. "Number one, the parents know nothing. Correction: the dad knows more than the mom and he doesn't know shit. Number two, when you're talking to a nineteen-year-old boy who's got nothing going for him, assume a drug connection."

That said, he apparently felt he had imparted something valuable, for he tossed a handful of nuts down his throat, crunched forcefully, and smacked his lips.

Paul liked Armano. He only hated the way he ate. "What's the blood evidence, Armano?" he asked eventually, giving him the chance to polish off a second handful.

"Forensics took some off the sidewalk, all his. No evidence of a fight. Nothing under his fingernails. Nothing like that. Just four messy shots."

"They find the casings?"

"Yeah, two lying on the ground near him. From the same weapon, a thirty-eight. One funny thing. One of the casings had a partial print on it. Turned out to be Taylor's. He said when he got outside and saw all the blood, he picked it up without thinking. With all the TV, you'd think people would know better."

"That's worth looking into."

"Taylor didn't shoot the kid. Roman would say so right off the bat."

"Your people go inside the store?"

"Had to interview Taylor in there. The store's kept really nice—you been in there? Painted blue all around the top of the walls with some nice-looking murals of fruit. He's got the veggies laid out in these little plastic things that look like grass, and he buys his produce from farms in Salinas, so it's good fresh stuff. Not only is it sweet-lookin', it's clean as a whistle. The guy takes a lot of pride in his business."

"What's he like? Taylor?"

"Normal. Businesslike. Trying to make money and stay out of trouble. We talked to a few of the people around that day. Nobody admitted knowing Roman but they might lie to stay out of it, or to protect Taylor. Then again, the store's on a busy street. I don't know how much repeat business the guy gets. Roman says he worked oddball hours, so he might not have been noticed in particular. We're believing Taylor until we've got a good reason to believe Roman instead."

"Why don't you believe Roman? He says he worked there. Seems like a strange story."

"Look, it wouldn't surprise me if Taylor slipped the kid a few bucks under the table and lied about that. He doesn't want to have any run-ins with the tax man. But, it's a fact that Roman got shot. It's a fact we found the kid lying on the sidewalk in front of the store. Whether he worked for Taylor or not is moot. He ran into someone who went joyriding with a pistol. I'm not even sure the kid's lying intentionally about being out there on the street. That kind of shock is bound to upset anyone. Now there was a theory floating around..."

"What theory?"

"Seems the owner complained to the cops several times about people taking potshots at his store. He's Anglo operating in a neighborhood where he's a minority. Maybe there is some tension. Maybe that's why he might hire Roman, who's at least partly Hispanic. But he says in this case, the guys pulled up, aimed at Roman, and shot. It's nothing to do with him. Course, if Taylor knew someone had a grudge and came after him, he might lie."

"Any estimate as to how far away the perp was when he fired?"

"Close. Maybe six, eight feet."

"Did he see the car?"

"Actually, no. Says he was in back. Just heard a car tear away when he came running out."

"What are my chances of getting something out of the medical examiner?"

"Susan? She's got a soft spot for you, Paul. All the muchachas do. I've been meaning to ask you about that..."

"Armano, you don't need any tips from me. I'm a two-time loser with wives."

"Who said anything about marriage, besides my mother?"

Paul jogged on the beach the next morning, working up a good sweat, running along Carmel Beach toward downtown, circling back, and running at the foot of Thirteenth. He was good and tired before he saw Susan Misumi making her way down a hillside pathway to the beach, dragged by a diminutive dog, a royal blue sweatshirt hood covering her head.

A woman of regular habits, she usually walked the beach very early in the morning. She was late. He must have run an extra mile. He'd skip tomorrow without guilt. He waved and ran toward her, slowing his pace.

"Son of a gun. It's been a while. Paul, right? After you quit, I thought you'd be heading back up to San Francisco."

"Where there's money, there's crime. Plenty of work for me right here. I could mention you're still here." He tried to catch his breath. He didn't feel very smooth with Susan. She was a type he found hard to understand, a woman happy in a man's job.

"Like you said, crime pays." She fell into step with him. They walked toward a large piece of driftwood and sat on it side by side. Small and delicate-looking, Susan did not look strong enough to cut through bone. "And I like my job." Her dog, a brindle-colored Lhasa apso, began a frantic search for something, flinging sand in all directions.

Paul moved out of the line of fire. "What got you interested in forensics?"

"In med school I quickly discovered my fatal flaw: I'm damned squeamish about cutting into living, breathing bodies. With dead people, you do no damage."

She looked up at Paul, grinning. "I've seen you on the beach a couple of times before, but you have that don't-bug-me-I'm-communing-with-nature look."

"Probably just in a hurry to answer nature's call."

Her dog must have known the meaning of the phrase. He raised his leg against the log a foot past Paul. Paul stood up and moved away. "Whew. Dangerous neighborhood."

"Speaking of which..." Susan said, apparently recognizing the lack of coincidence in their meeting.

"I'm working for Roman Maldonado's family. I wondered if you'd mind sharing a little of what's on your mind in that case."

"Oh, yes. What a mess. A drive-by, according to the police. Always hard to find those guys, unless they're dumb enough to brag about it. Amazing how many do."

"Did you go to the scene?"

"No. Earl Cummings from our office went over there because the owner of the store said the boy that was shot was dead. From what Earl said, and from the photographs, there's a problem with the blood at the scene."

"What's that?"

"There's blood on the sidewalk. Just not much. Strange, isn't it, when the kid got shot four times?"

"You think he was shot somewhere else and brought there?"

"No sign of blood in the store or the alley nearby. The first cop to arrive did a thorough survey of the area."

"How soon after the shooting did Earl get there?"

"About an hour. Should have been sooner. I've got a regular beef about that with Chief Carsey." She leaned over and scratched her dog behind the ears. His head moved ecstatically along with her fingers while his little body remained alert, the picture of eager anticipation. She got up. "Gotta go. Can't keep a good dog waiting."

She took off down the beach. Paul waved once more and then allowed his eyes to snap his standard body shot. She had good legs, muscular and balletic, a small waist, and long, developed arms. Susan was stronger than she looked. When she'd scratched the dog, Paul wanted to offer himself up for a good scratch, too. He watched her break into a carefree run. That woman probably plucked hearts out of men by the dozen. This level of cool, he could never quite approve.

After he had showered and dressed, he fired up his van and headed up 101 to Gilroy in a good mood, playing the radio and enjoying the cloud show on the green hills and dales flanking the freeway. He stopped at Chevy's for a breakfast burrito and drove up the hill toward Taylor's store. Parking in front, he noted the freshly painted angled spots and meticulously clean, well-swept walkway in front. No trees marred the shining asphalt with their leaves.

Armano hadn't exaggerated. Bert Taylor's market was definitely a cut above the average corner store. The windows sparkled, the floors shined. The area behind the counter looked like something organized and maintained by Paul's scrupulous Dutch grandmother, who had never made her peace with all the dirt in the world.

A woman with a baby in a stroller monopolized the man behind the counter for a good ten minutes trying to decide between what looked to be identically jumbo plastic packages of disposable diapers. One pass by the stroller, and Paul stayed away. Baby needed those diapers badly and had made bad use of them. Baby agreed, letting loose with a murderous howl. Her mother and the clerk ignored her, unconsciously adjusting the volume of their voices to be heard. Mom decided to take both packages, and then had the long job of figuring out how to carry them and push a stroller with a hysterical child at the same time.

"Bert Taylor?" Paul asked, after she was out of screaming distance.

"That's my name," said the clerk. Very tall, he would have been fairly good-looking except for a jaw that ended somewhere around his knees. The long face held an easy grin.

Paul introduced himself as an investigator. Taylor didn't ask him for further ID, assuming him to be yet another agent of law enforcement coming around to hear his story for the millionth time. Paul did not disabuse him of the notion, secretly marveling at how accepting people were when they shouldn't be.

Taylor was very interested in Roman's condition. "I coulda sworn that boy was dead as a doornail," he said in amazement. "I guess if you're here, he's not talking much. He remember what happened?"

"He's still confused. But he'll come out of it." Paul didn't know if that was true; he watched for a reaction, but missed it when Taylor turned away to adjust something on a shelf behind him.

Paul began to ask him a few questions, which Taylor answered. As they talked, Taylor moved stock on shelves, dusted for invisible dust, rearranged a sagging sign that read "If you look under a hundred years old, we want to see your ID for liquor purchases," and sprayed his counter with what smelled like poison gas, wiping it all down with an immaculate new sponge.

"A hundred?" Paul asked. "That's about how old I feel some days. You wouldn't really ID me, would you?"

"No," said Taylor.

"So why the sign?" Paul persisted.

"I put that sign up so maybe some people would quit making such a stink. You'd think they would be flattered I want to check their ID, but they get really ticked off."

The man's sudden show of anger piqued Paul's interest. "Ticked off enough to shoot someone?"

"No!" Taylor looked shocked. "That's ridiculous."

"So why make such a big deal about ID?"

"The penalties for selling to minors are fierce. Plus I'm not about to get in trouble so some sixteen-year-old can get loaded on my beer and crack up his mom's car."

Taylor swore Roman Maldonado had never worked for him. He said there were some rowdies who'd threatened him about being in the wrong neighborhood, but he wasn't about to cop to bullies. He'd opened a "dialogue," he said, and was working on making friends in the neighborhood. In general, he appeared to be a good-natured guy with nothing to hide. Only when he talked about Roman did he show his defensiveness.

"Look, I've seen him around, okay? I can't keep the kids from hanging around in front of the store. It's public property once they are out there. I've tried chasing them off, but I don't like to alienate anybody, especially potential customers. I turn a blind eye. But some of them are out there selling drugs, I know it and you do, too." He looked hard at Paul. "I bet you experimented when you were young. Most kids do."

"You're saying he was mixed up in a drug deal gone bad?"

"I wouldn't suggest that. I'm just trying to help you out, help you understand. He didn't work for me. If he had an income, that's one way people get it around here."

"When the Maldonados came by, you said you didn't know Roman. You lied, Bert. Why'd you lie?"

"They were upset. They remember wrong."

Paul wondered if they did.

On the way out of Taylor's, Paul ran into the stroller. Baby now sat quietly, calm as a cow chewing her cud, face covered with chocolate.

"Taylor sure keeps the store nice," Paul said to the baby's mother.

"Yeah, I hardly recognized it today. I'm here at least once a week. You notice when things change." She riffled for something in a voluminous straw bag, found what she was looking for, and brought out a crumpled cigarette.

"He really fixed it up, huh?"

"When he bought it, he put in the fresh food and painted the inside. I noticed today, the place is real clean."

"Ever see a big kid named Roman working the counter in there?"

"I don't want to get Bert into trouble."

"Kid got shot here a couple of days ago. Bert said it was a drive-by."

"Here?"

"Right in front of the store."

"Shit." She sighed, lighting up. "Might as well go out smoking."

Long shadows crept along the street shading the building opposite Paul's office, blurring as twilight hinted its approach. The shoppers were going home. If he wanted to make his evening walk on the beach, he would have to hurry. The thought, which ordinarily made him happy, irritated him for a moment. He didn't like routines. And he was tired of walking alone.

He called Taylor's insurance company, then pumped a workers' compensation lawyer he knew in Salinas for information. He had tried earlier in the day to talk with Roman again, but had another brief unenlightening conversation. The boy was in pain and too sick to talk on the phone.

But Paul was satisfied he had a solution. This wasn't the standard whodunit. The facts in the case had been deliberately muddied but he thought he knew now what had happened to Roman Maldonado.

Hurrying to his car, he clocked his trip to the hospital at four minutes. Another record.

Up in his room, Roman lifted himself out of his fog long enough for Paul to hammer the final nail in his solution: Taylor had a baseball bat he resorted to in a pinch to cool down hot-headed patrons.

He made the trip back up to Taylor's store, only once having to slip out of cruise control when a middle-aged flea marketeer cut him off at the Red Barn intersection.

"You again," Taylor greeted him. "Like Columbo. 'Oh, let me ask you one last thing.'" He laughed.

"That's right." Paul smiled. "I'm back and I'm bad."

"What's on your mind?"

The store was quiet, perhaps as quiet as the day Roman got shot. "Where are all your customers?"

"They come in waves. Sometimes we get ten people, then nobody for ten minutes."

"That way on Sunday?"

"Always is."

"That's right. There were no eyewitnesses. It was just you and Roman here, all alone. Just you two and a little under-the-table job, and a baseball bat." Paul strolled around picking a few things off the shelf, placing them carefully, neatly back. Behind the counter, he caught sight of the bat. "Self-made man," said Paul.

"That's right," Taylor said, wanting to throw him out, but nervous about it. "Nothing wrong with that."

"Self-sufficient. Hate hiring people. Bet you get worked up around tax time. Want to keep the government out of your business. Avoid insurance like the plague."

"Who doesn't?"

"I like that sign you've got in your window there. 'Survival of the fittest.' I've got to get one of those."

"Something I can help you find?" Taylor said impatiently.

"You know, I don't think so. This last thing I want to see here, I'll swear you haven't got."

It took him a long time to wear Taylor down, but in the

end he admitted it. Taylor just didn't carry what Paul was look-ing for.

The Maldonados were due in his office at about four o'clock. Stuck at a long light, he spent an extra minute on the return trip there, and ran up the stairs to make up the time. He was going to have to stop all these little games he played, find something a lit-tle more satisfying than competing against himself.

Puffing hard and inspired by the thought, he punched in the number for the medical examiner. Since that morning on the beach, he had thought a lot about Susan Misumi and that pip-squeak dog of hers.

She wasn't part of his grand plan, but dreams had a way of changing on you.

"Fancy an evening walk?" he asked.

She did.

The Maldonados arrived on the button. They took seats across from Paul. The long afternoon light from the window be-hind his desk slanted through blinds, striping their faces gold and gray.

"Did Roman tell you anything? We can't get him to talk. His mother cries when she goes there. It's tough, seeing him like that."

"He's confused about the details of what happened," Delilah said. "He remembers working behind the counter and he's sure he never stepped out that front door. Says he always used the back door. Too many smokers and winos hung around in front."

"So what the hell happened?"

"Victor!" his wife reprimanded.

"I'll send you a written report," Paul said. "But this was no drive-by shooting. There was no spatter on the wall, and at least some of the blood he lost ended up somewhere besides the side-walk in front of Taylor's store."

The parents looked at him, flummoxed. The father slammed

his open hand down on the Formica. "Taylor shot him! I didn't like him the moment I saw him."

"No. Taylor didn't shoot him. Roman says it was someone he didn't know. But Taylor's got plenty to answer for."

"Well, then . . . ?"

"Here's my take on it. Number one problem. Not enough blood on the sidewalk. That's easy. Roman was shot inside the store. Number two problem. Where's the blood? Well, we've got an immaculate store all of a sudden. Taylor's been mopping and scrubbing like a maniac. You said the day your son was shot, you got there and Taylor was cleaning. He probably had cleared away the blood seconds after Roman got shot right there behind the counter. Problem three. Who shot him? I don't think it was someone Roman knew. I don't think it had anything to do with drugs. I think Roman got shot the same way most people get shot in convenience stores. He got shot during an attempted robbery.

"My guess? It was a young-looking customer, a nervous one. Maybe put a six-pack on the counter thinking he'd get your son to open the register, then he'd make his move. But the owner's been on the warpath about selling to underage drinkers. Your son demands some ID, which is not something a thief is eager to show. The thief balks."

"Roman would stand up to the guy," Victor said sadly. "He's got a temper."

"So, okay, at this point Roman's already defensive, maybe a little mad. The customer looks young. Maybe he's a little fellow. And Roman's big, intimidating. Roman says Taylor keeps a base-ball bat under the counter in case things get rowdy. So, let's say, Roman reaches under the counter. Anyway, for that reason or some other one, the would-be thief gets nervous and pulls a gun. Your son gets shot. Happens all the time."

"It doesn't make sense. They found him outside."

"That slowed me down a little, too. That's where your friend Taylor came in. He moved him."

"He dragged Roman outside?" asked Roman's horrified mother. "After someone shot him?"

"Let's give him the benefit of the doubt. He thought Roman was already dead."

"But why would he do that, Mr. van Wagoner? Why leave our son dead on the sidewalk?"

"Bert Taylor didn't carry workers' compensation insurance. He knew he'd be liable if your son was shot in his store. Outside, he might be able to avoid any financial responsibility. He's not a murderer. He's just another small businessman trying to protect himself. Almost everybody lies to save money. He figured your son was dead already, so why invite trouble?"

"My God!"

"My ex-fellow cops are over there right now. I'm sure Taylor will be persuaded to help them identify the person who shot your son. He probably saw the whole thing."

"They better catch him," said Delilah, "before I do. Boys with guns. I never let Roman play with guns."

"By the way, I had a talk with Roman's doctor," Paul said. "In spite of being only a few feet away, the shooter missed anything vital. The doctor says Roman's as strong as a prizefighter. He'll be out of the hospital soon."

"Without a job to go to," worried his mother.

"No troubles on that score now. Taylor will make it up to him," Paul said. "I'll see to it."

"If he can't even afford insurance, we're not going after Bert Taylor," said Victor. "We don't want to put him out of business or anything. What he did was really low, but he didn't actually harm our boy."

"Oh, but Taylor can afford insurance. He just prefers to put his money into real estate. He owns a section of coastline south of Carmel."

"He can help us with Roman's medical bills?"

"I'll give you the name of a fine workers' comp attorney in Salinas who will make sure Mr. Taylor takes care of all Roman's needs for now and for a significant chunk of the future, guaranteed."

"You mean..." Delilah began, but her husband interrupted.

"Hot damn," cried Victor Maldonado, knocking the chair over as he stood up. "Roman's going to college!"

Dead Money

Through his sunglasses, darkly, Tim Breen watched Sunday-morning sun heat the fence outside the sheriff's office, sending steam off the fence and the roof of the town library next door. It had been raining for a month, but today would be clear.

All around the little Sierra foothill town of Timberlake the forest whistled and cawed, rustled and stirred. The gullies along West Main Street ran like creeks, splashing up water as the cars rolled by. He watched a mallard sail down one, making for the river, sun glistening on its iridescent green head. As it passed, it rasped out some quacks, like an old man laughing at him.

He watched the town come out to dry, thinking, Now they'll bring me all the trouble they've been storing up behind their screen doors. He liked it better dull and sleepy in the rain, nobody bothering him. He was burned out, and he knew it, but he hid it behind a lumbering good-natured facade.

Warm yeast smells drifted toward him from the Ponderosa Coffee Shop across the street. At ten fifteen, more or less, he was usually there, eating donuts and drinking coffee with Bodie Gates, the other deputy assigned to the tiny Timberlake station.

He still had half an hour. He pulled the missing persons report on Roy Ballantine out of his pocket, scanning it again.

Anita Ballantine had been waiting for him at eight when he rode into the parking lot in the patrol car, wound tight from anger or fear, he couldn't tell which. Inside, while he washed out the coffeepot and settled himself behind his old metal desk, she had told him about Roy Ballantine, who had gone AWOL in the night.

He knew Roy, the local agent for Gibraltar Insurance Company. Roy worked out of a storefront office three doors down and across the street.

Anita had said Roy never stayed out all night before. He had to be at work at eight A.M., and he never missed a day. He had taken the car about ten the night before, saying he was going to the liquor store for beer. The car, a 2002 Honda Accord, was in good shape, but maybe he'd gone for a drive in the woods, god knows why, broke down, and passed a cold Saturday night out there.

Tim had listened, noticing Anita had gotten thinner over the winter. Her skin was so white he could see the blue veins in her neck. He had written down the license number, and promised to check it out, telling Anita he was sure everything would be all right.

It was probably nothing, but he'd have to do something about it. He stuffed the paper back in his pocket, a little angrily. The duck floated out of view, ruffling its feathers, and he went into the station.

First he woke up Henry Salas with his phone call. Henry had been on shift at Timberlake Liquors the night before. Roy hadn't shown up there, for beer or anything else.

Then he drove down the highway, out of town, toward the Feather River Bridge, the tall firs along the road black against the strong sun. Across the bridge, six miles farther south down the highway at Camden, there was an all-night supermarket that sold Roy's brand of beer.

As he got on the two-lane bridge, forty feet above the swollen brown torrent below, he saw Roy's black Accord parked on the right, smack against the bridge railing. He turned on his flashing lights and parked behind the car.

Nobody inside. On the front seat of the unlocked car, Tim found Roy's wallet with twenty-six bucks in it. The back seat was covered with suit ties, paper cups, and burger wrappers, quite a few files, some girlie magazines. Like most insurance agents, Roy did a lot of business out of his car.

No blood smears, no sign of violence, but all wrong. Tim looked up ahead, looked back down the road.

Looked over the metal rail, about four feet high, coated with corroded green paint and bird guano, and down, to where the river poured by.

Back to the Accord. He searched it thoroughly this time. No note in the glove compartment, current registration above the driver's side visor. Keys in the ignition, shit. He got in and started it up, using his handkerchief. The engine roared. No breakdown here.

He called Bodie from his car radio and asked for backup and binoculars. Then he drove slowly the rest of the way across the bridge, searching with his eyes, and all the way to the Camden supermarket. The manager there made some calls. None of the night clerks had seen Roy. He had never made it that far.

When Tim got back to the bridge, Bodie was leaning over the rail, his hand shading his eyes. "Some good-sized trout down there," he said. His uniform hung on him. Still a growing boy, six feet four and rising, he weighed a hundred sixty pounds after dinner and cake.

Tim handed him the report from Anita, and said over the roar from below, "Roy Ballantine. He may be a jumper. But there's no note."

"I see the car keys," Bodie said. "I brought a couple pairs of fishing boots like you said."

"Let's get started, then." The two deputies climbed down the slick, weedy, muddy banks on the west side of the bridge, in the direction of the water flow, poking through the underbrush every few feet.

By noon they had covered both sides up to a half-mile down. They had found the carcass of a dog, about a million beer cans, and somebody's bra, and they were half-blind from the reflections off the river, but Roy hadn't turned up.

They went back to town, changed clothes, ate at the diner down the street, and called in a local construction crew to search the remaining half-mile stretch down to the falls. Anita called in and said she had had no word. Tim told her he'd have to hold on to the Accord for a while, and told her not to worry, but she was a smart girl. A few minutes later, he saw her in her old Mercedes heading toward the bridge.

The foreman of the crew came in at five to report that his men had searched the full mile down to the portage camp above Timberlake Falls, then hiked down around and had a look at the dense foliage at the bottom, where the rocks were. "Nothing," he said. "You're gonna have to bring in a diver. Why would Ballantine jump anyway? He was lookin' happy last Saturday night at the Elks, real happy. He won at least two hundred bucks playin' poker."

Tim said, "Thanks, buddy. Send me the bill," and then he went out on the front porch of the sheriff's office, where he had set up a folding chair, and thought.

The spring sun cast sharp shadows down the street, filtered here and there by the trees. He half-expected to see Roy come meandering down the sidewalk, returning from some backwoods bacchanalia, dirty and beat. But Roy didn't oblige.

Aside from the Elks Club and the Episcopal Church, the Ballantines kept to themselves. They had two kids in the elementary school. Roy and Anita had problems, but Tim had never received one of those late-night, help-he's-trying-to-kill-me calls. They had moved to Timberlake five years before, when Roy transferred in from San Francisco. Anita missed the big city. She still visited family there about once a month.

He left Bodie on the phone to his girlfriend. He felt tired, and he wanted to go home and hide like he'd been doing for a long time, but he had to talk to Anita again.

In the big white rambling Cape Cod on the edge of town, Anita sat in the dark dining room, curtains drawn, a bottle of expensive Chardonnay mostly empty on the table, a glass in her hand. She was usually careful about makeup and hair, but tonight she had pulled her long red hair into a ponytail and let the freckles show, and she was wearing one of Roy's old flannel shirts.

She jumped up when he came in, said, "Did you find him?" breathlessly, and when he had to tell her no, she sat back down with a thump and put her face in her hands while he told her about the search.

After a minute or two she stirred and said in a hostess voice, "I'm forgetting my manners. Let me pour you a glass of wine."

"Water or a soda would be fine," he said.

"Come on," she said. "You're off duty now. I heard you can drink the whole town under the table."

"I don't do that anymore."

"Oh," she said. "You got religion. How trendy. How middle-aged." She shuffled into the kitchen in her floppy slippers, came back with ice water.

"Ginny's out back," she said. "Roy rigged up a tree house for her and Kyle. Would you like to see it?"

"Some other time."

"I told them Roy had to go out of town. I didn't think I ought to—you know. Yet."

He had put it off as long as he could. "I'm not much good in the tact department, Anita. I hope you'll take this right. I need to know, has Roy been talking about suicide? Did he have any problems that were getting him down? Sleepless nights, signs of depression? Secrets?"

Anita said, "I've been sitting here all day, thinking about his car on the bridge. I suppose that's what Roy's done, committed suicide. I thought you came here to tell me you found his body."

"Did he give you any indication..." Anita cocked her head, raised her eyebrows, smiled brightly.

"Indication? No, he was actually quite specific. How he didn't love me anymore. How he hated this stupid town and all you rednecks riding around in your pickups. How if he never saw another tree it would be fine with him. He applied for a transfer, but the company's cutting back, and he was lucky to have this job. So he smiled and schmoozed all day and lay awake at night staring up toward the ceiling."

Having dumped its emotion, her voice trailed off.

"Funny. I thought he liked it here," Tim said.

"He was bored," Anita said. "Bored with me and the kids. Roy never wanted to sell insurance. He wanted to be sailing a yacht in the Aegean wearing a white cap with his arm around a teenager's waist. Then Ginny came. And Kyle the next year. How interesting. We're both talking about him in the past tense. He's probably going to walk through the front door any minute, pissing and moaning about his dinner being late."

"Was he a good swimmer?"

"What do you mean by that? He was trying to kill himself, so he wouldn't be swimming hard to save himself. Would he? And the water's freezing, how could he survive? He's dead, Mr. Deputy. Go find him."

"Keep your spirits up," Tim said.

"Actually, I'm drinking 'em down," Anita said, waving the wine bottle. She stopped herself after a second, and set the bottle carefully back on the table. "Whether he comes back or not, Timothy Breen, I don't want you telling anybody what I just said. About my marriage. About how Roy felt. I talked too much. Under the circumstances." She straightened up in the chair, put her hand to her hair. "Who knows. If he does turn up, mustn't hurt his business. Insurance agent, you know, he's like a minister or funeral director. You know, stable, good marr—marriage . . . Elks."

"If he's dead, that won't matter, Anita."

"It matters to me."

"I can't promise, Anita. But I sure won't hurt you unnecessarily."

She smiled humorlessly, put her elbows on the table and her head back in her hands. "All you care about is your stinkin' self," she said. "Gonna use my weakness against me."

He let it pass. She was talking to Roy, he knew that.

Just before six, back in town, he stopped into Gibraltar Insurance and talked to Roy's secretary, Kelly Durtz, the daughter of the mayor. Though she was eighteen, she looked about fourteen years old and had the brains of a pigeon. Roy would not have confided in her.

She let him go through Roy's desk. Everything was in order, more files on the desk, a pen set from his wife, certificates and family photos on the walls. No note, no private desperate musings stuck away in a corner of a drawer. Kelly locked up and left with him, walked toward home two blocks away.

Tim locked up, too, leaving his home number on the answering machine in case of emergency. Timberlake was too small to justify a 911 service. People were leaving, not arriving. Soon enough they would have to close the sheriff's substation there, and he would have to move somewhere or take up a new trade.

He drove home, five minutes away, off the highway and down two hundred feet of gravel road, startling a buck and doe browsing in the brush at the turnoff.

He really should get a dog. He turned on the lamp in the main room of his cabin, went into the kitchen, and microwaved three burritos. After setting them on his kitchen table, breathing in their beany aroma, he got the big bottle of orange Gatorade out of the fridge, not bothering with a glass.

He ate, watched TV, had a shower, got into bed with the old Ross Macdonald he was reading, keeping half an ear open for the sound of the phone or tires crunching in the driveway, but nothing happened. Nothing much ever did happen.

Right before he turned out the light, he thought to himself, I thought he liked it here. He hadn't really known Roy. No one had really known Roy, and no one really knew Tim.

And then he thought, if no body turned up, you have to wonder, what if Roy faked it? He lay there on the lumpy bed that gave him backaches and chewed on that thought for a long time.

As usual, he slept badly. Outside, the crickets built their wall of sound, the moths mated in a flutter of wings around his porch light, and a bullfrog raised his nightly ruckus down by the river, but Tim pulled the covers over his head, because he didn't want to hear it. The forest made him crazy, he didn't know why.

The next morning when Angel Ramirez opened up at the bank, Tim was there, and he got Angel to look up Roy's accounts without a warrant. Angel had that bad habit of driving to neighboring towns late at night and peeking into windows when the urge got too strong. Tim had helped him into a diversion program the year before, and Angel still saw Doc Ashland every week. If he was still peeping, he had gotten too discreet for Tim to hear a whisper of it.

"He has the individual checking account, in his name only, a joint checking account with his wife's name on it, too, a business account, and a trust account," Angel said. "Here're the last month's statements on each of the four."

Inflow, outflow, some bounced checks on the individual accounts. Like everybody, Roy and Anita spent more than they took in.

The trust account showed a big check being cashed for a client ten days before. "I'd like to see this one," he told Angel.

Made out to Roy Ballantine, as a Gibraltar agent, and Peter Bayle, jointly, the check was for two hundred fifty thousand dollars. Gibraltar Insurance had already cleared it.

"Settlement check," Angel explained.

"Why put Roy's name on it?"

"The company always puts both names on it so the agent can make sure he's got a signed release before the client can cash it. There'll be a release of liability form back at Roy's office."

"They both have to sign?" Tim said. He looked at the back. Two signatures all right, Royal F. Ballantine, as agent, and Pete Bayle. Different handwriting, the Bayle signature small and crabbed, like old man Bayle himself. "Who brought it in? I assume you cashed out a check this size yourself."

"Roy brought it in. Pete was holed up at home, nursing the broke jaw that got him all this big money," Angel said. "Broke jaw, bruised ribs, lost his spleen."

"He didn't have a lawyer?"

"Let some shyster take one-third of it? Pete's not that stupid. Roy took care of it," Angel said. "He made Pete a fair settlement offer. Gibraltar's insured was at fault. There wasn't any issue around it. Pete's got TMJ, has to have an operation on his jaw, and he's still gonna look a little sideways from head-on, even after the operation."

"What's Pete's number?" Tim said. When the old man picked up, Tim asked, "Pete, you get your check from Gibraltar yet?"

"No, and I ain't paid my rent in two months. I'm gonna call Ballantine tomorrow, kick him in the ass."

"You come to town and see me instead," Tim said. "In the morning." He turned the check over again, looking at the signatures. "Angel," he said, "Don't you ever do that again. Make sure both signatories are present."

"Well, I'll be lassoed and laid down," Angel said, his bug eyes through the thick glasses gentle and astonished. "When did Roy turn into a crook? He looked right in my eyes, asked me about the kids—I said to him, where's Pete going to take all that cash, over to the Wells Fargo Bank? And I offered to set Pete up for free checking, but Roy said, no, Pete's buying a hundred acres in Humboldt County, he's moving on—"

"Cash," Tim interrupted. "Two hundred fifty thousand. Roy stole it, and already spent it, and he killed himself when he couldn't pay back the trust account. Or else he faked a suicide. If he did, he's gone with the money, and his body won't turn up."

"What are you gonna do?"

"Have a donut," Tim said. He looked at his watch, and ambled across the street to the Ponderosa.

After a chocolate one and the kind with powdered sugar and two cups of coffee, he was ready to go back to the office. The sun had burned off the early mist, and he could see the plank floor needed a mop job. The red message light on the phone was blinking.

"This is Valerie at the store at the portage point. I found a . . . corpse down at the foot of the falls. I just left it, but I don't want any kids finding it, it's all beat up, so please come and—" The answering machine had cut out, but he'd heard enough.

On the car radio, Tim called Bodie and said, "Bring Doc Ashland and call Camden to send an ambulance." The donuts had reconstituted to hard round lumps in his stomach.

He had to admit, he was a little disappointed. A part of him that he didn't let anyone see had been rooting for Roy to make a clean getaway.

★   ★   ★

He turned right after the bridge and headed down River Road. Downstream about a mile south, a cluster of cabins sidled along the river, near the top of Timberlake Falls, and there was a store with fishing bait and supplies.

As he drove, he seemed to rush down the road at about the same speed as the flow of the river. He'd never seen it so high or so brown, so brimming with energy. What had made Roy jump in?

He parked in the mud in front of the store. The young woman who came out to meet him looked familiar, though her hair was longer, a nice brown instead of the yellow he remembered, and the plucked eyebrows and lipstick and earrings were gone. She was plainer than she had been, but she looked better, too, healthier. He remembered that line between her eyebrows, too, of chronic puzzlement or discontent.

"You took your time. I suppose you don't remember me," she said. "Valerie. From the year after high school, when we were both working at the supermarket in Camden."

"I knew right away it was you," he said.

"It's been a few years."

"Not so many."

"Come on in for a minute." She opened the screen door for him, and as he passed into the cool darkness he smelled her scent, vanilla and roses, seemed to feel her hair brush against him, soft as a spiderweb. She went around the counter and he sat down on a tall stool.

"This place hasn't changed in twenty years," he said, looking around at the old refrigerator unit that held the bait, and the candy bar rack, and the ice cream bin. "I used to ride my bike down here as a kid in the summer, sit out back under the trees and watch the waterfall. The fisherman used to set up nets there and catch the fish just before they went over."

Perri O'Shaughnessy

"My husband and I bought the store and the motel last year," Valerie said. "The rain's killed all the business."

"You look good." Her mouth, he remembered that, too, the taste of lemonade and whiskey.

"You, too, I think. It's hard to tell with those sunglasses on. I've seen you drive by in your patrol car. You used to be such a hellraiser, if you don't mind my saying so. You were so funny. I guess you must have got ahold of your drinking, becoming a deputy and all."

"I straightened up about five years ago. AA did it. Learned a lot. How about you?"

"I kept on until I hit a bad bottom. Went down to Sacramento for detox. That was two and a half years ago."

"You had any slips since?" Tim said. She was so different, calm, mature, not the frenetic girl he had known. He didn't feel inclined to hike down to the foot of the falls until Bodie got there, anyway.

"Slips? No, I watched my husband start down the tubes where I had been, and I thought for the children I better not give up."

"Whatever works," he said, and she smiled. "So you got married. How many kids do you have?"

"Two boys. They're little. My mom watches them while I'm working."

"Where's your husband now?"

"He just got laid off from his job in Camden. At the water company. Ed Strickland." She was still looking him over. She said. "You put on weight. You do look older, Tim."

"Last time I saw you, you were lying in the grass behind the market beating time with a bottle of vodka in your hand, singing every verse of 'Hotel California.'"

"I guess that was a good party," Valerie said. "I wouldn't know. I can't remember much about that year."

"I know what you mean," Tim said. He smiled at her, too.

What passed between them then was a recognition, hesitant, tenuous. Not like the old days, when the booze dissolved the barriers. They heard the ambulance siren.

"Guess we better go outside," he said.

"Sure. I'll take you down there."

She walked lightly, jumping along the rocks, wearing a long flowered dress and brown hiking boots. Bodie and Doc Ashland and the med techs followed behind her, carrying the stretcher, and Tim brought up the rear.

The falls dropped about fifty feet onto sharp rocks. It sounded like static, white noise overpowering everything else. The water went over fearlessly, even joyfully. He felt something inside himself stir in response.

They scrambled down the steep hill, following the water, out into the brush. "I was running my dog," she said breathlessly. "Over there, by the rocks. The river's so high it's flooded the trail, so we were bushwhacking. And I saw—that black foot sticking out. See it? I didn't go any closer. I just ran up the hill and called."

Tim just barely saw it, a shadow against other shadows. Valerie had sharp eyes. "You go back up, now," he said. "I'll talk to you later."

"He's dead. He went over the falls. I don't want to see the rest of him," she said. "Okay, then."

Roy Ballantine's body lay facedown in the mud, legs spread and knees drawn up. "In that wet suit, he looks like a big drowned frog," Bodie said. While the medics moved around the body, Tim and Bodie took pictures and hunted around in the bush. An hour later, they helped load the body on a stretcher. Black-bottomed clouds moved over the sun as the temperature dropped. They were covered with mud. "Let's go up to the store, see if Valerie'll give us some coffee," Tim said.

She did better, finding them chairs to sit on and letting them wash up, too. She had lit the stove, and they sat around it.

"More rain," Doc Ashland said. "It's a record year."

Tim told them about the money and said, "He botched his fake suicide, I'd say. He jumped off the bridge. He was going to climb out of the river downstream, peel off the wet suit, take the money, and leave town." He felt warm and comfortable. Valerie was behind him, but he could feel her eyes pressing, like soft curious blue daggers in his back.

"I've never seen the river this high," Bodie said. "He got carried down the stream and went over. I almost feel sorry for him. He had it worked out pretty well."

"He got bashed up bad going over, so I can't be positive, but I'm thinking all the injuries are consistent with the wet ride he took," Doc Ashland said. "I'll do a complete autopsy tonight. Idiot, thinking he could use the river."

"Good concept, poor execution," Tim said.

"The Great Escape," the doc said. "I thought about it myself, back when I was about to get drafted for the Vietnam War. Disappear, start over."

"We didn't find much around him or on him," Bodie said. "No money. If he had a pack strapped to him, it might be downriver. We'll start looking right away."

"He'd need transport once he got out," Tim said. "Bodie, you look hard for a car or motorcycle out there in the trees, too." He got up. "I'm going to have to go tell Anita. You coming, Bodie?"

The crew came back and searched the banks of the river for three days in pouring rain, but they didn't turn up a thing. Doc Ashland finished the autopsy, saying all he could add was that Roy didn't have any alcohol or drugs in his system. And that the cause of death looked like drowning, though Roy was so beat up from the falls he might have died anyway.

The fourth day, a man in a gray suit came driving up to the

sheriff's substation in a brand-new Jeep Cherokee. Tim came out to meet him. "James Burdick, Gibraltar Insurance," he said, shaking hands. "I thought you might have some sun this high up." Burdick was short and solid. He smelled of cigars.

"It'll be back," Tim said.

"I read your report. You sure your men have searched that river high and low for the money?"

"It's not there."

"Because if it doesn't turn up soon, I'm going to have to is-sue the old man another check. He's hired a lawyer this time and he's making a fearful racket. I don't work directly with the agents, so I didn't know Roy Ballantine. Did you ever think he'd do a thing like this?"

"I'd heard he was gambling, getting into debt. Maybe I should have paid more attention."

"If we do pay that geezer Bayle off again, we're going to try to recover from Ballantine's estate."

"Anita's going to need money. I doubt she'll be getting any of the life insurance he was loaded up with."

"She can always file bankruptcy," the Gibraltar man said breezily. "Can we go inside? It's freezing out here."

Anita came to see him the next day. She had fixed herself up, but the old spark had been replaced by something just old. Events like losing a husband could make a woman cross the line into age in one night. Tim had seen it before.

"Let's talk frankly, Anita," he said. Her eyes burned at him for a minute, then extinguished again. "I've been listening to the gossip. I heard some things I need to check out with you."

"Like what?"

"For example, that you were getting ready to leave Roy, take Ginny and Kyle."

"So what if I was?" she said. "So you've been listening to the

women in this town, stabbing you in the back when your husband's just died . . ." She started crying, lightly and easily, like the
rain falling outside the door. "He'd gambled away our savings.
He didn't care about me anymore. Yes, I was thinking about
leaving while I still had some self-respect. Of course, he's taken
even that away from me now." But the lift of her chin into the air
said, he can take everything else, but he won't take my pride.

"Did you know he was going to steal the money?"

"Of course not—"

"Marriage is an odd state. We let another person come so
close, they can read our minds," Tim said. "I think you knew."

"I can't believe you're saying this. You're accusing me of
killing him so I could have the money, like I dressed him in a wet
suit and tossed him over the bridge? He weighed over two hundred pounds. I don't have to listen to this. I'm going home."

"You might want to wait another few minutes," Tim said.

"Wh-why?"

"Because Bodie's out there searching your house and yard.
I'm sorry, we have to be sure." He handed her a copy of the
search warrant.

"That woman is so broke all we found was letters to her sister asking for loans," Bodie said later. "We dug around the backyard, knocked holes in the walls, tossed the garage. Found a
family of skunks. There's no money there."

"We had to try," Tim said. "You want to eat over at the hotel restaurant tonight? My treat."

"My grampa's in town," Bodie said. "My mom's making a
turkey. You're more than welcome . . ."

"No, you go on. I've got my heart set on a piece of apple pie
from the restaurant," Tim said.

He locked up at five. It was a warm clear night, and the street
was lined with the cars of the isolated cabin owners from miles

around who didn't get into town that often. He saw some loggers from Camden he knew, said hello, walked up the wooden steps to the Placer Hotel Restaurant.

After dinner Tim was trying to make up his mind whether to drive to Camden for a movie or to go home, when he saw Valerie's husband out front, careening toward his car. He hustled over and took his arm, saying, "Oh no you don't."

"Leggo," Ed Strickland said. He was a strong boy, but Tim got him over to the porch and half-threw him into the wicker chair.

"Stay there while I call a taxi. You can't drive like that," he said. Strickland's disheveled blond hair fell across his eyes and he blew out cheap Scotch vapors.

"I'll just walk back to the hotel, if you're gonna make a federal case out of me having a few," he said.

"You need to go home."

"The hotel is my home, Mr. Deputy Sir," Strickland said. "I moved here recently."

"Valerie and you . . ."

"It's all her fault," Strickland said. "She wanted to buy the damn place. Then the tourists stayed away because of the rain. I got laid off. Then she threw me out because I couldn't find any other work. It's not my fault. She's a hard-hearted b—"

"Watch your mouth," Tim said, cutting him off. "If you don't have any money, how are you paying to live at the Placer Hotel?"

Strickland gave him a sly look from under the hair. "You ever played poker with me? I have had one humongous streak lately. Best of all, she hasn't got any paycheck stub to look at, so she can't come after me for some of it. Can I go now?" He got up and wove across the street, waving away the traffic. Tim sat down, watching.

The next morning, early, he drove back to the portage point. Gray mist seeped around the dripping trees. Valerie opened the door to the motel office, looking surprised and maybe pleased to see him. She still wore her robe, a long blue silky thing. Her hair was wet from the shower. She hastily took off the specs she was wearing, invited him in.

"The kids just left for school," she said. "They left some eggs in the pan."

"Sounds good," Tim said. While he ate in the warm little kitchen, she washed the dishes. Finally, she sat down across the table from him with her coffee. She said, "I know you have some business or you wouldn't have come. So go right ahead."

"It's about Ed," Tim said.

"Ed? Did he do something?"

"I don't know. He says you and he have split up."

"Trust Ed to tell everybody in town," Valerie said.

"When did this happen?"

"Oh, I guess it was the day after I found Roy. Ed and I, we never were suited for each other. We were party pals, you know what I mean? When I sobered up, I found out there was nothing else between us."

"He's got a fancy room at the Placer Hotel," Tim said. "How does he pay for it?"

"Well, I can tell you he doesn't pay on credit. We have no credit," Valerie said. "He isn't working around here, or I'd know it. I suppose he's having a winning streak."

Her robe softened the hard planes of her face. Her damp hair shone like satin. He wanted to touch it. He drank some more coffee, and said, "I didn't know there really were such things."

"You stop believing in all that nonsense when the drinking stops," she said. "Yeah. He might be winning this week, but next week is another thing entirely. He doesn't think that way, though."

"Not like us," Tim said. "Upright and sober. I'm thinking maybe Ed found the body with the money before you got out there, picked a fight with you, and left."

Valerie's jaw dropped. She shook her head. "You mean he

might have two hundred fifty thousand dollars socked away somewhere? I can't believe it. He could never keep it a secret. He'd just have to brag about it."

"Now that you think about it, did you notice anything in his behavior that day, you know, going outside for a long time, anything like that?"

"Just the usual foul mood when he has a hangover," Valerie said. "I slept late that morning and didn't go out with Ginger for her walk until ten. But I still—"

"I hate being sober," Tim said. He rubbed his jaw, wondering what brought that comment on. She would understand, that was it. He could talk to her, and she would understand. "You ever feel that way?"

She stayed right with him, as if he hadn't suddenly changed the subject. "I know what you mean," she said. "It's like, you went to the optometrist, and he fit you with powerful glasses, and the whole world springs into this vivid focus. And it's the same old ugly world you drank to escape from, and you can see every dirty crevice again..." She looked around the shabby kitchen, at the cracked linoleum and the broken high chair in the corner.

"Yeah. Like you used to love riding the Ferris wheel, and now all you notice is the operator's tired and mean, hates his job, and doesn't like you," Tim said.

Valerie nodded. "I look back, and it's like we used to live in the night, under those romantic hazy-colored lights, and now it's daylight. It's too sharp and bright, isn't it?"

He sat there looking at her. She had that ironic, crooked smile he'd seen on so many drunks at so many meetings. "Yeah. They keep trying to convince you it's better," he said. "It's worse, but you can't escape anymore. You're gonna die if you keep boozing, shooting up, whatever you're doing."

"Condemned to real life," she said, laughing a little. "Forced to grow up."

"I could love you now," he said. "We've both been through it."

"Quit kidding yourself," she said. "You could have loved me years ago, when we were kids and drunk all the time, but not now. You can't fall in love unless you can get out of your head."

"Normal people do it."

"They're just born insensitive. Born lucky. So we sobered up, and you turned into a depressed cop. And I turned into an unhappy housewife. We're big successes now."

"There was something brave about what we were doing," Tim said. "You know? And now we don't even have that."

"We are the driest of dry drunks," Valerie said. She got up and came around the table to him. She took his big head in her hands and drew him to her breast, and his arms went around her little waist. "Maybe this will help," she said.

"Maybe."

"We could give it a try, anyway. Even if it only lasts a minute."

"Count on it lasting a little longer than that."

"Sobriety sucks, it really does," she said.

"Yeah. The whole situation. Take your panties off, okay?"

Tim put Bodie on Ed Strickland for the next couple of days. Bodie reported that Strickland sat in on three or four regular floating poker games at Camden and at Timberlake. He seemed content to hang around town, like he was waiting for something to happen.

After the second day, Tim got another search warrant, and he and Bodie tore up Strickland's room at the Placer Hotel. But they didn't find anything. The Strickland bank account contained about enough money for next week's groceries.

The Gibraltar man called. "Are you closing the investigation after the inquest tomorrow?" he said. "I need a final report for the records, so I can issue another check for Bayle and get this thing over with."

"You're going to give up on finding the money?"

"Let me put it to you this way," Burdick said. "You're Joe Schmoe with a mortgage, fishing along the riverbanks, and what do you snag but a bag full of a fortune in cash? What do you do with it?"

"You tell me."

"You dry out the bills on an inside clothesline. You wait a few months, and you start spending it slowly and carefully, and you thank your lucky fucking stars," Burdick said with a laugh. "We call it dead money. Now and then it slips through the cracks. You're never going to find it."

At the inquest the next day, nothing came out that Tim hadn't heard before. He gave his testimony, and they all called it a day and sloshed over to the hotel for lunch. The coroner's verdict was accidental death in the course of committing a crime, and Tim had no evidence to the contrary, except they still hadn't found the money.

He went back to the office, took care of other business, locked up, went home, and looked in the freezer. Burritos. One of those supermarket pizzas that tasted like paper.

He looked around the place. Something was missing. Oh yeah, Becky and little Dave. They had moved to Illinois. She had filed for divorce a month later.

He was sick of being struck with that thought ten times a day. Something was stinging his eyes. He was damn bored and damn lonely, and he was sick and tired of being bored and lonely, of listening to the forest outside and not being a part of anything.

Next thing he knew, he was on the phone to Valerie. "Can I come over for a while?" he said.

"Wait until nine or so," she said. "I'll get the kids to bed early."

★   ★   ★

He couldn't bring wine, so he stopped and bought her some flowers at the hotel. She opened the door, holding her finger to her lips, and led him directly into the bedroom. The sheets and pillowcases smelled like vanilla and roses, like her. She comforted him, and he did what he could for her.

Sometime later he woke out of a doze, to the clicking of a key being inserted into the kitchen door. Valerie woke up, too. He got up quickly, pulling his service revolver out of the holster hung on the bedpost. Valerie tiptoed behind him as he walked down the hall.

Ed Strickland had his head in the refrigerator. When he saw them, his bloodshot eyes went wide and he let out a strangled yell. "You been sleeping with him!" he said. "I'll fix you—"

"Shut up, you prick," Valerie said. "I'll sleep with him if I want. Get out."

"This is my house," he yelled, stumbling toward them, his fists up.

"Get away, Ed. Go on, leave," Tim said. He kept the gun down, but Strickland charged him, still yelling, grabbing for it. They locked in a furious embrace, Tim trying to keep the gun off him. Valerie ran over by the stove. Strickland smashed him in the face, a big dangerous drunk. They wrestled for the gun—

Tim heard the explosion, saw Strickland's head bloom out red on one side, and then Strickland crumpled on the ground, and the kids were standing in the doorway holding each other and screaming—

The sheriff, Bud Ames, came thirty miles from the county seat for the investigation. They took Tim's badge. Valerie backed him up all the way. The coroner called it an accident, and he got his badge back. But he knew that when the time came for layoffs of county staff, he'd be right up there on the list.

About a week after the Strickland inquest he went back to Valerie's. Her kids acted afraid of him. Valerie said maybe they shouldn't see each other anymore. The pain he felt when she said that shocked him. He hadn't known he was in love with her.

He went back to his routine.

April passed. The sun came out, the dazzling mountain sun that the tourists loved. He arrested drunks, rode patrol, issued citations, played dead. Or maybe he was dead.

He kept seeing the two deer when he drove home at dusk. They must have a nest under one of the trees not far from the cabin. As the weather warmed, the birds returned to raise hell at dawn.

On another Saturday night, he had just finished his dinner at the Placer Hotel when the desk clerk came over, the mayor's other daughter, the smart one. "I guess I shouldn't say this, but I hope you don't feel too bad about what happened," she said. "Strickland used to sit up in his room and drink, and then he'd lurch down the stairs looking for trouble. If you hadn't killed him, he might have killed somebody else, like his wife."

"I appreciate the thought," Tim said. He sipped his decaf, thinking about Strickland's face when he turned around and saw Tim there in the house.

"Why'd she call him?" the clerk said. "If I was separated from him, I would have left well enough alone."

"Valerie called him? At the hotel?"

"She called him that night," the clerk said. "You know, the night he . . . died. They didn't talk long, but he didn't look upset or anything when he came down. He left right after."

"Excuse me," Tim said. He picked up the check with trembling hands and took it to the cashier.

"You okay?" she said.

"Fine. Do me a favor, call Anita Ballantine and tell her I'll be over to see her in about ten minutes." He drove carefully out to the Ballantine house.

"Hello, Timothy," Anita said. "Do you have some more bad news for me?" She was haggard, her body lost in the heavy sweater.

He said, "Anita, did you get your March phone bill?" When she nodded, he said, "Go get it. Please."

When she came back, he unfolded it and stood there reading the numbers in the lamplight. "What is it?" she said.

"Nothing," he said. "Just something I had to check."

He drove out River Road to the portage point. The rain had finally stopped, but the roads were still slick. The motel sign was lit, and he could see she had a good crowd. He parked along the road and walked into the forest, toward the river, avoiding the motel.

The moon floated behind thin cirrus that veiled the stars, but he could see well enough. The pines were thick enough here that not much brush grew under them. He walked on, pushing away the wet boughs, his throat dry and something pressing on his chest, until he came to the clearing at the top of the falls.

Just before the drop-off, the riverbank rocks narrowed the river down to twelve or so feet across. He got down next to the narrows, felt around in the wet dirt.

The metal anchor in the ground was still there. He remembered how, as a kid, he had watched some of the men net fishing one summer. They had stretched netting across the river at the narrows, tying it firmly to the metal anchors on either side.

Those nets were strong, to catch many fish in a very fast current.

For quite a long time, he stared out over the river. Moonlight fell heavily on it, but it rushed ahead, dark and unstoppable.

He turned slowly and walked over to the motel that backed onto the clearing.

Valerie answered the door. She stepped back when she saw him and sent the kids off into the other room. The kitchen table was piled high with magazines. Tim went over and looked at the covers.

"Next time, please call first if you need to see me," she said.

"I already told you—"

"The Bahamas," Tim said. "I read those travel magazines, too. I see myself on a green mountainous island, sitting on the sand, looking out at turquoise water, with a pitcher of ice-cold daiquiris right next to me."

"What do you want?" she said.

"I like that flowered dress. I bet Roy liked it, too. That's the dress you were wearing the day you found his body."

"Is it?" she said.

"He called you four times in the two weeks before he died. Now, why would he do that?"

"Who?"

"Ballantine. Roy."

"No, he didn't call me. Do you have some kind of phone record? Maybe he called Ed. They were both gamblers."

"You're so beautiful. So harsh and so beautiful," Tim said. "How could he resist?"

"Me and Roy? Don't be ridiculous."

"He would jump over the bridge, and you would catch him at the narrows just before the falls and pull him out. He'd strip off the wet suit and you'd drive out to the airport with him and fly away from all the bad things."

"No!"

"That's what Roy thought, anyway. Was he willing to take your kids? Then when Roy was gone, were you worried that Ed would stay on your case, figure it out eventually? You remember old Ed, don't you? You called him at the hotel and asked him to come to the house. The clerk told me."

"No!" Valerie said, backing away. "You're crazy, Tim. Just because I won't have you after what happened— Calm down, let me make you a cup of coffee. Let's talk..." She reached up into the high cabinet and Tim caught a glimpse of the gun.

"Don't touch it," he said. "You think I'd come here unarmed? We searched this place. I knew you'd have it somewhere handy. Close the cabinet. Come toward me with your hands up."

"Tim—"

"No more bullshit."

Her shoulders slumped. She seemed about to fall. He brought her over to the table and made her sit, sat down across from her. Cracked linoleum; greasy stove, one soft flowing flowered dress to wear... "Valerie," he couldn't help saying, "I loved you."

She raised her head, and he caught something ancient and inhuman behind her eyes. It was the thing that had made her drink, still alive inside there. He had to look away.

"You were supposed to catch him at the narrow spot, weren't you?" he said.

She shrugged and said, "It would have been a very small risk. I knew how to use the net. Yeah. Catch him, and then we'd leave with the money. That was his plan."

"Did you try? You lost your grip, he went on by?"

"No."

He had to breathe a minute, hard, before he could say, "You let him go by, over the falls?"

"I let him go." Her mouth, that had kissed him so tenderly, saying those things—

"What did he do to you, that you would let him die like that?"

"It was what he would do to me someday. I thought it over. I just wanted to be alone."

She was alone, she would always be alone. "Why didn't you strip off the wet suit? I might have bought the suicide."

She backed away, saying in a hopeless, hostile voice, "I planned to. But when I saw him, the . . . injuries, I couldn't stand to touch him."

"You had it made."

"You know how it is, Tim. At the last minute, you sabotage yourself. You realize you're a loser, you don't have the strength to carry it off. Maybe if you'd been with me—but I wanted to be alone. That's all I wanted—"

"I'll have to take the money back," Tim said, interrupting.

"I don't have it." She had realized he wouldn't help her. Her mouth tightened, turned bitter.

"Of course you have it. He wouldn't risk floating down the river with it. No reason to. You were holding it. Go and get it."

"I tell you, I don't have it."

Tim said gently, "Write it off. It's dead money for you now. If you don't give it to me, I'll have to tear your house apart, dig up your land. If you tell me now, I'll say I found it somewhere else."

She said without any shame or guilt, "All I did was not save him when he was floating down the river. It's not a crime, is it?"

"I don't know. But stealing the money would be a crime, and I can't let you do that. And then, look what you made me do to poor old Ed."

"It's in the fireplace, above the flue. Get it yourself."

He made her walk into the small living room with him. He could hear the TV through the kids' door. "Is this all?"

"All except the back bills I paid. Are you going to tell on me? If you do, I'll just go on over the falls like he did."

"No. I'm not going to tell."

She stood in the doorway, glaring as he drove away. "Good-bye, then, you cold bastard," she yelled after him.

★   ★   ★

When he came to the bridge, where he needed to take a left to go into Timberlake, he took a right instead, and drove to the county airport, his right hand caressing the sooty bag. The Southwest Airlines plane bound for San Francisco was circling above, preparing to land. Through the open car windows, rustles and rushings and sighs drifted in on the wind.

He went into the dark airport bar and sat at a small candlelit table overlooking the runway. He placed the bag carefully on the table. "Drink?" the waitress said.

"A double Jack Daniel's, straight up."

He picked it up, savored the fumes—

Liquor, money, blurry romance, some faraway place—all he had to do was drink it down, have another, buy a ticket, and drop a postcard in the mailbox resigning as deputy sheriff—

"It's such a beautiful night, isn't it?" the waitress said. "I guess you're not ready for another."

Two hundred fifty thousand dollars. Two hundred fifty thousand dollars—

But it was dead money. He'd be alone like Valerie, resurrecting that presence in the back of his mind that made him drink—

He wasn't completely finished. He wasn't extinguished like Valerie; he could still love somebody. She had taught him that by making a fool out of him.

He was looking down at the table, staring at the little flame guttering in its holder. "Even the candlelight hurts tonight," he said. His voice sounded husky and strange.

She leaned down, put her hands on the table as she looked at the candle. "Blow it out, then, honey," she said. "Then the moonlight can come in from outside." She had a strong definite tone of voice and hair sprayed to stand firm against anything.

"You can take this drink away," he said.

"You're not going to have it?" Surprise lit her face.

"Not this time."

"Where you headed?" she said curiously. "San Francisco?"

"Not this time," he said again. As he climbed back into the patrol car and headed back to Timberlake, he glanced out the window.

Outside, the plane was landing, its red lights twinkling off the wet tarmac in the soft haze of evening.

O'Shay's Special Case

After they finished some initial paperwork, the interview proceeded in the usual fashion, starting with facts, ending up with emotional content, but something about the client made Patrick O'Shay uncomfortable, and it took a lot to shake him after all his years in the business. "You say you have good coverage?" O'Shay asked.

"Thirty years I've been their slave." Jeff Colby worked for Dunkirk Enterprises, a construction company that specialized in huge real estate developments. "Typical profit-driven corporation," he said, voice full of loathing. "Nobody gives a damn how the job gets done, long as it's done. I take the blame if anything upsets their damn schedule."

"You feel you aren't treated well?"

"Nothing to do with feeling," he said, angry. He looked around the rumpled, file-filled space, possibly wishing for something slicker. O'Shay's office didn't intimidate; its comfortable shabbiness welcomed workers from the farms ringing Salinas and the central valley. "They treat me worse than dirt."

O'Shay sat back in his chair. A big man with deep-set, piercing blue eyes women loved and men found scary or trustworthy,
depending upon their personalities, he was larger than life,
inches over six feet and well over the recommended healthy
weight for a man his size, although much of it was sheer muscle.
"Tell me about your injury."

And the litany began. Colby had worked there first the summer after high school. He had hammered flooring, Sheetrocked,
dug dirt, painted exteriors, framed foundations, poured cement—
he had done it all. He had built sprawling, spanking-new su-
burban houses for so long he had accumulated a million
indignities, all of which he unloaded on O'Shay—along with
resentment that ran so deep in him that his skin burned red as he
talked.

"Since I was seventeen, I worked," he said. "I started at the
bottom. I did what you might call shit work, what nobody else
wanted to do, and always slapped a smile on my face while I was
at it.

"My wife and me live in a cottage built in 1923 and looking
even older than that. That's what we can afford. Every day, I was
putting in new sinks, flagstone pathways, fountains, all for other
people." He almost spat with outrage. "We don't even have a
dishwasher."

"We need to pinpoint when the pain began," said O'Shay.

But Colby had been saving up for this moment, and he
wasn't squandering it by going straight to the point. "Time
went on, they put me in charge of a crew. Didn't pay much
more, but it was better telling other guys what to do, drinking
coffee, not coming home too sweaty to touch my kids. Then
one day they go, 'Sorry. The guys are complaining.' Well, yeah.
I worked 'em hard. Nobody got away with nothing. Hell, I
knew all the tricks to avoid working too hard. Bastards claimed
I lacked people skills." His laugh was ragged, angry. "They de-
moted me. I'm strong, always have been. But I'm forty-seven
now and haven't done heavy labor for years. Those jobs are for

younger guys and they know it. I think they forced me into that position thinking they could get rid of me once and for all. That I'd quit."

Something in Colby's eyes disturbed O'Shay. He looked in them and saw ponds full of scum, rough debris, hidden dangers.

Wide shoulders stretched the dress shirt Colby wore. "So last summer, August, I think, I was loading furniture from a truck for a model home. Even here in the valley, it can get hot. I bet it was ninety in the shade. Imports from Thailand, I think. Mostly, these designers pick lightweight stuff for these homes, keep them looking light and airy for buyers by using a lot of bamboo and cane but there was this armoire, a mahogany piece as heavy as a piano. Me and another guy were angling it through a narrow doorway and I heard this cracking sound like something rotten gave. My back hurt like a son of a bitch right away."

O'Shay had watched for signs of injury when the man entered his office. Colby had sat down easily, not lowering himself with the exquisite care of a man with a herniated disk or other nerve problem. His eyes looked clear and unbothered, not shadowed by pain, and nothing he did favored his back. "This man, your coworker, would he be willing to tell us about that day?"

"He's gone. Illegal, probably. Didn't speak much English. He split at Christmas for El Salvador or somewhere."

"Ah."

"I can't stand fully upright anymore," Colby said, "because I hurt so bad. I can't lift anything heavy. I can't do my job anymore. I can't even make love to my wife, although I'm not sure I want you to tell the court about that."

O'Shay made a note. "I want to know anything relevant," he said. "What makes you remark on that?"

"Well, you know. Positions. I can't do all the acrobatics I

used to." He snickered and crossed his leg with a graceful hoisting of muscled thigh.

O'Shay nodded.

"I heard you've been in business forever. Heard you go to bat for the little guy," Colby said.

"Twenty years in business. We have a lot of farmworker clients." And, oh, those people really suffered.

"I guess they get hurt sometimes, too."

"Sure," O'Shay said, scribbling notes, noting down the dozen vague problems Colby now went on to describe as unbearable.

"You say you don't get along with other employees."

"Buncha critics and complainers," Colby said. "When I do something right, there's people lining up to take credit." He had a mean line for a mouth.

"You've seen a doctor?"

"Several." Colby slapped a bundle of medical records down on O'Shay's desk. "I got one will swear I oughtta be dead."

According to their usual arrangement, Rosa knocked after twenty minutes had elapsed, and without waiting for a reply, entered the room. "Emilio Lopez on line one," she said urgently.

"Ah, thanks." O'Shay turned to Colby. "I have to take this. Let's talk again tomorrow morning. I need a list of all the physicians you've consulted and all the treatments you've had. Rosa, get the usual permissions signed by Mr. Colby before he goes so we can access his records, okay?"

"That guy," Rosa said after getting the forms signed and seeing the man out. She handed O'Shay a file that needed attention. "Another gray morning."

She talked that way, poetically. What she meant was, Colby was a loser.

"Should I dump these papers now or is he one of the unstable ones who needs to be let down easy?"

"Keep the papers. We're taking the case."

"No."

"Yes."

Nudging a loose pile of folders on his desk into order, Rosa said, "You're kidding, right? That guy could bench-press four hundred pounds without breaking a sweat!"

O'Shay shrugged.

Rosa put a hand on her hip. "He couldn't even keep a limp going all the way out the door. He was practically dancing the cha-cha out there, and you know why? Because he's lined up the best worker's comp attorney in Salinas. And why are you considered the best? In all these years, you've never taken a client who was blatantly faking. Everybody knows that and respects you for it. So what's going on?"

O'Shay didn't answer.

"Is this to do with your retirement? Are you worrying about that? Does his case mean big money?"

"Not likely, although that would be my wish."

His secretary stared at him, head at an angle, like a bird focusing on crumbs through a single sharp eye, hoping to see him better. "Then, don't do this," she said. "You don't take guys like him, a sleazebag. A phony. A greedhead."

"Rosa," he said, "open a new file."

She flounced out, leaving her perfume and disgust behind in equal measure.

In spite of the optimistic sounds the lawyer had made, Jeff Colby had seen the doubt in O'Shay's eyes. The man didn't believe him. Fair enough, Colby thought. He didn't believe O'Shay as far as he could toss him. So, he worked on Plan B. He could not, would not, go back to that soul-sucking job. He knew a lawsuit was a long shot, so plan for the short shot.

★   ★   ★

O'Shay spoke with Colby's doctor, the one who agreed to swear about Colby's on-the-job injury. He knew the man's reputation locally. Rampantly pro-worker and antiestablishment, the doctor nevertheless had a smooth professional manner, an excellent education, a thriving practice, and knew the right noises to make. What better could O'Shay hope for? Colby's doctor asked straight out exactly what O'Shay needed said to win his case. O'Shay gave him the details he wanted parroted back, anticipating the report to come, which would be shamelessly hyperbolized.

The doctor had friends also willing to swear for a price.

Further sinking below the mud line, O'Shay asked his old law school roommate out for lunch and plied him with flavored martinis, picking his brain.

"How you win a case that's unwinnable," Chuck said, sipping the cranberry-flavored concoction that was sure to send him heaving into the toilet bowl later, "is to invoke the everyman. Does your client qualify?"

"I guess. He has a wife and kids. He's worked all his life without getting fired even once."

His buddy shook his head. "No, no, no. Question is, does he look the part? Can he play an injury or not? And is he worthy?"

"What?"

"He has to get up there on the stand in a starched white shirt, slightly frayed, like he's making such an effort to look good but it's so hard. He has to speak English well, so we know he's not an idiot or some illegal just trying to finagle money out of the system. He should have bags under his eyes. Ditto for the wife and kids, if you can get them in there with you. He needs to show pain, and he needs to make that judge believe he hurts. He needs to look like a strong man knocked flat by the nefarious actions of his employer. He needs to look reduced from a major player to a husk. But you know all this already. You say he's white?"

"Yeah. Born in Oakland."

"Excellent. No offense to all those boys you usually represent, but nobody kicks in big bucks to the Mexicans."

Chuck read O'Shay's face, and shook his head. "O'Shay, O'Shay. Forget the liberal politics. Get real." He ordered another drink, this time vodka with orange juice, and nibbled on stale nuts. "Bottom line, you got a good thing going with this guy. I looked it up before I came today. His company takes care of their own. He's a movie star compared to your usual clientele, and he's got the backing of a major studio. Line up your experts. Practice with him until he's got the role nailed."

"You never asked me about his injury."

His pal, flirting with a girl at the end of the bar, waved at the bartender. "Isn't that kinda like asking a murderer if he done it? That's not the way of our people, O'Shay."

O'Shay paid for the drinks.

When he inclined toward optimism, which wasn't often, Jeff Colby indulged in fantasies about the family farm he would buy, maybe in the Caribbean, proving once and for all he was no loser. He would coddle his wife with cheap servants, get his kids into a school where they didn't know what gangbanging was, where they would learn to sail after school. Twirling the wheel of his Chevy Nova at a stoplight on Main, right before making a left, he indulged in a fantasy where he came to work and announced his swift exit. All the assholes he hated would be envious. He would prove he was somebody and not just the pathetic, powerless nobody they had made him into.

Back at the rental house on Blanco, he kissed Sandra, then took out his gun, loaded it, and went into the backyard, where the light was fading. He propped cans on the fence, glad as always that their small yard rose up steeply and was bordered by farmland, and shot, and shot, and shot, misses plunking into the dirt behind his targets.

He did well, annihilating dozens of beer cans. Back in the house, he emptied a few more, trying to blot out the image of his boss, Keith Landers, the smirk on his face when he told Jeff the news, and how Jeff had felt that night, having to tell Sandra. The look on her face.

He downed another one.

Landers generally got to work early, starting at the office behind the model home, flirting with the receptionist, hanging there as long as he could. The office was well-situated for visitors, close to the parking lot, and had plenty of windows.

The next week, O'Shay consulted with a retired judge, someone who had looked favorably upon many of his cases, someone fair. O'Shay laid out Jeff Colby's situation.

The judge, holding court at Dudley's on Main Street, nodded to a steady stream of hellos. His plate held three fried eggs, a pile of bacon, two pancakes, overdone, cheesy potatoes, plus toast. He called his order "heart attack heaven" and, stabbing a fork into an oozing egg, explained that his mother and father, both of them, lived well into their nineties and he planned to do the same. Slim, still walking five miles daily even though he was well into his eighties, he had O'Shay convinced that the usual rules did not apply to him.

"Okay, the way it happened was, this guy was faking an injury," the judge said, shaking out salt and pepper, eyeballing the shakers when they didn't seem to be applying themselves liberally enough. "The usual back thing. An invisible problem only God really could judge. I suspected he was a fake. I believed his attorney knew it. However, they found this amazing doctor, really, more a magician. This guy could make gold out of dog hair, I'm telling you." He bit into a strip of bacon, sighing with pleasure.

"Aw, I hate doing business when I eat. If I didn't remember your mother, O'Shay..."

"Thanks for seeing me."

"So, anyhow, a judge's duty is to weigh the evidence as presented. We're not really allowed leeway on that, you know? Instincts be damned. I have to say, like most people, I ignored that edict and did my own thing, but in this case, I had no choice."

"Why?"

"Overwhelming physical evidence, boy, and a doctor who could make you cry like a baby. Plus another doctor, less sterling, but confident, groomed. X-rays. Hospital admissions. Even the insurance guy couldn't get past the avalanche of evidence. You have to know, most cases are not so well-developed. Lawyers have lives, right? No time to track down several experts when one might do."

"Track down a dozen, check," O'Shay said, spooning brown sugar onto his oatmeal. He noted the name of the magical doctor and his friend.

The judge slathered strawberry jelly onto his side order of sourdough toast. "Not just any experts and evidence, O'Shay. Unassailable experts, with knowledge that will blow their Italian loafers off."

Back at the office, Rosa gave O'Shay the cold shoulder. After ten years, she felt he ought to listen to her. She knew him better than he knew himself, she believed, and she always let him know when she thought he was wrong about something, in her own way.

Do this, do that, he told her, and in return for his calm orders, she made his normally smooth life rough. The work she usually did on his files suddenly fell to him. Clients popped in unannounced all day until he reprimanded her sharply. She crossed her arms, grimly satisfied to have rattled him. He worked long into the night to get caught up.

The next morning, O'Shay arrived at the office slightly late. Rosa looked coolly upon his bleary eyes and awful mood. "Mrs. Olson called," she said. Mrs. Olson was his most challenging client besides Colby, and that was saying a lot. He handled hundreds a year. This woman made him crazy. Usually Rosa shielded him from clients like her. Not today.

"She has a new chiropractor you need to talk to. I told her you'd call right away, and get back to her, too. She's hysterical, could really use some hand-holding. Oh, and her husband called after. Yelling about something. I took a message." She handed him a pink slip of paper. "Really mad. I told him you'd call and explain everything."

He wanted to do something to stop the onslaught, kind of like his daughter had when she was a teenager and found something awesomely offensive, "No!" she would cry, fingers forming a cross, as if fending off vampires. Instead, he said, "Fine. Close the door behind you."

He did what had to be done. He befriended the prickly new chiropractor, talked down Mrs. Olson, empathized with Mr. Olson, whose wife made sure he shared every single pain she felt, and rolled through another six files.

Sandra Colby called. "I wanted to thank you for taking Jeff's case," she said.

"You're welcome."

"Because—he's not himself lately, you know? I don't think you're seeing him at his best. He's got such heart. He's an amazing, involved father, and really a sensitive husband. He cares too much is the problem. He puts on such a macho face, but that's because after all these years they've beat him down. I hardly recognize him sometimes." By the time she got off the phone with him she was crying.

"You make me tired," Rosa said, frowning, at lunchtime.

"I make me tired, too."

"What's going on, O'Shay?" she asked, her frustration evident in the way she persisted with him.

"I'm really hungry." He asked if she would arrange for a sandwich from the deli for him. She slammed the door on her way out.

Late in the afternoon, he tackled Jerome Castile, the insurance attorney representing Colby's company. "He's injured, with a ninety percent disability rating according to three doctors," O'Shay said into the phone.

"Come on, his injuries are almost all in his head, and you know we don't have to pay out psych cases anymore. Our doc says a maximum of twenty percent disability rating. Ten thousand."

"Trust me on this, Jerome. Lifetime medical, plus a ninety percent award."

Castile laughed. "You know, I expected better from you. There's nothing special about this case. Ten and a year's medical."

O'Shay gathered the X-rays, the hospital admissions papers, the medical records. He called a private detective. Finally, he called Colby.

"How's it hanging?" Colby asked.

"I need you to see a few people." O'Shay had made appointments Colby needed to keep, and went over the injuries Colby needed to be very clear about.

"Got it, man," Colby said. "I show up, shirt tucked in, fucked up like you wouldn't believe."

"Right," O'Shay said.

At home, Diana came after him. "You've always come on as such an idealist," she said. "I felt kind of mean-spirited next to you, wanting things. A little angry you never made the kind of money I thought you should, being an attorney."

He tried to hug her but she pulled away. "See, I consoled myself that I'd married a good guy. Now I hear you've taken on this client, and I hear he's been trying to wrestle money out of his employer for years. He's a fraud."

"You heard? Where?"

"My sister."

His wife's sister was also a local attorney. So the news had spread. He sighed. "He's a special case, honey."

"Yeah, he's special. He's putting all your years of hard work in the dumper." She gave up after a while, though, and O'Shay, so tired, read the newspaper in front of a cold fireplace. He crept off to bed after she had fallen asleep.

The next morning he ate bacon, eggs, and toast and got to the office before his wife got up and Rosa came in. He spoke with a few people, then called Colby. "I've got the experts," he said, "but you know, these doctors aren't willing to wreck their standing in the community for your sake. They will say the right things, but they have to convince a judge who understands every nuance, do you understand me?"

"You mean they'll talk careful and he'll hear that they're holding back."

"Right. Now, right now I can get you some money if we settle. That's the only sure thing right now. You probably should consider a deal."

"How much?"

"Maybe..." O'Shay tried to name a figure he could get "...up to fifteen thousand."

Colby snorted. "Half the price of a car and not even a luxury one at that," he said. "No, I don't think that's going to get me out of the hole I'm in. I'm not sure you appreciate exactly how serious my case is. And I'm beginning to question how committed you really are to my cause, O'Shay."

"Oh, I know it's serious, Mr. Colby. And I'm doing my best for you. I need you to believe that."

"Then don't hand me a bag of peanuts and expect thanks. I got lifelong disability. I got to go for the big money, O'Shay. Take it to trial."

"Jeff," O'Shay said. "I'm obligated to tell you if we go to trial there's a definite possibility we'll lose and you'll get nothing." A little of the old O'Shay poked through the Colby-induced fog of deceit and evil, and felt obliged to tell the truth.

Jeff Colby took a marker pen into the kitchen and marked the date of his trial on his calendar. The case was set for ten. Lander's office opened at nine. He needed to get cracking, but there was plenty of time to do the necessary shopping in advance.

"I can borrow from Daddy," Diana said, "if it's money you're worrying about."

O'Shay lay on a teak lounge in the backyard, admiring the fine job they had done with the plantings around the edge of their large lawn. A high fence plus fast-growing conifers made the yard very private. Sunshine spilled across the grass. He closed his eyes and smelled the blossoming lemon tree tucked at the back. "There's something ironic about invoking your dad in this case you think has so much to do with integrity. If I only understood irony better."

"Don't get cute, Patrick. Just don't sell yourself cheap."

He breathed the sunshine deeply. "I'll make sure we're well compensated."

"Don't joke about this!" she said, swatting him. "This isn't funny!"

Easing his bare feet onto the patio, he left her behind and walked across the lawn. He picked up the lemons that had fallen to the ground, and the ones that were ripe, holding as many as he could in his two hands. Back in the kitchen, he squeezed them, added sugar, and brought a glass out to her, along with a nice lunch which he laid out on the patio table.

While they ate, he brought up the topic of some thoughts he had about what they might do next summer for vacation. He thought he needed a decent break this year. He might even take three weeks this August. What did she think about that?

She didn't stay silent for long. Diana loved planning trips.

The next morning, O'Shay met with Jerome Castile in person at the insurance company's offices. They had nice rugs, he noticed, and original art on the wall. He admired the fresh green ferns. He and Rosa had long ago settled for artificial. "Here's the thing," he said, sinking into the soft leather cushion. "I have statistics illustrating a long pattern of patronage and unfair promotion practices at Dunkirk Enterprises."

Jerome definitely looked startled.

O'Shay flipped through papers that looked official. "Here the owner, Mr. Landers, hired his son, then his cousin, then his brother-in-law. Then his daughter. Not to mention his wife."

"It's a family business."

"Thereby bypassing my client and other worthy long-term employees."

"He gave the guy a chance at a better job, but he couldn't cut it. Nobody should be forced to keep an employee on when he can't do a decent job. Instead of firing him, they kept him on."

"Doing work he is no longer physically able to do."

The attorney took his time, flipped through his own irrelevant papers, and said, "Our clients have done nothing to be ashamed of, but more important, they've done nothing illegal."

"Oh," O'Shay said, "talk to them. They're locals, a major

employer, and so far, they have such a fine reputation. A short conversation with the *Californian* will blow all that. Because it's the tip of the iceberg, isn't it? There's lots to write about." He knew exactly how much more, since his own detective had done a fine job.

"You'd trash a major local employer who pays decent wages and provides good benefits for Jeff Colby, who's a notorious and classic disgruntled employee?"

"Yes." Play the game with a hardball, always.

"I had heard such good things about you."

"By the way, I have evidence that this cavalier disregard for fairness is a pattern with you people."

"Don't tell me you're gonna try to add in a bad faith allegation."

"Absolutely."

"So how'd it go with the insurance guy?" Colby asked.

O'Shay, alienated from his staff, unable to talk to his wife, found talking with Colby a strange relief. "Not so well," he said honestly. Almost immediately, he regretted his candor.

"More bad news?" Colby asked, his voice full of teeth.

"You never know until you are there in court."

"But no big settlement."

"No."

"Huh." Colby rubbed his chin and looked down, as if deciding something.

"Court at ten tomorrow. Be there on time?"

"Sure," Colby agreed.

The next morning, O'Shay dressed carefully. He wore a silk navy suit paired with an Hermès tie. He wanted to look subdued but successful. He had three doctors he ordinarily would never use who would testify about Colby's dire injuries. He had a rolling cart in the trunk of his car full of medical reports, job descriptions, legal pleadings, and law books. He had things on Dunkirk Enterprises Jerome Castile knew he would spill to the press, if necessary. He had the requisite chutzpah.

Diana handed him his laptop at the door, refusing to kiss him. "Don't sell out," she whispered, and he heard it, too, as he opened the garage door and left.

At the courthouse, early, O'Shay met with Castile one last time. He went to work on the insurance defense attorney, trying to reach an agreement that would set the Colby family up for life. They haggled; they fought; they got tough; they compromised; nobody gave enough. He tried again and lost. Bottom line was, the guy said he just didn't believe O'Shay would do what he was threatening to do. "You have a reputation to protect," Castile said smugly, "in spite of this recent, definite lapse in judgment."

"We're due in court," O'Shay told Colby on the telephone. "I'm on my way."

Something in Colby's voice screamed sirens.

Jeff Colby made a special effort with Sandra and the kids before leaving that morning, hugs and kisses all around, lots of positive words. "I'm stopping by the job site for a quick howdy before heading to the courthouse," he said.

"Are you sure you don't want us to go with you? Your attorney said it might be good for us to be there with you in court."

"No need, sweetheart." He kissed her again, holding her around her narrow waist, marveling that his childhood girlfriend had been so steadfast and true for so many years, and had stood by him through so much. He felt himself flinching at the thought of the next few hours. And he felt righteous.

"What's in the duffel?" his son asked as he walked out the door.

"Stuff and nonsense," he replied, smiling. "Good-bye, son."

"It's me, Patrick O'Shay. Is Jeff there?"

"He's gone."

"Where is he?"

"On his way?"

"You sound unsure."

"He was stopping by Dunkirk on the way to court."

"Oh, no."

"He won't be late," she said. "He's never late."

O'Shay got the insurance lawyer on line one. He had a new case just decided by the California Supreme Court to talk about.

"I'll call you back," Castile said. "Give me ten minutes."

O'Shay shot into traffic and headed toward Romie Lane, toward the scene of Jeff Colby's latest humiliation. He drove through the construction on Main Street like a man possessed. Somehow, he was not ticketed for turning illegally.

O'Shay thought about the list of people Jeff hated: the receptionist who mocked him; the stock boy who played malicious tricks; the boss who fired him . . .

Twenty minutes, and their case would be called. Barring a miracle, he couldn't make it back in time at this point. He pulled into the parking lot, frantically scanning for Jeff's car. He couldn't find it. Inside the developer's office, a man drinking coffee hovered over a pretty girl's desk.

O'Shay's phone rang.

"Jerome Castile here," the insurance lawyer announced officiously. "We need to talk."

★   ★   ★

A few minutes later, Jeff Colby pulled up three cars away, stopping to park directly in front of a bland stucco building sporting a boldly lettered sign which read "Dunkirk Enterprises." If he was surprised to see O'Shay sitting in his car so close by, he didn't show it. "Had a flat," he said.

"You should have gone straight to court," said O'Shay.

"Maybe."

Colby opened the trunk of his car, revealing a canvas duffel. "Why are you here?" he asked, tugging at the bag, bringing it out.

"It's over."

"What's over?" Colby, distracted, looked toward the entrance of the building, peered through the glass doors.

"Your case, Jeff. You beat them."

"I—what?"

"You beat them," O'Shay repeated. Since Colby seemed suddenly incapable of speaking, O'Shay outlined the details of the deal he had finally struck with the insurance company. They would pay for Colby's medical. They would provide a steady flow of income, a pension.

Colby fingered the duffel. "You wouldn't try to con me."

"No, I wouldn't."

Finally convinced, Colby was jubilant, ecstatic. He jabbered at O'Shay: he had pulled a fast one, showing them he could work the system just like the best of them! They would be buying his farm, his retirement, his security. They would dig him out of this hellhole. He could start fresh somewhere new. He finally had a stake. He couldn't wait to tell everyone, see their faces. They were stuck in that dump without windows, while he would be breathing the fresh air. Maybe he would spring for a trip to the Caribbean, just to check things out. He'd forgotten all about the duffel.

O'Shay drove away. He had won the biggest settlement he

ever had but he'd had to cheat and lie to get it. He had gotten others involved in his tricks. He had disappointed Rosa, Diana, and other professionals who had once respected him. Maybe he had compromised his good name forever.

But he, Patrick O'Shay, knew a special case when he saw one.

He shrugged, turned the ball game on the sportsradio channel, and thought about lunch.

House Afire

She cherished a picture of him at sixteen in summertime, grimy, wet with sweat, leaning insolently on the door of a Chevy. Every Sunday when she called him to talk, she would hold the picture in her hands, remembering the sun of that day, the baked smell of his skin, but she never mentioned it to him. Such intimacy would embarrass him. Their relationship, once so close that he was physically part of her, was now delicate, limited. When she got too sentimental, he rebuffed her. Every week, she vowed to herself that she would not pester him again with her chatter, and every week, craving his warm voice and recalling the concord of their heartbeats, she broke down and called him.

He was the kind of boy who had a list of safe topics ready for Mother.

She had raised him alone. For almost a year after separating from her husband, she suffered from a painful amazement that he could just walk away from their relationship the way he had.

How could you give up on other people? How could he abandon his home like that? Then for a long time she contemplated his rejection, wondering if there was some important conclusion to draw, but, in time, a very green spring came along. She revived her morning walks, only now she walked with the boy in a carriage in front of her. As the boy grew older, she clenched his cold, tiny hand in her own and they walked together.

Over the years, determined his father wouldn't miss out on his son's life, she had written letters. Her ex-husband answered a few times, at long intervals. One night when her son was three years old, after a movie that had left her crying, she wrote. "We are doing very well. They put balloons up all over the city to celebrate the Fourth this year. We got up early, before the children carried all the balloons off." He wrote back, "I miss you and the little one." Emboldened by this show of interest, she invited him to visit them. He wrote back quickly for once. He needed more time to sort things out.

One afternoon when the boy was seven and balky, she went browsing in a bookstore downtown and he disappeared. At first she hunted the aisles almost casually, certain he had merely wandered off. Then, deciding he was being deliberately rebellious she commanded him to return in her nastiest voice, plotting his punishments out loud. The other patrons scowled at her, but she hardly noticed. When her son did not come out of hiding, she left her coat behind and ran down the street screaming his name until her voice left her.

Back at home she caught her breath in her chair, watching out the window for his return. The late afternoon heat poured over her. She tried to think of the next sensible thing to do.

When the boy returned after dinnertime, he woke her up. She had been frowning, he told her. Snoring, too. She tried to grab him, hold him close, but he stood woodenly in her grasp, angry about something. When she let him go, he closed the window quietly, shutting out the evening wind.

She knew he would have special needs, growing up with a single parent. Trying to forestall future problems, she arranged his room in a bedroom at the far end of the house so that he would have privacy when he needed it. Once he got over his fear of the dark, he shut the door to his room and kept it shut.

When he finally asked, she tried to explain why his father had left them. "We were very young," she said, and for the life of her couldn't think how to explain the inevitability of that cataclysm. "He wanted to see more of the world. And he was homesick for where he used to live."

"What did you do to make him leave?" the boy asked, turning his gaze full on her for once.

"Nothing."

That was not entirely true.

She and the boy's father had never fought. They had lived a quiet life in a quiet town together until one summer day, sick to death of the hot, dry weather of the West, he pulled up stakes, taking her and their infant with him. They moved to a town on the shores of Massachusetts, where he had grown up.

The Northeast did not agree with her. She wilted in the humidity and missed the usual smells, the yellow grasses. And her husband, never much of a talker, sank into a rocking chair stupor out on the porch, emerging only for meals and work. Three months later, she flew herself and the baby home and refused to return. Her husband stayed in Fairhaven. In his first letter to her he described the flowers in bloom, the million shapes and colors; in his second, he raved about the white buds of summer jasmine, about how short, intense, summers were tolerable, even delightful in their transience; in the third he enclosed a brightly colored maple leaf. Then, except for those rare replies to her letters, he stopped writing.

The truth was, she could not make herself stay with a man who inhabited such an inhospitable nest. And she knew it was not the weather or the pretty colors or scents of the seasons that kept

him holed up somewhere in New England. He had simply extended his hibernation into the realm of the physical.

As a toddler, her son never talked much. She liked to talk, and
he made a good listener, so she told him what she felt about the
day, or the people nearby, or the news. He seemed content as her
audience. When he did feel moved to share something, an obser-
vation, a revelation, about what had happened that day with the
teacher, something that scared him, his perceptions filled her with
pride. She felt very lucky to have such a sensitive and intelligent
child.

As he got older, if she questioned him too much, his face
would fill with reproach, so much so she wanted to laugh, although of course she didn't. He had given her that same look
years ago when he was three, when she put too much weight on
one side of the teeter-totter, sending him sailing too high, making
him cry. She guessed that he had inherited the need for a private
safety zone from his father, but by then, she had grown accus-
tomed to speaking her mind to him, to having him as a silent but,
in her imagination at least, sympathetic, witness. She had to make
a conscious effort to gear her stories to his disposition, to stop
when he looked bored or the least bit angry.

He never seemed entirely happy, but if she asked, and he
replied, he would say but of course he was a happy boy. When he
did appear cheerful, he would laugh to himself and refuse to explain why. If she insisted, he would launch into a long story, intentionally boring, she decided, devised to discourage her questions.
So, over a period of years, in a process unfortunately parallel to the
one that had derailed her from her marriage, her questions dried
up, and so did her stories. She curbed her tongue, keeping her topics to the practical and trivial.

The day he left for college, for just a moment as he stepped
toward a waiting car, she forgot all about the distance between
them. The rangy six-footer disappeared and in his place stood
a small boy in a doorway, angry and sad about something she

could not fix and did not understand. She cried, clinging to him. "Don't make a scene, Mom," he said, gently lifting her arms off him and taking his leave with a casual wave. She finished off that afternoon with whiskey and a mystery story. She cooked no supper. She drank lukewarm coffee from the breakfast thermos and watched the sun go down.

During his college years, they spoke once a week. She confined herself to the kind of anecdotes he tolerated best, short, funny ones. He didn't share much. He had homework, a test. A pile of books to read. "Which ones?" she might ask, and he would answer vaguely, "Oh, some philosophy. Some physics." Something she could not sink her teeth into. "I saw a movie," he might offer, and she would jump. "Which one?"

"I forget. A shoot-'em-up. Great special effects."

The years passed. Then, one weekend, busy with picking weeds and selecting ripe strawberries for dinner from her garden, she forgot to call him. Sunday slipped by. On Monday, she didn't know where he would be. So went the rest of the week. The following Sunday, she fully intended to call at the usual time, but Mrs. Peters from next door came by asking for advice on killing gophers in her yard. Happy for the company, she offered a piece of poppy seed cake. She kicked herself later, as Mrs. Peters ate two pieces, all the while implying that her own efforts to control the gophers had in fact caused an infestation in Mrs. Peters's yard. She felt too upset to call her son that day, too upset to make small talk.

The following Sunday, as she whiled away the afternoon with the papers, he called. "Mom, where have you been?"

"Right here."

"I've been so worried! I almost called the police yesterday!"

She had forgotten to call him for a couple of weeks. How surprising! Still, it was probably a good thing. Time was passing. He needed to get along without her. By habit, she reached for the picture of him leaning on his car, but it was gone from its usual spot. She must have stowed it during the dusting on Tuesday. Rummaging in a desk drawer, she found it.

"I haven't gone anywhere," she said. "I'm still sitting in my blue chair and talking to you."

"The blue chair," he said. "You've had that forever. That's where I found you . . . remember that time I ran away?" he asked.

"Of course I do." But how funny that he did, and funnier still that he would mention it. He had been so little then, still able to stand under her outstretched arm.

"I was really scared."

"This was a small town. I knew you'd be okay."

"Why didn't you try to find me, Mom?"

"But I did. I searched for hours."

"Then you gave up."

"I waited for you at home. I hoped you'd find your way back. And you did, didn't you?"

As time went by, and the phone calls grew ever more erratic, she lost interest in gardening. She would force herself outside, but the leaves became dry and brittle before her eyes, the landscape drained of its usual colors. She called old friends, but found herself wanting to hang up almost immediately. Their conversation, friendly enough, proved as insubstantial as the local ocean fogs. There was no intrinsic value in these relationships, she realized, letting them lag. She quit reading the news, stopped watching her evening shows. Life reduced itself to an egg in the morning, cleanup, sandwich, cleanup, and long periods when she stared out the window, mentally vacant.

Then one night, she took out some pills and set them on her bed stand. She poured herself a glass of water, opened the bottle, and hesitated.

She would wait for one more phone call, then end it.

Strangely, the sight of the pills on her bureau gave her

strength. Over the next few days, she conversed cheerfully with neighbors, and, full of purpose for a change, tidied her papers and her life. Her home looked almost happy.

On her birthday, an intolerably smoggy day a month after he graduated from college, he called.

"Happy birthday!"

She couldn't speak for a minute. Sitting down on the bed, she fingered the pills. Her last day. He would be sad, but he would rough it, as she had. These blows that knocked you down only bruised and battered. They did not stop you cold. You went on. He was so young still.

She roused herself. She knew what she should say, but they didn't have that kind of a relationship. Maybe, she decided, as he told her about what he was up to, she would leave him a letter. She could write at her leisure, explain things somehow.

He talked, and she found herself nervous, the warm ocean wave of his voice on the other end, usually so important, receding on a tide. She found his meaning hard to extract, although she tried, shifting her attention from the pills, from the window and the clearing of the sky outside, white clouds consuming the yellow haze, back to him.

Odd the way the usual quick hang up did not happen. He talked about the smell of the ocean breezes and the din of the weed cutters in early summer. She couldn't help noticing how remarkably like his father he sounded, picking up on the sensory details of life as though entirely untouched by them. The similarity unsettled her, reminding her of another leaving a long time ago. This was different, she told herself, because his reaction would be different. Hardy, she hoped. He was an independent soul, she felt, although she was guessing.

She listened now without listening for content. She pressed her ear to the receiver, eager for something besides words. She listened for rhythm, for a thrumming, for a bigger meaning. It took a minute for her to realize what she wanted. She was asking a lot of this final conversation, wasn't she? She urgently wanted to make final contact with his heart.

What she heard instead was a young man's awkward voice, her distracted chat, and punctuating silences between them. But that was who they were, she thought, realizing she didn't have to hear its beat through the phone, or even in the words he said. His heart continued to beat inside her, alongside her own, out of sync.

She knew she must sound funny, but she couldn't help it, as things large and painful moved inside her own heart.

She swung her attention back to the conversation. She had expected to say good-bye by now, but then questions began, like, what was the weather like there today, and how big were her beefsteak tomatoes this year?

She wouldn't tell him she hadn't planted any. "Oh, not as big as last year's. But when did you start to worry about my garden?"

She could hear the silence ballooning, as it so often did, full of all the things they would never say to each other.

Then, he exhaled. "I've met someone."

"Someone?" she asked stupidly.

"A girl named Tammy."

A gusher of something, her blood pumping perhaps, made her suddenly dizzy. "Hang on," she said, then took a sip of water and four deep breaths. "Honey," she said, "what does that have to do with my garden?"

He wanted to tell Tammy about her tomatoes, he said, because she complained that all they could get were ones that tasted like cardboard.

He had a girlfriend.

How long was her hair? What kind of clothes did she wear? Was she tall? Thin? Pretty? Freckled? Plump? Sweet-natured or cross? Smart? Foolish? Fun? Serious?

A student? Older than him? Younger? An only child?

Sterile?

Sick?

Big-bosomed?

But he would hate her questions, and so she didn't ask them. "I've got to go," he said, as he always did when he had had enough.

"Okay, dear," she said, as she always did, careful to keep the leap of frustration she felt at this abrupt pronouncement out of her voice. This time something new crept upon her—fear. She stopped all such feelings and thought about her last words to him. Nothing came to mind. She couldn't show what she felt without scaring him, too. "Have a good evening."

"Oh, that's weird." He laughed slightly. "I almost forgot to say why I called! We're flying out for her dad's birthday next weekend. Would you come?"

"Her folks live out here?"

"Yeah."

"Where?"

"Real close to you, actually."

Surprising herself even more, she said immediately, "Of course I will."

"I'll pick you up."

"Okay, honey." She waited for his good-bye, picking up his picture to look at, hoping she would not cry.

He hovered on the phone. She could hear him breathing. "Honey, are you still there?"

"Yeah."

He breathed in and out, and she followed the rhythm like a jumpy little tune. Why didn't he hang up?

"It's a double celebration. Mom, we're getting engaged."

"Oh, honey!"

"Marriage next June, if that works out."

"That's wonderful news."

"And she wants to settle near her parents. We'll be able to visit more often than I have lately."

"That would be really nice, dear." A vague picture arose and

sharpened in her mind, of roses, of arbors, sunshine, smiling people, a happy event in her very own beautiful, flower-soaked yard.
"How did you meet? At school?"

"No, she worked in a copy place at night putting herself
through college. I was always in there in the middle of the night."

"Who spoke first?"

"You obviously don't know her or you wouldn't bother
to ask."

She heard a tinkle of laughter in the background. So Tammy
was there, listening. "What's she like?"

"Oh, she's a riot. Has a story about everything. Kind of like
you, Mom, although she talks more. Much, much more."

He yelped and dropped the phone. "Oops," he said, "sorry."

"Will she be with you when you come?"

"Yes. And, Mom. I tried to resist, but she begged me. And I
gave in. I told her all about you."

"You have?"

"She knows all your secrets."

"Really."

He laughed. "I'm sure there are a few left you can tell her
yourself, if you can get a word in edgewise. You two are gonna
get along like a house afire, Mom. That, I promise you."

He kept her on the phone for a very long time. She heard
love in his voice, and hope. Listening to the emotional outpour-
ing, her heart pumped faster. Her eyes welled up. They made
plans for his visit, then she said good-bye and hung up.

Sun came through the window, spilling butter on the bed,
warming the skin of her arm. Outside, blue skies, puff clouds, all
kinds of prettiness.

Plans to make.

She needed to make the place beautiful with her flowers. It
wasn't too late to put in some azaleas for a fall bloom. She stuck the
pills into her bedside drawer. Dusting his picture with a dishrag,
she gave it a kiss and put it back on the desk.

She remembered the day the photograph had been taken, how eager he had been to change the oil on his first car, how she had begged him to read the instructions in the manual first, how he had gone ahead and got more of it on himself than into the pan. How hard she had laughed.

When they came, she would show the picture to Tammy. And then, Tammy would ask about her son's interesting expression. She would tell her all about it.

And then, Tammy would talk.

His Master's Hand

I am a cultured man. I am a lonely man. I am a nefarious man. My liver is healthy, and I expect to live well into my eighties.

I have my pleasures, and I enjoy my work.

Have you heard of Peter the Gravedigger? No, you have not and you never will because if the authorities ever realized I existed, they would staple my face onto every post office wall.

My profession is a solitary one. Oh, I am not the first. There are a few rudimentary practitioners in the Valley of the Kings, where there is a long history of my line of work. And of course, there is the woman. She is not in my league yet. I am the specialist, a professional with the highest standards. My work demands a strong back and a scientist's curiosity, and . . . but let me give you an example.

In the summer of the year 200–, I needed funds. My bank account at the time would appear large to you, but my interests are expensive. A generous contributor to several charities and a certain political party, in that pivotal election year I had outdone myself in more ways than one. Christie's chose that moment to announce a forthcoming auction of an incredible treasure—the manuscript of Dostoyevsky's *Notes from Underground,* written entirely in the Master's hand, which I had coveted since reading a copy as a boy, sitting beside a fresh grave while my father dumped dirt into a neat pile beside me.

In that chilly Upstate New York village of my origin, I began my odyssey through life, my small steps accompanied by the sound of a shovel, a man grunting, moist soil, and the gaping holes that receive life's detritus. My father, whose broken English inspired such derision from the locals, taught me after school in our shack on the edge of town about Tolstoy, Stendhal, about that European culture which America has so hastily forgotten . . . and about Dostoyevsky.

The Master's story, the spewed-out vitriolic phrases, laying bare the hypocrisies of the Establishment in his day, had turned my staid world upside down. And now his ms. was available to the highest bidder. To me!

Gates might acquire his Leonardo for $30 million, Spielberg could keep his Holocaust memorabilia . . . for me, the supreme collectible has always been the paper upon which was penned the immortal ruminations of the nineteenth-century Russian novelists, Chekhov, Tolstoy, and . . . the most tortured of them all, Fyodor Mikhailovich Dostoyevsky.

I had to have it. I contacted my New York agent for more details and found out the manuscript's probable cost. One lucrative job plus my current liquid holdings would suffice.

After driving to the library of the large university in my city one humid Sunday, I immersed myself in the academic journals. What I needed to find were the latest historical academic brouhahas. The Egyptian controversies I skipped; a one-man operation is unsuitable for an Egyptian project.

The University of Missouri *Journal of American History* mentioned a dispute over John Wilkes Booth's body. Certain academic factions alleged that Booth was not buried in his grave, but instead had fled to the Wild West after being—oh, please!—unjustly accused of the assassination of Lincoln. It had possibilities. Speaking of Lincoln, the old controversy as to whether he suffered from Marfan syndrome had heated up again. Then I waded through the usual Napoleona. Cause of the stout little general's death has never been indubitably established—a trip to the Isle of Elba might be pleasant.

Then I found it: a most acrimonious debate. The *National Review of Musicology,* a new publication of the Juilliard School with a slick cover photo of Mahler in his slippers, smoking a pipe, contained an intriguing series of letters. A Juilliard professor, Anton Sabatich, expert on eighteenth-century opera, was embroiled in a wintry and progressively more impolite exchange with Professor Arnhem of the University of Leyden concerning the cause of Mozart's death.

Sabatich refused to believe the young genius died of any illness, much less the atypical tuberculosis theory advanced by Professor Arnhem. The American, influenced perhaps too heavily by popular media, opined that Mozart had been slowly poisoned by his rival, Salieri, probably with arsenic. It's well-known that Mozart died penniless and was buried in a pauper's field.

I faxed Sabatich my standard letter:

Dear Professor Sabatich:
Regarding the death of Mozart: I can make you privy to
incontrovertible scientific evidence as to the *causa
mortis.*
Please fax me to arrange a meeting.
Sincerely,
Peter C.

Before lunch I had my reply, a very good sign, and I duly flew to New York City for a consultation. We met in the VIP waiting room at La Guardia. Sabatich was a short, hawk-nosed man glinting with fanaticism behind his spectacles. He never opened the heavy briefcase, presumably full of learned papers, which he held tightly on his lap. I discussed my ways, my means, and my price, ignoring the gaping of his mouth and the paling of his skin. By the time I finished, he had recovered his normal floridity and fallen under the calming influence of his own avarice. He agreed to my terms. He had money or the intensity of his need had overpowered his good sense. Usually, they try to dicker.

I caught the next available flight to Vienna, checking my long, heavy bag of equipment. In first class, the charming flight attendants kept my glass full of mediocre champagne and provided me with a blanket when I grew fatigued. I arrived, still weary, in the small hours in the heart of the old city. A taxi took me to the Wienerwald Gasthof, a homey jewel amid the soulless international hotels near the Ring.

Later that morning, after a hearty *Frühstuck* of fresh eggs, black bread, and strawberries, I made my way along the cobbled streets, an inconspicuous if unusually broad-shouldered tourist, to St. Marxer Friedhof, where the young composer had been buried without ceremony in a pauper's unmarked grave.

Of course, it was raining. A funeral party brooded under black umbrellas, issuing low wails. Urns of red plastic flowers and a horseshoe wreath of white and yellow mums had been arranged in the general area of Mozart's final resting place, as though others had tried to pinpoint its location. A smashed can of Heineken beer formed shallow puddles over the spot that I knew, from information gathered years before by my father's father, held the body. A low black fence surrounding an area nearby invoked a grassy yard where the composer's youthful spirit might still wander.

I remained awhile paying my respects, hat in hand, rain dripping off my nose, eyes busy. A security guard drove by at 10:20 and again at 10:35 and 10:50. Out of such routines are crimes born.

After a while, the cold having prowled through my skin and taken hold of my bones, unwilling to admit a slight unease, I explored further, walking to the far end of the cemetery at the edge of a misty forest. A pile of loose earth fast turning to mud indicated recent maintenance activity—brush clippings, shreds of winding-sheet. I looked more closely, a fractured humerus and knobs of knuckle—the gardener had been tidying up, all too assiduously. The clippings, dry under a tarp, would make excellent fill, if need be.

Reductio ad absurdum.

As I replaced the tarp, I caught movement on the periphery of the forest. Something light in color, a large animal perhaps. A deer? But it was my experience that wild animals will leave if you approach them, which I did, waving my arms a little foolishly, shouting, I admit. A slow withdrawal into the murk of the dark green marked its exit, nothing more. I was loath to follow. The dark of the day and the sucking sponge of the ground below discouraged me. Can you blame me for a moment's unprofessionalism? I am not immune to the emanations of human fragility such a place provokes. I left quickly, leaving the forest to its mystery.

Back in the city, I joined a bus tour with my fellow Americans, enjoying the sights of the capital, including St. Stephen's Cathedral and the vast Schönbrunn Palace, where, as a six-year-old, the prodigy Wolfgang Amadeus astonished Empress Maria Theresa. In what was for me an unusual flight of imagination, I could imagine the small feet tapping across the shining floors, and the small fingers, cold as mine today in the graveyard, whispering over the keys, the fresh music of a young genius resounding through the hard walls. Too young to have any idea of how short his life would be, he would have been feeling immortal, maybe dreaming of puppies as he played for the jaded oldsters who barely preceded him into a coffin.

Refreshed with my thoughts, as I always am when I consider mortality and how it brings all of us, sycophants, tyrants, and talents, to the same home, I found a candlelit dining room and filled up on delightful Viennese schnitzel. The continuing drizzle that had escorted me to the hotel did not dampen my spirits.

My plans floated around my head, suspended like the soft eiderdown under which I later went to bed. I saw myself as I drowsed, spiraling down toward the cemetery, then veering toward its forest. Once there, in the shadows of my dream, I thumbed through the cracked yellow pages of the Dostoyevsky opus that would soon be mine, the glare of his haunted intelligence my night-light, as exciting as good sex.

At three A.M. I arose. Putting on the rain gear and boots I had left beside my bed, I shouldered the long bag which held the tools of my trade. The walk to the cemetery took forty minutes, with only one policeman to avoid. Even the taverns had closed and a cool vaporous rain obscured the severe gothic lines of the granite buildings so favored by the city burgermeisters.

The lock to the main wrought iron gate I picked without incident, and made my way within, treading cautiously along the graveled path, words of the Master lingering in my mind: "I know that I am going to a graveyard, but it's a most precious graveyard."

At Mozart's grave, I swiftly unpacked my spade and dug. Several hours passed. I had stripped to the waist, oblivious to the cold. If the cherubim in the sky lamented, if the composer himself watched infuriated, I remained oblivious, chained to my task, intent upon my work and its own rhythms. Only an amateur would allow the cries of owls to suggest such things. Only an amateur would shiver at the gauzy haunts that passed through me as I worked. The regular chink of the spade followed by the sifting sound of dirt falling in a pile were the only sounds I heard, and they were cozy sounds, soothing even, sounds of my father, sounds of my youth.

Flashes of movement near the trees, I could swear I saw them, but the coffin came into view, and all such childish imaginings fled at the sight of it.

Made of flimsy wood and rotted through from two hundred

years in the dank Viennese earth, the box was quite deeply em-bedded. I had to climb into the hole to get closer. From my small dirt ledge, I lifted the lid with my spade handle, and gazed upon the composer.

Like all the rest, a grinning skull, bones enfolded in half-disintegrated bits of frippery, lace and velvet and . . . A short sword, still entangled between the fingers of the right hand, lay along what had once had been a thigh, a final gift, no doubt, from some noble friend. I could not resist. I took hold of the hilt and tried to disengage my prize from its encumbrance but to my dismay the desiccated appendage detached itself at the wrist and came loose with the sword. Surprised, I cried out, then brought myself under control, removing the musician's possessive palm and fingers with gentle force. I held his hand for a brief moment in my own, mar-veling at the small size that had exerted such crescendos of origi-nality in life, before returning it to its owner. I then climbed out of the pit and thrust the sword into my pack.

Back again into the boggy grave I crawled, snipping a bit of hair that clung to the grayish skull and scraping bits of bone into a zipper-lock plastic bag. My task was almost complete. Standing for a last moment in the grave I decided to examine the coffin lid further. Were those words I saw there? Last bits of wisdom to consider? In a foolish gesture that cost me everything, I bent and was struck from above.

No, I did not die, although my dream died. I awoke covered with earth, my bones commingled with Mozart's, his cold and disturbed, mine fortunately still ignited by flesh. I was only loosely coated with the earth. Above me, dawn spread, a faint streak of red after rain. Taking the time only to replace the lid and grab my spade, failing to bid my usually gracious adieu to the man who owned this spot, I climbed quickly out.

Gone! Pack, tools, samples—and sword! Gone while I had succumbed to a moment of humanity, a craving to know more than I needed to know. All that was left above was my spade and a flashlight. I freely confess I danced around the grave shouting obscenities and kicking the spot where there should have been a headstone for some minutes, but my rage was soon replaced by fear. Even my shirt had been stolen. The gray light of morning crept up around me and the morning rounds would soon begin.

Gathering my wits, I shone my flashlight along the ground, observing impressions in the mud, small boot marks. Haunts did not wear boots. If they did, they would be larger, I said to myself, picturing the thief and the laughter. An easy job, taking full advantage of my overconfidence.

Shaken, but determined in my task, I started back for the grave. A shout and heavy footsteps turned me away. I ran, following the tracks that led away from the grave, diminutive footsteps deepened by the heavy pack and easy to see. Strong, swift, silent as death she had been...remarkable in every way. My heart pounded as I visualized her, trim in her jeans and boots, observing me from the trees, watching the rain stream down my straining back, joyful at outwitting me...

I flew back to New York the next morning, scrutinizing my fellow passengers, alert for the small, smart, strong, and solitary female. But she had too much sense to take the same plane.

Sabatich, my unhappy client, got a refund. Two weeks later I fought melancholy, with the news that a Japanese corporation had purchased *Notes from Underground* at a record auction price for a literary ms. of $1.2 million.

I took comfort in three observations. First, Professor Arnhem published no further attacks on Professor Sabatich's arsenic poisoning theory. Clearly, the samples she provided had tested positive, and the man had some modicum of professional honor.

Second, I now know I have a female counterpart in the world. In her no doubt exquisite home hangs an old decorative sword, casually displayed, its value, its meaning, known only to two people in the world. Her, I shall seek out and...ravish, yes, ravish as I ravish my graves...

And third, Mozart's last sad gesture inspired an idea, and led to pleasure far greater than the mere handling of the Master's manuscript. A whole new level of collecting—

Direct from my recent nocturnal visitation to the Tikhov Cemetery in St. Petersburg—

I am caressing it now, running my hand over its bony yellow protuberances—

The Master's hand!

Gertrude Stein Solves a Mystery

Gertrude Stein and Alice B. Toklas during July of 1933 motored to the new country house at Bilignin in their ancient Ford named Godiva during a hot spell when there was no there at 27 Rue de Fleurus in Paris. At this time Gertrude Stein was still only a legend in her own mind and perhaps the minds of Picasso and Matisse and young insecure black haired Hemingway and Fitzgerald who had long known her crew cut immensity but before the year was out she would become definitely a legend and not perhaps a legend.

At Bilignin Gertrude Stein and Alice B. Toklas had servant trouble. The servants were sickly and sickly servants serve badly and must go so they went.

At this time near the new house at Bilignin there lived a mannish neighbor who wore the pants and her dear friend a not so mannish Englishwoman. The mannish neighbor offered to help find a housekeeper and gardener a local couple married if possible for Gertrude Stein to hire as servants.

This offer caused Alice B. Toklas to invite the mannish neighbor who wore the pants and the not so mannish Englishwoman to tea at the new house at Bilignin tea of the broad shouldered English kind in hopes that good servant advice would be given.

On this fine July afternoon with some humidity so that a storm was expected the four ladies drank English tea on the lawn at the new house at Bilignin. Alice B. Toklas had to serve it herself but the not so mannish Englishwoman helped with the cleanup while Gertrude Stein and the mannish neighbor discussed the servant problem with reference to Marx Voltaire and Emerson. Soon however Gertrude Stein saw the expected storm and the seeing made them hurry inside from the lawn outside the new house at Bilignin.

Eau de vie a colorless liqueur tinged with the fragrance of raspberries was served in the parlor by Alice B. Toklas who by now was glowering at the serving but Gertrude Stein in her immensity did not notice. Typical remarked the not so mannish Englishwoman to Alice B. Toklas we have to do all the work while they discuss the servant problem eh Alice.

To which remark the broad shouldered mannish volatile neighbor whose name was Madame Caesar and who wore the pants replied you are lucky I keep you you English sheep I have seen you seeing little Fleurette at the post office in Bilignin. And it was true the Englishwoman had the melting eyes of a sheep whether French or English.

On this fine July afternoon with increasing humidity as if summoned by these harsh words a pretty little bicycle bell was heard outside the new house at Bilignin causing Madame Caesar the mannish neighbor to drop her monocle in the seeing that she was having.

The seeing that she was having was of little Fleurette of the post office at Bilignin dismounting from her bicycle and being seen by the not so mannish Englishwoman whose seeing was a glint and a fish and a rose and a bicycle. And this vivid English seeing was seen very well by Madame Caesar who said what the hell is that girl doing here.

She can cook said the not so mannish Englishwoman with a petulant toss of her head well that is a start said Alice B. Toklas gathering up the bottle and glasses onto the tray and Gertrude Stein heaved her imperturbable ego off the parlor sofa and said let us talk to her why not.

Then little Fleurette of the post office at Bilignin stepped up prettily into the parlor and inquired if a housekeeper was needed for twenty francs a week she could cook and keep house and Raymond her brother could garden the roses badly needed cutting.

During this speech little Fleurette's lubricious sharp black eyes stayed fixed on the melting sheep like eyes of the not so mannish Englishwoman as thunder rolled across the sky because in surreal fashion they were back outside again staring at the threatening clouds perspiring in unladylike fashion from the humidity.

Let us go inside I feel the influence of an extraneous literary movement said Gertrude Stein whose eyes were also sharp under the tanned brow and gray crew cut and while they hurried inside Gertrude Stein saw and could hardly believe and looked again and without question saw and could hardly believe she saw the not so mannish Englishwoman reach out a white heavily ringed left hand and pat the charming bottom of little Fleurette of the post office at Bilignin.

Gertrude Stein's seeing was not a glint a fish a rose or a bicycle. It was an oh shit trouble ahead kind of seeing because the mannish neighbor with the volatile temper named Madame Caesar had also seen. And so under a threatening sky they all hastened to follow the charming bottom of little Fleurette into the new house at Bilignin some with placid thoughts some with calamitous thoughts.

Deep within an overstuffed chair leaning forward her hands

on her soon to be legendary thighs as painted by Picasso and Vallotton and sculpted by Lipschitz Gertrude Stein quizzed little Fleurette about whether she would mop and cook and sew and scrub for twenty francs a week and whether her brother Raymond would garden while weather sounds of a moist plopping nature were heard through the open door. Alice B. Toklas made a sound at the answers of Fleurette an approving sound heard by Gertrude Stein.

So little Fleurette with her tender buttons and sharp black eyes and charming bottom was hired on that no longer fine July afternoon with numerous small wet objects beginning their falling. No one stared at the sky as they had all hastened inside.

When little Fleurette left a vivid argument erupted between the mannish neighbor who wore the jodhpurs and the not so mannish Englishwoman who by the way wore a cream colored georgette shirtwaist with a peach colored cameo at her white neck. This argument was much more vivid than a glint a fish a rose or a bicycle for after all such things are charming things like the pretty little bicycle bell bottom of Fleurette but now Madame Caesar and the not so mannish Englishwoman with the white neck accused each other of many things that were not charming and many domestic failures.

A flush mounted to the white cheeks of the cameoed Englishwoman as Madame Caesar accused her of having the hots for little Fleurette and causing her to be employed chez Gertrude Stein where her charming bottom could be seen by all who wished to be seeing especially certain sheep eyed neighbors.

At this the plump lip of the not so mannish Englishwoman trembled and she flung out her heavily ringed left hand and cried your jealousy makes me sick knocking over the bottle of eau de vie concocted after many failures from ripe raspberries grown at the new house at Bilignin the previous summer by Alice B. Toklas.

While Gertrude Stein generally enjoyed a fine argument even a drunken confrontation among geniuses on a hot July afternoon with wet objects falling outside she had a rule in her perhaps legendary immensity and this rule had to be observed by all she invited including mannish neighbors in jodhpurs and not so mannish Englishwomen with flushed cheeks and this rule was that anyone who upset Alice B. Toklas who by now was sitting on the floor amid spilled eau de vie her eyes threatening to let fall small wet objects must leave right now and no more gracious hostess.

The volatile neighbor in black linty jodhpurs and her dear friend who were no longer speaking to each other were seen to the door by sullen exotic Alice B. Toklas who was not speaking. No one was speaking on this moist July afternoon though little Fleurette's bicycle bell could still be heard down the lane for those who were hearing.

What ill behaved women lovey said Alice B. Toklas swabbing at the oriental rug in the parlor and Gertrude Stein said well pussy at least we have servants coming tomorrow Fleurette can vacuum with the new vacuuming machine and Raymond the brother can trim the roses. But the august tanned brow of Gertrude Stein was obscured by a line of worry as Gertrude Stein looked out toward the neighboring house obscured by the dropping of wet objects. And even the knowing by Gertrude Stein that she was perhaps a legend to Joyce her archrival and Lawrence and Sherwood Anderson who at this time was at the height of his fame did not ease this line of worry.

Next morning a scream was coming. The scream was coming from the neighboring house so in haste Alice B. Toklas in her exotic wrapper and Gertrude Stein following in her brown corduroy robe and sandals slogged through the mud caused by abstract teardrop shaped objects falling to the jodhpured neighbor Madame Caesar who was pointing to the ditch by her house her eyes wide with horror.

Meantime a bicycle bell was ringing and some were screaming at the seeing of the not so mannish Englishwoman lying in the ditch shot twice in the right side of the head the muddy gun still clutched in her right hand her sightless eyes as moist and abstract as the sky.

The line of worry obscuring the august tanned brow of Gertrude Stein deepened. Gertrude Stein made a sound and the sound was heard by Alice B. Toklas who made a corresponding sound. The soon to be legendary writer and the long nosed companion saw the constabulaire in its arriving and returned to the new house. Numerous wet objects were still falling and it was still a hot July.

Are you thinking what I am thinking pussy inquired Gertrude Stein as Alice B. Toklas ruffled the wet gray crew cut with a towel in front of the fireplace in the parlor. Are we thinking that Madame Caesar used and then put the pistol in the hand of her dear friend replied Alice B. Toklas. Just so said Gertrude Stein and they both had a hefty swig of eau de vie.

In two days the inquest was over in its overing and the verdict was suicide.

Twice in the head not likely said Gertrude Stein as the two ladies motored home from the inquest in Godiva the ancient Ford. We shall stay away from the jodhpured one she won't be invited to tea don't worry exclaimed Alice B. Toklas. That evening Gertrude Stein called a French lieutenant named Rambouillet whom she met in the Great War and learned that military men always shoot themselves twice in the head if they can manage it so for the evening she stopped thinking the thing that she had been thinking.

And all this would have been and actually was merely a curious footnote in the vivid life of Gertrude Stein except that little Fleurette started work at the new house at Bilignin the following day and exhibited the troublesome charming bottom which was hard not to be seeing as she bent over frequently.

And even the devoted proper immense crew cut Gertrude Stein who was rewriting her legendary never ending thousand page book in the upstairs bedroom during this French summer was distracted by the bent over bottom and for a moment intensely wished to reach out and pat it and even extended her right hand which caused her to remember that the charming bottom had been patted by the left hand of the no longer living Englishwoman.

Pat with a left hand shoot with a right hand. Right shoot pat left. Ditch right pat heavily ringed sheep bottom. Left fish bicycle hand pat shoot right bell. No. No no not likely. Gertrude Stein observed but did not pat the calamitous bottom of little Fleurette while dust bunnies disappeared into the efficient maw of the new vacuuming machine which made a loud and unpleasant sound in the French afternoon unlike the pleasant whisk whisk whisk whisk of a good French broom.

She did it pussy it was Madame Caesar the neighbor but we'll never prove it said Gertrude Stein putting down her pen while Alice B. Toklas looked down from the upstairs window at Raymond the gardener who was clipping the roses with a snip and another snip and all the snips were precise. The Englishwoman was left handed and would not have shot herself with her right hand that is that is that but the right handed Madame Caesar will just claim the Englishwoman was right handed and the Englishwoman had no other friends here to say otherwise Gertrude Stein continued picking up her fountain pen a green marbleized Schaeffer and writing a homespun phrase over and over on a piece of paper which she then added to the immense stack of papers on the desk.

Perhaps someone else did it and placed the pistol in her right hand I have seen Raymond the gardener seeing la petite Fleurette also and there is something about his seeing that smells like a fish or you know a bicycle and so on mused Alice B. Toklas whose mood had reverted to the placid practical usual domestic mood of Alice B. Toklas.

So he is not the brother of Fleurette and he might be jealous of the attentions of the cameoed one with the plump lip nodded Gertrude Stein and reflected awhile. And as Gertrude Stein stared out the upstairs window at Raymond the gardener who was a good looking bootblack type as has also been said of Picasso Gertrude Stein made a sound that was jolly and robust and which came from the belly.

But he is left handed too look how he snips his snipping clears him. He would have remembered even in haste to place the pistol in the left hand of the cameoed one things sometimes come clear in a simple homespun way if you have been seeing what there is to be seeing and that is that is that is that said Gertrude Stein interspersing her statement with many more jolly sounds from the belly.

That is a relief I would hate for him to be sent away he snips the roses so well and there is such a servant problem said Alice B. Toklas who failed to see the humor as always.

That is not the point pussy the point is that definitely it was the right handed volatile Madame Caesar who killed the English-woman said Gertrude Stein. Will you please send Madame Caesar our calling card stating Gertrude Stein declines any further friendship.

Yes of course I shall send the card Raymond can take it but should we not also notify the constabulaire asked Alice B. Toklas.

Regrettably we cannot prove anything but we have at least solved this small mystery to our moral satisfaction which is a relief replied Gertrude Stein. You see pussy all is mystery we live in the middle of something grand and terrible not knowing where we came from not knowing where we are going not knowing what we are doing here or if there is a here here. However in solving the case of the sheep eyed Englishwoman we are comforted by uncovering the small vivid truth which incidentally explains why the mystery story is the grandest and most cathartic of literary forms.

Upon completing this statement the mood of Gertrude Stein darkened suddenly in the manner of geniuses. Gertrude Stein pooched out her lower lip while gazing upon the stack of papers and rubbed her august brow with her right hand muttering perhaps I should throw all this away and write a well plotted conventional mystery and made a sound of despair.

There there let us forget it if we can't prove anything we can't prove anything replied the placid practical no longer sullen Alice B. Toklas who had a small dark downy mustache growing. Come here lovey look at the size of that rose he is cutting is it a rose it is as big as jodhpurs or a fish or a bicycle.

A rose cannot be a bicycle observed Gertrude Stein rising from her chair and looking down from the upstairs window.

A rose is a rose you can say that again said Alice B. Toklas stroking her upper lip where there was definitely a mustache growing.

There is always something more if you have been seeing what there was to be seeing responded Gertrude Stein in her monk's haircut which imparted a dignity like that of Joan of Arc. I need to go back to my writing now pussy I think I am onto something that I am thinking and what I am thinking has to do with what you just said something about roses.

Picasso and his second wife will be arriving at dinnertime said Alice B. Toklas do not forget. And we have to buy two chickens at the market Picasso likes my recipe for roasted chicken.

Okay okay okay said Gertrude Stein. You made me forget what I was thinking something about roses I almost had it but now the thinking has turned to Picasso so shall we go and get the chickens.

And they motored in the ancient Ford to Belley to buy chickens and perhaps they are still driving there talking about bells roses and bicycles. On the way Gertrude Stein who always drove and dreamed for the two of them turned to Alice B. Toklas and said will you always love me pussy even after I am dead and Alice B. Toklas replied oh lovey yes I said yes I will yes

But that is another story.

The Furnace Man

Mrs. Rodriguez had her hand on the doorknob and had just swung her purse to her shoulder when the phone rang. She considered leaving it for the machine. But couldn't it be Geraldo, calling to tell her he was sorry? In spite of the unlikelihood of it being Geraldo, who didn't operate that way, who generally fumed for a few days, then brought her flowers, but never ever admitted any wrongdoing, she ran back into the kitchen and picked up the portable phone, out of breath.

"Uh, hello, Mrs. Rodriguez. This is Clean-So-Well Heating and Plumbing. How are you today?"

She was disappointed. You like to think a man can grow and learn. Why should she always be the one to make peace? She did a fine job running the house, and if once in a while, she blew the budget, well, that was life. Something of a crapshoot. But her husband didn't agree. He disliked uncertainty, and, even more, debt. So they couldn't pay off the card this one month. How frivolous was it for her to buy some clothes she needed, and the kids needed, that they could afford, that they could pay back next month out of his raise?

She heard the breathing of the man on the other end of the phone. She never knew what to say to these strangers who called. Was there some polite way to tell them to get lost? "Fine," she said, stalling.

"We have a sale on. We'll inspect and clean your furnace and your ventilation system for sixty dollars off this month."

The house had central heating, and she vaguely recalled a furnace in the basement. She supposed these things required maintenance. In their five years in this house, she could not recall any occasion when they had had the system cleaned. This was their first real home, and she'd talked Geraldo into buying it against his instincts, back when he would still cave in to her sometimes. How she loved it, with the red geraniums in window boxes outside her kitchen windows, and three perfect bedrooms, one peach, one blue, and one pink; with its white see-through curtains in the living room and the worn golden maple of her mother's dining set. Probably, they ought to try to keep the air fresh during cold weather, when all the doors and windows would be closed.

"Time to think about cranking that thing up for winter, wouldn't you say?" the furnace man went on. He had an unusual voice, nasal and unpleasant, almost funny if it wasn't for his deadpan delivery.

"Well, I don't know." She was acutely aware that her mother was waiting for her. Wednesday was grocery day, and she always took her mother to the shops to help her get what she needed. She always did her best for everyone. Why couldn't Geraldo see all that she did to make everything nice and homey for all of them? She would do anything for her family, anything.

"You know how dusty the vents get," he said as if she hadn't spoken. "There's fire danger, of course. We'll replace the filter as part of the service."

She felt helpless in the grip of such certainty. This was exactly how it went with Geraldo. He would bully and insist. She would give in, because most things weren't worth fighting about. And she only got her way if she was willing to put up with the flack that followed any decisions she made without his sanction. "I'll think about it," she said.

"Why don't I call you again in a week or two, then?"

"Whatever," she said, hanging up with relief, practically running out the door.

Two weeks later, she returned exhausted from her shopping trip with her mother, made a pot of coffee, and sat down with the morning paper to give herself a break before the kids got home from school. Her mother had been really aggravating that morning. Physically a very large and intimidating woman, she had lost the good humor she used to have, and was awfully cranky and difficult on these outings.

Today, she had jumped on a grocery boy for the way he stacked cans up too high for her to reach. When he shrugged in answer, she pulled a can out of the middle of the stack, sending the green beans rolling around the floor, stepping neatly out of the way herself while the boy took a few on the legs. Really, it was a sight, Elena thought, able to laugh a little now, all those dented cans rolling up the aisles toward the other outraged shoppers. Her crafty mother had run to the boy full of charm and gracious apologies, a game she played to keep people off balance and off her case. By the time they left, the manager was thrusting free canned foods into their bags.

Her mother's policy was do whatever you have to do to get what you want.

She sipped her coffee, worrying about Geraldo. He had come home late the night before, as he had for the last several weeks, ever since that big blowup about money. This time, there had been no flowers. And now she had the hassle of knowing the credit card bill would be coming again, maybe today, and he would see more charges there that they could not pay. She didn't understand it. She did everything she could to keep things going right. How could it all be going so wrong?

Her job was to keep the household in order. He didn't understand or appreciate what that involved, no man did. How could you clean windows without paper towels? How could you eat without napkins? He suggested rags, like his mother had used, and cloth towels, which needed laundering, soap, and more time she felt she didn't have to devote to such a level of trivia. He wanted her to be at home with the kids, he said, but they couldn't afford it, now that the kids were in school. He kept mentioning how their neighbor Rosa had found a job at the unemployment department, like he wanted her to do that. As if she could possibly hold a job now—doing what? Work as a secretary again for low wages with some jerk boss, and then come home and keep everything organized with three little kids? He was dreaming!

Who would get the clothes clean, the beds made, the groceries bought, the house tidy, the record-keeping done, the phone calls made? Who would be here when the kids got home, when the cable repair-people came, or the washing-machine repair-people, or the delivery people? Who would make sure they all ate fresh-cooked, healthy foods, and make good lunches to take to school? Who would make breakfast, with her up and running to get out the door at the same time he did every morning? Geraldo? She didn't think so. She hopped up, heading back into the kitchen to rinse out the pot and figure out what to give the kids for a snack. The phone rang.

"Mrs. Rodriguez? Fare-Thee-Well Plumbing and Heating here. I talked with you a couple of weeks ago about cleaning your furnace, and you asked me to call back and remind you."

She instantly recognized the voice. But could she possibly have asked this man to call back? They couldn't afford to have the furnace cleaned.

"You'll save money on your heating bills because your furnace will run more efficiently with a new filter," the horrible voice continued, sounding like Pee-wee Herman, exaggeratedly insinuating. How did he know what she had been thinking at that exact moment? It was eerie. If only Geraldo were as tuned in to her thoughts.

She giggled.

"When was the last time you had your furnace cleaned?"

She had no idea. Probably never. But if she admitted it to this man, he would have her where he wanted her. "Recently," she said firmly.

"This is something you should do every year," he said just as firmly.

"I'll have to talk to my husband," she said, mad at herself the second she spoke the words. She hated women who resorted to this old cop-out. As if she couldn't decide whether to have the stupid furnace cleaned if she wanted to.

But here was an excuse that always worked with men. "I'll call back then," he said.

"No, don't!" she cried into the dead phone.

That night, for the first time since they had gotten married, Geraldo didn't come home at all.

"Mrs. Rodriguez? How you doing? Do-Well Heating and Plumbing here. You wanted me to call so that we could schedule a time to clean your furnace and ventilating systems."

He had awakened her. It was the middle of the afternoon, rainy and gray outside. The kids were going to after-school sports, so they would be having dinner late. She hadn't been sleeping well since this trouble with Geraldo, so she had put her head down for just a minute, after washing the kitchen and bathroom floors.

She had been dreaming about something—oh, yes. In her

dream, they lived in a house surrounded by green hills, with church steeples in the distance, like a picture out of her youngest son's fairy-tale books. She had found an extra room in this dream house, a room just for her, where she could keep her things. She had been gathering her things when he called, her photographs, the little desk where she kept her bookkeeping and coupons tucked, a comfy armchair. A large picture window in the room looked out into the distant half-green, half-blue landscape. If she could just get all her things in there, into this haven of peace and isolation, everything would be all right again...

"Have you talked to your husband yet?" he asked.

His affected voice had taken on a new, familiar tone, as if he were inquiring as a friend.

"No," she said, still not quite awake enough to tackle him straight on. She sat up, rubbing her eyes, throwing the sheet off her legs. "I forgot." She stifled an idiotic impulse to apologize.

"I'll call again," the man said. "How about next week?"

"Look, why don't you give me your number and I'll call you?"

"You can't call me," he said. "I'm on the phone all day. So I'll just give you a call..."

"Don't call back!" she said quickly, before he could hang up, before they had a plan together.

"Well, now, why is that, Mrs. Rodriguez?" the voice said, hurt.

The nerve!

"Good-bye!" she said, hanging up the phone. She fell back onto the pillows, and pulled the sheet, then the comforter up around her, mad that such a nice dream had been interrupted like that. Didn't these people realize you had a life outside of their problems? From his point of view, she was this lazy good-for-nothing housewife who had nothing better to do than spend all her time considering what else needed doing to perfect this house that took all her time already and was eating them up with its needs and its extravagances!

Was it her fault the roof leaked? Was it her fault mice had crept into the basement and were nesting in the old dryer down there? And heating cost so much? Was it all her fault they had three children who needed a safe, warm house, clothing, food, books, and a father once in a while?

She couldn't get back to sleep. Combing her hair, she stared into the mirror at the face of a woman she barely recognized. She had gained a lot of weight since she had married. Diets didn't seem to help. Age had taken the soft prettiness Geraldo had once loved and left a middle-aged lady with hard lines around the eyes and mouth, in a housecoat in the middle of the day, hardly able to get out of bed. Geraldo had noticed and judged.

Funny how he remained so possessive of her, quite jealous of men on the street who caught her eye, cockadoodling like a rooster if she even once looked back. Old habit, she guessed. He could get really angry and impossible, irrational even, on the topic of other men, so she was always very careful not to trample his male ego. Yet here he was anyway, slipping away from her.

She could get him back. Rallying, she put on some tights and a big clean T-shirt. She would hop on the Exercycle. She had just enough time before the kids got home.

Propping a book on a stand near the stationary bike, she began pedaling. She pedaled hard, so that the sweat broke out on her forehead and ran down her face. With one hand, she picked up the book, turning the pages as she finished, skimming, mostly absorbed in the workout her body was getting. Geraldo deserved something better from her, a better devotion. She knew it. She loved him and she was making him unhappy. She needed to work harder, do better. He had taken her checkbook and her credit card that morning, and left her with just a little cash. She had resented it, yes, but she would rise above it, not letting this petty garbage get between them.

Sweating, pedaling, breathing hard, she resolved to work off the extra pounds, keep the house cleaner, even scrub the damn toilet bowls more often, and quit spending extra money he didn't think they could afford, even if she disagreed. It wasn't worth losing her marriage, just because he was a skinflint in some ways, and nagged her so much about her spending habits. He was a good father, the best, and had always been an attentive husband until recently. She would promise him no more wastefulness, no more frivolity, and stick to the bargain.

She didn't think there was another serious woman in the picture yet. She still had time to work things out with him.

She would get the kids to bed early tonight, put on a pretty negligee, and perfume. He had said he would be home early, so that they could talk. Instead, she planned to show him she remembered how to be a wife to him, in every way.

She had answered the door without hesitation, thinking Geraldo must have misplaced his key. A strange man in a uniform with an emblem sewn above his pocket stood on the porch, staring at her nightie.

"Mrs. Rodriguez," he said. "It's so good to meet you in person."

She knew the voice, but couldn't place it. Aware of the darkness outside, the hour, and the skimpiness of her clothes, she tried to close the door, but the man had a toe in the way.

"I'm here to clean the furnace," he said. "You made an appointment with me for tonight." She couldn't see him too well on the porch, but what she could see matched the voice: a pockmarked face, a short body, a certain twist to the trunk that suggested something not quite right with his posture.

Had she made an arrangement with this man? She had drunk a few glasses of wine that evening, waiting for Geraldo, who had said he was delayed, quite a few glasses, and those phone calls just weren't all that important. She couldn't remember exactly what she had said. She got a lot of calls from solicitors, and at the moment, she had a headache and a certain amount of blurriness.

"This is a bad time," she said.

"I'll have to charge you seventy-five dollars for a house call whether I clean the furnace or not, at this point, Mrs. Rodriguez. It'll only take fifteen minutes. Might as well let me do my job."

Seventy-five dollars! For fifteen minutes of work! Geraldo would kill her! Lost in her thoughts, trying to figure out a way to make this whole thing palatable to her husband, who should be home any moment, she let the little man in.

He brought some tools in a canvas plumber's bag. While she scrambled for a robe, he picked up dirt and lots of clinky bits of debris from the vents in each room, snaking a long vacuum hose a long way down, except for in the children's bedrooms, even though, as he said, those might be the dirtiest. Kids stuck all kinds of things down there. But she didn't want him to wake them up.

Then he needed to get into the basement. Geraldo insisted that she unlock the basement for workers, and never give out the key to anyone. To get there, they had to go out the back door, and down a steep hill alongside the house to a half-size door that led underneath. She put some shoes on, and turned on the outside lights while he waited, watching her. She pulled a jacket on over the wispy robe she had found, tucking her wallet into its pocket, and led him outside. She wasn't letting him back in the house.

He followed her down the steep hill, slipping and sliding in the mud. She had trouble with the key; it took forever to get the door open. The cold night air worked on her, and suddenly clearheaded, she remembered the phone call. She hadn't told the furnace man to come at all.

He followed her through the door.

She flipped the light on by the door, exposing the dirt floor of a hillside basement and showed him where the furnace was, in the farthest corner, while she tried to think about what she should do now he was here and had already done some of the work. He fiddled with the furnace for a couple of minutes, maybe five total, and announced that he was done.

"You said you would replace the filter," she said. "I didn't see any filter."

"I don't have the right size. Anyway, yours is in good shape. You don't need a new one."

She hadn't needed to have the furnace cleaned, either. And she could as easily have vacuumed the vents.

"I'm not going to pay you," she said. "You didn't do anything. And I didn't ask you to come here tonight."

"Oh, but you did, Mrs. Rodriguez," he said, coming close enough so that she could smell the alcohol on his breath. Maybe he could smell hers, too. "You wanted me to come. And now you owe me."

"I'm not going to pay," she said. She took a step back. Her foot caught on a box, and she started to fall. The furnace man caught her in his arms, one hand still clinging to a heavy wrench that she hadn't seen him use.

She pulled away, shaking him off like dirt.

"Where's your husband tonight, Mrs. Rodriguez? Working late, huh?" He blinked brown eyes as solid and impassive-looking as thumbtacks. "He'll pay if you don't. I'll just wait with you for him to come home and we'll tell him all about it."

She was walking toward the basement door, with him following a few steps behind. She whirled to face him. "We're not going to pay! I never asked you to do anything!"

"Look at it from my point of view," he said, taking that wheedling tack that she just hated. "You have this nice house in a nice neighborhood. I come and do some work for you: I expect to get paid. Is that so hard to understand? Don't tell me you can't afford it. Not too many women can stay home these days, but you do. You're home all day, aren't you? Plenty of time to take a little nap, get out some frozen food for dinner real quick before everyone comes home. It's a nice setup."

"What do you know about me? You don't know me at all."

He laughed, and the sound sent a chill up her bare legs. "I

know enough. You had a dirty furnace and I cleaned it. Now you owe me money." All in that nasty voice of his . . .

"You can't stay."

"I'm not leaving until I'm paid."

She wanted this settled without him making a racket and waking the kids and her neighbors. They were standing at the basement door. She took her wallet from her jacket pocket. "Look," she said. "Just take a look. I only have twenty dollars. How about if you take that and go away?"

"That's not enough," he said.

"You hardly did anything."

"The job is seventy-five bucks. It's a deal. A sale." He set his bag down, with the wrench on top of it, as if he were resigning himself to a long wait.

"What's the name of your company?"

"Goodwill Heating and Plumbing," he said.

Huh? For the first time she realized he had never given her the same name twice. He was making things up as he went along. Why, she'd bet he didn't even have a shop! Coming to her house like this, in the night, uninvited . . . probably just set off in his truck with no idea who would be foolish enough to let him in, no business address, no records of any kind . . . She should never have let him into the house. "Send me a bill. I'll get the money and send it to you."

"Cash on completion," he said.

"You have got to leave. My husband is about to come home. If he finds you here . . ."

"What?" he asked innocently. "Didn't you tell him about the furnace?"

She wanted to scream at him. My God, the man was unreasonable. He was making her crazy! He had no idea! Geraldo might be home any minute! Her husband would be wild, finding her dressed like some floozy, and a man hanging around. He could ruin everything worth anything in her life with his impossible demands! "Get out!"

He folded his arms, and stood there with a little smile on his face. He had her. The men always did get their way . . .

She grabbed the heavy wrench off his bag, raised it in both hands, and brought it down on his head, while he stood there, goggle-eyed with surprise. He had never expected such a thing from her, that was for sure. He knew nothing about her, nothing. She had to hit him several times before he stopped moving and thrashing around on the ground.

She went back up to the house to get a couple of big trash bags out of the kitchen drawer, put some yellow plastic dishwashing gloves on, and bagged him up, using tape to seal the bags. She made a quick trip to the garage for the shovel, and went to work, digging a fairly deep hole, one that would cover him nicely, in the soft loamy soil at the middle of the basement. She buried him with his tools.

With a bucket of cold water, she went to work on the blood that had spattered the basement wall. Cold water on blood. She wondered if men knew that.

She had a good marriage. She would do anything to save it.

She wondered if Geraldo knew that.

Trio

"Don't ask me that."

"Why not? You love me. I'm waiting for you to say you don't love me."

"Please."

"I didn't come all this way to let you off easy. You have to decide."

In the kitchen, the teapot whistled. Victoria slid in her socks across the green linoleum floor toward the stove, gripping the telephone in her left hand. She touched the sizzling handle of the pot and pulled her other hand away quickly. On the wall beside the sink a hotpad hung, oily and besmirched by a thousand meals. She couldn't put her hand inside it.

"Ouch," she cried, moving the pot to a wooden cutting board as fast as she could.

"What's the matter?"

"Nothing."

"Is he there?"

She marveled at how the voice on the phone of a man she had loved so dearly a few months before had devolved so insidiously into a whine.

"No."

"Vic, I want to marry you."

It was not an invitation, a plea, a question. It was an edict. She found a chipped mug in the cupboard, reasonably clean, and set it on the drain board. In the cabinet, she located a tea bag and placed it delicately into the cup. She used a dish towel found near the plumbing under the sink to protect her hand from the steaming kettle while she poured the hot water.

The water wet the leaves inside the translucent bag, making them soggy and a darker color, sending up a smoky drift of Lapsang souchong. Why did he have to want her now? She had run away, found someone new, and now all of the sudden, Jason couldn't live without her. It struck her as all wrong. His words were as murky as the contents of her cup.

"Why?"

"I can't live without you."

Good answer. "You know," she said, then blew on her tea while she paused to think, "I didn't do any of this to hurt you."

Silence on the phone. While her words sunk in, she wiped the drops of water from the scummy counter. Sharing a kitchen with male roommates, it turned out, was no picnic. When the lights went out, the roaches scurried around the room, proud owners of the night. She reached under the sink, past Luther's gallon of half-drunk gin, and found some cleanser which she sprinkled liberally around the countertop.

"Is he better-looking?" Jason asked.

Tom was taller. His hair was darker. He looked good. The regularity of his looks, the cragginess, the nasal sound of his voice, these flaws reduced him to human, while his aspirations and intelligence elevated him.

"No," she said.

"Then, why?"

She took a tentative sip of her tea, which was still too hot. Hardening herself against the pain, she let her tongue scald as the second, longer sip traveled toward her throat.

Because, she thought, I let go. I finally did. After years of holding on, dreaming, accepting lies as truth, she had let go. And now, too late, here Jason was, exactly where she had wanted him a long time ago. It was a pyrrhic victory. Now, she felt cold and distant from him. How to tell him? He had been her skin. He had held her soul together for years. She puzzled over the words she should speak. Should she tell him it was over? How could he understand that? Clearly, he clung to the idea that she was still accessible to him. Where was the grace in this situation? How did you tell someone that the passion between you, once so palpable, had burned to dust? Another man's smell, his sex, his squarer jaw, was now as established as her skeleton.

"I'm coming over," Jason said, as if tired of waiting for her to say something.

"No!" she said into the dead phone.

By the time Tom came home, she had sizzled frozen corn to perfection, chicken-fried two steaks, and poured an entire bag of prepared salad into a bowl and drizzled it with dressing from a bottle. One of Tom's virtues was an undemanding palate. He ate to live, unlike Jason, who lived to eat very well.

Jason had not shown up.

They dined by candlelight, a stick dribbling over an old wine bottle at the table in the worn kitchen, any romance derived from the shush of wind and rattle of old glass in the windows. They turned on an old movie, but within minutes, were making love in the attic room he had painted in shades of blue.

She was on top because he liked it that way, and she was

exploring some unfamiliar realms of feminine pleasures up there, when suddenly, the door flew open.

In stepped Jason.

But she didn't notice immediately. She was licking Tom's shoulder, relishing the salt and sweat of it. She only noticed when Tom stopped moaning and then stopped moving entirely.

"Get out," he said distinctly.

She turned and saw Jason.

He stood frozen in a corner by the door, glows from a canister candle on the dresser bleeding red light down his cheeks. How long had he been there watching them?

"Jason?" she said, lifting herself off Tom and turning to look at him. "Who let you in?"

Immediately, she knew the answer. Luther had let him in, too drunk and oblivious to consider anyone else's problems, and too lazy to announce a guest.

Jason said nothing and everything. His eyes had assumed a largeness beyond normal, and the clenching and unclenching of his jaw scared her.

"You have to go," she said before Tom could do anything. How must he be feeling, nude, wrapped in her body, totally vulnerable.

Jason swayed in the doorway. She saw for the first time a glinting in his hand. A gun? But...how could this be possible? She had loved him. She had given him everything, her entire heart and soul, and he had repeatedly trampled on them. He had stomped them until they didn't have a breath of life left.

All this thought was reduced to a moment of breathless suspense while she waited to see what he would do, feeling Tom's innocent blood pumping in the heart that was still close enough to her own to feel.

★   ★   ★

She had met Jason when she was in college in Los Angeles. He was her best friend Carol's buddy. She heard about him for months before they met, and that was exactly the source of all the trouble. What she heard from Carol, about his wit, his warmth, his loving family, she incorporated into a mythology. She invented a perfect man in her mind, smart, sensitive, funny. Creative. Against that, she didn't have a chance. At their first meeting, she fell, and she fell hard.

"What do you see in him?" Carol asked her, strangely upset.

"What a question. He's your friend. You like him, don't you?"

"Well, he has his problems."

"Of course he does. He's human."

But she didn't really believe it. Suddenly Carol, formerly Jason's biggest fan, became his biggest detractor. "He's too short for you," she would say. "He's sleazy," she said once. "Can't you see it?"

She couldn't. She liked his compact size, which made him less threatening. He was muscular to make up for a lack in height, and had a lovely narrow waist and dark, masculine whiskers that he had to shave daily. What did Carol mean calling him sleazy, she puzzled. Was it possible Carol was jealous?

She tested the theory and found it untenable. Jason had made a play for Carol ages ago which she had rebuffed. He flirted shamelessly with her on every occasion, and she discouraged him with playful insults, as sexually interested as a sister would be in a charming but disgusting younger brother.

Then she considered the idea that Carol was jealous of their growing closeness, because Jason had sniffed out Victoria's excitement about him immediately, and began to circle in an ever narrowing spiral.

"Just because I like Jason and he seems to like me doesn't mean we won't still be friends," she had told Carol.

Carol broke into a big belly laugh. "What a relief!" she had responded. "Gee, then I can be honest with you? You won't turn on me if I say something negative about him? I just hate friends that pull that kind of shit, loyal to the boy, even when it means sacrificing a sense of humor or perspective."

"Just what is it you don't like about him?" she had asked one night after sharing a joint in Carol's living room.

Carol thought for a long time. "Jason's okay, running around with lightweights. But Vic, you're not like that. You're going to get in there and scratch his insides. It's you two together that feels dangerous to me. Somebody could get hurt."

She dismissed Carol's worries right then and there. "Deep is good and right. Who wants a shallow life? People are emotional creatures. We've got to give that full scope, don't we?"

"See what I mean?" Carol complained. "Everything is so heavy with you. You go too far. Most people aren't cut out for high drama."

She had shaken her head. "Hurt is human. How else do we know we live?"

"Vic, you drive me crazy, and I bet I'm not the only one." Carol had left it at that.

When Jason and Vic finally went to bed together, a month after their first meeting, Vic was deeply, hopelessly smitten. In love, in the worst possible way. Awash in sexual chemistry, she felt satisfied beyond reason with his lovemaking, which later she might have called calculated. The tiniest touch of his fingertip sent gushers of hot blood flooding through her body. Sex synthesized her into an unthinking organism, which exploded fertility, big as a season, bursting with buds and pollinating the universe. She wanted to own him, possess his soul and every thought.

And Jason was an eager colluder. He wrote poetry and songs for her, oblique metaphors which were really all about him and not about her at all. But that was fair, in fact, because all her thoughts of him were really all about an idealized version of herself. She was in love with her own creation, a consummate specimen of humanity, and not with Jason at all.

This went on for quite a while, lots of letters, feverish phone calls in the dead of night, passionate meetings on a cold, sandy beach, on a roof still radiating heat after the sun went down, against the dirty wall of a garage. She didn't want to contain their lovemaking. She desperately wanted to be out of control emotionally, and so she was.

Jason, perhaps, came along for the adventure.

They wore out. Six months of mindless doggy happiness and two years of self-imposed blindness passed before reality began its inexorable drip, smearing her fresh, perfect painting of relationship bliss.

A weekend came and went without a letter. That Sunday night, her frantic worry had given way to a dark resignation. She called his house, even though he preferred to call her.

"He's not in," said his mother. "Who shall I say is calling?"

As if she had no idea who Vic was. As if nearly three years hadn't registered with her.

When he did call, he was full of newsy gossip about his weekend. He had studied hard on Saturday, and taken on his brother's paper route for fun on Sunday. They did the route in his battered Karmann Ghia, high.

"So two hours kinda morphed into three." Jason chuckled.

"Just you and your brother?" she had asked, unable to stop herself.

He changed the subject, and she knew, somewhere in the infinitesimal portion of rational thought still accessible to her, the colors in her mind began to blur, and the brightness toned down just a hair. She knew, but for a brief time, she ignored what she knew.

The fights began.

Victoria came from an argumentative family. She knew how to argue, how to wield sarcasm, how to twist facts. She had a terrible tendency, she was the first to admit, to bolster her opinions with specious facts.

Jason had a more subtle style. He opened his eyes wide, convinced with a guileless air of calm reason. Which made her crazy. And made her throw things.

Deterioration, particularly when he responded in kind.

He had another lover. She knew it. He knew she knew. The entire thing made her so tired, she spent days when she didn't have school lying on a couch with a blanket over her, moping and crying. He didn't call, just came by occasionally wanting sex. She gave him bitterness and grief.

After a few weeks of this, she came to her senses. She didn't wait for the usual call, the tentative plans that were dependent upon how cheerful she was willing to act. That morning the sun spread down the sidewalks and crept happily over the bushes and trees. Her usual place on the couch, in a cold, shadowy corner of the living room close to the phone, held no appeal.

Like a car in drive, inspired by the impulsive lurch of sunshine outside, she packed a bag with lotion, a paperback book, and a towel, popped sunglasses on her head, and hitchhiked to the beach. The day passed in a pleasant pageant of blue and white, with a touch of orange sun when she tilted her head a certain way. She swam out beyond the breakers, and had a conversation with a recovering heroin addict that made her glad to be alive and not addicted.

Jason was waiting on the porch when she came home. The ex-addict had taken her home on his motorcycle. When he saw Jason, he stopped short at the gate, gave her a wave, and jumped back on his bike and roared away.

She unlocked the front door, wondering what to say.

"Have a good time at the beach?" Jason said, and she heard caverns of unhappiness in his voice.

She let him inside.

"I've been trying to reach you all day."

The accusation stood there naked for her to see. Seeing it, she didn't like it. "Want something to drink?" she asked. "I'm so thirsty." She didn't wait for an answer. Tossing her things on the floor, she went into the kitchen and reached into the freezer for ice. "Beer?" she asked. He liked beer.

"Okay." He drank the beer.

She put on some music, sat down next to him on the couch, and drank wine. While the music wound around them, tight as his arms around her shoulder, he drank another beer and another. Then he tried to steer her into the bedroom. She was surprised to discover she did not want to go there with him.

"Time to go, Jason," she said, trying to disentangle herself from him.

He planted his feet in her living room. First, he flirted. She was lovely tonight, her skin glowing with the day's sunshine. When that didn't work, he pleaded. How far it was to drive home. He was tired. She didn't want him driving when he was so tired, did she? Then he got demanding and things got ugly.

He tried to force her.

She kicked him in the nuts.

He bellowed with pain and left enraged.

It being the end of the school year, she moved back home to San Francisco. Although her parents in Palo Alto offered her a safe haven, she checked the want ads in the *Chronicle*. Tom lived in a nice big apartment near Nob Hill with one other roommate, Luther. They needed another person to share the rent.

She liked Tom instantly. She even liked the way he answered the phone. "Whee!" he said. Later he explained that he was taking French, and she had misunderstood the word *oui,* but by then she was already captivated by his devilish smile and the cute room at the front of an old building fronting a Wayne Thibault–style San Francisco street, all flat planes leading straight up. She put a chair in the middle of the bay window and made that her power spot in the apartment, strewing newspapers, books, and dried coffee cups.

Jason wrote from L.A., and oh, could he write. His letters arrived almost daily through a slot in the front door, and his words balled up her insides until she stopped reading them. So he called. He told her about his fellow workers at the ketchup factory, making fun of them with a fondness that reminded her about the bigness of his heart. He engaged her in the furies of his creative struggles, made her laugh.

During the day she worked in an office, busying herself with the futile task of organizing other people's chaos. She missed Jason, the intimacy. His phone calls, when she took them, had the safety of distance behind them. She felt free to fantasize again, to imagine a closeness between them, to wonder about a future. But on the foggy summer nights, it was Tom, sipping Scotch out of thin glass, who radiated like a heater and drew her closer. Only the rude blare of the telephone could upset the peace when they would sit together at the table playing cards or trading jokes.

"You going to answer that?" Tom would ask.

Sometimes she answered, sometimes not. Always these calls from Jason were awkward because Tom sat there sipping or snacking, his warm, brown eyes fixed elsewhere, but every molecule of his body spinning in her direction.

One night in August, Tom went to a party with an old friend, a social worker named Peggy with muscular legs and a wide smile. Victoria spent the evening fussing, due to return to school in September, to L.A. Did that mean she returned to Jason, too? What about Tom? Tom's absence from the kitchen made her cranky, and when Luther came in to pour himself a little gin, not even drunk yet, she said nastily, "Oh, why bother with a glass when you can take the whole bottle?"

When Tom came home, late, she was waiting for him in the kitchen surrounded by the dirty dishes and cockroaches that had crept out, unafraid of the still, fuming woman at the table.

Tom lounged against the table, bubbling a little, as if the alcohol slogging inside him continued to brew. Ordinarily shy and wary around her, he reached a long arm out to snag her, pulling her close. Sniffing her hair, he said, "Ah. I knew you would smell just like this."

Maybe if she hadn't been so jealous of Peggy, maybe if her nightly phone joust with Jason hadn't left her angry at herself for leading him on when she suddenly did not want a future with him and dreaded leaving San Francisco and the life she now led, she would have pushed Tom away. She valued their friendship. She did not want to jeopardize that by jumping into bed with him.

But the charged bolts of energy sizzled around them and she couldn't let go.

That first night, she let Tom hold her close.

The next night, they made love in his moody blue room, with the windows open and the cold night air seeping around and between the heat of their bodies, and she was hooked. All feeling for Jason faded into memory, into embarrassment. How could she have loved him? Examining the picture he had sent in a frame, she realized Carol had been right.

He was sleazy. He had little piggy eyes, and he had cheated on her and lied to her face.

The next time Jason called, she told him she didn't want him to call again. Frantic at her rejection, he stepped up his campaign, sending flowers, even a telegram. I LOVE YOU STOP

When she stopped responding, he had flown up. "I'm coming over..."

Life moves. That's the essence of it, force forward into progress, like mad lines of ants marching along, individual, mobbed, compelled. Yet, at that moment, while Jason's gun glinted in the corner of the attic room, and Tom moved out from beneath her, nothing progressed. Stalled, frozen, paralyzed, all these words did not do what happened justice. An eternal moment passed. She had time to assess the fundamental nature of the situation.

Jealousy.

Two men, one woman.

Elemental and immutable.

In her naiveté, she had not understood completely that they were not playing. These romances constituted the essential nature of life. Childhood was over. Adulthood was life itself, happiness, children. There were no higher stakes.

The gun glinting, as Jason raised it . . .

When she was very young, very very young, she played with dolls. She invented worlds where men were not necessary, where the characters reproduced asexually. They lived on the moon, powerful and unchallenged.

What happened in real life: staring at a gun. Something over for good. Accepting it.

"Aaaa!" she cried, then repeated herself. Jason's hand quavered. He stared at them. Blood bloomed on the chest of the man she loved.

"My fault?" she wondered, staring into the black hole of the barrel Jason now pointed at her. Everything on this warm, wild earth froze.

His hand wavered and his piggy eyes fixed. He brought the gun back, opened his mouth, and shot red all over the blue wall behind him. He slumped down on the rug, leaving behind two dead bodies and one living.

During the time their lives passed from active to inactive, she hesitated like a bee above a flower. Something was pending, something always hovered, and it was her life, lingering.

They died, they both died, and she stayed on to fly around in the sunshine and ponder that moment for the rest of her short days.

The Second Head

Neurons splintered, shrapnel flew, bombs exploded. She woke up in the middle of a war, only the war was not happening outside. The war was happening inside her body. Cells died, screaming as they went down. Reinforcements crept out of ditches and met resistance. All around, flashes of light and noise . . .

They wheeled her out of the operation.

"Pain. Pain. Pain," she said. She had no idea if these words were a murmur or a scream. She opened her eyes to a blur of people in hallways and an elevator. "Pain," she told them. "Pain," she tattled to anyone that passed.

Hours later, she saw her husband. "How are you?" he asked.

"In pain." Her voice came out as a croak. Oxygen flowed into her nose through tubes. Another tube ran through her right nostril and straight down into her stomach, draining any liquid she took in and scratching the back of her throat. He gave her ice chips to roll around in the dry world of her mouth when she needed them and the clear tube bubbled them out to a machine on her right side. She watched the moisture move out.

She made the decision early to use every bit of pain medicine that came her way. They hooked an IV up next to her bed and placed a button in her hand that would give her a dose every five minutes. Every time she thought of it, whether or not five minutes had passed, she pushed the button. The drug did little to disrupt the skirmishes inside of her. Instead it made her not care. In one druggy dream, she saw earnest people in white clustered around a conference table. "Do we numb the hurt or make the patient not give a shit about it?"

They had chosen to attack her spirit.

Her bed, a white-sheeted machine that contorted into any shape, was her foxhole. A remote control twined over the silver side rails hovered near her right hand. If she wanted to sit higher, she pushed the top right button. To rotate the entire machine, she pushed the third button from the bottom. She learned the sequence for how to sit up. First, second button on the left until the bed stopped. This button brought the bed down close to the ground. Then, the third button on the left until the bed stopped. This rotated the bed up until she was practically sliding out of it. She played with the first on the right and fourth on the left throughout, adjusting the head- and footrests, then sat, sweating, heart beating, sutures weeping, until she gathered the energy to grasp the side rails, spread her legs apart, and heave herself upright.

Pre-op, the anesthesiologist, Dr. Phelz, had asked questions to determine her overall hardiness. "You seem to have a strong constitution. You might heal without this procedure," he said, as if questioning her decision to have the surgery.

The car accident had turned her easy life topsy-turvy. She could skip the surgery, and maybe continue a downward spiral that she was convinced would lead her straight down the pit into death. Or she could take the risk.

She hated having to make the choice. She wanted to revenge herself on the cause of all this agony. She had made no threat, she had spoken no words in anger, but a plan grew with her pain, and with the impending operation. She must not only punish, but punish with impunity. That was not easy, considering the state of her health after the accident. She counted on more strength and her unshakable resolve to see her through the aftermath.

"I do not like thee, Dr. Fell," she had thought, gazing up at the anesthesiologist's handsome face. It was a nursery rhyme she used to read to her children. "The reasons why, I cannot tell," her mind ran on as he spoke, reassuring her, attempting a bedside manner. "But this I know and know full well. I do not like thee, Dr. Fell." The rhyme rose and fell behind his words like a tank rolling over hills.

It was obvious to her he did not like her, either. Possibly, he, too, did not know why. He visited her the first day or so after surgery and she thanked him very genuinely because, like her or no, he gave her a moment of heaven in the midst of sheer hell, and he managed to keep her alive. Later, the surgeon said that he was quite an "interesting guy." Since she respected the surgeon, she reconsidered. Dr. Phelz was whole and fit. She was lying on the table, a disorderly blob, about to be gutted. No doubt the contrast had affected her judgment.

She did not fear death by anesthesia or heart failure. She did not even fear pain. She had given birth to four children without medication. She imagined she knew all that pain had to offer. She was ignorant, but her ignorance made her calm and strong and helped her survive the battles ahead. This same mysterious thing inside people sent young people to war with a secret in their hearts, a yearning for adventure and glory.

She was just being human, denying the facts that stared her in the face. She did not climb mountains too high to ascend or march off to meet enemies who wanted to kill her. She walked into a hospital where sharp knives waited, sterilized upon a table.

The day before the operation, she spent hours completing a battery of tests. Questions, many questions, but never the right ones. Why had she walked in front of the car? They did not ask. Why had the young man who hit her been without insurance?

Why that split-second mistake? Why all that pain? During the months of her recovery she thought of little else, except holding him accountable for ruining her life. She was a teacher. He needed a lesson he could never forget.

A few forms, to hold everyone else harmless. Then they needed her blood. "It's very hard to find a good spot on me," she warned them. They patted, then slapped the inside crook of her elbow. They put a heating pad around it. They called in an expert. The phlebotomist, a young woman with scraggly black hair, took six tubes of her blood out of one thin vein, chattering, trying to keep her placid as the red fluid oozed slowly up the plastic piping.

The third day after the operation turned out to be a terrible day. Where the IV entered her hand a bruise had formed, and her hand was bloated. They had once again called the meager-haired woman, who had moved the needle into her arm. Now her arm had bloated, too, and a foot-long red trail under her skin ran from her wrist to her elbow. She had cellulitus, and required more medicine.

She passed much of that day watching the red establish itself under the wan white of her skin. After lunch, which she didn't eat, she eyed her stack of books, wondering if they held enough power to distract her from the heat of the needle and the lead rock in her stomach. When her mind cleared enough, she could think of nothing but the purity of vengeance. She pictured his death. She thought of the story, the one where the one bent on revenge walled another one up alive.

She would like to do that. She would listen for the scream that never came, the jingling of the bells, and mortar the last brick into place anyway.

For months before the operation, while making up her mind to go for it, she had read stories about mountain climbers, trying to read between the lines to find what drove them to take such insane risks. Was it courage? A vain hope for life without pain, without the terrible outcome of a very bad moment?

For her hospital stay, knowing she might have trouble concentrating, she had instead stocked up on best sellers. She picked up one from the bedstand, read a page, and put it down. The downfall and redemption of this character unfolded in her thoughts like a Hollywood movie, so tight. So unreal.

The third evening, still groggy from the abundant course of treatment she had self-prescribed, a man with pocked skin was on duty: the attendant.

Most of the hospital personnel were women. The nurses were typical American types, with the exception of the nurse on graveyard, a large East Indian woman named Mercy, who embodied the night perfectly, muttering incantations as she checked the IV, replacing the bag of fluids and the vial of medication. The orderlies and aides were female immigrants from South America and Thailand, sweet people willing to wipe dirty bottoms and powder flesh that had seen better days.

The exception was Mike.

He came in to check her blood pressure. His reading was different than any other she had had—which she mentioned. He didn't laugh when she joked about it. He slowly pulled out the cuff, fumbling with her arm, and tried again. And again. And then he entered figures she knew to be wrong into his log. That evening, she needed help in the bathroom. He helped her and she didn't care that he scared her a little with his moodiness and the unusual seriousness of his temperament. She didn't care that he was male and black and she was female and white. She needed him and he helped her.

The next evening, she made her husband come earlier so that she would not feel so helpless, and so that she would not have to depend on Mike. Mike came in very quickly, took her blood pressure, and left. She remembered the car coming and the look on the boy's face as his car came forward as if powered by the stars, a machine bent on devastation.

"What did the doctor say when he came out to tell you about the surgery?" she asked her husband. "When you were out there in the lobby, waiting for me?"

"He said you were in recovery."

"Did he say I was okay?"

He looked confused. "I guess he must have."

"What else?"

"I asked if there were any surprises."

"And?"

"He said, and this was strange. Just last week, he had been reading about people with an unusual anatomical feature, an anomaly. He was wondering why, after doing this operation on thousands of patients, he had never come across it. And then you came along, boom."

"What was it?"

"I don't know. A long name."

"I want to know."

"You can ask him later. I was thinking about other things..."

"Should I be scared?"

"No. It's gone now. He took it out. Something vestigial. A leftover from when we were apes that's useless to humans." He laughed at the thought. "Like too much hair."

After he left, she drifted into a haze, locked on the idea of a piece of herself, now missing. She had something in her body that had performed an ancient function but was no longer considered useful. There were other body parts like that, she knew. The appendix, of course. The coccyx.

Maybe they still performed an essential role. Medical science wasn't smart enough to know everything. The body was a mysterious thing. All these inbred instincts, behaviors, things that seemed ill-suited to contemporary people, maybe they were needed, somehow. Maybe, by defining them as useless and removing them, humans ran the risk of making themselves less human. Sometimes she suspected that a piece of her had already gone missing when she landed against that curb so very, very hard.

Friday, the surgeon tiptoed around the idea of her leaving by Sunday, an idea she instantly vetoed. She was terribly injured. She couldn't possibly return home, back to the life she remembered from the past, maimed as she was. Why, she couldn't even bend down to tie her shoes yet or reach up for toothpaste in the bathroom cabinet. She needed more time to adjust. She felt so abnormal, practically crippled. She didn't want to see anyone or be seen. Plus, although she did not say this, there was a day of reckoning ahead and she wasn't quite ready.

She knew where he lived, the boy who had hurt her.

The doctor nodded. He would not force her to leave until she was ready.

Something vestigial should have told her she did not want to kill anyone.

But they had removed that, right?

That same day, they removed her IV. The nurses were amazed that one so drug-friendly could switch readily to milder oral medications, but she had breezed through the transition. She had her wits about her for the first time in days. She took note of the room, a large room with a blue sofa underneath a picture window that spread out a view all the way to the Golden Gate Bridge. Her husband had sat on that sofa nightly exclaiming with pleasure at the view. All her visitors also exclaimed at the view. She couldn't see the bridge from her bed, but she could see a wall-sized array of stars at night, and streets dotted with red and white lights rising into hills.

Her battles with pain were receding. Medicated, she verged on comfortable for the first time since the accident.

She had spent many a night imagining the damage she would do to the boy who hit her. She would teach him what it meant to be less than utterly responsible. She would hit him in the night, on a dark street—she imagined the crunch as his bones disintegrated. She had the whole thing worked out. She could not wall him up, but she could wreck him.

She flipped on the television, not for the first time, but for the first time since she had become coherent again. She found nothing very exciting. On the public station, a show ran about World War II that included formerly secret Allied and Axis films, and she watched it with half an eye, watched a former German U-boat captain saying, "We were young. We didn't think about what we were doing. We didn't think about the consequences of our actions. We couldn't think of anything more fun than going out and sinking ships."

Mike came into the room, wheeling his faulty blood pressure machinery in front of him.

He stopped in his tracks, eyes riveted on the show. "That reminds me of my dad." He watched for a few seconds. "I was just a kid. Nineteen fifty-five, we got our first TV."

Funny, she wanted to say. We also got our first TV around then. Or was it a year later, on Ceres Street in Whittier? They must be about the same age. She wanted to tell him, share this coincidence, but Mike seemed absorbed in the flickering images on the screen above them and she did not want to interrupt.

A German boat submerged. Cut to the men inside, lowering a periscope.

"Friday night on Potrero Hill. See, that was payday," Mike said, one hand on his hip, more animated than she had ever seen him. "He'd go out and buy himself a few beers . . . get a few beers in him." He stood between her and the television, concentrating on the screen as he spoke. "We had the five hamburgers for a dollar.

"Yeah, he'd get a few beers in him. Those were his favorite shows. *Victory at Sea,* you know? Black and white. All that old war stuff. He was Army. Friday night, that's when all of us gathered around the new TV."

Mike began to pace in front of the television, slapping his

knee. His voice, an emotionless, unaccented one, changed to a Southern dialect and rose in pitch. "See up there," he said, parading, prancing back and forth, and she could see his father forty years ago, proud of some remembered or imagined glory. Mike lifted an arm straight up and pointed to the set, still talking in his father's voice. "See, kids? That there's Guadalcanal..."

"Mike, where are you?" said a voice over the loudspeaker.

He startled, putting his hands to his sides as if standing at attention.

"I'm taking Ms. Watkins's vital signs," he called out.

"Could we borrow your muscle for a minute?" the voice said. There was affection in the words.

"Sure thing." He walked out the door.

While he was gone, she noticed the pile of best sellers on the refrigerator. She didn't want to make an extra trip back to clear them out when the time came to leave. She had her toiletries, the flowers...too much to carry in one load, even with her husband helping. Once she left that room, she never wanted to return. Maybe she could give them away.

Mike returned almost immediately and started toward her with the cuff. As he adjusted it around her upper arm she said, "You a reader?"

He stepped back from the bed and fiddled with his machine. "Oh, I sure used to be," he said. "As a kid, I read everything. History and science were my favorites." He flipped a switch, punched a few buttons.

"Because I wondered if..." she began, but Mike was still talking.

"But I don't much anymore. Got bad eyes," he said.

She was thinking, how strange. They were so alike, and she had thought them so different. Her dad bought steak on payday and the kids ate take-out burgers for a treat when she was a kid, and now she had two pairs of glasses, one for distance, and one for close-up. Neither one seemed to work worth a damn.

"I was in Vietnam," he said.

The mumbling of visitors in the rooms nearby grew louder, and the bright stars outside looked brighter. Her mouth was open, but she closed it without speaking.

Mike was lost in thought. Suddenly, he turned his back to her and reached behind his head. "See this?" He pointed up at the back of his skull to a lumpy scar, significant-looking. About six inches long, it curved like a long evil smile above his neck underneath his nubby hair.

"Yes."

"I spent eighteen years in the hospital," he said. "There was shrapnel stuck back there and they couldn't take it out. Looked like I had a second head. Couldn't go anywhere, anyway. Looked like a freak."

He turned sideways for a moment, long enough for her to imagine behind him, his second head.

He put the cuff on her arm, puffed it up, and watched the red numbers on his machine going down.

"Had me on psychotropic drugs. Everything. Because sometimes, I'd feel bad about what I missed."

The highest reading ever. He noted it on a piece of paper.

"Then they found a way to take it off."

He pushed the machine toward her door. "Sometimes I think about life," he said, passing under the television, "how much I missed."

She would leave the thrillers behind, she decided, find something better to read now that her mind had awakened, something like the books she had read in the summer. She had learned in those books what made mountain climbers climb and people go to war. Not courage, she had finally decided. A mysterious force drove them on. That same mysterious force had motivated her to go under the knife—something beyond survival, some greedy spirit full of valor, something vestigial like her anomaly, something as outlandish as Mike's second head.

She lay back against the pillows watching San Francisco blink, and thought of a young man and how long life should be and what it should be. Her husband came into the room, greeted her, and pulled a chair closer to her bed. He took her hand. "How are you?"

She squeezed his hand. "Better," she said. "They say I can go home on Sunday." Days, as opposed to years...a lifetime that could so easily be cut short by misery, bricks, metal.

Let the kid live. He had been hanging from her like shrapnel, but Mike had cut him off her.

"But...you're ready? They won't make you leave if you aren't ready..." She saw now how afraid he was. "Why are you smiling?" he went on.

"Come here." Her husband bent down and she kissed his bald head. "Because the operation was a success."

Chocolate Milkshake

One night, after a movie, she and a woman friend dropped into one of those anachronistic ice cream parlors modeled on the fifties, where an actual soda jerk in a white cap sponged behind the counter and silver-haired denizens licked their spoons as they no doubt had been doing for years. They sat across from each other in a mahogany booth. Her friend ordered a root-beer float from an ornate leather menu. That started her thinking about when she was sixteen and Charlie Almquist took her to the Bob's Big Boy on Willow Street and they ordered the most wonderful dripping burgers and huge thick chocolate milkshakes with whipped cream. For old times' sake and in a spirit of middle-aged daring, she ordered the chocolate milkshake, thinking you can't bring back the past and that she must be out of her mind to order such a mountain of calories. When the milkshake arrived it was better than the Bob's, taller, with cream that tasted freshly whipped and semisweet chocolate tempered to bland mild perfection with milk. She sipped it slowly through the straw, finding it difficult to make conversation because it had been thirty years since anything tasted this good. When it was all gone she was full, really full, her brain still savoring the taste and her cells still lapping up the cream.

She did not dare to repeat this experience, nor did she tell her husband about it, because although they had smoked pot and even sniffed cocaine once in younger wilder days and had drunk about a thousand bottles of wine together, this was an experience he could never share with her, a truly illicit, downright obscene pleasure, and besides he was a saturated fat and salt eater, who at night in front of the TV snacked on salted nuts and nacho chips, while she usually tried to content herself with tea, since she gained weight easily and had to be careful; but after the milkshake experience she began sneaking Hostess Cupcakes in the kitchen, eating two sandwiches in the daytime when he and the children were not at home, and having a second breakfast of microwave waffles with loads of real maple syrup, which helped her sleep better and maintain the bland sweetness which he and the children needed, deadening her to the irritations and lack of money and the fact that she really didn't seem to care about her husband anymore; and then she started to put on weight, and she had to buy some bigger clothes at the Penney's on their charge card, which is how he first noticed she was getting fatter.

Meanwhile she felt deeply ashamed, as though she were having an affair, which began to be quite unlikely, as she was really piling on the weight, having stored the scale in the garage so she wouldn't have to think about it after it read two hundred one morning; but eclipsing her shame was an exhilarating feeling of fighting back, an obscure defiance, and also that delirious pleasure of letting go completely and filling up, so much better than sex with her husband, who had no idea how to please her even after all these years; so she just wanted to continue eating brownies and corn bread and her children's dreadful cookies which had to be constantly replaced; she stopped looking in the mirror and there was an extra layer between herself and her husband when they made love, but they didn't talk about it; never anything to worry about there, her husband was as faithful as the lighthouse light; he would never leave her; they had married for life and they both believed in the sanctity of marriage.

After six months she had gained eighty pounds and decided she had to stop; people were staring at her thighs on the street and she was getting embarrassed to go out to the grocery store; she had to drop out of coaching the school play, which disappointed her daughter and the teacher, and when summer came she had to avoid the swim club, where she had spent years chatting desultorily with the neighbors; tennis with her husband was out of the question; so she joined a diet center, and for four months, until Christmas, she starved herself faithfully, castigating herself after each tiny slip, suffering horribly from hunger, until her hair was falling out in little clumps and the skin under her arms hung in small quilted bags, but she was no longer fat.

Then at a Christmas party down the block she noticed she was looking longingly at the husband of her neighbor, admiring the blond downy hair glowing on his forearms, and he noticed her looking and pushed her into the kitchen with him and ran his fingers up her now thin thigh and stuck his tongue into her mouth, all slimy and tasting of beer, until she finally pulled away and headed back into the living room where people smiled at her, and she found a tray of small quiches, spinach and Monterey Jack, and she had a couple, which sent her off and running again.

After that, in the middle of the night sometimes she would gently slide out from under the comforter and flit to the refrigerator while her family slept, and the day came when she could wear nothing but muumuus and it was hard to fit into her chair at the dining room table, and all the while her husband tried to be nice and pretended things were like before, and was supportive about her therapy, which gave her a weekly excuse to visit the McDonald's for an extra lunch of two Big Macs and a large fries, even though sex with him was really impossible by now and he was depressed, but trying not to show it, loyal and true man that he was.

As the fat enfolded her legs, her arms, her neck, even her fingers and toes, she continued to eat assiduously, not for the taste or the feeling of fullness but because she had to, the fat had taken on a life of its own, and within she had shrunk to a mere pinprick of existence; she found it hard even to make the school lunches and to wash the dishes, but her husband took over these chores as he had taken over the laundry and vacuuming and bed-making; at this point all she could get up for was the cooking, and the meals she produced were odd, even she knew it, buttered garlic bread and noodles in oily pesto and chocolate cake, and her husband never got the dishes he loved anymore.

Then one evening, he caught her in the bedroom eating a dozen Mounds bars under the covers, dropping melted chocolate onto the clean sheet he had patiently fitted that morning before work. At six P.M. he was hungry, as he always was, but she hadn't started dinner and although it was obvious she was in no shape to get up, he wouldn't leave her alone; he burst into tears and told her she was killing herself and had to stop, and, the words disgorging from somewhere inside she blurted out: you could leave you know, and he sobbed, oh, no you don't, marriage is forever, we agree about that, and the children were whining in the kitchen for their dinner, their voices piercing as bird beaks, pecking at her, and her husband pounded on the dresser, saying, why, why, why, and it sounded to her like I, I, I. She felt muscles under her fat tense as every ounce of her shook, and he made the mistake of pointing his finger at her like he was pushing a cap into a dynamite stick, and she was exploding, they were killing her so in pure self-defense she took her husband's loaded gun out of the bedside table and shot him, and when the children came running with shrill shrieks she shot them, too, until the whole family had shut up.

She pulled herself up laboriously from the bed and, stepping over the bodies, wrapped herself in her men's extra large parka. Wiping her shoes on a dish towel, she found the keys to the car he had left, a cheap Japanese car they had bought when they were first married. She drove straight to the ice cream parlor, wedged herself into the booth, and ordered the chocolate milkshake. Beige-gray in color, like mud or weak vomit, the milkshake had a sour aftertaste. After the one sip, she pushed it away, asking for the check. She wasn't hungry. Back at home she put her key in the lock, peering in, but they had not stirred. She heard no TV. No high sharp voices demanded her attention.

Cool silence seeped into her. She sucked in the quiet gratefully, allowing it to invade and fill her, standing utterly still in the dark hallway, savoring every last drop.

The Young Lady

Roo arranged to meet him in the parking lot after the game. She wore a carefully tight cropped knit top, yellow, with white shorts that she hoped showed off the golden glow of last weekend. Standing under a lamppost, she observed as the crowds poured into the parking lot. "They won," shouted the running back's father to someone, tossing a cap into the air. "Helluva game!" The students seemed more subdued than their parents, but Roo knew why. Their celebrating started later, out from under the glare of adult eyes.

Roo watched for Newell's blond head. He would be happy. Good.

After the crowd thinned out, Newell finally appeared, his hair wet. He found her under the light, gathered her up, and kissed her. "Sorry I took so long. Grabbed a shower." He steered her over to his car, a blue Cavalier, closing the door behind her with a hard thump.

They drove down the dark streets of their town and up the

hill, winding around until the lights flickered like sparks through the trees. Coming out to the clearing, Newell parked the car. Usually the place was packed on Friday night. "Jeff's having a party. Didn't I mention it?"

"You don't want to go," she said. "Do you?"

"Not really." Newell put his arm around her and reeled her in close. They kissed awhile, then he watched and waited while she pulled the crop top down into a kind of belt around her waist. "Just a minute," he said then, his breath a loud exhalation. "I need to tell you something."

"I thought we decided," she said, pushing him down, leaning over him. "Tonight's going to be so special . . ."

"Roo . . ." he said, and then he said her name a few more times.

Newell started the car up and rolled down the hill. He had to be home by ten. He had promised.

When they hit Main Street, he broke the silence. "Last night my parents got really mad about how much time we're spending together."

"They finally know about me? About us?"

"Yeah. And I guess you know how my dad is. Don't you have him for English?"

Roo nodded.

"He gets on my case and won't let go. So I blew it. I couldn't help it, Roo. I told them how much I love you," he said, reaching a hand over to stroke her hair. "How I'd do anything for you."

"Bet they didn't like hearing that."

"No. They told me they're sending me to an aunt in Sacramento until school's out. Summer, we're going back East. Renting a house in Truro."

She didn't know where Truro was, but she could imagine the clapboard cottage overlooking a blue blue sea, sunshine, and pretty girls all in a row.

"Well," she said. "At least we can write."

"No. They said no."

He didn't look at her, and Roo knew why. Newell was basically a coward.

He told her how he had fought them, and how only his mother's tears and the whiteness of his father's face had convinced him that this might be a good thing for both of them.

"God, Newell. You could have told me before we . . ."

"I know," he said. "Sorry."

Well, she couldn't blame him. For months she had teased him. She knew how he felt. He had earned her, with all those dates, the flowers, the whole romance thing. She sighed. "You told them who I was?"

"Yes. Don't worry, though. My dad would never use it against you in your grades or anything. Never. He's scrupulous when it's easy. He's just a weasel when it comes to the hard stuff."

"You shouldn't talk about your father that way."

"Yeah, yeah."

"You should have told them I didn't mean a thing to you."

"Why would I do that?"

How could someone with his grades be so dense? "What else did you tell them?"

"My father asked if we'd had sex."

"But we didn't until tonight."

"No. That was lucky, wasn't it?"

While he faced the windshield, driving carefully, as he always did, his eyes swerved over to watch her. He drove her all the rest of the way home in silence, probably wondering why she wasn't crying.

In June, while sitting behind a tree at lunchtime listening to a gaggle of teenagers chat, Carl Capshaw found out exactly what his girl students thought of him. They loved having him for English.

He looked like Ben Affleck, tall and dark. Deep. Also, they said, he seemed very young, although how could he be, being Newell's dad? He had to be in his thirties, at least.

On the way back to his classroom, he reran the conversation, feeling pleased.

Carl taught English literature, a sometimes arcane and dated subject, according to his students. He used any means at his disposal to keep the kids interested, including his smile, if it worked, or a sharp, mean bark if that worked better. The old songs and dances no longer did the trick. You had to work at penetrating their generally unfocused and overstimulated minds.

Passing by the lockers, waving at a few of the kids, Carl thought this year was winding up rather nicely. A group of his senior English students had rewritten *King Lear* in the style of Harold Pinter, full of pauses and portent, and would be staging their version next week. The junior students had just finished *The Crucible*, quite swept up in witchcraft and hysteria themselves, poor things, victims of spring fever en masse. They had stories to turn in at the end of the quarter.

He taught five classes and directed sixth-period study hall. According to Cath, he didn't make enough money to compensate for the aggravation factor, but then nothing he did lately satisfied her. As time passed, he had begun to wonder if anything would diminish the magnitude of his transgression, and her shocked memory of finding that motel slip in his pocket.

He didn't know why it had happened, except that Shelly, the school counselor, got so drunk that night. She had come on to him after a school board meeting, when they had retired to the bar to indulge in the general gossip and backstabbing they all enjoyed in mild forms, and he had done what was indefensible but entirely natural. He hadn't even come home very late. But, confronted with the evidence by Cath the next day, he confessed immediately.

Now, nearly a year later, at breakfast sometimes, he could see shadows of doubt and pain in Cath's eyes. The crisis in December with Newell had helped them to forge an uneasy alliance, raising a hope in him that someday she would love him wholeheartedly and without reserve again, as she always had before.

At his classroom, he stopped and fiddled for his keys. He had been taken off guard by the whole situation, surprised at himself, and surprised by the powerful aftershocks that had almost toppled his marriage. The truth was, from the moment he had that second drink with Shelly, Cath had flown out of his mind. He had never meant to hurt her. He had never even considered her.

He crumpled his lunch sack, threw it into the plastic container beside his desk, and took his seat. Somehow, he could never get being a couple exactly right. He felt like hell about it. His only consolation was the assurance he made to himself and to Cath that it would never happen again.

This virtuous thought left an indistinct emptiness at the same moment it soothed him.

As the kids raised hell and found their seats, he paused to consider the mighty pines outside the bank of windows his desk faced. He had watched them grow from seedlings. He had watched Mr. Cahill, the school gardener, prune and nurture them for his whole working life through those windows. He had watched the man's hair go gray and fall out.

Fourteen years of a man's life were summed up in those big old trees waving in the wind, looking so happy and well-fed. You could grow plants in any room in this school, as a matter of fact, particularly his classroom, he thought whimsically. You could fill the place up with hothouse flowers, the girls displaying bright blossoms, the boys buzzing around their heady perfume. When they had decided to send Newell away in December, he had tried to remind Cath about how mature seventeen felt, how full-blown, how physically electrifying. She told him Newell was just a pup, in spite of how he looked. That girl had seduced him.

Her naiveté never ceased to astound him.

Carl had met his wife at fourteen and married her at twenty-one. He had enjoyed returning to her cool gravity and good sense after a bevy of selfish, bullheaded college girls. He had experienced enough high drama between fourteen and twenty-one to last a lifetime—at least he thought so until the Shelly incident, and more recently, the escalating scenes with Newell.

At least Newell, being amenable to bribes, had been easy to fix. The promise of a trip East in summer and maybe his own wheels spun his attitude around fast.

He shuffled the papers on his desk, waiting for the kids to settle down. The air in his classroom, thick with evaporating body fluid, stinking of adolescent sexual glory, sometimes made him want to throw his arms around the kids and dance naked with them in circles around a bonfire. More times, it made him sick with longing for the sweeter smells found elsewhere.

Class began. The fifth-period juniors read minimally coherent essays on Miller in monotone, a low roar of voices their accompaniment, until he could stand it no longer. He stormed, raining down until they sat silent and he was spent.

"Capshaw's still pissed about Newell and Roo," he heard the whisper as they scurried to the bell. "Dude's lost it."

He cleared his throat to say over the din of their leaving, "Miss Fielding. Please stay after for a moment."

Roo stopped in her tracks, shifted her books, marched back to the front row, and sat down, feeling curious but acting blasé.

"You're not turning in your work," Capshaw said, when the door slammed.

Roo knew from the girls' bathroom mirror she had eyes round as plates, edged in red. She looked emotional, dramatic. She hoped he noticed. "I'm sorry, Mr. Capshaw," she said, but he wanted an explanation. He waited long enough to make her uncomfortable.

"You made As all last year. Now you'll be lucky to get a C this last quarter. Want to tell me what the problem is?"

She looked at him, thinking about Newell. Then she talked about what a mess her life was lately, how her mom was on her case, about how her dog had died. Tears dribbled down her cheeks.

Mr. Capshaw frowned. He handed her a tissue.

"I just miss him so much," she sobbed. "It's nothing to do with English. I'm doing badly in every class. I just can't seem to concentrate." Her body shook. This room always felt hot, since the first day of school. Mr. Capshaw kept the windows closed most of the time, to keep the noisy equipment and traffic sounds out, he said.

"I'm sorry for your loss, but we've got another problem here. I'd like to help you. You could bring your grade up to a B with this next story. It's the last creative writing assignment for the year, so I expect everybody to do his or her best work."

She wiped her face with a tissue. "I sit down to work. I start something. I end up crying. My mom says she cried the whole last half of her junior year. She says it's hormones."

"Did you tell your mom about you and Newell?"

"No! She could never understand."

"Think about telling her. And think about this story. You're going to find it hard to swallow, but you need this grade. You need it to get into college. It's dumb, but your future's riding on it."

She stood up. "I know, Mr. Capshaw. I'll try."

"Can you get me a preliminary proposal by Friday? It can be about anything."

"Sure," she said.

Friday afternoon, Carl had Roo in his sixth-period study hall. She came in looking bedraggled, her face flushed pink with heat.

"Where's your proposal, Miss Fielding?" he asked. "That is due today, last period. I thought I made that clear."

"I'll work on it right now," she promised. "I'll get it to you by the end of the day." The bell rang. The other students hustled to the oak tables, hanging backpacks on chairs, littering the floor with notebooks. He sat at his desk, trying hard not to notice Roo, whose pen hovered over her paper for minutes at a time, unwavering, while she stared at the neck of the boy in front of her. When the bell rang, the fog left her eyes. She looked up with a start and caught his eyes on her face.

"Your story concept?"

"Not done."

"You'll have to stay after today, Roo. I'll help you if I can."

Roo called her mother from the office so that she wouldn't panic when she came home late. "I'm working with Mr. Capshaw on finishing something up, Mom."

"He's that cutie from open house?"

"My English teacher."

"Newell's father, right?"

How was her mother always so clued-in? "Yes."

"Where'd he go, anyway?"

"Who?"

"Newell. You went out a couple of times, didn't you?"

"He's at another school."

"Private school, I bet. All the public school teachers send their kids to private, the paper says. They're canceling Honors English at Obispo next year. I'm just disgusted."

"Can I stay 'til five? I'll unload the dishes when I get home."

"Okay, honey. Need a ride? I don't want you to walk home alone, young lady."

"Don't worry so much. I'll find a ride."

Roo managed a poor rehash of a story she had written in eighth grade for something to give Mr. Capshaw. He didn't really do anything to help, just sat there at his desk pretending not to look at her the whole time. She finished by five. She asked him for a ride home, explaining that her mother worried. "A guy pulled over off the road once. He got out of his car and followed me for a few blocks. Asked me if I wanted to go for a ride. I was only thirteen. Since then, Mom's a maniac about safety."

Roo had worn the lightest cotton she could find that morning, a sleeveless red blouse over sparkling white slacks. Her mom had helped her to twist her hair into a French braid, but by now she had a curly halo around her face, too messy, she felt. She excused herself for the bathroom and wetted some scratchy paper towels, getting her underarms with one, smoothing back her hair with another. She dabbed a dry towel over her washed face, licked her lips, then glossed them. She was ready.

Mr. Capshaw had parked his car under the row of eucalyptus by the far lot. By the time they got there, she was sweating again. "I hope you have air-conditioning," she said.

"I do. My wife says it's an unnecessary extravagance this close to the coast but after all day at school, I'm ready to be pampered."

"Me, too," she said, wondering what his wife looked like. Maybe like Nicole Kidman, with that narrow face and rat's nest of hair. "I live kind of up in the county land. It's not quite two miles. Sorry to take you out of your way." Newell had always raved about how pretty it was up there, how woodsy and pleasant compared to the flats. He must hate Sacramento, with its heat and tract houses.

Mr. Capshaw turned the air on full blast and rolled open the sunroof. "Is that okay?" he asked, and she nodded, half-closing her eyes as they swerved out of town.

"Last time I came this way," she said dreamily, "was with Newell."

Carl could smell Roo, a kind of gym class sweat he remembered from his son, mixed with a lusty odor he tried not to think about. She seemed to have fallen asleep, her head tipped back against the seat. Awkward. Beautiful.

He remembered his body at seventeen. He recalled a day stepping out into the sunshine, fresh from the shower, the sun petting his skin, the licks of air, the rank smell of wet dirt. His own juicy youth had filled him up, flooded him. For one luscious moment, all was perfection. Then, knowledge returned like a slap and woke him up. The concrete burned his bare feet...

"Shoot. Roo, wake up. We're lost." He could see the Pacific below the road. He'd overshot his turn. He'd gone too far.

She breathed deeply and raised a hand to her cheek. "Where are we?"

"I don't know," he said. "You're the one who lives around here. Could you take a look at the map in the glove compartment?" They climbed steadily up a winding road to a dead end.

"I can't figure this out."

"I'll look," he said. Stopping in a shady spot high above the ocean, he turned off the engine, turning the map over to find the town. "Okay, the high school, right here." He traced their route. "There's where I turned wrong." She moved in to look. "We're five miles off base. At the bottom of the hill, I go left. Then back to Foothill. Left again onto Crocker."

"I live right there." She drooped a long thin arm over his arm to point. Her breast pushed against him, lightly, innocently.

When she removed her hand, he folded the map. She stayed close, looking out at the trees. "Can I get out for a second?" she asked. "I want to peek at the ocean."

"Okay," he said. "Quickly, though. Let's not give your mom anything to worry about."

She walked over to where the land dropped away. On top of the hill like this, the wind off the ocean hit full force. Her hair slapped and blew like sails. She stayed so long, raising and lowering her arms in the wind, that he got out to get her.

She was crying again. "I'm so lonely," she said. Carl put her head against his shoulder and let her cry.

After a while she quieted down. She sat on a rock, still clinging to him, holding his legs. She looked up at him once. She reached up.

"No," he said. "Roo..." He stood with the wind to his back, as lovesick as any seventeen-year-old, as deeply moved, as heartfelt, as pained.

They made love, the teacher halting the compelling rush of his lust just long enough to witness himself there, hanging over the ocean, his body disappearing into the girl's body, his past resurrected, his future destroyed.

"Did you see this?" Cath said Monday morning, holding up the "Living" section. "You give a drug addict all the drugs he needs to be satisfied, and he is not satisfied. You give an alcoholic access to all the alcohol he wants, and he is not satisfied."

"And...what conclusions do they draw?" He had slept poorly this weekend. He sipped his coffee slowly, savoring the flavor, savoring his wife who sat in a patch of sun at the table.

"Same thing with chocolate," she continued, "even in unlimited quantities."

"So..."

"So the point is, people who crave a substance can never get enough."

He found it hard to come up with the right thing to say. Absorbed by guilt, he wasn't really following. "This is not news," he said.

"No, wait. Nothing satiates the craving. A lot of crank doesn't do any better than a little. There's no satiety. Anticipation is what drives them on. Hope."

"Always chasing the high."

"But the chase keeps 'em going, get it?"

"Uh huh."

"That's you."

"What do you mean?"

"You feel stuck in your job. Sometimes you feel stuck with me."

"Cath..."

"You've always been the seeker. Like Emerson's traveler, who is never happy. The spot you are in is never quite good enough."

"What are you talking about?"

"Something's wrong, isn't it?"

He stood and tried to put his arms around her but while accepting his embrace, she sighed deeply.

"Nothing's wrong. It's the last day of school before finals. I'm distracted," he said.

"That's not it."

"Nothing's wrong, goddammit!"

The look she turned on him proclaimed exquisitely the depths of her understanding and grief. He had done nothing different than he did any other weekend, but his wife was already mourning over some unknown catastrophe. That's what a real marriage was, understanding too deep for deception. Well, he had a real one, didn't he, and now he had blown it, along with everything else.

He knew he should tell her before word leaked back, as it surely would, and soon, but he couldn't. He knew that he would try to explain, and he knew he couldn't. Cath's simple values were admirable, but there were things in his world that could not survive such astringency—delicate, complex things. Nothing could make her understand how wrapped up in that moment he had been, how obliterated he had been. How impersonal it had been. He had wandered outside her framework, and was lost to her comprehension.

He kissed her good-bye, lingering, wrapped in the smell of her shampoo, doing his own mourning in advance of the news.

In the car he tuned the radio to an all-news station all the way to school. Pasting a composed look on his face, he greeted the other teachers in the hallway with the usual salutations. They greeted him back.

So Roo hadn't said anything yet. There was still time.

Once in his classroom, he opened up the briefcase he was carrying, removed his gun, and tucked it into the bottom drawer.

"Final projects are due this morning," he started off in first period, second period, third period. "You had the weekend to finish up," he said while he flitted between heaven and hell.

At lunch, he sat under a tree, itching in a patch of cut grass, his paper sack untouched beside him. The gardener came unpleasantly close with his rake a few times. The teachers would not tolerate the noise of leaf blowers, so disruptive to the calm of academe. Mr. Cahill thought their position made his life harder and made his opinion known however possible. A horde of little children skating, followed by a troupe of mothers, screamed by on the sidewalk.

Another bell rang in fourth period and then there was the senior class parody, which was witty enough to shake a few nervous laughs out of him.

Fifth period. Roo.

She walked into the classroom with her friend Jayne, and sat in the back row until class started, chatting quietly.

"Stories to the front, please," he said, amazed at his own cool. How did he do it? How could he function in the middle of the worst crisis of his life? Cath would leave him, if she knew. She would never trust him again.

He watched to see if Roo had something ready. She did.

"I need to see you after class, Miss Fielding."

She nodded, and her eyes returned to her book.

"Now read this Katherine Anne Porter, the last story in your lit book, and answer the questions at the end. As you are reading, I want you to be thinking about how she generates a theme. What are the elements? What role do characters, plot, and detail play? Pay attention to the ending and the beginning. Look for parallels in the structure. Oh yes. We've talked a lot about point of view. We'll be talking about that again at the end of the period."

The class groaned.

"Thought you could take it easy just because it's the last day, huh?" How normal he sounded! How pathetic and irrelevant everything he said sounded!

He had staved off the inevitable over the weekend, because he was afraid. He had justified his hesitation by telling himself he had to see Roo one last time to apologize, and that's what he would do, wasn't it, even though something sharp and nasty in him wanted to take her down with him.

He tried to write to Cath, but ended up throwing the pages away. He could not face her with this. He could not face the pain of her humiliation, and his own public downfall.

The world sucked. Everything was bound to appear so sordid, when it had been nothing but a spring day, the sunshine, the trees in an ocean breeze. Ah, how the world sucked.

Blurry in his thoughts, looking for something to get himself through to the end of the class when he would get Roo alone, or himself alone, or both of them, he hadn't decided, he picked up Roo's story and began to read.

"The Young Lady," a new title, headlined the page. She hadn't used her synopsis at all. Roo wrote well; he usually enjoyed her assignments.

A clutching at his heart reminded him, and his moist fingers left marks as they traveled down the side of her paper. His time was up. He had done something others would see as deplorable, selfish, vile ... the respect of his colleagues, the admiration of his pupils, all that would be lost along with Cath, as soon as they knew.

Was Roo's time up, too? Did he have to decide this minute, or was the decision made the moment he pulled off the road that day with her? His heart began to thump. He worried someone might hear it, might find him out before he could escape.

A squirrel ran down a tree outside. A few of his students turned to watch.

The gun in his drawer made that side of the desk feel warmer, like a hearth, so he leaned that way as if its comfort could pamper him through the last few minutes of class. But as he read, he forgot the desk; he forgot the gun. His fear continued to sit in his stomach, indigestible as coal, but he gave it no attention.

He found himself driving along in a car, a young girl, feeling the pressure of an older man's eyes on her skin as she feigned sleep. He took in the fine sensory details of her clothing, her perception of this man, his handsomeness, his strength, his intelligence. She had such a crush.

And slowly, he began to understand.

Roo's story was the story of his seduction.

Way back at the beginning of the year, Roo had decided to go after him. But Carl, well-schooled in how to handle students with crushes, had not taken her bait. He threw out his arsenal of defenses to frustrate her. Nothing she did caused even a flicker of interest in his eyes. Nothing she wore made him look any closer than he looked at all the other girls.

So, she had developed a plan. She would seduce Newell. She reasoned that would draw Carl's attention. She didn't care what kind of attention she got. Negative was okay for a start. She just needed a way to rise above what she called the "herd of anonymous cattle" in the classroom. If necessary, she would sacrifice her grade, but that direction had not come until later, when Carl continued to ignore her.

With fascination swinging toward dread, he read on, recognizing only snippets of the situation he had lived. The English teacher in him marveled at the point of view, so distinct, so different from his own. Moments he remembered had been distorted into something completely unfamiliar.

Roo's girl was ready to explore a bigger world. She had put her own physical feelings on hold long enough. Her character cited Margaret Mead on the subject of adolescent sexuality.

Carl read on. Appalled by the cold analysis of her seduction of his son, he flipped a page and stumbled into her version of his own. There it was, a "tryst" on the cliff, romanticized and glossy as a magazine cover.

The story was a message to him. A confession. She wanted him to understand. She wanted him to see it from her point of view. "The young lady had a different tale to tell," she wrote.

He sat back in his chair and felt a glimmer of hope.

She would not tell Cath. This life that he loved so much would continue. For a long time he looked out the window, watching Mr. Cahill trimming pine branches outside with a long pole.

He would not lose his job. The gun . . . he would not have to use it.

He picked up a pencil and went to work on her story. Mechanically, he marked spelling errors in red while his mind kept up a chorus of protests at trivializing the contents.

Contrast POVs: his story was the story of her seduction.

She would never tell anyone, the last few lines read, and she told "the man" to keep silent. His victim did not accept her victimization.

What a gift. He wanted to stand up and cheer, he felt such a gush of relief. This was better than sex. Better than falling in love. She had given him back his life!

At the end of class, she walked up to his desk. "Mr. Capshaw, how'd you like my story? Did you get a chance to read it yet?"

"I did. It's on the racy side of good taste, Roo, but you worked hard on this and I'm sure your grade will reflect that." He struggled to maintain his poise, but she undid him, opening her mouth a little to reveal her sharp, newly minted caps. As she ran her tongue self-consciously over them, eager to hear more, he found his attention riveted on the perfect white rectangles that were all for show, not for biting better.

"I like the way you developed your theme," he said finally, then sat back in his chair.

"Great," she said, nodding. Her eyes said nothing special to him. Only her mouth's half-smile appreciated the joke.

"You have summer plans?"

"My relatives have a house at Tahoe. I got most of my finals done early so that we can leave tomorrow, all except for this class, and I thought you might pass on requiring a final, Mr. Capshaw. I mean, you know what I can do well enough already, don't you?"

"The final's a big part of your grade."

She shrugged. "My mom's decided to enroll me in private school next fall. So this is my last day here. Could you possibly double the credit on the story? I worked *really* hard on it." Her words, her posture were as always. Only the force behind her words betrayed the sea change in their relationship.

"I guess I could. Yes. Well, we're really sorry to lose you, Roo. Stop in to say hi next year. And you have a nice summer, now."

"Have a hot one, Mr. Capshaw."

He watched her leave, closing the door on his class for the year. Outside, Mr. Cahill, taking advantage of the school-wide exodus, started up the leaf blower. Ignoring the din, Carl rushed to clear his desk. He wanted to get home early and curl up with Cath in the hammock. He needed her to steady him, to bring him down from the lunatic elevation of his thoughts. Because there was no tragedy here. No harm done to anyone! No suicide! No murder! Looking around the classroom, he allowed the prosaic sight of crooked desks and beat-up linoleum to mute the twanging of his heart.

He dismissed his sixth-period study hall early and finished marking his students' stories. Before leaving, before putting the gun in his pocket to stow in the locked box at home, he reread the ending of Roo's tale.

"She would dispense with her mother's criticism, that she was a greedy girl, that nothing satisfied her. That breaking the rules led to heartache. How worth it it was to have a hope, play it out, and blunder. What did her mother understand about the moments that fed a girl's soul and in between, the pleasurable hunger of her waiting?"

She needed to cut it. She needed to tone down the florid language, be more subtle. He wrote on her paper to "watch the fragments" and gave her an A.

Laughing to himself, restored, he wondered how she would interpret her grade.

On the way home, he stopped to buy roses, yellow ones, Cath's favorite. He felt such love for her, such appreciation. He couldn't believe his luck, but he was so thankful for another chance. It had been an aberration, he said to himself in the car on the way up the hill to his house. He would never, ever do it again.

"Cath," he cried, throwing open the front door. "Cath?"

A yellow note, very brief, had been stuck to the front of the refrigerator.

She would not be back.

Juggernaut

From the Hindi, *Jagannāth*. A large, overpowering, destructive force or object—an idol of Krishna which is drawn on a huge cart during an annual parade, under whose wheels devotees throw themselves to be crushed....

The first accident gave Neal the idea for the second accident. He had spent the evening of the first crash pouring coins down the throat of the Silver Ghost, the name of his favorite slot machine at Harrah's Tahoe. As usual, when he was about to give up, eager, in fact, to watch the cherries, plums, and jackpot signs line up, signifying nothing, three bars kachunged into place and seventy-five dollars in tokens pinged into the bin. It was not a big win, considering his investment that evening, but it was enough to keep him going until his eyes were bloodshot and the free drinks from earlier in the evening had invaded his bloodstream and slithered over his brain stem. Now he felt tired. Exhausted. Oh, how he could not wait for bed.

His car was hard to find because he had not parked in the usual spot, so he floundered around the lot looking for it under stars bright as burning spear points, shivering. Up here in the Sierra, November always came as a rude shock. October blew through like fire, all reds and oranges and gusting wind. Winter chased right behind it like a hound from some bone-biting, cold hell.

Finally, he found the Toyota crouched in the far end of the lot, almost touching the dark forest beyond. He wished he were drunk, but no such luck. The abysmal state of his stomach had kept him prudent, along with the hot cups of coffee toward the end of the session.

Too bad, because a clear head brought him around to thoughts of Juliette, who would be waiting at home, mad because once again—once again, she would say, in that new and strident tone he hated—she had to spend the evening alone. Of course, she wouldn't say that at first, she would stand at the kitchen counter watching him with her mouth sullen, refusing to talk, refusing to respond.

As he started the engine, he drifted into a pleasant fantasy. She would decide for once to treat him right. He would come through the door and find her sleeping in a pretty pink negligee like the one she wore when they were first married. He would crawl into bed. Her fragrant arms would rise to pull him down beneath the cool white sheets. Not a word would be spoken; no guilt would be heaped on him.

Checking his rearview mirror for oblivious drunks, he backed out slowly, drove through the valet parking area and out toward the street, where he stopped to wait for a break in traffic before entering. It was while he was there, mentally with Juliette, imagining what they would do in bed, that a stretch limo roared up behind him, screeched its brakes, skated into a skid, and slammed into him with the force of a locomotive.

The next day he awoke in the hospital, loaded up on Darvon. He had jammed his foot on the brake and been thrown forward, almost through the windshield, he was told. Luckily, car traffic along the highway had been light, so no other car had been involved. Aside from a moment of paralyzing fear as he saw the car sliding along the ice toward him in his rearview mirror, he remembered almost nothing of the accident.

He was shook up, that was all. The doctor and the chiropractor he found later legitimized the exaggerated backache and the jaw trouble. His lawyer settled for twenty-five thousand from the limo company, and with another twenty-five hundred thrown in by the casino for nuisance value, he had enough for bills and gambling money until February.

To add to his good fortune, there had been that moment when Juliette arrived at the hospital, her blonde hair shimmering down her shoulders like the falls near Emerald Bay, gorgeous and young. He basked in the envy of his fellow patients and for just a few moments there at the beginning when she thought he was really badly hurt, he basked in the glow of her concern.

"Your hands?" she had asked first thing and, for a second, he couldn't think why she would care. Then he remembered. He played the piano in the bar at the casino, didn't he? When he had a job, which she thought he did.

"The doctor says no permanent damage," he told her.

She pulled his hands to her chest and left them there to feel the pulsing life underneath her sweater. Five years of her, and he would never get enough.

The windfall caused problems. Soon after he got home from the hospital the fights with Juliette resumed. She wanted the money, wanted to put him on an allowance, wanted his paychecks, wanted to save for a future, and yammer yammer yammer. He never could hold his own in an argument with her. Her words pounded on him like a club, so he hurt her back the only way he knew how, with the back of his hand and sometimes when she just would not shut up, with his fists. He always regretted it, always begged for her forgiveness, and she always came through after a day or two.

If she ever left him...but he would not allow her to leave. She knew that. He would hunt her down and bring her back. He had done it before, and she knew he would do it again. Marriage made two people one. He would no more let her go than he would let his left leg walk off without him.

Nothing meant more to him than Juliette. She was his biggest score, the one he would hold on to.

One day, a few months after the first accident, Neal went shopping at the jewelry store at the outlet center for a little present for her. He wanted something that would tell her exactly how bad he felt about a minor fracas of the night before. The saleslady pulled out a display of glamorous-looking gold necklaces. All the glitter in one place made him nervous—he turned his back briefly to count his money.

He had spent most of the insurance settlement, so he counted out his singles. When he was satisfied he could just swing the thinnest gold chain and was about to say so, the saleslady said, "Let me show you some other necklaces I think you'll love!" Sweeping the expensive chains back underneath the counter, she came up with another display that looked identical to him. Leaning in conspiratorially, she had said, "Vermeil. All precious metal, of course."

"Gold?" he had asked.

"Sterling silver with a fine layer of gold on top. Better because it's just as beautiful and has the same intrinsic worth, but is more reasonably priced."

"I'll take it," he said, selecting a thick, flashy one he knew Juliette would love. He would tell her it was solid gold. She would never know the difference.

While the woman stooped under the counter finding paper to wrap it up, he happened to look out the store window. Out on the highway, a Caddie was hanging a left in front of a beat-up white Pontiac coming down the opposite side of the highway.

Only the Pontiac couldn't stop, not with the icy sleet coating the road. There was that same eerie moment of screeching brakes and watching a quarter-ton of metal sliding forward on pure inertia. Then crrrunch!

The Pontiac driver got out, rubbing his neck. Lucky break for him.

That moment, an idea that he had nursed like a seed since November sprouted into full foliage. Here was real money, ready for the taking. Risky, but a much better bet than the slots. A way to bring peace back home, enough to please Juliette, enough to get him out of hock, enough for a few more games, any one of them a potential big winner.

All he had to do was make sure whoever hit him next time was massively insured. And make sure he didn't get killed.

And he knew just the man to help him out.

The saleslady handed him a small package wrapped in metallic paper. "She's going to love it."

"She will," he said. "You are so right."

That afternoon, after he gave Juliette the necklace and collected his thanks from her, he said casually, "Why not call Lenny and Carol? Invite them for dinner tonight. They haven't been by in quite a while."

They were sitting together on the couch in the living room. A rare fire burned, and Juliette's cheeks glowed as orange as persimmons in the light. She had been studying for a test at the kitchen table. An older sophomore at Lake Tahoe Community College at twenty-three, she wanted to better herself, she always said. Still holding the chain, she turned to look at him. "But you hate Lenny."

"Correction," he said. "Your big brother hates me. Always getting on me about the way I treat you." He had a lock of her hair between his thumb and forefinger. His hand slipped along like it used to slide over the ivory keys a long time ago when music had seemed to have a direct line from his imagination to his fingers. He laughed, although he didn't feel funny. "He had you all lined up to marry some straight little civil engineer, some meat loaf who would agree with everything he said, yessir, that's right, Lenny, uh huh, you are so smart..."

He waited for her to say she was glad she'd married him but she was silent, looking into the fire.

"Old Lenny doesn't get it," he went on, annoyed, but aware this was not a good time to pick a fight. "How close we are. How well we fit."

"No, he's never understood it," she agreed, and her hand tugged on the new necklace.

The words grated, and the feeling behind the words grated more. Was there the tiniest suggestion that she, too, didn't understand it? He made his voice calm. "But hey, he's family. We should see them more."

She had turned back to him. He put a lot into the smile he gave her. She smiled back tentatively, then jumped up to make the call. She thought this was a peace offering like the necklace, another part of the "I'm sorry" game. Fine. Whatever it took.

He hoped she would cook something tasty, something to take his mind off those dark, glowering eyes of Lenny's, and Carol's jittery chat.

They arrived about seven, stomping the snow off their shoes in the entryway on a thick rug Juliette put there for that purpose.

"Sonofabitchin' cold night," Neal said, holding the door, giving them a big smile.

As usual, the wrong thing to say. A thought-policeman, Lenny was already glaring at Neal. Lenny thought he was better than Neal, better educated, more intelligent, classier...just thinking about it made Neal angry, but he kept his smile locked in place.

Fortunately, Carol and Juliette smoothed things over, making those female sounds that reminded Neal of spicy smells, permeating the air with promise but ultimately just amounting to a lot of warm air breezing through the room. They made it through dinner with just one really bad moment, when Lenny mentioned that he had spent some time down at Harrah's one night with some out-of-town associates—only reason he'd ever go into one of those nasty places—and was so disappointed that Neal was not, as advertised within the family, playing in the piano bar. "Asked the bartender," Lenny had said, shoveling in a mouthful of cacciatore. "Told me they hadn't seen you in months."

That made Juliette send Neal a visual promise that said, Later, honey, you will make me believe he is mistaken or this lovely evening that started out so well will be spoiled. "That guy must be new, Lenny" was all she said. "Neal's been working steady, haven't you, Neal?"

"You betcha." Below the table, he had her hand in his and had to repress a sudden desire to crush her knuckles until they cracked. She had married a musician, an artist, for Chrissake, not some poor slob with a routine job. She needed reminding. His fingers were strong. No doubt one hard squeeze would take care of anything further she might care to remark if he wanted to stop her.

But Carol interrupted his thoughts with a surprisingly welcome suggestion. "How about a movie? There's one at the Y I'd love to see."

Juliette brightened, withdrew her hand from his, and ran for the newspaper to check for times. Lenny continued to separate items on his plate, prissy and offended-looking at the green spreading of the spinach. "I'll pass," he said when Carol returned.

"Aw, Lenny," Carol said. "Live a little."

"Go without me. I have some paperwork."

Lenny worked for an insurance company, strictly a nine-to-five job that involved no late nights and no overtime. He just said things like this to make himself sound like a mover and shaker to others, the phony ass.

"Nothing that won't wait," Carol said to her husband.

See, now, this was exactly the kind of thing a man could not let pass. This was direct confrontation. Lenny was pussy whipped, the dry little shit, and he didn't even know it.

"You girls will have a better time without us," Neal said. "Go salivate over Brad Pitt. I'll give Lenny a lift home. Then I'll put in some practice time."

Token protests, but eventually the girls drove off in Lenny's car. Lenny finished his dessert and coffee, eating methodically, not saying a word, then got up. "Gotta go," he said.

"Stay for a drink," Neal said, pouring Lenny's favorite poison into two small glasses. "Cheers."

"Yeah," Lenny said, lifting his glass and draining it.

"Another?"

"You're driving," he said.

"Oh, thanks for reminding me," Neal said. "But don't let that stop you. Have a drink for both of us."

Neal managed to get three more stiff ones down Lenny and got him talking about his work. And over the course of the next hour, by prodding and pushing, he extracted the names of several prominent Tahoe people who carried especially good policies, Lenny's best clients.

"See, here's the thing," Neal told him then. Lenny's normal reticence had relaxed as he related exciting tales of his exploits in the insurance business. He was stretched out on the couch, glazed and receptive, just like Neal needed him to be. "Here's the thing, Lenny. I'm really glad you stayed tonight, because I've got some bad news and I didn't want to talk about it in front of the girls."

"I knew it," Lenny said. "You had to be up to something. Well, I don't have any money to lend you right now. You can forget it. I'm scraping by myself, if you want to know."

"Oh, Lenny. Man, I don't want your money. No. It's—it's a medical thing." Neal explained about the carpal tunnel syndrome the doctors had diagnosed in the hospital that would make it impossible for him to use his hands in the future, and watched

Lenny's mediocre mind attempt to take it in. That's right, Lenny, put it together, he thought. Musician, hands, carpal tunnel. Ah!

"But this is terrible," Lenny said, the light finally penetrating his thick skull. "You won't be able to support Juliette."

Well, he didn't really anyway, hadn't for a long time, but Lenny didn't need to know about that. He didn't need to know how the music had left Neal one day, never to return. The music had gone. He couldn't even hold his own in a lobby at a Nordstrom's these days. His reputation in this little town was right down there with the dirtiest rat in a Dumpster.

Lenny didn't need to know that Juliette was clerking in a real estate office part-time mornings to pay their rent. Juliette wouldn't tell him.

Neal laid it on thick, so thick, he had his wife and him living out on the streets within the next month.

"Then you'll live with us," Lenny said, horrified. "I'm not going to let my sister go down, Neal. Never. If you can't be a man and take care of her . . ."

"That's a very kind offer, Lenny," Neal had said hurriedly, striving for a whipped puppy effect in his voice. "But you know how proud Juliette is."

Lenny knew. How Juliette bragged about her husband the artist. She lorded it over her brother in this one regard, and it was the one thing that Neal felt kept her by his side and protected from criticism sometimes, his mystique as an artist. She really respected Neal's talent. And now that talent would be gone, laid waste by a devilish medical fluke! Lenny was eating it up.

"This will kill her," Lenny said, sounding truly miserable. "She'll have to quit school. Neal, I don't have to tell you how disappointed I am. You promised our mother and father, bless them both, that . . . You must have some fallback!"

"I have thought of something. It's—an unusual opportunity. Only it involves you. You've got a lot of guts, Lenny, and I know you're going to pitch in to help us so we don't lose our home."

"Anything for Juliette. Count me in," Lenny said, relieved.

To seal the deal, he offered his glass up for an unheard-of fifth snort.

But the details of Neal's plan shocked him. It took the rest of the evening and some careful manipulations before Neal eventually wore down Lenny's resistance. At first, Lenny agreed only to help with research. He refused to play an active role in the accident. He would help Neal with the setup because his sister needed help so desperately, but he did so only under the most indignant moral protest. There, his involvement must end. They went back and forth. Neal needed him to get in the game. Otherwise, the authorities might suspect. Lenny couldn't see why Neal wouldn't simply apply his brakes, get rear-ended, and collect without Lenny's involvement.

"Got to make it look good, Lenny. Gotta make 'em believe."

"You're good at that," Lenny said then.

"What do you mean by that?"

"You got my sister, didn't you?"

Neal laughed, even though inside he was fuming. He hadn't acted to get Juliette. She loved him for who he was, not who he pretended to be. All the smoldering fireworks between the two men flared up at that point, and it took Neal's return to cold logic to convince Lenny that, in fact, his plan was the only way.

"It's dangerous, Neal. You realize you could be badly hurt."

"I won't let that happen."

"You won't be able to control it!" Lenny yelled.

"Quit worrying. That's my problem. And whatever happens, Juliette will be set for life."

Those words worked like magic. Lenny didn't give a damn what happened to Neal except as it related to Juliette.

Even so, Lenny hadn't given in easily, although after that point, he had most definitely stepped on board the bus. Before he settled down, he asked a million questions: Couldn't Neal just slam on his brakes in front of someone and leave it at that? Why did Lenny have to cut him off? Wouldn't it look suspicious? Would Neal wear a seat belt? Did it matter if the accident happened in California or should they go over the state line into Nevada to maximize how well they would do in a settlement?

"Lenny, take it easy. I'm the one who's going to get hurt, not you and not Juliette, remember?"

Lenny broke out in a cold sweat at that, so Neal had to soothe him yet again, patiently breaking through his objections, pouring the liquor, painting comforting word pictures for Lenny, keeping things at his level. "Two things are absolutely all you have to do, Lenny. Cut me off, so people see I stopped for a reason. And find me a juicy mark. Has to be a drinker," Neal said. "I talked with my lawyer this morning and asked him a few things..."

"You didn't tell him!"

"No, no. Just got him talking generally about my old case. He said if the limo driver had been drinking, well, that would have opened up a whole new pocketbook."

"Gross negligence?"

"Punitive damages, my man."

Three weeks later, they were set. Lenny had chosen some client with two DUI arrests in her background, who had just bought a big, heavy Mercedes and played roulette at Caesars every Friday night with two of her lady friends, but always drove home alone.

They had worked out every detail. Once in, Lenny was a meticulous planner. He drew up careful diagrams on paper they burned in the fireplace afterward, listed time frames, pulled out charts that gave some information on what speeds were most likely to cause lethal collisions, and bogged them both down in trivial issues until Neal was bored silly.

"We'll have your car serviced the day before," Lenny had said, "so there's no confusion about some mechanical failure."

"Sure, Lenny."

"I've got a great mechanic. Let me make sure it gets done."

"Fine, Lenny." Anything to shut him up.

They waited on the highway side of the club in the whizzing

traffic. The mark, who Lenny said was a widow, always used valet parking and always made a left out of the lot, then drove two miles before turning off the highway. That gave them plenty of time to get the game in place.

Neal had parked two blocks up, Lenny three. When Neal saw the bronze Mercedes pulling out of the lot, he swung out ahead of the mark, motioning to Lenny as he passed.

Traffic was perfect, busy but moving well, and there were nice long stretches on the road where you could get going pretty fast. Lenny would have no trouble moving into position when the time came. Neal felt like his nerves had moved to the surface of his skin, he felt so electric, so alive. To keep his mind off the pain to follow, he flashed to the penthouse suite at Harrah's he and Juliette would rent for a month or two, about the new car he would buy, about all the hands of poker he could play without gut-tearing fear... He'd never humiliate himself at a piano again, never put up with some slobbering lonely heart who wanted to hear him play the same old song again and again until he thought his fingers would crack into pieces... Who knew crashing could be such a high?

She was weaving, he noted with satisfaction, glancing into his rearview mirror. She had the visor down, so he couldn't make out the face, but her arms were slim. She looked young. For a moment he wondered about her, about what he'd be doing to her. He slowed and behind him, she slowed. He sped up and she sped up. They were dancing together, and she never even noticed the choreography. Like an automaton, she followed his lead until he knew he had her. All so smooth, so perfect... and then suddenly, bursting ahead like a true maniac, all his timidity apparently left behind when he got behind the wheel, good old Lenny blew out in front to cut him off. As planned.

And Neal jammed his foot on the brake.

★   ★   ★

Emily Chuvarsky, the widow, could not tell the story without crying. She sat in an orange client chair across from Nina Reilly, petite and perfect in her jeans and turtleneck sweater, shaking her head and interrupting herself, and tried several times to come out with it, but broke down every time. Outside, snow blew at an angle away from the lake. The drifts along the road were five feet high and Nina was thinking about closing up early to be sure she made it home to her cabin on Kulow Street.

"This car cut him off. He just . . . he came to a dead stop, right there in the middle of the road. I barely had time to brake. And so I hit him! His c-car burst into flames!" she cried. "I got out and ran up to see if I could do anything but the flames had reached the front . . . someone pulled me away. I heard him screaming. I dream about it. I heard him . . . and then the car exploded."

Nina looked down at her desk. "The police report says he had a five-gallon can of gasoline stored in the trunk of his Toyota. His wife said she didn't know he kept gasoline in the trunk, and if she'd known would have asked him to remove it."

"What a horrible way to die." Letting her head fall back, Emily screwed her eyes shut and covered her face, her shoulders clenching tightly. "My insurance company is negotiating with his wife. But my policy only covers two hundred fifty thousand, and she feels she should get much more because . . ." She stopped, and her arms fell down into her lap. "She lost her husband. I do understand. But I don't have that kind of money."

Nina said, "You were drinking that night?"

"Wine with dinner," Emily said. "Three miles home on a road I've driven a million times. Maybe I had one glass too many but I wasn't falling-down drunk. I went to a seminar on living trusts once and the lawyer mentioned that if you're ever picked up for drunk driving to refuse the Breathalyzer test, so I refused when they asked me. They took a urine test a couple of hours later."

"The results on that won't be in for a few more days," Nina

said. "Refusing the Breathalyzer won't make any difference. They'll just extrapolate back to the time of the accident, using your weight and the elapsed time."

Emily said, "I ought to just take my medicine, you know? Go to jail for reckless driving, file for bankruptcy. The guilt is horrible. I don't sleep. There can't be anything worse in this world than killing a person, an utterly innocent person who never dreamed his life would be cut short like that—it's a nightmare! It's over for me, I'm going to hate myself for the rest of my life. But . . ."

Nina listened. After several years of solo practice in her Tahoe office, it was something she was finally learning to do. She didn't offer words of comfort or false assurances. She waited to hear it all first. Emily opened her purse and her wallet and pulled out a small photo. Nina took it.

A little girl, Eurasian, bright-eyed and still with baby teeth. "She's deaf. What money I have from my husband's life insurance, I need for her education. I want her to have the best. Right now, she's in a wonderful school. They do whole language training, a mixture of signing, lipreading, and speaking. She's thriving there. I can't take her out. I can't!"

"What's her name?" Nina asked.

"Caitlin." Emily returned the photo to her wallet.

"You saw the man—Neal Meurer—get cut off?"

"Another car cut right in front of him. I don't think the driver even knew what he did. He was long gone."

"Do you remember anything about the car?"

"A sedan with ski racks," she said promptly. "Wait a minute. I remember the license plate had three eights. I noticed that because my late husband was from Hong Kong. He told me how lucky the number eight is considered to be in China and I just had time to think, what a lucky license plate . . ."

"That's great." Nina wrote that down and thought, Amazing. Nobody ever noticed license plates.

"I just thought of it."

"Be sure to go to the police station on Johnson Boulevard tomorrow and tell them you want to add that to your statement."

"I'm not positive. I'll think about it a little more."

"What about the man in that car? You're sure it was a man?"

"Oh, yes. He had a mustache. They're out of fashion now, so I noticed."

Nina wrote that down, too. After a few more minutes and settling the business of the retainer agreement, she followed Emily out to the parking lot of the Starlake Building. Then, buffeted by the storm, she fought her way down Pioneer Trail in the Bronco. At the corner of Golden Bear a pickup suddenly spun out in front of her. Pulling sharply to the right, she hit the snowbank. Behind her, brakes squealed.

But the car behind her didn't hit her, just honked savagely and continued on its way. Very cautiously she backed into the darkening street and drove home, teeth gritted, furious because sudden chance events that ruined lives weren't acceptable to her. Nina didn't believe in accidents.

A few days later, with light snow still falling, the lights were on in the middle of the day at Lake Tahoe Community College. Nina caught Juliette Meurer coming out of her poli sci class with a tall, bespectacled young man who had his arm around her and was kneading her shoulder.

"Oh," she said when Nina introduced herself. "Am I allowed to talk to you?" Standing near Nina, who was on the small side, she towered. She was almost as tall as the man standing with her.

"It's not a lawsuit yet," Nina said. "It might help."

"This is my friend Don."

Don shook hands, saying, "Juli's been through a lot." He seemed cool and kept his distance. Without asking, he tagged along to the Bronco, climbing into the back seat behind Juliette.

Nina drove them to the Pizza Hut near Ski Run and the three of them sat down in a booth and ordered coffee.

Nina started slow and easy, letting Juliette Meurer relive the moments after the Tahoe police called her, listening to her talk tearfully about Neal's incredible talent, his charm, how she missed him so much . . . In spite of the reports of frequent brawls at the house, a few of which resulted in calls from the neighbors to the police, she sounded very much in love with her husband. Don glowered next to her, saying nothing. The two of them went together very well, Nina couldn't help noticing, both handsome, athletic, blond, and long-haired.

"The gas can in the back," Nina said. "It bothers me."

"Neal was stupid about cars. The weather has been so bad, if you ran out of gas in the mountains you might freeze. Maybe that's what he was thinking. Poor Neal. But he would have been fine, except the woman—your client—she had been drinking, hadn't she?"

"Mmm," Nina said. "But the thing about the gas can, you know, is that it had prints on it that weren't Neal's."

"What?" Juliette looked stunned. "Why would the police take fingerprints?"

"Oh, to be thorough. What's amazing is that there were prints left to take. Luckily, they found a fairly large piece intact ten feet away in a drift."

"Those prints probably came from the guy who sold Neal the gas," said Don. "Where's the big mystery in that?"

"Well, at first I thought that, too, and it was hard to check because the can didn't have the store sticker on it or anything. But this is a small town. My investigator managed to locate the fellow who sold that gas can. They weren't his prints. He remembered selling one three days before Mr. Meurer's death, at the Chevron at the Y, and he recognized it by the bits of paint color left on the metal piece the police found. That can was the only one he could spare that day, a really old one."

"So?" Juliette said.

"Well, the thing is, I showed him a picture of your husband just to confirm everything. And this fellow who pumps the gas says it wasn't Neal Meurer who bought it."

"He's wrong."

"Said all he could see was the man was short, with blue eyes. Like everybody else around here, was mostly covered up. Wore a parka, muffler, ski hat. But Mr. Meurer had brown eyes, didn't he?"

Juliette nodded.

"Strange, don't you think?"

Don's blue eyes stared at her. "You can see what she's doing, can't you, Juli? She's weaseling her client out of trouble. She sees disaster heading straight their way. It's her job to do anything to head it off." He half-rose. "Let's get out of here."

Nina shrugged. "The gas attendant could be wrong but the fingerprint expert isn't. Your husband never touched that can."

"Then—the rescue workers!"

"They had a fire and your husband to deal with."

"Oh," Juliette said, "this is too much. You're trying to tell me somebody else put the gas can in the back? That Neal was murdered? Well, who—who would have put the can there except your client, then? Nobody forced her to run into Neal that night."

"Who would want to kill Neal, Juliette?" Nina asked the girl. "My client says she never even met your husband. And I hear there were a few domestic problems between the two of you."

"Your client is responsible! She ran into my husband and killed him!" Juliette wailed. "She was drunk! God, are you serious about all this?" Don yanked her to her feet.

"Come on," he said urgently. He looked down at Nina, who was calmly sipping her coffee. "I detest you shysters," he said in a thick voice. Then he was pulling Juliette away toward the exit. She looked back once, her face a mask of anguish, blue eyes filled with tears.

★   ★   ★

Nina's investigator, Tony Ramirez, spent a week working on the three eights.

Tony, who was on the shady side of sixty and had the relaxed attitude to prove it, hailed from the low-tech school of investigation. He could have worked with the police to obtain a list of hundreds of people in California and Nevada with triple-eight license plates, and things could have gone on for months, but, as he put it, he liked to use his noggin to save himself work.

"Neal's sister lives in Illinois with her husband and five kids and hasn't talked to Neal for years. She's off the hook. There's no other family. So I looked to the workplace. Turns out Neal didn't have a workplace. I checked the license on his last supervisor at the casino—no eights on his plates. I checked Neal's gambling buddies and his bookie. No triple eights. Then I looked for Neal's women. There weren't any recent ones I could find and lately he stuck to his wife like a leech."

Nina read through the police report again while Tony stood at the window, flipping through his notes.

"So maybe he just pulled a Pinto," she said. "Emily gets a personal judgment for wrongful death against her for about a million dollars and goes to jail for reckless driving, and her daughter leaves school."

"When you put it that way I feel like I better hustle back out on the street and do better," Tony said.

"At least her blood alcohol was only point-five," Nina said. "She wasn't impaired as a matter of law; not this time anyway."

"The fingerprints came back from NCIC. Whoever bought that gas can has never had trouble with the law and ain't in the system."

"Juliette gets the money. So we check out Juliette. We look at her friends and family."

★   ★   ★

South Lake Tahoe is a small town, and Nina knew Lenny Dole, who was her brother Matt's auto insurance agent, as well as Juliette Meurer's brother. Lenny's office was at Round Hill Mall, around the lake on the Nevada side. He was waiting for her, and he was terrified; she could see that.

Short, not much taller than she was, according to Tony he had triple-eight license plates on his sedan. That plus his obvious terror excited her. She couldn't believe he had agreed to see her without consulting his own lawyer first, and she wanted to be very careful.

No need. Lenny proceeded to spill his guts, and it wasn't a pretty sight.

"When I told Neal I'd do it, I was drunk," he said. "The next morning I called his house and left a message. 'No way,' I said. Neal would understand what I was talking about."

"But he talked you back into it?"

"No! That's what I'm saying! I refused! Absolutely!"

"But it was your car," Nina said. "A witness saw the license number: six-K-L-S-eight-eight-eight," which was a slight bending of the truth, since Emily had remembered only part of the license, but he didn't need to know that.

"It wasn't me. Somebody must have taken my car. I parked it out front all night—it was snowing..."

"You left the keys in it?"

"Those Cutlasses, you can hotwire them in three seconds..."

"So you're claiming someone tried to frame you? Who else did you tell about Neal's plan?"

He gaped. "Nobody!"

"You didn't tell Juliette? Or your wife?"

"I..." He shook his head weakly.

Nina took out a portable fingerprint kit. "Lenny," she said, "if you're innocent, you'll do this."

Looking guilty as hell, he shuffled up close. When he looked up she saw brown eyes and thought, Phooey.

★   ★   ★

The snowchains requirement had snarled traffic into a pile of stationary ski racks, but somehow Tony Ramirez made it up the hill from Reno to bring the print comparison back to Nina's office a day later. This latest Sierra storm had dumped two more feet and South Lake Tahoe looked as quaint as Santa's village.

The expert had found no fingerprint match. Lenny Dole hadn't left his prints on what remained of the gas can. Nina had also obtained prints on coffee cups from Don and Juliette, and those results were in, too. No match, no clue. Nina studied the whorls and notches and lines on the blowups as if they were hieroglyphics that might reveal a hidden story. "Tony," she said. "I just can't put this together."

Tony pried off his hiking boots and sticky, wet red socks, complaining about having to get out of the car to put on chains. "Can I?" he said. She nodded and he laid them across the heater. The smell of wet wool spread through the hot office.

"We're making progress," Tony said, drying his toes with a tissue from her desk. "There was a conspiracy, whether Lenny stayed in or not. Emily was set up, no doubt about it. Lenny or somebody cut Neal off deliberately per the plan and Emily was the scapegoat."

"But nobody would be stupid enough to arrange a rear-end collision with five gallons of gas in his trunk," Nina said.

"A double cross," Tony said. "Neal's partner decided to make it permanent."

"Juliette would get the money," Nina said. "She's at the center of it. But whose prints are these? Who bought that can of gas? Some short, blue-eyed ghost. None of these people is short and blue-eyed. Juliette must be nearly six feet tall. Who drove the Olds Cutlass that cut off Neal Meurer? A man with a mustache, Emily said. Nobody I know in this case has or had a mustache."

"A buck sixty-nine at the joke shop," Tony said. "Cheap whiskers for kids four and up." He rattled the keys in his pocket and looked worried. "Nina, don't drive yourself too nuts with this stuff. Our job is to do our best, then let the chips fall."

"I can't do that. I feel responsible for Emily. I feel if I push harder, work smarter, and go that extra step, I'll arrive at the heart of the matter. That's the only way to a just outcome. Then there's nothing to regret."

"Just don't expect thanks when you've killed yourself for months and you hand over the bill for your outstanding service."

Nina sighed.

"C'mon," Tony said. "Let's continue this conversation over at Passaretti's. A glass of red wine and something smothered in olive oil and fresh pesto will put things back into perspective. What do you say? Let's get fed."

"What about your socks?"

He pulled the boots on over bare feet and stood up. "Keep 'em for a souvenir."

Nina got home about seven thirty. Her dog, Hitchcock, and her teenage son, Bob, were out front under the floodlight. Bob was making a snowman, a very peculiar snowman with a rubber dog ring on top like a halo. Hitchcock ran to the truck and gamboled around it while she swung down and shut the door. "You know he's going to jump on it and destroy all your work," she called to her son. "He loves that ring."

As if taking note of her words, Hitchcock turned abruptly and made a beeline for the snowman. Bob grabbed for the ring, snatching it off the snowman's head just before the dog made contact. "What's this, boy? C'mon, what's this?" He waved it at Hitchcock, who jumped vainly, tongue lolling, for his toy, until finally Bob put it back on top of the hillock of snow that made up the snowman's head. In one final heave, Hitchcock leaped valiantly into the air, landing with an audible "oof" near the top. His jaws closed around the ring. Bob jumped on, too. For an instant he clung to the hard-packed snow, arms circling the head as if to protect it. Then the whole shebang, snowman, dog, and boy, toppled into a cloud of snow.

Hitchcock chewed vigorously on his ring, having destroyed an hour of hard work. Lying in the white powder, Bob laughed helplessly. Destruction was still far more gratifying than building.

Nina went into the cabin. Bob had made himself frozen burritos as she had instructed, but appeared to have had a run-in with the microwave in the process. She found that mess easier to clear away than Emily's. Removing the cracked glass tray, Nina swabbed down the insides of the microwave almost gratefully.

By ten o'clock, Bob had been nagged through his shower and into bed. Nina sat on the rug in front of the fire with her glass of sauvignon blanc, comfortable in her silk kimono. She was trying to think, but the thinking kept turning into a kind of dozing, a hypnagogic dreaming. She kept thinking about the rubber ring and Hitchcock, such a patsy, going for it, doing his dogged doggy number, until he actually got what he wanted...

So easy to know what he wanted. In the end, so simple to get it.

"I'm sorry to disturb you," Nina told Carol Dole the next morning. Carol was in a plaid wool robe and glasses. Nina had watched from the Bronco while Lenny drove off to work.

A small woman, Carol had blue eyes behind the specs that were blinking against some strong emotion right now. She tried to close the door, but Nina's six-hundred-dollar Manolo Blahnik boot heel was wedged between the door and its sill.

"Ah ah ah," Nina said. "It's me or the cops. You'll do better with me."

"Go away."

"It's cold out here. Twenty degrees and dropping, I'd say. We can talk with the door open and run up your heating bill or you can let me inside and we'll both be better off."

Carol looked once more at the boot in the door and gave up. "Come in," she said ungraciously, opening the door and turning her back to Nina.

The house showed a lot of pride around its shined surfaces. On the walls, signed lithographs hung: a gaudy Peter Max, an English cottage scene by the guy who billed himself as the Painter of Light in his TV ads, and a Picasso scribble showing hands passing a bouquet of flowers. Showy knickknacks decorated the bookshelf.

"Lenny says he told you about Neal's plan," Carol said. She was sitting on the white leather couch, bare legs crossed. Her robe gaped a little, exposing an angular bosom.

"How did you get involved?" Nina said.

"He was too worried to keep his mouth shut about this."

"Lenny saw an opportunity in Neal's plan, didn't he? He could set his sister up for life and get rid of her troublesome husband, all in one stroke. Did he ask you for help, or was it your idea to buy the gas can and put it into the trunk? Neal had no idea it was there, did he? But you and Lenny had easy access to Neal's car, and you fit the description . . ."

"You're barking up the wrong tree. Lenny and I had nothing to do with it."

"Short and blue-eyed. That's how the person who bought the gas can was described," Nina said.

Carol Dole shook her head. "Have you taken a good look at your client lately?" she asked with a smile as wide as a half-moon. She tipped her head back so that Nina could follow the long line of her throat. It reminded her of Emily screwing up her eyes, closing them, leaning her head back . . .

Emily, petite, blue-eyed.

"Em was my best friend in high school," Carol said. "That's where she and Neal met. Then just a couple months ago, after her husband died, she came across him again."

Carol's meaning hit Nina hard. Emily had lied to her. Well, clients lied. She knew that. "So you know Caitlin," she said.

"Who?" Carol said, and Nina felt like she was drifting off into some kind of space, only it wasn't calm and peaceful there. Supernovas were going off all around her. Through the distant chaos she heard her voice saying quite normally and correctly, "Emily Chuvarsky's little girl?"

Carol's laughter brought her back to earth.

"Em a mom?" Carol said. "You have to be kidding. She hates kids. It was Neal she loved after her husband died. Neal knew it, and he played her for a lot of money before she realized he'd never leave Juliette. She used to go listen to him when he was playing piano, before he got fired. Music is the way to so many women, have you noticed? Neal sure used it that way, when it suited him."

"If it was Emily, then she was working with you or your husband," Nina said. "Triple eights."

"So she was the one who made up the story about our license plate? You really scared Lenny with that one. I thought it must be her. I remember one time she said we were lucky with the eights."

"You're saying—do you realize..."

"All I'm saying is, I didn't do a thing to anybody."

"Did you tell her about Neal's plan?"

"Just to show her she was better off forgetting about him. I didn't know she was the patsy."

"Emily?"

Nina's client looked flushed and pretty, as if she had walked all the way to the office. "Yes?"

"I talked to Carol Dole about you."

"Oh," she said, all her prettiness falling behind a frown.

"You lied to me about Caitlin."

"I always loved that name," she said after a pause. "She's cute, too, isn't she? I found the photo stuck inside a book I bought at the Salvation Army."

"You lied about knowing Neal, too."

She tapped her foot, examined her fingernails, and didn't say anything for a long time.

"Maybe you need to find another lawyer, one you feel comfortable telling the truth to."

"I just—everything I say to you is confidential, right?"

"That's right."

"I guess you already figured out most of the story. Might as well know the rest. I did know Neal. He was a liar and a cheat. He gambled away a lot of my money. He hurt me . . . drew me in and made a fool of me."

"You hated him."

"No." She breathed in short breaths, impatient to be understood. "I never hated him."

"Carol told you that Neal had come up with a plan."

Emily studied Nina awhile, then seemed to come to a decision. "When I heard about his idea for a crash scam, it set off something in me, something I didn't even know was there. I started thinking, wouldn't it be perfect if he should get his while trying to screw yet another unsuspecting victim? Almost a biblical justice."

"You put the gas in his trunk."

She shifted her body in her chair, looking uncomfortable. "I was over at Carol's when Lenny drove up in Neal's car. He had just had it in for servicing and was about to take it back to Neal, but we were all hungry, so he left the keys on the counter in the kitchen while they went out in Lenny's car to get us some food.

"It was fate, you see? I saw those keys lying there . . . I thought about Neal, how horrible he was to me. I felt such pain . . . and I picked them up. I didn't even think. I just took Neal's car and ran over to Chevron for the gas. Disguised myself a little. Then I hid the can under a blanket in the trunk before Carol and Lenny got back. It was cold and I wore gloves. If I thought at all, I guess I thought the car would be destroyed in a crash."

"You wanted to kill him." Nina was thinking about the fingerprint leading nowhere. A helper at the gas station? A previous customer?

"I loved him," she said simply, as if even a child could see that explained everything. "But he hurt me so much. So I...engineered a little divine intervention. God rode beside him that day. If he had done nothing wrong, he would have lived, you see?"

"But you hit him, not someone else."

"My rotten luck," Emily said with a bitter laugh. "After that last DUI, I needed new insurance. Carol talked me into buying from Lenny, and he sold me a big fat new policy! So here I am driving home one night and suddenly Neal's in front of me. It happened so fast! I didn't realize it was him right away, but something struck me funny, so I followed close behind to try to see him better. Next thing I know, I'm stepping on the brakes, but the road's so slippery, I slide right into him! God—what a riot—isn't it funny? I can't stop laughing—the bad luck part—but you know, it's a small town—the bad luck part is, Lenny, who had me fresh in his mind and never liked me, must have picked me to be the mark! And I didn't know when they were planning the crash!"

"The triple eights..."

"Oh, Lenny was there that night, whatever he and Carol say, whether I saw him or not. He's the one who cut in front of Neal, wearing a mustache that hung crooked, just like everybody in that whole damn family, including my so-called friend, who never could keep a secret, even when we were thirteen. Oh, God. They'll never be able to keep quiet about this."

"You realize you're in serious trouble now, Emily. The system doesn't forgive murder."

"Yes, thanks for nothing! You could have just helped me, forced Juliette to settle within the policy limits instead of dragging up all this old business!"

She didn't really appreciate the extent of the calamity she had set off yet. Her first mistake had been a headlong, thoughtless rush into the fray, but her biggest mistake had been involving Nina.

Clasping her bag, Emily stood up. "I suppose I will get that new lawyer."

"Good idea." Nina also stood. "I'll sign the Substitution of Attorney as soon as it comes in."

"Carol and Lenny have figured everything out by now, thanks to you. They'll hurry to protect themselves. No doubt the cops will follow close behind."

They would, and they would get her, too. She should have forced her insurance company to settle with Juliette. She should never have put herself in front of the legal machine because now Nina had turned on the ignition and the wheels had started up. They would roll inexorably from here on out until they crushed her beneath them.

"Here's a check," Nina said, scribbling one out and handing it to her. "Your retainer, less my expenses."

Emily took the check, studied it, and frowned.

She went out the door. "Shyster," she said, pulling it shut behind her.

When Nina got home, Hitchcock made a rush for her and began licking her stockings. "Get off me, you damn hound," she said, making for the upstairs bedroom.

She lay down, imagining what the courts had in store for the impetuous Emily. She wondered if she'd ever feel the desire to get up again. She wondered if there was still a Peace Corps and if they had any openings in Gabon. Maybe the villagers there would thank her for doing a good job. Maybe there, passionate women did not plot against ex-lovers.

"Mom," Bob said through the door, "I made a tuna casserole."

"You're kidding!"

"In the microwave. It's steamin', Mom. Plus I poured you a glass of wine out of the bottle in the fridge. It's on the kitchen table. And the news is on."

Nina opened one eye. White fell through the twilight outside the window.

"Mom?" At the same moment, Hitchcock barked. He wanted to come in, and he wouldn't take no for an answer.

"I'm coming," Nina said. She got up and opened the door.

The Couple Behind the Curtain

Craig settled himself into the small, battered chair beside her hospital bed and punched his cell phone.

"I don't think you're supposed to use those here."

He shrugged, put a finger up, and listened. He shut the phone. "There wasn't a sign around here. Maybe that's just for intensive care or emergency."

"Water," Gretchen said. "I'm going to need some."

He set the phone beside his chair, picked up a miniature plastic pitcher on the table beside her, walked over to the sink, flipped a lever, and collected cold water. The pitcher spilled a few drops on the way back to her bedside.

"Better wipe that up," she said, handing him a tissue. "Someone might slip."

He took the proffered tissue, bent carefully after pulling up his slacks to protect the crease, and dabbed at the spots. He tossed the tissue into the can nearby while she drank. "You know when they call these floors dirty, they mean dirty with a capital *D*?" He shuddered. "I hate thinking what's been down there." He picked up her book, her discs, her music player, and the headphones that lay littering the counter under the window and stuffed them into her overnight bag. He searched under the bed, and pulled out a hair tie and a sock, holding them between his finger and thumb, like dead rats. He zipped the bag shut, then looked hard at her. "Shouldn't you comb your hair? Start getting ready? You need to comb your hair."

"My hair is fine, Craig."

He found her comb, got behind her, pushed her shoulders forward, and began to comb it.

"Well?" Gretchen asked, wincing as he yanked through a tangle. "Talk, why don't you? You want to talk. You insist on talking. I'm a captive audience."

"How's the leg?"

"When I move, it feels like it's in a meat grinder. The bones are loose inside. Don't ask me about it. I feel feeble at the moment, not myself. I want to cry."

"Have you taken your pills?"

"An hour ago. I'm in my prime, in terms of being pain-free. Another hour and I'm going to be chewing the sheets. Then there's that final glorious hour, when I'll be murderous or in tears."

"Another hour and you'll be home."

"I don't think I'm ready."

"The doctor said you're ready."

"I don't believe other people anymore. I believe the evidence of my own senses."

"Gretchen, don't be difficult. They kept you in one night and all day today. Now you can go home."

"I have a temperature."

"A low temperature is common after surgery."

"Craig, they put a plate in my leg! This is not a normal situation!"

"You panic too easily." He examined her hair critically, gave it another rough swipe, and put the comb away. "You overreact." He sat on the edge of her bed, near her hurt leg. "I need you to be reasonable, here, okay?"

"What's going on?"

"It's about us."

"You were trying to tell me something at the dance when I fell."

"That's right. And that was a pretty severe reaction you had, falling like that, breaking your leg. I guess you knew somehow what I needed to say was very serious."

"Maybe the anticipation was too much for me. You've been wanting to tell me for a long time. I thought you might never get up the courage. You're seeing someone."

He moved away from her and took a breath. "You know?"

"Don't tell me about her, Craig, okay? I really don't want to talk about her."

"You knew and you didn't tell me. It's been so hard, Gretchen. Do you know, there's never a good time to tell someone something like this. Never! Not when she's brushing her teeth, not when she's putting on her nylons in the morning. Not at dinner when she's tired." He smiled a rueful smile. "Not when she's dancing, obviously."

"I agree. The dancing started out so promising. I was enjoying myself."

"But you knew all along," he said.

"I didn't want to know."

"Now you do."

"Now you've unloaded, can we just forget about it?"

"Gretchen, it's over between us. I'm leaving."

"No!"

"I packed yesterday."

"While I was in surgery?"

"I know . . . it's low. But I've been trying to move out for weeks, and you stall me, and you act so horribly nice, or you get sick or have a rotten day at work. Don't tell me you didn't know things were bad. You act like a clown, stumbling around, just wild. You'll do anything to avoid facing this."

"You think I broke my leg on purpose?"

"You're a good dancer."

"You think that?"

"Well, did you?"

"You've got such an ego. I don't think I ever realized. I'm seeing a side of you that I don't like very much. And when did I become a clown in your eyes? After you met the lovely alternate lady?"

"She really has nothing to do with this."

"Liar. If you hadn't lined her up, you couldn't leave. You're no one unless you're with someone."

"See what I mean? Why would you want to hold on to someone like me? I'm a big nobody to you, a parasite. You've lost all respect."

"I've heard about this happening to people. I just never thought it would happen to us. Marriages have ups and downs, that's natural."

"We've been down so long..."

"I know what you're going to say, that dumb thing, it looks like up to me. It's awful when you can predict every word someone's about to say! But, Craig, you always told me you loved me. What about our baby?"

"You're pregnant?"

The lengthy pause made him drop his cell phone. "No," she said finally. "But I thought we were ready. You said we were ready."

He pushed hair off his forehead. "Scared me there for a minute." He picked up the phone, fiddling with it, opening it, and closing it. "Touché."

"Are we fighting? I thought you were telling me something."

"We don't have to fight. You're right."

"But if you insist on talking about this . . . aberration . . . I need an explanation. You married me for a reason. For life."

"We've been married ten years."

"Not a long marriage . . ."

"A very long time. Listen, this was a bad idea. Let's get you home and talk there. They're doing the paperwork. Why don't you put your clothes on?"

But Gretchen picked up a magazine instead.

He peered into a brown paper sack on the floor beside him, then tossed it onto her bed. "Please, get dressed."

"The paperwork could take hours."

"Or a few minutes. That nurse looked efficient."

"I'm tired. I just had a damn operation. And now you want to take me home so that you can leave me there alone. How am I supposed to cope? I can't even walk!"

"Gretchen, you said you needed a ride, so I came. I'll rent you a wheelchair. We'll call your mom, locate a goddamned attendant. You'll be taken care of, I promise."

"I had to beg you because otherwise you wouldn't have come, would you?"

"I don't have much time. I want to get back. And you know I hate these places. Don't you want to go home? You'll be much more comfortable there."

"I need more time. I have a lot of pain." A bulging white splint covered her left leg all the way down from the knee, but she wasn't looking at it. She was looking at him.

"Hospitals are full of sick people . . ."

"That time I sprained my wrist, you got Mom to bail me out. I guess I'm one of the sick ones, again, huh? You'd rather avoid me completely."

"My policy is, and always has been, get out as soon as you can. Get home to your own nice clean sheets, fresh pillows . . ."

"Were you hoping she'd be waiting for you out there?" She

looked out through the large window into the mucky yellow puddles of the dark parking lot. Headlights lit the blue plastic curtain behind her and made the branches of a sprawling oak tree outside blobs against the night sky. She had turned off the light over her bed, turned off the television. The only light aside from a reading light over her book came through the window. "Well, were you?"

"No."

"Where do you think she is right now? Praying I'll let you go? Is she the one you keep calling?"

Three discreet knocks on the side of the open door announced the arrival of another gang of medical personnel, an attendant after blood, a nurse to pull out Gretchen's IV, a helper to knock around the dinner tray. They marched in and out of the room, as strict as army troops on maneuvers.

Gretchen pushed hard on the cotton they left behind on her hand where the IV had entered. "It hurts," she said. She started to cry. Craig stood up, put a hand on her shoulder, and held on while she shook.

A sudden commotion escalated the echoing in the hallway. Several people burst into the room, boisterous as a theater troupe leaping onstage for a bow. The lights blasted on, and the softness of the moment was destroyed by the details, the look on Craig's face, so put-upon. The wrinkled sheets, all balled up at the foot of her bed. The huge white bandages on her left leg. Gretchen stopped crying and Craig left her side. A young girl, black-haired, pierced with metal loops from her eyebrow right down to her sandaled toes, pushed the blue curtain aside, came over to the bed, and looked sympathetically at Gretchen.

"I'm guessing I'm your roommate. Katie. What happened to you?" she said, her eyes brushing over Craig to Gretchen and back again.

"I broke my leg."

"Ouch," she said. "How'd you do it?"

"Dancing."

"Really? Well, that's almost cool."

"What about you?" Gretchen asked.

"I have an abscess on my boob." She disappeared behind the curtain. A woman with short, wispy, gray-blonde hair smiled apologetically. She wore pink lipstick, and a matching sleeveless blouse that showed loose skin under the arms. "Can I have your extra chair?" she asked.

Craig nodded. The woman, Katie's mother, possibly, pulled the chair to the foot of the other bed. Katie's skin was brown, the woman's was stark, glaring white. A big, dark, bearded man with a British accent filled up another chair.

Gretchen pulled the curtain so that only the lower part of her body remained exposed and she could not see her neighbor's head, although she could see most of the bed and the rest of the room. Craig, sitting toward the foot of her bed again, could see almost everything, although the curtain provided a psychological shield. Everyone acted as if they were in entirely separate realms.

A discussion started up on the other side of the room. With help, the girl climbed on the bed and promptly started to whine. "I'm so hungry," she said. "Why can't I eat something? Mother, have you got anything I can eat?"

"I'm so sorry, honey, but you have to wait," her mother said. "They won't let me feed you."

"They'll give you anesthesia before the . . . they fix things up," said the Brit. "They don't want you tossing up food in there."

"Why did this have to happen?" the girl asked. She slurped water noisily. "This hurts, you know. I feel like utter crap. I might as well be dead."

The Brit winced and reached out a hand to her. "Don't drink too much. They said not to."

"Oh, honey," the girl's mother murmured. "They'll take care of you soon." She crawled up onto the bed beside her daughter. "Daddy and I will make sure they do."

But the whining intensified into pained bleating, and no one came. After a while, the dad left to find someone, ostensibly to demand an explanation for the delay, but Gretchen and Craig knew why. Her surgery was unscheduled, not an emergency. She had to wait her turn. Daddy just had to do something. He couldn't bear to see his girl suffer.

Gretchen's eyes filled. She spoke softly to Craig so that no one else could hear. "I want you to tell me...I need to know. What happened to change my life so I can't recognize it anymore?"

"Gretchen," Craig's voice was so low she could barely hear it, "I consider the matter settled. This isn't a negotiation. It's just upsetting for both of us and gets us nowhere."

"I don't recognize myself in this."

"People change," he said. "You're hard to live with. Up, down, all over the place. Mad for no reason. Jumping out of your skin and all over me. I never know what you might do next. I feel ungrounded. I just want a happy life. Peace."

"Did the feeling just...shift, like a dog jumping over to another lap? Did you tell her she's irresistible to you, like you did me?"

"Hush, now." He pulled the sheet down. "Get up, Gretchen. Let's get going."

"Did you think, oh, here's someone prettier than Gretchen, someone who will hold me in high esteem. Someone who won't nag me to work harder or slob around in an untidy house without lifting a finger to pick up."

"Please put your clothes on."

"How can you love someone and then not love them?" she asked. "I don't believe it's possible."

Craig opened the brown sack, pulling out a blouse. He untied the threadbare blue print hospital gown that encased Gretchen and tried to pull it up over her head. She resisted, arms down at her sides, steely.

"You can't just stop loving."

"Come on," he said. "Come on." When she continued to resist, he dropped his arms to his sides. He put one in his pocket.

"You wish it would ring, don't you? There's a woman out there, you're thinking. She'll welcome me without any pressure. But what I want to tell you, Craig, is that that's a temporary state in a relationship. It's after six months that matters, when you see the man's pores, and dirty underwear on the floor, when you notice he never flosses...I love you, defects and all. I love when you make a racket blowing your nose, and when you fret about the newspaper being late, and when you criticize me, then say it's because you care so much."

The girl in the next bed whimpered, then moaned. Her cries were muffled, presumably by the arms of her mother.

"I decided"—Gretchen pulled her knees up to her chest and hugged them—"that she must be hotter in bed, something along those lines. So last week I conducted some scientific tests. Remember, by the window? And then at the beach that Thursday morning. So early, fog everywhere...I may not have proved anything to you, but I proved a few things to myself. You're older, and you hate getting older. I mean, forty isn't so old, even though you feel it is. But there's such a thing as being graceful, you know. We could be graceful together."

"Don't do this," Craig said.

"Like during the dance, I felt happy with your arms around me, the love I felt for you right at that moment. I felt like it didn't matter that I'm not a perfect person. I felt accepted, for just a moment. Then...you chose a bad time to tell me, admit that. You're slightly guilty in that respect, too."

"I never said a word!"

"You were going to. It felt like a truck crossing the centerline, coming at me."

"You were drunk, just like you were the night before, you know, when you went to stay at your mom's. You were mad for days before I even said a word. Don't tell me you blame this situation on me."

"Of course I do. I wish you would say you were sorry for everything."

"If I say I'm sorry, will you get up?" He picked up her clothes, then set them down on the bed again. "And put on these god-awful clothes you brought?"

"No."

"I'm just trying to . . . it wouldn't be respectful of me not to tell you, would it, Gretch? To live a big lie?"

"You show your respect for me by cheating?"

"Is it cheating if I tell you about it? We aren't even sleeping together yet."

"Yet you want to move in with her."

"Everything's in the car, ready to go. Now you know it all."

"You plan to sleep with her tonight, if all goes well here. You expect to find her sitting by the fire, combing her neat hair, wearing the kind of negligee you like, something frothy and girly. She'll jump up, arms raised to hold you . . . It's a charming fantasy. I can't compete. I drink too much, I have no fashion sense, and at the moment, I can't even reach you to hug you without using a crutch."

"I don't want to hurt you. You're hurting yourself."

"Not true. You want honesty? I stumbled at the dance. I felt faint when I realized the moment had come and you wanted to end things. I simply fell. I didn't try to evade the truth. Although I was afraid, yes."

"Tell me you'll be graceful now, Gretchen."

"You want it easy."

"Tell me we can get beyond this."

"To a divorce? The house is mine. Where will you live? In some dingy, little apartment in a bad neighborhood?"

He looked startled. She had scored. "Let's not get into that. The lawyers will work things out so that they are fair."

"Did you tell her about the back taxes we owe?"

"I refuse to talk about this. That's business. Right now is personal."

"Okay, it's personal. You want to leave me for a younger blonde with black roots and a quiet voice."

"How do you know all that?"

"No great detective work involved there. She's blonde with roots because you like blondes, and I'm blonde and no woman over twenty is a natural blonde. She's quiet, the better to listen to her hero. No doubt she drinks too much, too, or sings too loud like I do? She fancies herself in control, but sometimes she does outrageous, unbelievable things? She has to do something obnoxious."

"No, she doesn't."

Gretchen threw her magazine on the floor. "I really don't want to know about her and her delicate sensibilities!"

A drawn-out wail from behind the plastic curtain split her sentence in half.

"This isn't the place," Craig said.

"It's the only place. After tonight, you won't see me. You'll be busy with her."

"Please, Gretch, let's get going." He punched the cell phone again. Again, there was no answer. He stood, shifting his weight from one foot to the other, one eye on the window. "Where's that damn nurse?" He checked the clock on the wall.

The Brit returned, successful, with a resident in tow. He sat back down in his chair in front of the sink. The mother removed herself from the bed. The tall, thin doctor, black bags big as old-fashioned doctor satchels pouched under his eyes, leaned momentarily against the wall for support, then moved toward the bed. "Where does it hurt?" he asked.

"It freaking hurts there, and there! It hurts all the way underneath!" she said. "I went to this clinic last week? And they gave me painkillers, that's it! Can you believe it? And now I end up here!"

"When did the pain get really bad?"

"Two days ago."

"And when did you originally injure yourself?"

"Last weekend, on Saturday night. A week ago."

"How did you do it?"

"I was frolicking," she said. Weirdly, she giggled. "I was frolicking in the bushes, and I fell, and a twig or something caught on
my nipple ring, you know?"

A shocked pause stopped all activity for a few seconds. The
resident, who probably had seen it all and heard it all, paused in
his scribbling. Even he seemed rattled. Gretchen held herself
utterly still. Craig's mouth hung open, stalled at the start of a sentence.

"I never frolic," said the doctor, and the relief in his voice—if
such was the result of frolicking, then by God, he was glad to put
in thirty-six-hour shifts for the rest of his natural life—shook the
other people in the room, on both sides of the curtain out of their
momentary arrest.

"Too busy to frolic," the mother said. "You must work very
hard."

"Yes," he murmured. "Um, you'll need to remove your jewelry for surgery, Ms. Heller."

"All of it? Some of them won't go back in. They're permanent."

"Okay," the resident said. "Fine."

"They made me remove my wedding ring," Gretchen whispered to Craig. "Said you can't have anything metal in the operating room."

"They don't want to tangle with her," Craig said. "Don't
want to get stuck with something sharp. Holy Christ, what's
the matter with those parents? She looks completely savage. Her
parents ought to be teaching her more about what it means to be
human."

"You're how old?" the resident asked Katie.

"Twenty-one."

"Smoke?"

"Yep."

"For how long?"

"Since I was ten. That's...uh..."

"Eleven years," her mother offered helpfully.

"Right. Eleven years."

"Drink?" the resident, from here on out unflappable, said.

"Yeah, to excess, regularly."

Craig, listening across the curtain, ruffled his hair again, clearly quite upset.

And despite the obvious heat of the story bubbling behind Katie's words, the resident ignored the implications and moved right along. "Anything today?"

"No."

"Street drugs?"

"No."

Craig snorted. Gretchen put a hand to his lips to shush him. "Yeah," he whispered, "she was running naked through the bushes and she doesn't take drugs. Right."

"I imagine the staff know instantly what lies are being told. Like when they asked how much I weighed..." Gretchen said. "They can probably tell by looking."

"Oh, you. You don't lie very well. Every crazy thing you do, you eventually confess."

"You didn't know I knew about your girlfriend."

He shrugged. "Maybe I didn't want to know. Maybe I wasn't ready until now."

"Prescriptions?" the resident continued with the girl.

The father stood up. "I've got the list," he said. "Already gave it to the nurse."

The resident's head stayed bent over his clipboard. "Read 'em off."

Katie's father listed at least a dozen medications in a clear English accent. The first ones, familiar names like Xanax, came out brightly, as though he were reciting a list of breakfast cereals. Several others he had trouble pronouncing, but he struggled until he had conveyed the information, and put the paper back into his pocket, satisfied.

"Okay, I was wrong," Craig said. "She didn't need street drugs when she could get high legally ten different ways every day."

"Diagnosis?" asked the resident through the curtain, a paragon of dispassion.

"Bipolar," Katie said, sounding almost happy at being truly pegged. "And..."

At this point, Craig bumped into Gretchen's table and upset the water pitcher, so they didn't hear the rest of the diagnosis. But the next question from the doctor regained their attention. "Are you sexually active?"

"Not anymore," Katie said, again filling her words with portent.

"One of those drugs that's supposed to make her sane must inhibit her libido," Craig said, keeping his voice quiet, obviously fascinated.

"Where can I get some?" asked Gretchen. "Stop you from wanting to screw your newest blonde and any other willing women in your future. Nip your desire in the bud. Make you act your age."

"Don't be bitter, Gretchen. That's ugly."

"I'm not pretty but you used to think I was. I guess now all your blind loving goes her way. Now you think she's pretty. Now you see me in front of you, faded. I thought you had more character, Craig. You could have resisted."

"I couldn't. You think you can control everything."

"I do have control, Craig."

"Nobody controls life."

"I make a dozen decisions every day to regulate my behavior, to keep to the path I've picked. I don't grab for the man making eye contact in the elevator, even if he's handsome, and I'm lonely and ignored. I don't steal at the store even if it's something I want and nobody's looking. I won't sell my soul for a nickel!"

"Here you go again, hysterical. Souls at stake, instead of a failed relationship."

"Out-of-control is so easy. You didn't make a conscious choice when you looked too closely at a woman and started noticing her perfume, and then took it further and talked to her. Touched her."

"Gretchen, it isn't as if you don't do crazy things. You know you do when you drink."

"I'm not proud of that. It's not who I really am."

"You had to know eventually. I'm glad it's out."

"I didn't want you to tell me. I wanted it to burn out. Now, you've told me, it's real."

"She's just a place to go for now. It isn't what you think."

"Should that make me feel better? That you didn't even fall in love with someone else? You left me for nothing?"

"I didn't say that..."

"Romance is fantasy, you know. You think there's a special woman out there for you when it really all amounts to the same thing, a woman, a sexual attraction, connection. Doesn't matter what woman. It might as well be me as her."

"I need something different in my life."

"Question," Gretchen said. "If you don't love me, how do I feel about you?" She started crying, but really it was her leg killing her now. The dull pain sharpened and struck, and the long bone that had broken burned inside her leg like a molten sword. She took her other half pill with a piece of leftover bread, and pushed him away when he fluttered around her, looking angry. He hovered between her and the window, casting shadows on the bed.

On the other side of the curtain, a nurse announced that they had squeezed Katie in next for surgery. With much effort and many encouragements from her parents, a crew of family and hospital personnel helped her onto the gurney. They took her away. The room quieted for a moment.

"The squeaky wheel," Craig said dismissively. "Wonder what other poor schmuck will have to wait while they fix her miserable, self-abused breast." He walked to the foot of her bed and held the metal bar, looking at her. "If you'll get ready, we'll go. If not, I'm leaving."

She knew he didn't mean it. "I need more water. One more, okay?"

He started over to the sink, but before he got there, two people arrived with armloads of fresh linens and began to make Katie's bed. Silently, he watched. After they left, Gretchen pulled back the curtain and watched him pour her water, then wash his hands.

"What a sordid little life. I guess those people were her parents. What losers," he said, handing her the glass.

"How do you mean?"

"Smoked since she was ten. Where were they?" he asked. "Lots of teen piercings. Nipple rings."

"She's an adult. She's twenty-one."

"And free to act like any old adult fathead, apparently. They popped her out and gave up. Let her roll in the slop on the floor."

"You don't know what they've been through with her. Maybe this is the best way. Maybe being forgiving, unconditional... people can do that, love unconditionally."

"To hell with her pain. I'd have had her over my knee. I'd be ripping the damned 'jewelry' out one by one."

"I got something different," Gretchen said, reaching into the bag for her clothes. She pulled the hospital gown down onto the floor and threw on a sweater.

"Oh? What did you get? That they're such good people because they let her ruin her life? Come on, you were as staggered as me about what a waste she is. She won't live to be thirty."

"She seemed very young to me. Immature, and very, very desperate. She was hurting. The dad kept track of everything for her. He ran out to find help. The mother cuddled her because she needed that. They forgave her everything, every dumb thing she did."

"They're irresponsible idiots. People like that should never be parents, and that girl had no business living, she was so screwed up."

"How is it you're so responsible? Remind me. I forget."

"My life is honest, at least. When I knew I had to change things, I told you."

"You always overrated honesty. What matters isn't what you say, it's what you do. I don't think you're responsible at all. I think you depend on other people too much, and I think your ego gives you the idea you're running your life independently, when you don't. You need me. You always will. You've got to face that before you can understand real love." Gretchen pulled on her underpants carefully, up and over her injured leg. He came over to help her with her sweatpants.

"No."

"That looks awkward. Let me help."

"You'll push too fast and it will hurt. Please don't. Leave it."

"I'll be careful."

"No!"

He stared at her.

"I'm too pissed now. I don't want you to touch me, okay?"

"Okay."

"I can see we're going nowhere. It's like you said, this isn't a negotiation, and you're not changing your mind without leaving here tonight. You won't let go of her and come back to me yet, which is what you should do. So do something else for me."

"What?"

"Go, Craig."

"I'll take you home. I said I would."

"I don't want you here right now. You need to grow up. See what's in front of your face. That she's not real. I am real, and I am here for you when you figure that out."

He loved the idea; she saw it in his eyes, but the well-trained gentleman in him rose to the occasion, offering up token arguments which she easily dismissed.

"How will you get home?" he said, finally giving in.

"Don't worry. I can take care of it."

"It's very . . . generous of you, Gretchen."

"No, it isn't. It's pure selfishness." She was adamant, and he was eager to get back to his new lover. He left, cell phone open, finger punching away.

Katie's mother came back into the room looking vaguely around. "Forgot her apple juice," she said, checking under the sheets. She finally found what she was looking for on the counter beside the sink. "She loves apple juice."

Well, Mom did seem a little on the dim side, Gretchen decided. Nobody left apple juice in bed.

But she sure loved her wayward, screwed-up daughter.

Gretchen swung her leg over the side of the bed and pressed the red button to summon a nurse. Somebody needed to get her a wheelchair, to push her out to the curb. By the time she got home tonight, Craig would have gone to Julie's apartment.

What would Craig do when Julie didn't answer her door? Probably the same thing he had done all evening with the cell phone. He would try and try again. At some point, maybe days down the line, he would get it through his thick skull that Julie was gone.

She hadn't been hard to take care of. Soft, not a suitable match for Craig, Julie wasn't someone with the strength to prop him up. She was certainly no match for Gretchen.

Gretchen had followed her and Craig on Friday night. They went to a restaurant, the restaurant where Gretchen and Craig always used to eat together. Now Gretchen couldn't go there anymore. She would be too embarrassed for their waiter, Harold, to witness her humiliation.

To Gretchen's surprise, Craig hadn't gone home with Julie. At least he had told the truth about that. He left her at the doorway to her building. They kissed while Gretchen watched. Then she followed his new woman all the way back into the dinky, dark apartment house. Gretchen knocked on the door and Julie answered.

Flimsy, insubstantial person. Gretchen would have known better. She had all night to finish, because she and Craig had fought earlier about her drinking. She had stomped off to stay at her mother's, supposedly. Julie's kitchen was full of things Gretchen knew how to use, even if she didn't usually use them.

That Saturday night dancing with Craig, she had seen the specter of Julie coming toward her in his eyes even though she knew it was impossible, that Julie was gone, but with that traveling car wreck of a thought, she had fallen. In that moment, she had succumbed to fear and weakness, and this was her punishment. She accepted it. She took responsibility. She didn't have to like it: visible injury. Weeks of disability. So she learned her lesson. You take control; you accept consequences.

Would he come back begging? Or would he waste a lot of time searching for Julie first?

Maybe he would call the police.

But they would never find her. No one would ever find her. Julie, as it turned out, was a clean freak. She had more bleach stowed below her kitchen sink than a hospital. And Gretchen, messy in her own life, knew how to clean, she just didn't like it much.

He had no one else. She had also spoken the truth when she said he wouldn't have had the courage to leave Gretchen without someone waiting in the wings to substitute. He needed a woman to anchor him. He would be unhappy without one.

Gretchen would think some more on unconditional love and forgiveness. She would forgive him his infidelity, and he would have to forgive her, too. Maybe she would tell him someday exactly what she had done with Julie when things were settled, after she was pregnant and he was happy with the outcome of unveiling all these secrets, even if he didn't much like knowing them. Well, she didn't, either.

She made a mental note that he would have to take some parenting classes before the big event. He didn't seem to understand that you have to let people be who they are and love them anyway. You forgive them their piercings, their abscesses, their strayings, their excesses, their lack of control. You love them anyway, with your whole heart.

She leaned over to use the bedside phone. She punched in a nine and then the number.

"Mom?" she said. "I need your help."

Sandstorm

JUNE 3

At night I take pills to sleep. They don't go very well with the brandy I drink starting at eight or nine. When the alarm clock goes off at six the next morning and my husband gets up, swearing, to take his shower, I rise painfully and put on my glasses. Even so, as I make my way into the kitchen, I can't seem to make my eyes focus.

By seven, though, I am dressed and presentable in my high heels and my suit. My hair is clean and curled, sprayed so it will not stray during the day. I have cooked breakfast for my husband and packed his lunch, and he has left for work, ten minutes late as always.

Time to wake Abe and Molly. I bring their dishes to the table and they eat, gloomy and half-conscious, complaining. They dress and pick up their heavy packs and leave for school. I feed and walk the dog, throw a load of clothes in the washer to dry tonight, sweep the floor, unload the dishwasher, call the repair shop about the car, and stamp the letters my husband asked me to send to his relatives in Michigan. I have almost forgotten to get the chicken out of the freezer to cook tonight. Taking one last glance around, I lock up and walk down the path, which needs weeding, toward the car.

It is time to go to work.

The radio weatherman says it's going to be a hot summer. Summer, winter, the seasons don't matter. All that matters is the traffic, the dog, Abe and Molly, my husband—and Leo, my boss.

When I arrive at five past eight, they are all waiting for me—Leo and Carol, who is Leo's secretary, the students who are helping with the phones, the stacks of papers, the phone messages. Leo is the community college president, and I am his executive assistant. I work for Leo from eight to five every day, and from eight to ten in the evenings, trying to catch up, and on Saturdays, when Leo has his meetings to get ready for the Accreditation Committee. The Accreditation Committee is always coming and we are always preparing for it.

During the lunch hour, I go to the grocery store. Carol fills in. Lately she has been getting messages wrong and spending too much time smoking in the ladies' restroom. She has problems at home. Leo is threatening to fire her. She sits in my office and cries and I try to comfort her.

The student workers never last long. Only Leo and I are always here. I have actually been here longer than Leo, almost twenty years. For ten of those years, Leo and I had an affair. I wonder now how I found the time.

I believe my husband knew about the affair, but he runs the local Ford dealership and Leo has referred many customers to him over the years and buys his cars there himself.

Anyway, Leo moved on a long time ago.

Leo wants to become chancellor of the district community colleges. He is very busy with meetings with representatives and he travels a lot. When he is gone, I run the college for him.

It is two thirty. Leo is still at lunch. I have called back twelve people, most of whom were not available, met with representatives of the local Latino group regarding hiring more Latinos at the college, prepared the paperwork to fire the food services manager for drunkenness, and prodded our business services manager regarding the delays in preparing next year's budget. More people are waiting outside. I am dictating memos to Leo about all of this.

The day passes as usual, in a blur of frantic motion. I have accomplished much, but I don't know what, exactly.

Due to construction, it takes almost an hour to drive home.

Molly does not come home after school. She has been sleeping with her boyfriend for five months and she chooses not to follow parental rules anymore. I make calls, find her, and go pick her up, her face sullen and hostile. Abe is in his room, on the Internet, where he stays from four to twelve every day.

I cook chicken and rice and make a good salad. Molly will not eat because she had a hamburger after school. Abe takes his food to his room after a sharp exchange with his father. My husband sits down in his La-Z-Boy and picks up the remote, and I settle down at the kitchen table to write a short speech for Leo to deliver over the weekend to the Association of Realtors.

About eight I start drinking my brandy. By eleven I have finished the speech, washed two more loads of laundry, given the dog a bath, and nagged Abe into taking out the trash.

I open up a book. I used to love to read, a long time ago. The words swim before my eyes.

JUNE 10

In two days summer vacation begins at my college. Leo is reviewing his commencement speech, which I completed last night. I am helping the students sign his name to the certificates of graduation. The acting director of food services has walked off the job, so I have to get over there and figure out how to serve two thousand people at the reception on Saturday night.

JUNE 12

Leo's speech was very well received, and he was complimented many times on how well the reception was organized.

The students are gone. In September they will return, blurred, interchangeable.

Molly has left for New York City with her boyfriend. She left a note saying she would be in touch. I call her boyfriend's parents and we talk for a long time, but can't decide what to do.

JUNE 13

Today is Sunday. It is quiet at my house. My husband is selling cars and Abe is in his room clicking his mouse at the computer monitor. Laundry, the floors, the bathrooms, dusting, the windows—Sunday is the day I clean house.

My father, at the convalescent hospital outside town, has just called. As always, what he said makes no sense whatever. Alzheimer's is a devastating disease. Abe says he can't stand to see the old man, but I go when I can.

I begin mopping the floor. Soup for tonight is on the stove. A lot of little bugs have gotten in through the screen, looking for coolness, I guess, and will have to be dealt with.

Molly's room is a mess. Her baby picture still sits on the chest. I look at it for a long time.

I notice I am wearing my nightgown, though it is afternoon. This will never do. I go into my bedroom and look in the closet, at the large overfull hamper. I have forgotten to take the dry cleaning.

I look in my drawer and find a pair of shorts and a T-shirt. My legs are thick and white.

I sit down on the bed. The soup burns up. The dog knocks over the pail of soapy water on the kitchen floor. I lie down on the bed. The smoke alarm goes off. Someone puts out the fire on the stove.

I close my eyes.

My husband comes home, wanting his supper.

The bedroom door is locked. He pounds and threatens.

"I am thinking," I tell him.

JUNE 15

"Leo," I say, "I am taking a leave of absence."

"You can't do that," Leo says. He sits me down and tells me to get ahold of myself. I tell him I will finish out the week. He asks me just what he is supposed to do about the Accreditation Committee, the food services manager position, the projected loss of A.D.A., the lawsuit by the disgruntled faculty member, the speech he has to deliver next weekend to the Rotary, travel arrangements for his trip to the Grand Tetons next week, and so on. I am silent.

He cajoles. He threatens.

I leave the office.

He runs after me and fires me. I go home and tell my husband.

JUNE 16

My husband is storming around the house. I am vacuuming. There are cobwebs in all the corners. I clean house from sunrise to sunset. Then I drink my brandy. I still can't read.

★   ★   ★

JUNE 18

My father calls. I take the call in my bed. "When are you go-ing to get me out of here?" he asks.

"Soon, Pops."

"Who are these people anyway?"

"I have no idea," I tell him. "I'll ask around and call you back." I take some pills so I can go to sleep. It is one o'clock in the afternoon on a Friday.

When I wake up, Abe is sitting on the bed, angry. "Mom," he says, "I'm hungry."

I get up and make an exquisite eggplant parmigiana from scratch. Abe takes his plate to his room. My husband and I sit in silence. Fi-nally he says, "Aren't you going to ask me how it went today?"

I look at him. His eyes are bloodshot, and the gray has thick-ened around his ears. I realize that I have no idea who he is.

JUNE 19

I leave. I bring shorts and toothpaste. I clean out the checking account on the way out of town. I drive for several days. I stay at the Motel 6's along the freeway. A couple of times I call my father, and he always says, "When are you gonna get me out of here?" I think about going to get him, but then he says, "Who are you anyway?"

JUNE 23

I am tired. I stop. The sign says I am in Barstow, California, Gateway to Death Valley. The motel room is dusty, but I am too tired to care. I go to bed.

★   ★   ★

July 25

The maid cleans every day. I eat bread and cheese and drink coffee from the coffee machine. I rinse my shorts out in the sink. I stay inside and sleep a lot.

Over the phone, I tell my father I'm living in a desert, and he replies, "You and me both."

August 10

There is a shaded concrete walkway in front of my room and a metal chair. I have been sitting in that chair, watching the people come and go. They never stay more than a day or two, because they think there's nothing to do here.

But I am very busy. I have thought through my life to about the age of ten. It is amazing what I can remember. I have discovered how good cool water tastes, and I drink a lot of it. Although I only leave my room to pick up food at the convenience store across the street, these trips overwhelm me. Crossing the hot asphalt and avoiding cars, all the choices, the customers in line, the dash back...I am knocked off balance and have to rest afterward.

Molly's baby picture sits on the windowsill. A woman is holding Molly in her arms, smiling. Who was that woman?

A cactus grows on the other side of the parking lot, and then a long sweep of cacti recedes into the desert as far as my eyes can see. In the afternoon a wind comes up, swirling the sand. I never noticed the wind at home. There must have been some. This wind is the enemy of the cactus. It beats relentlessly against the cactus from afternoon until evening, twisting its arms into bizarre positions over time.

The days are long, and I look forward to the hour of sunset. So much happens during this hour. The wind dies down at last.

The air cools. The shadows lengthen. The light dies down from steady and bright to sparkling black.

I have learned some amazing things. For instance, I can touch my own body and feel it. It feels good to rub my two bare feet together. The skin on my arms is dry and smooth. I look at my wrists and am astonished at their fine modeling. My hands are the most remarkable machines.

AUGUST 15

I took my first walk today, out into the desert. It was early, still cool. The sky is not very deep—I felt the top of it was right over my head. A vulture passed overhead, quite beautiful with its ruff of white feathers. Every morning I'm going to walk, and sit down—here—on this spot of sand, in the shade of this cactus. I have gotten up to my adolescence in the remembering. My mother died during this time. I had forgotten about her. Poor Abe. Poor Molly.

AUGUST 18

My father makes a lot more sense lately. He is always cheerful. He thinks my mother is still alive, and in a way she is. I talk to her myself.

Sometimes in the afternoon as I sit in my chair, my head begins to nod. Smoothly and imperceptibly, a sweet peace steals over me. My thoughts swirl round and round like a whirlpool and down I go. I sink into sleep. I never slept before during the daytime. I'm sure my body wanted to, but I never let my body make a decision about anything.

Sometimes I don't get hungry all day. I always ate three square meals a day. I even found out my body sometimes wants to have a bowel movement at a time other than six thirty every morning. I mentioned this to my father. He laughed, and I laughed, too.

My body is a great silent companion. I follow it around. It knows what it wants.

Sometimes as I walk in the desert, my long shadow beside me, I look down at the ground and it is very far away. I feel vast, like a mountain, aware of how the bacteria view me. I'm like a tourist in the head of the Statue of Liberty, looking out through Liberty's eyes across the sea.

This morning I stepped on an anthill. The ants were deflected only momentarily from their purpose. All of them together seem to make up one body.

A long time ago I read that the greatest evolutionary step occurred when primitive spirochetes swimming around encountered the precursors of sperm. They attached themselves to the end of the sperm and their flailing tails allowed the sperm to move. Which is how human reproduction became possible, but that is not what interests me. What I think about is that my millions of cells are descendants of free swimmers banding together into an organized and complex universe. I am not trivial; I carry many beings within me. I deserve to survive.

AUGUST 24

It is hot even in the mornings now, hot blue above, hot yellow below. I go out now before the sun tops the black Nevada mountain range on the horizon. In the afternoon the wind whips the sand into stinging clouds and I stay inside.

I give the maid a few extra dollars. She thanks me in Spanish. Spanish is a very courtly language, musical, like water over stones. Leo always complained that the Latinos were trying to take over his college. I wonder why he hated them so much.

In the quiet evenings, the air-conditioning whirring and the shades drawn, I lie on the bed and think about the college. I think how we trained people to become just like us. This kind of thinking is very hard work, but when I have a thought it sticks to the grain of sand that is my soul.

AUGUST 26

Leo and my husband are at the door. When I open it, they look stunned and step back.

They are looking at me. I see myself their way, disheveled and plain. No mask of makeup, no curls, no shoes. My legs are brown now and strong.

They are both sweating in their suits.

"We've come to take you home," they say. My husband starts to cry. They follow me into my room and sit on the bed, their eyes raking around the furniture, looking like tarantulas. My husband is still crying angrily.

"Who do you think you are?" he asks.

Leo says, "The new school year is starting next week. Everything is a mess. I'm willing to overlook this irresponsible behavior."

They do not wait for me to speak. They rush on, whining.

I shake my head, and I hear the tone change, becoming sinister. They are talking about nervous breakdowns. My husband says I can't abandon my children. Molly is back and she needs me.

I shake my head.

Leo takes my arm. He says I need a doctor, and tells my husband to help him. My husband looks at him, at me. Now he is the one who smells of brandy.

"Go away," I say. They pick me up and carry me to the car. Leo drives and I am firmly strapped between the two of them in the front seat. We drive out the long flat highway. It's got to be a hundred ten degrees out here. I see my cactus receding in the distance. The wind is blowing up a real sandstorm.

Leo turns on the wipers and peers out the front window, going slower. My husband is telling me that they had to do it for my own good.

SEPTEMBER 10

I am back at home. I am seeing Dr. Bernstein three times a week. My eyes feel gritty, as if sand were blowing through my head. My soul may already have blown away. My father asks on the phone, "When are you gonna get me out of here?" His voice sounds weaker.

I don't think anymore. Dr. Bernstein says it would hamper my recovery.

SEPTEMBER 12

I am back at work. Leo has started an affair with his secretary. My husband says I better get with the program and start cooking again.

I wake up with a start, my throat dry, my eyes stinging. My husband is snoring. He has drunk a lot of brandy.

I'm rushing into the sandstorm. The wind shrieks and picks me up and tosses me into the howling chaos.

I tumble out of bed. I blow into the kitchen, past the sandy, dirty pots and pans and the sandy, filthy floor, and out the door to the garage.

Wind is roaring through my head. I tote the can of gasoline into the bedroom and pour gas all around the bed. Then I climb up quietly and take the batteries out of the smoke detector. I light the match and toss it toward the bed. There is a blast of heat and more wind.

I have made my own desert.

I force the bedroom door shut on the flames. I walk out into the night in my nightgown, but now the desert is gone, only the darkness remains, there's only confusion, confusion, confusion.

My body gets into the car, carefully setting the can of gasoline onto the passenger seat.

Where are we going? I ask, turning the keys in the ignition.

A siren sounds in the distance as I turn onto the boulevard.

It seems that we are going to Leo's.

Tiny Angels

"Look, Danny! Can you see? This is so fabulous." Laura leaned back. Her neck cranked around like an alien's, all the way behind her and to the left. They were seated over the wing. Daniel assumed she could see better out the window behind her. He couldn't see out and he didn't care.

He wanted to say shut up, but his wife's excitement kept him kind. For so many years, Laura had stayed home taking care of the kids while he worked and traveled. This time, for the first time, when she asked to come along, he had said yes. He had agreed for reasons other than timing: a woman who took women's magazines too seriously, that night when he got home she had removed her robe to reveal a sleek black nightie that slid like oil down her ample curves. Wrapping creamy thighs around him, mouth cold and sweet as chocolate ice cream, she had made him beg, and she had made him promise.

He had no trouble begging, no trouble promising, because he had another motivation. Laura made good cover for this trip. He was a husband taking his pretty wife down to the islands for a vacation. Their wool coats were stuffed in overhead bins. He wore a rayon shirt with palm trees splattered across it, and she wore heeled sandals and a sleeveless cotton shift sprinkled with minuscule blue flowers, hidden at the moment under a sweater against the airplane's chill.

"All that snow, see it? Going, going...Gone! Good-bye miserable cold! Bye-bye, irksome children." She let out a giddy laugh. "I can't believe your mom took them. Has she ever before?" Her head cocked to one side. "I don't think so," she answered herself. "She was willing—almost. I'd suspect you put her up to it but you wouldn't do that just to take me on a trip, or else why would it be three years since we went anywhere alone together?" Possibly to soothe the sting of this implicit criticism, she wound her husband's arm through her own and gave his wrist a squeeze.

Laura spent most days wrangling the kids like an expert cowboy on horseback, cracking the whip without ever harming a hair of their valuable pelts. He never saw her read a newspaper, he never saw her relax, yet she seemed remarkably tuned-in. She knew current movie stars, and cannily guessed outcomes for the Friday night video rentals he usually slept through. Maybe she listened to public radio in the daytime. Maybe the kids connected her to deeper meanings, or some earthy mom-blood-dirt-detergent-kid link he couldn't comprehend. She continued to have the one thing going for her he had always admired, the ability to say things that surprised him, a good thing, since her chattering need to include him in the running drama of her thoughts often drove him crazy.

He called what he felt for her love, but differentiated it from what he felt for his children. That feeling, aroused a few times when they were little—when one ran ahead in the store or got away on a busy street just long enough for him to feel desperate, animal, and basic—growled in him, sharpened his teeth, revealed an ungovernable violence within. How could he use the same word for the sexual thrall that kept him with Laura?

She'd had trouble giving birth to Joey. When he entertained, for one second, the idea that she might not make it, he became efficient rather than terrified, resigned rather than angry. He didn't think he could have been so philosophical if Corinna were the victim. No, he didn't.

So call what he had with Laura a loving connection rather than the intense, crazy aura of fun he had once fantasized surrounding marriage. Their tie now only allowed him a certain amount of leeway before it dragged him back. He needed her, appreciated her abilities as a parent and as an easy, sometimes ingenious lover. Without her, there would be no flowered curtains on the windows, no soap-smelling, happy children running to greet him at the door when he did come home. There would be no tease, no mystery. She kept the mysterious machinery of their marriage oiled and operating. He played worker bee. Somebody had to.

But here today, once again, Laura had shown her strong suit, intuiting correctly. He had, in fact, intervened with his mother, Olga, telling her she had to watch his children at their house in Lincoln for the very short time they would be away or Laura wouldn't feel comfortable going. He needed Laura, ergo, Mom had to comply, but Mom never gave in without a fight. He'd had to hire her full-time help for the duration, and had promised to pick up the cost of her housekeeper for three months.

Too bad he had to keep Laura in the dark about the brevity of this trip. She expected a week away; he planned to finish his business by the time they got off the plane in Puerto Rico. Guilt burned his stomach, a feeling so familiar he barely registered it. He would make it up to her somehow, which was always the follow-up thought, which didn't stop the pain but weakened it like drinking milk. He pushed hair off his forehead and felt sweat beading on his brow, so he reached up to twist on the plastic fan over his seat.

He wondered if he could declare Mom an expense. Picturing Curtis Patchett in the accounting office of the bureau scrutinizing his report, he felt as giddy as his wife sounded. Curtis, formerly a field agent like himself, would chop him into a hundred pieces and hang the bits on the wall as a decorative advance warning to any potential future jokers.

The plane ascended through a soupy, oatmeal-colored mass of cloud. Settling in, Laura said, "Olga had her hands full raising you, and you were only one kid, but I read ours the riot act and told them if they didn't behave, I'd make them stay until they got it right." She giggled. "Not that they don't like your mother. But she can be a pill." She pulled down her tray table, then pushed it back into place, clicking the lock in place with a satisfied, "Ah. I can't wait to eat."

Daniel glanced around his newspaper at the woman with frizzy brown hair, whom he had already mentally named "Curly." Tall and lean, her head way up on the seat headrest, she adjusted a pair of black corduroy slacks she was wearing that matched a fitted black blouse as she jiggled a baby's hand in her own. The baby made long, up and down sounds like the beginnings of a song sung off-key and minus rhythm. After a while, Curly pulled a windup musical toy out from her carry-on to amuse the child, then played peekaboo with a black and white killer whale puppet that resembled one his kids had when they were little that they had dubbed "Shamu."

Laura bent over him to look. "A little over five months old," she noted. "Good age for a traveler. They can smile and almost sit by themselves, but they're tied to Mama. They can't escape."

Daniel pushed her gently back into her seat, resisting an urge to shout at her. "When was the last time you ate a meal on a plane, honey?" he asked her. "Don't expect gourmet. The food stinks."

"If someone else cooks it and puts it in front of me, well, I call that delicious."

He had a good view of the three women and their babies. Due to the arm-wrestling contest his boss had won with the airline, they sat in rows close by but in front of him. They all had the putative mom's own requirements: getting in and out to change or walk the babies would be easier. He could observe relatively discreetly, since the plane, an Airbus A300, held two seats on each side, four in the middle. There weren't that many places to look, and the movie would play soon, offering him unlimited, anonymous viewing pleasure.

The three drooling babies, roughly the same age, appeared happy and well-fed, so distinctions were going to be subtle. None of the mothers was breast-feeding, which would have provided a definite clue that they were not the bad one.

The bureau had identified a few other people with small kids on this flight, but the kids were too old or too young, or the father was along to help. They knew the target was traveling alone with a baby who was not yet crawling. They also knew the mom was white and that Daniel had to identify her before she left the terminal in San Juan so that the locals, who had been alerted by the bureau in advance, could help him grab her before she disappeared into the forgiving sunshine of the Caribbean. She could fly right out of their grasp from San Juan. She could run for Tortola, St. Croix, Nevis, any number of welcoming islands.

Daniel peered up the aisle.

Without tearing her eyes away from the airline magazine she seemed to be studying, Laura said, "That one's sitting up already. Six months old, I'd say. But then, our two were so precocious. Joey sat up earlier than Corinna. Hard to tell if it's a boy or girl, all wrapped up like that."

The baby faced a second woman wearing a leaf-patterned yellow sundress, thin cotton, just right for the tropics. He wondered how she had managed in that dress. Must have brought a fur coat along to get herself on the plane in Boston.

She had long blonde hair twisted into a short braid that fell over her left shoulder, but most of it escaped, floating beyond her skull in a permanently windblown state. He code-named her

"Fan." When the baby slept, minutes at a time, she leafed through a movie magazine, looking irritated. If she had looked bored, he might have found her attitude significant; but she didn't. When the baby fussed, she was right there, kissing its cheek, letting it attempt to stand on her knees, generously supported by her.

"What a sturdy little neck," Laura observed. "Remember how Cori's neck flopped?"

The flight attendant, a thin, graying man, asked if they would prefer lasagna or meat loaf. They both preferred lasagna.

"Meat loaf?" Laura scoffed. "What do you suppose they put into it?"

Laura made terrific meat loaf. She folded in bits of whole wheat bread with the low-fat turkey grind, fresh tomatoes, garlic, mushrooms, apple-chicken sausages, zucchini, yogurt cheeses. Somehow, the mishmash tasted great. He didn't expect the same from the airline.

Their red blobs of goo arrived. Dan couldn't eat his. Laura tucked in.

The third mother, "Mole," black-haired and blue-eyed, with a flesh-colored mole at the tip of her chin that extended her face into an exact triangle, bottle-fed her baby throughout the meal, eating nothing. She sipped from a bottle of water she had stowed in the back of the seat in front of her. Whenever her child began to move even a little erratically, she picked through a big bag and stuffed a pacifier into its mouth, or dangled a toy provocatively above it. The move seemed to work, as the baby interrupted its near meltdown, satisfying itself by sucking hard on the rubber nipple. The target wore a pair of lightweight jeans with a baggy pink shirt over a tight white T-shirt.

"These young moms are so attentive," Laura said, observing his focus, "which is good. It's a blurry time. You're afraid and confident all at the same time." She put a finger to his cheek. "They're just so darling, such tiny angels. Remember Cori? How she slept for the first three weeks and I had to wake her up to eat?"

It was a blur. Daniel couldn't believe they had two children. The only way he could cope was to immerse himself in work. He was not cut out to change diapers. The smell nauseated him. He couldn't understand how Laura could pick up a steaming, reeking soggy pile and casually rinse it in the toilet. The process, so primordial, made him glad to be civilized, and after the first time he was left alone to cope, gagging with revulsion, he sprang magnanimously for paper diapers.

He was proud of the kids, of course. Symbolizing his success as a man, they were his seed. You only had to look at Joey to know that. Daniel supported them and their stay-at-home mother. He would put them through college, by God.

Laura pulled her hand back and her eyes looked inward. "I thought she might die of hunger. I cried. I was worried. Funny, huh? I mean, now I worry when she eats fast food. She's not thin like you might expect. She's sturdy-looking, even though she exercises constantly."

Daniel crushed his napkin and put it onto his plate so that the flight attendant would get that he was done. They were firing up the movie, a comedy featuring Ben Stiller. Every time he thought he had seen every Ben Stiller movie, another one gushed along, about as entertaining as a broken water pipe. He put his headphones on, pretending to adjust the channels, but instead turned the volume down to nothing.

"He's not handsome," his wife announced. "Why is he a movie star?"

Daniel tidied his tray.

"Well," Laura went on, "it's that false vulnerability. He believes he's clued-in to what's happening. Truth is, he isn't. He doesn't understand that women need, first and foremost, his attentive regard." She messed with her controls. "These Hollywood guys, what they care about is big breasts. Hence the over-endowed lead actress. If she has anything else going for her, Ben'll never notice."

He felt irritated but forgave her. From what he could see, movies reflected life: women flitted along the periphery. Even his target was not the main player in this incident. She belonged to someone. She did what she was told.

Read history, he had said to Laura so many times. Women played support staff. Their memorable accomplishments related to raising heroic soldier boys.

The flight attendant came around with a plastic bag to collect trash. Daniel handed his plastic plate and tray to her, heavily loaded. Laura's tray was as clean as if she had licked it.

"That baby," Laura said, pushing her tray table up, "see how he sticks his toes through the holes in that knit blanket? Just like Joey. His baby blankey? Still on his bed. Did you know that?"

Joe had always clung tightly to his mother, listening too intently to her, laughing at her jokes before she reached the punch lines. He went to her with problems. He avoided Daniel because, Daniel suspected, he found his father harsh and uncompromising.

Daniel found all forms of anodyne unpalatable. He didn't offer Band-Aids, he offered solutions which were painful and sometimes left you bleeding underneath. When would the boy get free of her soft umbilical pull? He was almost fourteen. Adulthood belonged to the hardy. Children and their mothers needed protection, loveys, comfort. Men required weapons. He needed to spend more time with the boy, let him know which side was up before he ended up as naive as Laura.

Four rows ahead of him, Fan sagged. The baby, toes tangled in a blanket as Laura had described, was pushing tight against Fan's right shoulder. It closed its eyes. Fan's mouth gaped. She snored.

Damn. No ideas occurred. What mom wouldn't take advantage of an unconscious baby to cop a snooze?

As the movie screen brightened and Curly's baby tired, the mother and baby stuck together like pages of a book, related, but individual. The baby's eyes closed so tightly its little face smoothed over like a marble sculpture. The mother rested her head against the hard curved portion of the seat that substituted for a travel pillow. She breathed fast when she slept. Was she pretending?

Mole watched the movie, even chuckling sometimes, headphones on her head while her baby slept peacefully. Nothing suspicious there. No reason not to embrace a serene moment.

He turned up the volume and listened to Ben Stiller, eyes still on his prizes.

"She's too pretty for him, and way too bright," Laura said, interrupting a bad movie joke.

Daniel pulled out a notebook and took notes. Fan dozed while her baby sucked on a bottle, Curly wiggled the baby on her knee, Mole's baby adjusted itself and continued to sleep.

"Did you ever think, 'Oh, I wish I had it all in hand'?" Laura asked him.

"I do have it all in hand."

She was quiet for once.

Most of the passengers had pulled down the plastic screens over their windows so that the movie could be seen, which dipped them all in gloom. Hollywood droned on. A few people snickered. Very few laughed outright.

Daniel punched the buttons on the seat beside him, lowering the volume back to nil. He watched the women, annoyed with himself. He had remarkable instincts. Everybody said so. Why, then, so much trouble today?

All mothers looked alike. The thought sneaked in and he laughed. A few people looked at him. He examined the thought, found it unworthy, and laughed again. Well, he said to himself, once he was able to get himself under control, better locate some differences pronto.

Beside him Laura, who had been so critical earlier, laughed at bumbling Ben.

After the movie, the attendants came around with more drinks. Passengers were advised to use the facilities before landing began. Each of the three moms took a turn in the bathroom. He timed them. Each took about the same amount of time.

He strolled the aisles, taking a closer look. He couldn't tell one baby from the next, much less align its features with its purported mother.

The three moms all seemed equally nurturing, nervous, tired, concerned. They all, despite relative youth, had dark bags under their eyes. After the movie, the babies all began to fuss, one more than the others, but the mothers' anxious ministrations all seemed equally determined, loving, and calm.

The babies all cried during the landing. All the moms shoved bottles at them, and all the babies batted the bottles away, faces purple, ears apparently popping.

Laura, after exclaiming over the view of the islands on the way down, hadn't said anything in a long time. As they stood in the aisle waiting for the signal to disembark, he reached up into the bins for their winter coats. She said, "I've imagined this moment for so long. When we get off the plane, it's gonna feel like heaven should feel. Like velvet. Warm, silky, soft air." She sighed.

"It'll be hot all right," Daniel agreed, then he turned his attention back to the women. Fan, one hand holding a bottle, had her baby tucked up on her shoulder facing to the rear. Now quieted, it peered confusedly at the people standing behind her in the line. Curly, grappling with a massive carry-on, was still seated and trying to get organized. The woman beside her was holding the baby while Curly apologized and stuffed toys, diapers, rags inside the bag. Slightly ahead of her, Mole stood, baby neatly tucked into a fabric sling over her stomach, her bag on rollers behind her.

"Why did we come, Daniel?" Laura stood in front of him in the aisle, where the passengers were lined up like airplanes on the runway awaiting a signal to go.

Trapped.

"You don't give a damn about the weather. You don't care where you are. You haven't looked out the window once."

"Laura," he said urgently, keeping his voice down. "Not now."

"You don't care about me." She was bristling like a terrier.

"Oh, geez. Not true."

He saw hurt and anger in her eyes and he didn't have time for this shit right now.

With relief, he saw the line ahead of them stirring. He could still pull this off. He considered shoving past his suddenly difficult wife, but with all the luggage jamming the aisle, he didn't think he could do it without raising some kind of general alarm, the last thing he wanted to do. "Please. Let's just get out of here. I hate being crowded."

Laura set her carry-on down on his foot. Hard.

"Ow." He kicked it off.

"I'm not moving until you tell me what's going on."

Fan was making her way toward the front of the plane.

"Shit, Laura! Go, will you? You're holding all these people up."

"I was so excited about this trip, the two of us. Only I expected everything to be different. I bought a new bathing suit. I thought we'd snorkel. Play. Love each other."

Curly shuffled ahead, apologizing, knocking into people with her bulky bag, disappearing into the business class section.

He nudged Laura with his hip. "Honey, move it!" When she didn't move, he tried going around her. She turned to face him, stretching her arms out to block him.

Up ahead, Mole exited, her pink shirt flapping behind her. "Christ!" he said. "Please, Laura!"

Behind them, other passengers began stealing across the middle aisle to the other side of the plane.

He considered bolting, but only for a second. The look in her eye riveted him.

"It's one of those women, isn't it?"

"What?" He wanted to laugh but he didn't have time. "No."

"It's her," she said. "The pretty one."

In spite of his consternation, he had to ask, "What are you talking about?"

"The one with the bogus baby. Did you think I wouldn't notice?"

"Notice what?" He felt his heartbeat all the way down to his fingertips.

"What's she, an au pair? A babysitter?"

"Who?" he asked urgently. "Which one?"

But Laura was on her own jag. "You had me so thrown off, the way you eyeballed those other two mothers. But you're devious, I guess I know that because of your work. Maybe you imagined you could throw me off that way? And for a few minutes there, I tried to think they just reminded you of... of me, when I first had our children. I thought you were remembering what I was remembering. I imagined tenderness." A tear hung in the corner of her eye.

Registering it, he felt forced to ignore it for the moment. "You said bogus baby. What are you talking about, Laura? It's important."

"At first I thought she was just another mother. She had me fooled for at least five seconds."

"My God, honey, help me here. Which one had you fooled? Who?"

"Don't lie to me. You bribed your mother. I wanted to think it was for us. Now I know it wasn't."

The three moms would be in the terminal now, buying tickets to places where the palm trees could hide them forever, waving down taxis, catching rides, out of his reach unless he could find a way out of this mess right now.

"Which one?" he yelled, grabbing her arm.

She pulled it away, reached down, and unzipped her bag. She pulled out a big straw hat. "I'm going down that gangplank onto the tarmac. I'm going to feel that sun-soaked air, and I'm going to love it. And I'm going without you."

"For God's sake, Laura! Which one? Which one is bogus?"

The line behind them emptied as their fellow travelers continued to skulk furtively over to the next aisle and out the front.

She gave him a hard look and saw something new. Her expression changed. "Oh, Daniel," she said, worriedly. "I got it wrong, didn't I."

"You sure did!"

"It's work, isn't it? My old familiar rival. Same old, same old."

"Yes, yes. It's work! Now who the hell is she?"

"Tell me why you need to know."

But he was not supposed to tell. He couldn't share such things with her. She stood in one place, he stood in another. They stood frustrated in the airplane aisle, immobilized by her recalcitrance and his stubborn maleness.

"Tell me."

She knew little about his work, except that mostly he did things he couldn't talk about.

He had no choice, and for once, he had no doubt he was doing exactly the right thing. "It's a kidnapping, Laura. She stole the kid."

Laura's reply came instantly. "The one in the yellow sundress."

Fan.

"Go get her." She stepped aside.

He ran.

The authorities in Puerto Rico arrested the woman in the yellow sundress just as she was trotting toward a plane for St. Kitts, ran her face and stats through their computers.

Fan was their bogus mom.

Baby was returned home to his, as it turned out, frantic family in Somerville, Massachusetts.

Daniel and Laura flew to Tortola and stayed for three weeks

at a villa near Smuggler's Cove, Olga be damned. Laura loved the air, the humidity, the silver waves. Daniel loved Laura.

"Now," he said that first night, the one where she wore the slinky black nightie until, four piña coladas past the yardarm, he tore it off her with his teeth. "How did you know it was her?"

"She got off the plane with a baby on her shoulder and a bottle in her hand. So where was her diaper bag?

"No insecure new mom goes anywhere without a pile of changes, activities, toys. She had one diaper, two bottles, no bag. I couldn't help wondering, where's the stuffy, the rattle, the plastic key set? Where's Shamu the stuffed whale?"

Daniel said, "I owe you, honey."

"Then pay up," Laura said, and he grabbed her.

To Still the Beating of Her Heart

Leaving the shop behind, Claude stepped outside onto the street and took a deep breath of car fumes. He wrinkled his nose and finding that insufficient defense, blew it on an immaculate handkerchief. He zipped his new leather jacket, walked toward the subway, then stopped, laughing a little at himself. Habit, old scripts. He had plenty of cards and cash nowadays. He scanned the street for taxis, but saw none. Hands in his pockets, he reflected on the circumstance that had led him into the perfume business. He loved the smell of women. He drank in their radiant skin the way other men guzzled fine wine. His father, trained at the Henri Jacques Parfum House in France, had left him the San Francisco shop when he died, probably worried about Claude. "A man needs an occupation," he used to scold, "even a gentleman." After the inheritance, crazy in love with Clea, with an excellent education in French literature but no calling, Claude discovered the latent talent hidden in his untrained but eager nose.

He waved a yellow cab down, got inside, and shut the cold wind out. Today had been unusually successful. Four Asian females, all beautiful, all petite and dark with hair that gleamed like dripping oil, had bought out the majority of his stock of his most precious French scents, the ones he had manufactured especially for his shop. He had a special connection to the factory outside of Eze. The town hovered pretty as a sprawling vacation villa above the Mediterranean, and was very near where his father's relatives all lived, and where he had spent the majority of his childhood until the divorce, when his mother had brought him to the States to live near her family. He thought perhaps something floral would suit them, heavy on the tuberose, beeswax, and rose de May, with a slight tickle of sweet honey.

Bantering, friendly, fun-loving, these Asian customers knew how to make a good day great, how to flirt with a man, how to make him feel—manly. On the way out, the prettiest of the group slipped her business card into his pocket, whispering, "I'll be back at the hotel by eight tonight. Call me."

Unbidden images invaded his mind. Six years of happy marriage had inured him to such invitations, but recently, he felt pulled in an unfamiliar way. He felt a weakening, a lack of moral musculature where there once was brawn. Still, he did not want another woman. Another woman would not be Clea. He wanted Clea back, the way she was the day he met her.

The trip to their home in Noe Valley shouldn't take more than ten minutes from downtown San Francisco, but tonight, with rush hour in full roar...the halts and jerks of the cab irritated him, obliterating the last traces of his good mood. He began to picture Clea, at the window at home, waiting for him, her beady, unmascaraed eyes never wavering from the street.

Beautiful, she had been, with her flaming red hair, her perfect body and intense intelligence. Passionate, loving, the ideal model for his products, Clea was his vision of female perfection. She looked as she was, like a woman with a career of her own, thoughts, opinions, life, so much life. Everything a man could want, she had been.

No longer.

Now she waited for him, and he felt her waiting like a cable car slipped off the track on Powell Street, going downhill and coming at him. He would show up in the taxi, pay the man, get out, and wave at her face in the window. He would try not to look, but he would feel the onslaught of her need. He saw it coming, and he was paralyzed in its face. He would be flattened, reduced to a blot of blood in the dirt between the tracks.

As he paid too much for the taxi, he steeled himself for the charge, turned, and smiled at the pale moon-face that glowed like a headlight.

For a long time after the accident, he had believed Clea would get better. Her doctors told them there was hope that she would improve over time.

They lied.

Hurting, he watched the changes reduce her. Her skin, once a lovely pink, drained and tinged to blue. The cantering of her mind—they had taken so much pleasure in the evenings together talking by the fire, entertaining each other with tales of their days and the people that mesmerized them like the characters in her films—ceased. Conversations drifted away, sabotaged by a narcotized mind. She slogged behind him now like a snail, leaving a sticky trail of regret for what was, and what would never again be.

Where before, Clea held his heart in her hands, his worshipful attendance on her after the accident had subtly altered the balance of power and thrown the weight of their lives entirely upon him. He toiled in the world, she stayed home. He brought whatever life there was to this house which would otherwise fall rank with decay as a deserted shack. Once upon a time, she could inspire a frenzy of lust with a brush of eyelash upon cheek. Now when her eyelashes brushed her cheek, he felt only relief. Would she fall asleep early? Could he, just this once, sit in his study and read the newspaper, like a normal man in a normal house?

So over time, he who swore eternal love faltered. Grated to shreds with emotion on a day when she had cried inconsolably for two solid hours, he decided to tackle the issue coldly. Like a scientist collecting data, for the past few weeks he had observed his reactions and Clea's; he graphed them, and now he had reached a conclusion.

His feelings had altered, inexorably. His perfect wife had become his gothic madwoman in the attic. Her tiny moans worked on him like screams in a horror movie, making him jump. No matter how well he kept the elements of his life separate, smiling through his days in the city, stronger by the minute in his business, every day when he came home, she shambled from the background into the foreground and choked the screen with her colossal presence.

He hated her.

However, the more he considered, the more he wanted to preserve the idea of them as they used to be. Clea must never know what the graph showed, its remorseless descent. That would break her heart. She deserved love, and he would continue to make her believe in it as a tip of the hat to their past shared happiness.

If along the way the effort had become exhausting, if, in spite of his best efforts, cracks had appeared in his facade, well, he was human. He had seen her tilt the angle of her head at the sight of the new model, for instance. He had seen her moment of uncertainty, and his pity welled at the sight.

As he pulled his keys from his pocket and opened the front door to the claustrophobic miasma of antiseptic, bleach, and sick, he promised himself he would renew his efforts to keep her happy. Later tonight, after she fell into her usual drugged stupor, he would give her a last chance. He would examine the emotional graph one last time, inspecting his heart for dishonor. He would convince himself that killing her was by far the best solution to her problem, and she would die securely in the warm bosom of their love.

Sad, things coming to this. If only he hadn't taken on the role of white knight. He was ill-suited to the position, he knew now.

Right after the accident, Clea had wanted to die. As soon as she had regained some mobility, she tried to overdose on pills, then tried to drown herself in the low laundry sink, holding her head underwater until she passed out and he had found her. She cried nonstop. She tore at her hair. She screamed at him. She hurled herself to the floor, and one time, tried to roll herself down the stairs. After that, they kept her on the first floor. When she couldn't do it herself, she begged him to help her die. Fortunately, or so he thought at the time, she hadn't done any real damage to herself. These incidents, coming during the full flush of his savior complex, made him feel protective. He had thrown all his energy into making her feel cherished so that she would never consider such a thing again.

Stupidity. Clea had been right. She foresaw the bitter ending before he did.

They could not continue like this. He hated the man she now made of him. He hated their life together. But what other life was there for her without him? He had taken the truth away from her. The lie she lived rendered her unfit to participate in these painful deliberations. As he had several times before, he pictured telling her the truth, that he didn't love her. A vision of her face hearing the news flashed before him. This repulsive image filled him with businesslike energy. He would decide what constituted a merciful future for both of them.

He cleared his throat, the better to inject false joviality. "Clea," he said. "Darling." He leaned over to kiss her lips, still soft, closing his nose against the smell of her, the dirty-hair smell the nurse had not managed to eradicate, the smell of ointments, emollients, and chemicals, with no aesthetics, no pleasures for a man with an educated nose.

★   ★   ★

The sight of Claude outside made Clea's heart pound shallow and fast. With him, came pressure. When he leaned down to kiss her, she felt afresh the wheelchair, the indignities of the day, her pain, her fears. She breathed harder, her asthmatic lungs contracting with her emotions. He floated in on a wave of fresh air, smiled, and made her wonder at his horrific tenacity. When had his love become such a burden?

He loved her so much and he so depended on her. Even in her immediate hysteria after the accident, she recognized that she had to protect Claude. Claude was squeamish in a way a woman never would be. He found earthly things squalid. He read the newspaper for its politics and sports, skipping over headlines of mayhem and crime. Everyday domestic demands puzzled him, laundry, dishes, cleaning. They didn't fit in to the picture he had of life, a kind of impressionistic bliss, removed from drudgery. Really, it was lucky, his father leaving him the shop. Perfume sugarcoated his world, keeping it sweet the way he needed it.

Unfortunately, Claude was more figurehead than business-man. The shop operated at a loss, and she did all of its business even now, figuring the accounts, writing his letters, signing paperwork in his name, covering his debts. She never publicly acknowledged his failures. In fact, she collaborated with him on his public pose as a success. She didn't mind. She felt useful in this one regard, and it did help keep Claude happy.

Soon after her injury, after recovering her spirit, she decided to stake out his arrival home from work with unwavering loyalty. She owed him that, even though many days, waiting endless minutes, often in pain, plastering a grin on her face at the sight of him while screeching inside, her daily waits for his return from work had become as much ordeal as tradition. He seemed to love the formal reception, saying once, "I feel so cherished," and another time, "You are everything to me."

Clea appreciated his devotion and knew she needed to show an equal commitment, but she wasn't foolish. They would never regain the closeness they had lost. They weren't two peas in a pod anymore. She lived in one, in an arid, harsh garden. He flourished nearby, in another universe where there was shade and moisture. She depended on him for nourishment, for things as basic as water.

She depended too much on him. That eroded everything every day. That compromised her love.

Nowadays the only acting she did was to maintain this sham of a relationship.

Awful the way things changed...

Agitated, as she always seemed to be in his presence these days, her heart continuing its erratic flip-flops, Clea could barely catch her breath to speak. "Claude?"

He nodded, but continued on his way toward the bedroom.

"I need to tell you something. I've made a decision."

"Okay," he said. His voice muffled as he went into the bathroom. He closed the door. She heard running water.

She wheeled herself away from the window, where air slipped through cracks and made her shiver, toward the fire. She ran into a plush armchair, one she used to sit in in the evenings, studying her lines and chatting with Claude. Joking, laughing, crying over a lost role, griping about her colleagues. He would sweep her up in his arms, turn on some music, and they would dance...She tried to kick it, but her foot ignored the message of her emotions. She passed by the chair consumed with frustration, settling in as close as she could to the fire without getting burned.

The nurse, an unkind, competent woman named Lucy, started toward her with a glass cup and a handful of pills. "You need to take these."

"Not now," Clea said.

"Doctor says," Lucy began.

"I don't give a damn what 'Doctor' says," Clea said. At that moment, Claude came into the room.

"What's this? Ignoring Doctor's orders?" he asked, a tease in his voice, a finger lifting a lock of hair out of her eyes.

"We need to talk," she said stubbornly, pleadingly. "Those pills knock me out. Claude, I want to talk. I can't stand the way those things make me feel."

"Doctor says she needs to take them three times a day." Sensing an ally, Lucy added, "She already put me off an hour. Plus he's been calling and she won't talk to him."

"He checks up on me. He's a diligent guy," Clea said. "I'm not sure I need that anymore. And you came home later than usual," Clea told Claude.

"I'm so sorry, honey," said Claude. "Today was amazing. I don't think I've had such a major sales day since you were..."

Something showed in her face because he stopped talking, but her thoughts rolled on: Since you were whole, intact, able. Since you were our model, the symbol of beauty for our product.

She had been replaced by Lucia, an expensive Italian model. One day the previous week, during a brief business meeting at the house, Clea had intercepted Lucia's come-hither glance at Claude. On the way out, when Lucia bent down to say good-bye to Clea, Clea had whispered, "Go after him and I'll see you dead. I have friends." She had no friends, but relied on her stereotypes of Italian culture to make her point. She had smiled when Lucia jumped back and flounced out the door without another word. The threat made her feel powerful again. How she missed that feeling.

After Lucia's brusque departure, Claude wheeled Clea into his study and took her on his lap. "You're my dream of a woman. No one can replace you," he said. Had he seen the look? Had he heard the whisper? If he knew anything, he had had the grace to ignore it.

"Tell you what," Claude said now, apparently rushing to change the subject. Any mention of her past life was tricky and she guessed he didn't want to set her off. "Take your pills like a good girl. Have a good nap. We'll talk before bed."

"But..."

He whispered in her ear. "Remember that summer night when you lit all the candles and we went out onto the deck with our champagne glasses? Hmm? Remember what we said? We will take care of each other and now I'm taking care of you, like I always do..."

His chant had the desired effect. She felt less urgent. Still, they had to talk. She didn't want to continue like this. She had made up her mind. They had had their six good years, a sweet feast of love. Now, in utter rationality, she was ready to say good-bye to Claude and salvage the clean memory of what they had shared before the present ruined it.

She wanted to tell him she could survive alone, now, even in the face of continuing deterioration. She had accepted her disability in a way he never could. In a surprising way, she welcomed the woman she had become, relishing her new self, this mature version of the silly girl she had been. The challenge had been awesome, but she had risen to it, and she was proud. He would never understand this. She didn't expect it. Maybe she didn't want it. He was no longer the man for her. Whatever time she had left, whatever quality of life, she needed to experience it without him.

Such poignant truths, but she was scared to death to tell him. She did not want to puncture the illusions that kept him going.

She opened her mouth to speak but he and Lucy were intent upon their task. A red pill made its way toward her, onto her tongue and down her throat, to be followed by a blue one, a green one, etc. She closed her mouth obediently upon each pill, swallowing, her gums shriveling from the sour flavors.

Before she passed out completely, they lifted her onto her bed. Claude left for a moment to find her hairbrush, and Lucy, ever ready to undertake the chores Claude could not face, rose to the task, gently changing Clea into a fresh knit gown.

Clea entered a new state, close to sleep but not quite there. The drugs ripped crudely through her body like tiny dynamites.

They hurt her all over in order to help her, or so "Doctor" explained.

"A broken back is cataclysmic," he had said. And so it was.

For the first several months, they had encased her in a body cast. During that enforced rigidity, she explored in excruciating detail the moment when her whole life went bad. Her anguished regrets were equal to her pain, and could not be anesthetized. They woke up with her. They sang her to sleep at night.

Why? Why had she done it?

The answer wasn't hard. She had it the instant she posed the question. Hadn't she acted a dozen roles where the outcome of the story hinged on this very same tragic character flaw?

She fell victim to hubris and ruined a beautiful happiness.

She had been such an athlete when she was young, fleet of foot, coordinated, and although her schedule eliminated many opportunities for her to maintain that toned physique and physical grace, she hung on to an athlete's most useful trait too long: physical risks did not scare her. She was fearless.

That May, the whole crew spent a week up at Strawberry Lodge, many complaining about the empty swimming pool and noise from the traffic. Others loved the area and went for hikes when they had precious time off. Claude had stayed behind in the city. Her room had yellow walls and a view of trees and a creek in back, and she called him every night to talk for an hour, missing him.

The scene on that Wednesday morning was set for Pyramid Creek. The crew hiked up single file, most still sleepy-eyed, quiet, but everyone in a fine mood in spite of the heavy equipment they were packing. This beat the studio, they all agreed. While the crew set up the camera and sound, and quickly storyboarded revised camera angles based on the stark sun and shadows, she had drunk coffee from a silver thermos, sitting on a rock, swathed in down. Because this was spring, a few hardy high-altitude flowers were struggling up. She picked a purple lupine still glittering with melted snow.

When they were ready for her, she stripped down to shorts and a T-shirt. Suddenly, through the magic of film, it was summer and the cold breeze was a hot one, and the long slanting sunlight harbored scorching heat. Her skin did not know this, however. The director decided to make the longest shot fairly wide to include them both, fortunately. The goose bumps on her arms would not show then, or later when they moved on to close-ups on her face.

She knew her lines. Her "husband" was rocky, however, so they did several takes of the violent argument that took place at the end of the trail. Evan, her costar, had smiled and thanked her for her patience. "My wife's pregnant and nervous. It's our first child. She kept me up all night last night on the phone."

Evan was strong and handsome in his hiking boots and khakis, and was also one of the least self-conscious actors she knew. He treated his looks as a joke and the adoration of the press as aberrant. She remembered thinking, someday Claude and I will have a baby, too. I will keep him awake all night and he will calm my fears.

Their argument scene took all morning, and at one point, when Evan pushed a little too hard, she ended up puncturing her shorts on a sharp boulder. She changed into another pair, and then they ate chicken sandwiches with avocado and tomato and drank lemonade for lunch. The sun rose in the sky, warming the day slightly. After lunch, they would film action to follow the argument. She would run into the creek, crying, stumbling. She would turn and shout at her husband, who would notice that, in her rage, she had gotten too close to Horsetail Falls. He would swoop down, intending to rescue her, but his sudden movement, her suspicion of his motives, and their unresolved argument would inspire her to step back even farther. Then, the script read, Evan would reach her and rescue her. They would reconcile, all the discord of the past erased in their shared recognition of this nearly fatal moment.

The camera crew set up the shot, and everyone took their positions. And the stuntwoman who was due to replace her after her first rush into the stream started throwing up.

"I can't breathe up here. It's like there's no air," she said, crying.

The director stomped over, talked with her, found her a drink of water, waited for her to recover. She threw up again. The director said she had better get down to the lodge. One of the crew offered to accompany her, and the director, by now unable to speak directly to the stuntwoman, nodded, his face purple.

As she stuffed a small bag with water and a snack bar, everyone sympathized. They agreed it was the altitude and dehydration. Once she was safely out of sight down the trail, they grumbled about the amount of wine she had consumed the night before.

The director, able to talk again, pitched a fit. He had funding problems, timeline problems. They were wimps, shits, losers. They now had a full crew and no shot, and did they have any idea the cost of this setup, this day? He was so screwed.

So she had stepped forward to save the day. A hero.

An idiot.

She ran into the creek once, twice, three times. They shot again and again. The director stroked his chin, shaded his eyes, suggested some minor adjustments in the camera angle. They shot until her legs froze up and wouldn't move. They warmed her up and shot again.

And then he announced a final take. The last take, he swore it. The light was fading. The shot looked beautiful, though. They had to get down the hill before dark. He called for action.

She ran into the creek, crying. She turned, shouting at Evan. He chased into the water after her. She stepped back, stumbled, and fell one hundred feet.

★   ★   ★

When she woke up, she had tubes in her nose and a room full of flowers. The doctors told her how lucky she was that two men on the crew were experienced climbers, and somehow managed to get her out of the pool she fell into. As mindful of her injuries as they could be under the circumstances, aware of the grave risks her battered body faced, they lashed her to a makeshift gurney and rushed her back to the lodge.

"They did everything they could do. You could have died."

She wished, then, that she had died.

Claude came and cried with her, and begged her to live, not to leave him.

When, at last, the cast came off, they had all hoped so much ... the surgeon's face had told her right away. As each instruction he made to her failed to elicit the proper action, the corners of his mouth dipped and solidified a little more. The look on Claude's face when she could not move her body from the waist down had crushed her.

Now, observant but druggily detached, she watched as Claude pulled the cover up to her chin, and kissed her cheek warmly. "Love you forever and forever," he said, as he always said.

"It's been so hard for you," she said, only the words slurred.

"Go to sleep," Claude soothed.

She saw her early past, her first high school part in *The Importance of Being Earnest.* She had flubbed her lines, but got laughs in the right places. *Arsenic and Old Lace,* off-Broadway, she played one of the elderly aunts in a wig that itched. She took her clothes off for a revival of *Hair* and sang in *Les Mis.* She ran through her lines, reinterpreting.

Claude got up and the bed moved as he rose. She awoke and opened her eyes. "Comfy?" he asked her. "I'll turn off the light."

"Lonely," she said, "don't go. I have to tell you something ..."

She realized she had forgotten what. What was it she needed to tell him, something important? She tried to apply her mind to the problem, but the problem slipped away with Claude, on tiptoes. The light went off and she returned to her dreams.

Lucy left at nine. She had a family and didn't like staying so late, but she had a stolid sense of obligation. She was a saint, unlike Claude, who closed the door behind her, sighing with pleasure at a moment's solitude.

He drank a strong whiskey with ice and poked at the fire. In a flash, like the flash of a dry ember igniting, he realized he had already made his decision, and that it was the right one.

Clea should die.

She should die knowing she was loved. The falsity of his feeling would never get strong enough to penetrate the soft cloud of her belief in him.

The decision fell over him as gently and moodily as rain. He knew it was the proper choice under the circumstances. Clea would want him to have a happy life. Her love was unselfish and pure, unlike his. If only the full picture of the situation would not cause her such emotional harm, she would concur, he was certain.

The only question left was how?

He pondered alternatives. Suicide—there was plenty of evidence that Clea had been suicidal in the past, so why shouldn't she be suicidal again? Their neighbor Mrs. Winters had helped him get Clea fixed up after she had tried to drown herself when the nurse was out to lunch. She could testify. Lucy would, too. She didn't like Clea, he suspected, but it would have to happen off her watch so that she didn't look bad. Maybe Clea stockpiled pills? He liked the peacefulness of pills. She would go quietly, kissed on the forehead by him, loved to the end. But sometimes people threw them up, didn't they? Sordid thought.

A knife? During those early scenes, right after she got out of the cast and into the chair, they had taken pains to keep knives out of her reach. Since then, they had relaxed vigilance. A large knife like one used to slice a melon? Something with a sharp tip.

Ugh. He didn't think he could stab her, not even if he put her to sleep first. The police would be very suspicious with a stabbing.

Hanging? He got out of his chair and wandered around the entire downstairs. Hanging was out. She couldn't reach anything high enough that would hold her. A doorknob? No.

He had a baseball bat, and had played in high school. He knew one fell swoop could deck her. Then, push the wheelchair down the stairs. But she didn't go upstairs anymore, everyone knew that, and those clever forensics people might be able to identify a bat indentation or something.

Okay, asphyxiation. Didn't people tie plastic bags over their heads or something when they wanted to self-asphyxiate? Clea had the ability to do that.

But it was so ugly!

Yet this idea drifted like feathers into something better. Yes, he thought, suffocating her would solve a number of problems. With her asthma, the doctor would have no trouble assuming a natural death. Her memory wouldn't be sullied by suicide, and he could grieve normally, a real widower.

She would die believing in the integrity of their love. Didn't this ending do proper justice to their incredible romance?

Excited, he decided it would. He would serve up a lovely dinner, then death. Something elegant was at work, something which would move the poets and playwrights she worshipped.

Clea awoke at eleven, a terrible time. If you had nightmares, eleven was too early to provide a useful buffer from a night of misery, and too late to promise simple sleep. Lucy was gone. She tried to maneuver herself into her chair, a daunting, if not impossible, proposition. She could not turn over at night, worrying that she might end up facedown on a pillow and unable to shift, but sometimes she could find the strength to haul herself out of bed. Moving the covers off her body, she scrutinized her lower legs, wasted-looking, and dragged herself into the chair. The effort took several minutes, in darkness, without support. She wheeled herself into the bathroom and applied the unusual blackberry-colored lipstick and blush he had brought her recently while on a business trip to France. She needed to look her best for tonight. She required feminine courage. She listened for something from the study but if Claude was in there, he was very quiet.

Primed, minutes later, she appeared in the study.

"Hi, you," Claude said.

"Hi, you, too." Somehow, he didn't notice she had put herself into her chair. He missed seeing what strength she had, and that, more than anything, had finally decided her. He saw her as weak and helpless and he seemed to love her more daily. She was his weakling patient, his darling small child, vulnerable being.

She had to put a stop to all this . . . nonsense, even if it broke his heart.

She settled near the fire. She felt tuned. Once, years ago, she had taken speed with an aspiring actor and stayed up all night, clearheaded, doped to the gills, unreal but blazing with sensation. That was how she felt now. The only uncontrollable thing was the way her heart shuddered in Claude's presence these days, never relaxed or steady, ever alert to the tiniest change in the size of his pupils, or the distance between his brows. She didn't know when that had started, but it affected every thing about every day. He came into her placid pond and stirred up a swirling maelstrom.

"Clea," he said.

Preamble to what? She didn't want to deflect herself from her own thoughts by reading something into his tone. "Um," she said. "Got any whiskey?"

"Is it okay for you to drink?"

"*Das machts nichts,*" she said, an old joke they used to share, that's irrelevant, who gives a damn no matter how serious the situation.

He poured her a minuscule whiskey.

"More."

He poured another dollop.

She picked it up and drank. "Ah, now that's a drink."

He cleared his throat raucously, something he did more often now, kind of like her old grandpa used to do. Living with her was aging him prematurely. He didn't deserve that.

An image of herself in black stockings and nothing else, Claude astride her, both of them drunk as skunks, music loud, bed rolling on castors across the floor, assaulted her. They hadn't made love properly since before the accident. When she tried to talk about it, he sloughed her off. "I love cuddling," he would say, his eyes guileless. "It's enough for me." She didn't know if he believed the kind white lies or merely wanted her to believe them.

She drank some more, letting the liquid ooze down her pipes, heating her insides. "So, you had a good day."

"Yes."

He sounded surprised. She didn't know how to get to the topic at hand. Sober and not seriously doped-up at this point, she entertained the brief delusion that he would understand and accept her decision without argument.

"These ladies from Taipei," he said. "Shit. They do spend. Coming back later in the week, too. They want something exotic. Challenging. I told them I have a new shipment coming in. You have such a nose, Clea. Any suggestions about what might arouse them?"

She wanted to say, we have enough money. You don't have to kowtow to anybody, but the words stuck in her throat. The money was hers. Naturally, he took pride in what little the shop contributed. She put excitement in her voice for his benefit. "Big money?"

"Ummm," he said, as if savoring a particularly delicious slow-melting chocolate.

The sound unaccountably brought up a moment from the first night they had shared. Confessing to a failed relationship, he had kissed her on the nose. She had wondered what the hell. Why her nose? Endearing, she had decided. A small, touching gesture that reached into her in a way a more expansive move would have pushed her away. Only later did she realize the fundamental nature of the nose in Claude's world, and only now did she see that kiss for what it was, sensorial, not sensual, as mindful as his reaching down to pet a cat.

"Claude?"

"You know what I would like," he said, reaching over to hold her hand.

"What?"

"Simplicity."

Before she could react to that mysterious sidetrack, the phone rang.

Claude picked up the phone and looked at the display. "Your doctor." He pushed the button. "Hello?"

She rolled over and pushed the button down.

"Why'd you do that?"

"Because . . . I want to talk to you. Right now."

He put the phone down, looking puzzled but patient.

"Do you remember?" Clea said, getting ready for the next line, which would tell him something was happening, and he didn't know what it was.

Did he, Mr. Claude.

He pulled the lines of his mouth up into a sort of smile. "I remember. All of it."

The full force of his words stopped the torrent of her thoughts momentarily. They both remembered the good, but how well did Claude recall the bad and the ugly? He seemed to frolic in a yellow glaze of sunshine while her days alternated between gray, the bad, and bloody red, the ugly.

Why was this so hard? "I was going to say, do you remember Lucy said the doctor was trying to call?" she said.

"Oh? Well, we can call him back tomorrow. Unless it's an emergency?"

"Not that I know of."

"Why won't you talk to him?"

She said honestly, "I get so tired of focusing on my health. I like to think I'm normal."

Sympathy flickered in his eyes. Just what she didn't need. "But... Clea. Darling. Of course."

"No, you don't understand, do you? I just saw him yesterday, and I'm sick of seeing him and talking to him and chewing over every word he says. All this attention on my body saps me. I want to be strong."

She could read it in his eyes, the patronizing flicker of pink-cheeked health as he reflected upon her afflictions and the hopelessness of her case. That's the way he saw her, a drowning kitten, helpless in a bag, scratching and biting her way all the way to the mucky bottom of the pond. Hell, sometimes she thought he actually liked her weak! He enjoyed taking the lead and having all the control...

No, stop this, she commanded. You are trying to get yourself mad enough to do this thing you have to do, and it isn't necessary, and it isn't fair. He doesn't deserve this anger. "I've been thinking about us, Claude."

"It's been so beautiful," he said, his face suffused. "And I hope you know, my feelings have never changed. In spite of everything that's happened, I love you with all my heart. You believe that, don't you, Clea?"

Oh, this was her fault. She had set herself up for this. To punctuate his statements, he leaned down for a kiss, which she gave without hesitation, leaving a slight berry stain beside his mouth. Then she remembered she hadn't brushed her teeth since the medications she had taken earlier, and how they must smell to him.

Oh, God, she wanted him gone. He made her uglier and more miserable than her circumstances ever could.

"Don't you?" he asked again.

"I do believe it," she said, "but...Claude, you must know this. You married a different woman. I'll never be the person I was again, no matter what happens to my health from here on out. And sometimes I think...you love her, not me."

"Silly!" He ruffled her hair. "I love you. Warts and all."

Another old joke, remarkably ungraceful under the circumstances, but it just pointed out how upset he was by the direction she was taking. His charm was buried behind the urgency of the moment.

Still, she plowed onward. "And your love is so strong, I'm knocked down by it. It's too big for me, the woman I am now. I can't stand up to it." Literally, she thought, her pulse stuttering. This was the closest she had come to honesty in months, and she felt the gusher ready to pour out a flood of real feelings. With effort, she restrained herself and stopped her mouth.

"You don't have to stand up alone. I'll help you. I'll be with you to the end, Clea. Now, please. Stop these dark thoughts. Have you been taking those antidepressants they prescribed? Because..."

"You've made me so happy, as happy as a man could make a woman. You're a wonderful man." Damn her traitorous emotions. She jabbed at the tears with a knuckle, continuing in her mind what she found impossible to say: "I find our relationship *draining*. You hold me up higher than I need to be held, and I pretend, God help me, wishing that I could love you the same. I can't. I'm not capable. We're no good together."

Too late. He had seen the tears. He licked them like salt, greedily. She could almost see his body puff up with purpose. "I'm here by your side, like always." He stepped in closer, placing a gentle hand on her shoulder. "Tell you what. Let's talk to your doctor tomorrow and together we'll get things straight, okay?"

"Don't do this..."

"I'm making us some dinner," he said. "You must be starving. I know I am." He squeezed her shoulder.

Leave this house, she thought.

If only the strength of her decision could communicate itself through her thoughts, but except with perfumes, where every subtlety registered, Claude was not a sensitive person.

If she had the guts to make the demand, how would he react? She knew. He would be grieved that she could make such a suggestion, then he would suggest calling the doctor sooner, to get a read on where the medicine was failing, because it had to be failing or she could never entertain such thoughts.

And then, if she could make him listen long enough to register that she meant what she said, he would refuse to leave. He couldn't imagine her living without him.

The house belonged to her. She could make him leave legally. She imagined calling the family lawyer, the scenes. Why, they might even call in psychologists, because she must be insane to think she could make it without this loyal, loving man.

And then there was the injury she would inflict on his heart . . . how could she find the words?

In their shared silence, they both remembered it all.

He plucked the empty glass out of her hand and headed out of the room. "Let me get you some water, darling, to wet down that whiskey. I don't think that was such a good idea. I've got halibut, artichoke, lemons. Sound good? Let's see what other goodies Lucy has stocked for us. Good food will get us back on track."

She watched his back go and her glass bobbling away.

In the kitchen, rendered immaculate by Lucy, Claude rinsed his mouth, and then his face all the way up to the roots of his hair. That kiss . . . but, on the whole he felt things had gone rather smoothly. He had said the right words, communicated the heartfelt commitment he felt to her, maybe for the last time. Her tears proved she was with him, entirely with him, as she should be.

He carried a tall glass of ice water in to Clea, handing it to her without a word.

Rooting around in the refrigerator, he found a few things he could use, some fresh herbs that smelled of garden parties, fresh salmon, which smelled of the sea. That would go down even better than halibut. Humming to himself, he grated some bread crumbs, mixed them with dill, rosemary, and a number of other more obscure spices she loved, and set the salmon on to broil. Ordinarily, he would grill the fish, but it was very late. He could see from the bags under her eyes Clea was tired. She would not make it much longer. He wanted this dinner to wow her. He wanted the last image on her eyes to be its beautiful color, its smell to wrap her in all the enticing spices life had to offer. He wanted the last thoughts she had, the last tastes she savored on her tongue, to be his perfect creations.

While the food cooked, he set the table in the dining room very carefully, using the ironed white cloth, the hammered silver candlesticks, the best silver, her family silver. He lined the implements up neatly beside porcelain plates and studied the results. Something missing...out in the backyard, with the help of a flashlight, he discovered a few silver-colored roses drooping on a bush, at that perfect, ripe point in their existence, redolent with the heat and lazy summer days past. He stuck his face in the bouquet and drank their scent before arranging them neatly in a clear glass vase.

"Darling, it's ready," he announced.

Clea rolled up to the table. "I'm not very hungry," she said tentatively.

He understood, oh, he did. Overcome by the emotional weight of the moment, she felt unable to carry it. Ignoring her worries, he served up the dinner along with some good gossip, calling up his most entertaining self. She ate hungrily, like someone unable to resist, eyes on him, smiling here and there at his jokes.

He felt satisfied.

She would go to bed full. She would go to bed with all her

recent, unsettling foolish notions put to rest, emotionally and psychically fulfilled.

Only one more thing to make a perfect happy ending.

She did as much as she could to prepare herself for bed without his help. She wheeled herself into the accessible shower, a concession to her disability she thought Claude would never accept but which her mother had insisted upon. She brushed her teeth ferociously, but retouched her makeup, remembering nights long ago when she never went to bed without renewing it.

Putting on her easiest nightie she waited for him to help her heave herself onto the left side of the bed.

He splayed an arm there, awaiting her head.

Hell.

Do I open the conversation, or not?

Do I allow the time to pass? Because many nights, in spite of her own obligations, the nurse stayed. Claude paid her enough to stay, stay, stay.

They were not alone so often.

The salmon balled in her stomach like sludge. The salad, made of the freshest ingredients, made her think she might need the bathroom.

She resisted. This fight she could wage. She needed to control things, her digestion, her wasting limbs. Why, lately, she had enjoyed a faint reminder of her old life, when her foot would jerk or a leg would feel tired. She knew the doctor called this "phantom," and what an apt description that was.

"Claude, are you awake?" She thought she could detect the quiet of his non-sleeping.

"Mmm," he said.

"Have you ever thought of living without me? How it would be?" Silence. "You could be free again." No response. She assumed he was listening by the expectant hush of his breath. "You don't have to worry. I would give you money." This crass reduction of her complicated feelings to words made her cringe with self-disgust. After speaking lines of grandeur and wisdom all her adult life, when it came to providing her own script, she bombed. "I don't mean it that way," she said. "That's not what I mean. I mean, we've been happy, haven't we? And now, it's time to move on. This is not about me being depressed, or you leaving some feeble woman behind. This is about us moving on, making new lives and new happinesses. Claude?"

She hated him for his silence. Rigid as a plank on the floor she awaited his reaction. Now in the pureness of a dark room, without the distraction of color and light, he could hear her clearly. He could react honestly, without defensiveness.

Nothing.

His breathing was so soft, she must have missed it, the tide rolling in and out. He was asleep.

She reached over his chest and spread a hand over it. Usually, that was enough to wake him. But nothing changed. She couldn't remember. Did he drink more than usual tonight? Yes. Well, it had been a long day.

She felt very alone. She lay in the dark with her eyes open, drowning in the bottomless well of her unhappiness. How could she put herself through another day like today, waiting to speak? Then the delicious dinner wine worked on her, and the blackness of the room deepened. She dreamed about the waterfall, the one she didn't recall in real life. She dreamed of falling.

Claude drank orange juice, unsettled. His idea of the final act had been quite different from the reality. He remembered falling asleep to a murmuring, like a bedtime story being told, words slipping over him like a refreshing breeze from the window. About four in the morning, when no one was up to hear, and nobody did anything but dream dreams bad and good, he awakened, picked up one of her pillows, placed it gently over her face, and pushed down.

How she struggled.

How she fought.

She tried to scream, and he heard cries like a mewling baby's through the feathers.

Witch.

She had never, ever, been easy.

In the morning, after he awoke on the couch in the study from the stupor that had overtaken him, he peeked in on her.

Eyes closed but without tremor.

Skin, once translucent, a blue-white opaque.

Unmoving.

The smell—actually, he had feared that the most, that there would be something putrid happening by morning. How long did it take? He thanked his lucky stars that the night was chill, and her death seemed storybook and odorless.

He could not bring himself to touch her or to get too close. He thought he sensed just the tiniest bit of deterioration. Before bed, he had noticed she smelled of the perfume, Entracte, he had had specially formulated for her as a gift years ago, an aromatic citrus-herbal mix of jasmine, cardamom, tangerine, and cedar moss. He would never again sell that perfume in his store. What a perversion that would be, to sell the smell of her death.

After the juice, he felt the need for coffee. He drank deeply.

She slept like the baby they never had, he decided. She slept peacefully, in the full knowledge of his love.

He picked up the phone. Weirdly, there was no dial tone. In fact, he heard a sound of waiting.

"Hello?" he said.

"Did you try to call me?" an amazed voice asked.

"Who is this?" he said.

"Dr. Bartholomew."

"Clea's doctor?"

"Yes. I'm out of town and..."

"You've been trying to reach us."

"Yes."

"You must have called just when I picked up the phone. Strange, it didn't ring."

"You're Clea's husband? You're Claude?"

"Yes."

"Well, I'm glad we're in touch because..."

"I'm so sorry. I don't have time to talk to you right this second," Claude said.

The word the doctor uttered sounded like the outcome of an unexpected punch.

"I need to make another call. It's urgent. Sorry."

"No—" said the doctor. But Claude hung up.

Claude called the emergency number, watched the ambulance arrive, smelled antiseptics along with the soapy clean of uniforms. "Can you save her?" he asked, watching them carry her out, confident that they couldn't.

"We'll see, sir," they said. "Now please, make way."

Standard response to a dead body, Claude realized, stepping out of their path. Don't fry the relatives with news that will change the outcome of their lives. "She doesn't look good," he noted for the record. "Please tell me she won't die!"

He watched the emergency technician figure out what to say next. They told him not to lose hope and advised him to follow them to the hospital in his car. He told them he couldn't come immediately, he was too shaken. He would come along later. The hospital will be in touch, they said kindly. Get someone else to drive you, okay?

Instead, he made toast and sliced a grapefruit. She would never come back. The one great love affair of his life was over. He had a good cry, saying good-bye to her, whispering last words of love. Oh, Clea.

★   ★   ★

He avoided making calls to relatives and family, unable to face their suffering. He didn't answer any calls until late afternoon when he felt he could muster appropriate responses. He almost didn't answer then, but Lucy had shown up, pitching a fit when he had to fire her without notice, and he wanted the distraction, so when the phone rang in the middle of her harangue, he picked up, expecting a sepulchral voice verifying Clea's death.

"Claude?"

Shock ran through him like a ragged shard of glass. "Who is this?" he asked. He waved Lucy out of the room and shut the door in her face.

The voice was weak, but undeniably hers. "It's Clea."

Speechless, he sat down in the desk chair, feet on the ground, one hand clutching the desk for support. "Clea? But . . . they took you away. I thought . . ."

"Can you come get me, please?"

Clea hung up the phone. Claude had thought she was dead. To all appearances, she had been. The doctors said she had survived a massive asthma attack. When she stopped breathing at one point, her heart had stopped, but they had somehow miraculously managed to revive her. Now that the attack had been controlled with medication, she could go on, out of danger for now. They advised her to see her own doctor as soon as he returned from his vacation, and to keep her inhaler close by in the bedside table.

She did not remember the asthma attack. When she thought back to the moment when everything stopped for her, she saw Claude's face hovering above her, then the pressure over her face, a pillow pressing down.

A nightmare?

Had she filled that consoling, longed-for peace with this— hideous manifestation? Did she create this evil being out of her resentment of Claude's pity and kindness to her?

Tubes up her nose and a needle in her arm, she told no one

about these images. Once she regained her sense of equilibrium and was breathing normally, they removed their equipment and said she could go when she felt ready. She let a couple of hours go by while she reflected. Should she revisit their past together, reinterpreting? Were his kisses obligations, his eyelid twitches, the ones she thought were his way of controlling his pity, cringes? Was the past year all lies and betrayals? Had he tried to kill her the previous night?

She was filled with disbelief, even horror, at her suspicions. Should she believe the evidence of her own senses or had her psyche become as frail as her body? She pondered telling the doctors about these dark thoughts, even imagined a conversation with the police. They might not believe her. She didn't believe herself. Should she subject herself and Claude to outside scrutiny, and perhaps misunderstanding? No.

Did Claude want her dead? The idea bounced around, bruising everything inside her. He would be happy to control the money at last. He would know the doctors would put her death down to natural causes, asthma or some other health problem.

If she had died, he would have gone on living without her. The women would flock to console him, because he would mourn her deeply. He would convince himself that he had loved her dearly, to the end, then tell himself her death was for the best. Yes, that was Claude. He saw her deteriorating. Her face, once lean, was now bloated, porcine, from the steroids. Her body, well, no need to make comparisons. They were obvious. He probably thought she hated herself as much as he must hate her.

What an eligible widower he would make, with his charm and her money.

What perfidy, these traitorous thoughts. He had been nothing but kind, and this was how she repaid him, with doubt, suspicion.

Fear assailed her, confusion.

Swallowing water, letting the cool liquid flow into her living body, hoping for cleansing, the dark moment returned.

Pillow pressing down on her face. Those eyes of his, gleaming, black as a raven's. Breath gone, agitated heart stopping... Yes. Clea's eyes squeezed shut, her mouth trembled. He would certainly try again.

Claude made quite a fuss over Clea's homecoming. Lavish flower arrangements graced every vase, and he had only the warmest, murmuring, loving things to say. He wanted a quick bite, then bed, but she nixed the idea. "I have chores."

"Leave them to Lucy," he said. But she wheeled into the kitchen and began wiping the counters.

Well, let her squander her last moments on trivia, Claude thought, stomping out of the kitchen. So be it. Ignoring the ringing telephone, he sat down with the newspaper, aware he would try to kill her again that very night, but not obsessing over the fact. Why drag things out? So the first attempt ended badly—so what? Clea was a ghost to him now. The decision had already been made; she was as good as dead. There in the study, considering his options, rather worn out from the ordeal of the past night and day, he waited for the phone to stop ringing and ordered take-out Thai for dinner. Clea loved sesame noodles.

"I've been a good wife to you, haven't I?" Clea spoke these words after dinner, gazing across a candle at him, decaf coffee untouched before her.

Actually, Claude felt miffed. Clea had eaten almost nothing. She had, in fact, been terribly nice all evening. She made things so difficult, with her capricious moods. He had a simple plan for the night. He would use her very own suicide stash of pills, oh, yes, he had found those long ago. He would crumble them into a hot bedtime drink, and she would go peacefully to sleep. No need to go through that awful struggle of the last attempt this time, or a reprieving vomit. He would prevent nasty surprises by using enough to slay a horse. Confronted with an overdose, he would admit to her serious depression, and he would not admit knowledge of the extra pills. Lucy would confirm Clea's previous suicide attempts.

"Clea, you're the most wonderful woman in the world. You always have been. You always will be," Claude said, tired of saying this sort of thing, but rallying for one more try.

She nodded. She must be satisfied with the sentiment.

Lucy had left a few hours before, with a malevolent glance in the direction of Clea's room. "She's alive. What a miracle. How we should thank God." The words held a cold affect of which he did not approve. He wondered if Lucy would regret her attitude tomorrow.

"You've had it hard, Claude," Clea now said. "You've never liked involving yourself in the running of a household, have you? I guess you were raised that way."

Oh, why did she have to get into this now, too late? Why not spend these final hours in calm realms beyond the irritating day-to-day? "No," he said firmly. "Everything about us is right." He approved of the statement, so simple, so encapsulating.

"Sure it is," she said.

In the study, post-dinner, she offered him a brandy, insisting on getting the bottle and pouring it herself, refusing his offer of help. She poured two glasses, and took one. "You used to love brandy," she said. "Remember how we danced the tango, and how drunk you were, and how I fell to the floor when you let go?"

He laughed obligingly, hating the reminder of himself at another time in another state of mind. He drank the brandy, mindful of these final statements. Would he spend the rest of his life going over this evening? He thought not, but you never knew.

"Tell me this, Claude," she said, fixing steady eyes on him.

Her insatiable needs hurtled toward him once again, too fast, and he felt suddenly shot with fear. He would be glad never to see those beady eyes open on him again. "What is it, darling?"

"Have you ever sorted one load of laundry in your life?"

He had to laugh.

What an ending to their six years of love and trial. He had expected more of her, he really had.

The funeral home had wanted to know, did she want a graveside ceremony or something more traditional? Did he wish to be remembered some other way?

She instructed them, and went all the way down to the city cemetery to pick a discreet granite gravestone, paying with a check from her own account.

On this day, the day Claude would be buried, she arrived early, wanting it all to go without a hitch. His family, the French and the American sides, wailed like people in a melodrama when they saw the casket hovering above the hole. His friends and acquaintances, mostly lovely customers, were even less restrained in their mourning.

While a priest who had never known Claude eulogized him, book in hand, Dr. Bartholomew drooped a weighty arm upon her shoulder.

"So especially sad," he whispered, "considering the circumstances."

Clea heaved an appropriate sigh, thinking about how hard it had been, crushing so many pills, mixing them in the brandy.

"I'll always feel just a little at fault," the doctor went on. "Please forgive me for asking, but I understand he left a note. Why would a man like him, in his prime, take his own life?"

She examined the doctor's face for suspicion, but saw only a disturbed sadness in it. "Apparently," she paused to choke the words with emotions she did not feel, "he felt terrible about some rather serious business losses. He had hidden so much from everyone for a long time." Handy, her acting ability. Handy, her signing all those letters for all those years. His signature on the suicide note, and his motives had not been questioned. If the police even once suspected her condition had anything to do with her husband's unfortunate death, they had generously kept it to themselves.

"I've been calling," the doctor said, looking strangely relieved, as if he, too, found the contents of the note reassuring. He put a hand to his beard and pulled. "Why didn't you call back?"

"What does it matter now?"

"Because I don't get many patients like you. Patients who survive a fall like that." He cleared his throat. "I imagined you might be our spokesperson. Yours is such a success story. That kind of injury to the back, well, there's not usually such a stunning outcome."

The priest had stopped talking. People threw flowers on the casket. Clea, admiring the pretty colors and the largesse of the splashy bouquets, barely registered his comments.

"I mean, usually patients like you die or otherwise screw up. It's not easy to adjust to such massive injury when you're so young."

"I feel myself going downhill," Clea said, sure of herself. "Do I have long to live? Am I dying?"

The doctor started. "What?" he said. "Not at all."

"Doctor, there's no room in my life for pretending anymore. I'm getting worse. There's such pain, more every day. My emotional problems are affecting me physically. Although I've been pretending to myself that I am a strong person because I've needed that to go on, in reality, I feel less physically able every day."

"You don't know?" he said, shaking his head. "You really don't know? I hoped maybe you suspected. I thought you refused my phone calls because you needed time to adjust to the thought."

Clea squelched her irritation with the man. No wonder she had avoided his calls.

"I tried calling to tell you the results of our last tests. Remember? You complained of phantom pain in your paralyzed legs."

"Yes."

"Well, although some pain is normal, yours seemed exceptional, and the fact that you described it as growing...I had my suspicions, which I didn't share, but I needed to do some more sophisticated analyses. You remember the most recent round of tests? I believe you found them rather grueling. I'm sorry about that. I guess you suffered. But the results were so astonishing... I wish I could have told you earlier. I regret your husband never knew..."

"Astonishing?"

"You're in full recovery," the doctor said flatly. "You're a textbook case of spontaneous recovery. The pain you feel in your limbs? Part of the healing process. Your limbs aren't permanently paralyzed. You were laid up for such a long time, there was some debasement in your functioning that will take a lot of physical therapy to overcome."

"But...my legs don't do what I want them to do! I can't even move them!" Clea cried.

"Now that you know you can, it will be easier, I promise. I expect great progress from here on out. I didn't want to confirm with you until I was sure. I guess it wouldn't have changed what has happened. Life's so unfair. I'm so sorry about your loss."

The doctor stepped back as two men took hold of the ropes that kept the coffin aboveground and lowered it until it hovered just above the neat dirt hole. Clea concentrated, watching as Claude descended, feeling regret, not for his death, but for the months they had both wasted. Someday, she would reminisce about the good times, she hoped, but in the meanwhile, she had to admit it: her husband's absence left her lighter. Her heart beat steady and strong, her breath came in long, refreshing draughts.

She smelled earth. Expecting something rancid at the scene of a burial, she was pleasantly surprised by a scent like one in their garden, a piquant freshness.

As the men paused, everyone stepped forward for a last good-bye before the coffin would be lowered below the surface. She tossed a silver rose at Claude, inhaling the clean, grass-perfumed air. She needed to move on, and something about the day, the clear air, its sweetness, suggested just the scent to enthrall the Asian ladies Claude had said would be coming back, her favorite, Entracte. Cheeky and green, like today, and so perfect because, although only today could she fully appreciate this, her life with Claude had been an interlude, hadn't it? Only that. She would call the shopgirl with advice as soon as she got home.

So many flowers decked his coffin, all kinds, carnations, gardenias, roses, lilies, some in fussy arrangements, many flung loose, too many scents intermixed, so untrue to Claude.

Could the doctor be right? she wondered, gazing one last time upon the mahogany box that held her husband's cold body. Could she be getting better? The idea was so big, she couldn't approach it with anything less than staggered wonder. She rolled in closer as the coffin paused, half in, half out. She looked down at her thin leg. She commanded her foot.

The kick, as slight as a twitch, left a smudge on the satiny wood. Then someone pulled her wheelchair back, but she was still watching, fascinated, as the curtain fell.

Lemons

Toward the end of February, Doris noticed that the lemon tree in the backyard was heavy with lemons.

She opened the door to the back porch and stepped out into the thicket of pampas grass, forging a trail almost to the fence line, and stood looking at it. In spite of her complete neglect, and some damage to the trunk, the tree had somehow hung on during the dry Salinas summer and cool winter. Hundreds of lemons, big, round, so ripe they were colored almost orange, scented the air around the tree, weighing down the low branches. The tree sprawled across the yard, green and disheveled, propped up against the redwood fence. In the shadows underneath, more lemons lay half-buried in the moist dirt.

Lemons were useless fruit. Fresh lemon juice with water and sugar wasn't half as good as the store-bought kind, in spite of the chemicals they added to concentrate. Who made real pies these days? She had a faint memory that her mother had made one once but she didn't have the slightest idea how to make a lemon meringue pie. And then, didn't she read somewhere you could put lemon juice in your hair and bleach it? But her hair was black streaked with gray.

She returned to her work at the computer, billing out Dr. Pelosi's medical services and stuffing the printed-out bills into the window envelopes. At two o'clock she stacked them neatly on the kitchen table, as always, and stretched out on the couch with the Mickey Spillane she was reading, her tray of cheese and crackers right beside her. The fact that she liked violent crime novels was one of the many little secrets that no one knew about her. She had switched from Agatha Christie last year, when Gene died.

At four she put the envelopes in her briefcase and pushed her arms into the blue suit jacket she always wore to go out, hunching her shoulders a little to adjust the fabric in back and buttoning the bottom two buttons. She blended in better on the street in her jacket, like any businessperson on an errand, and no one cast a second glance at her. She liked how safe that made her feel.

She locked the door and walked down the hill to the post office, because you had to get your exercise, and found her place in a short line. She let a girl with a package go in front of her. Otherwise she would get the red-haired young man who kept up a steady stream of conversation, asking her questions about her day that always made her feel a little upset. As if he were her friend! What did he care!

At the supermarket on the way home, she bought herself some Tiparillos so she could have a smoke after supper. Right before bed she washed the dishes. The yellow curtains above the sink reminded her of the lemon tree. She pulled them apart and leaned over the soapy water, peering out into the blackness. She couldn't see it, but she knew it was there, bulky against the night sky. What a shame she couldn't think of a single thing to do with all those lemons!

Like always, she slept on her side of the bed, even though

Gene had been gone a year now. He wouldn't like her spreading out too much on the bed, wanton and sloppy. Her side was big enough to hold her, and that was all the space she needed. She groaned a little settling in, and remembered it was the only sound she had made all day. At least she didn't talk to herself. She would call someone tomorrow, maybe the doctor about her stiff neck, or the technician at ComputerFix to talk about the keys sticking.

Gene had once handled such outside business for her. She had grown used to staying home, taking care of him, letting him handle all the little hassles other people represented. As he got sicker, though, he had gotten meaner, and she hadn't much wanted to deal with him, either. At the dinner table, toward the end, they had read, the business section for him and a murder mystery for her. His funeral service had been hard on her, having to socialize with relatives Gene wouldn't speak to when he was alive. It was a relief when he was finally laid in the ground and she could go home and shut the damn door on all of them.

The next day, after she finished the billing and she'd had her nap and cup of coffee, she took some paper bags out back and started picking lemons. You couldn't just let them rot on the tree. It would be a ridiculous waste. The lemons had grown so ripe they tore at the base as she plucked them, so a little skin came off. They would have to be used quickly. She picked two large sacks, but only one fit into the refrigerator, so she set one sack out front until she could figure out what to do with it.

That night, she couldn't get to sleep. Her neck and shoulders ached. Early in the morning she rolled herself out of bed and took a hot shower, letting the scalding spray loosen up the tight muscles in her shoulders. She skipped brushing her teeth and looked for a long time into the foggy mirror. Not much to see, just the same old face looking back. She could hardly believe she'd ever been young. What was the point of getting dressed?

The point was—she had forgotten the point. She shook her head, chastising herself for the interior blabberings, watching the woman in the mirror straighten up, push her chin out, and firm up her mouth, but could do nothing about something furious in her eyes.

At four o'clock, as she locked up and picked up her briefcase, she saw the old couple walking up the street, just like they always did. Ten years before, they had come to the door to introduce themselves when she and Gene were moving in, but Gene had made it plain he and Doris were not the kaffeeklatsch type. They had better things to do than sit around with geezers nattering about the weather. The couple walked downtown every day, just like she did, and sometimes she couldn't avoid passing them. Then the old woman would say "Hello there," and she would answer with a half-smile that meant she was trying to be polite but after all she was a busy woman, and continue on her way.

This particular afternoon Doris stood back in the shadows of her front porch and watched them. Where did they live, anyway? To her surprise they turned into the driveway of the house two doors farther up the hill.

That night, she found herself thinking about the old couple. She had snubbed them about a hundred times, and they still said "Hello there."

Maybe she would give them the extra sack of lemons. They would be thrilled at her friendly action, and ask her to stay for a cup of tea, and they would all have a nice chat about something or other. Visualizing herself holding a china teacup, sitting in their armchair, telling them about the lemons, made her notice something tight and hard in her throat that made it hard to swallow.

The next day it rained, and the old people didn't go for a walk as usual. Doris watched some nature shows on TV, but she couldn't stay interested. She was feeling anxious about the lemons. She could just set them out on the curb and somebody who knew what to do with them would pick them up, and she would be done with the problem. She actually hauled the sack out there, but with the rain falling on the sack she had a bad feeling no one would take the lemons after all, so she brought them right back and set them by the front door.

On Friday at four fifteen, at the post office, she looked at the smooth hands of the woman postal clerk, wondering if she would like the lemons. "Fifty-eight cents," the clerk said, and Doris stared with fascination at her face, which resolved just for an instant from the general blur, so that she could see the clerk was a soft-skinned woman of about forty, motherly somehow, with chapped lips and long dark eyelashes. As she got out the exact change, Doris lowered her eyes, feeling as though she had been intrusive to look so closely. "Have a good day," the woman clerk said, and Doris could just make out as she turned quickly away that the clerk was smiling.

Rain gave way to a gray overcast which faded into darkness by the time she finished her supper, and here they came, the old couple, walking slowly past, toward their house. She felt like running out with the sack and giving it to them, but at the same time she had begun to feel very worried about actually talking to them after all these years. What if they were pests, and started coming to her door all the time? She would have to move, which would involve moving men and having her references checked by cold-eyed bankers . . . These thoughts were very frightening, so she stayed inside, watching them turn into their driveway, watching their lights flick on at the top of the hill, bright in the dusk.

The house had grown cold but she didn't feel like making a fire just for herself. She had her smoke and finished her novel by about seven, and then there was nothing to do. Should she have a hot bath or turn on the TV? Dismayed, she looked around for some activity to grab her and involve her, but it was all so familiar, she had used it all up, seen thousands of programs, read thousands of pages . . . she stepped outside into the cold night without her jacket and pulled the door shut without locking it, picked up the sack of lemons, and sped up the hill.

No bell or buzzer, a locked screen door. She stood there, waiting, as though they must feel her presence, the loud unseemly emotion rediating from her, but they didn't come, so she rapped her knuckles against the screen. An interior light came on and before she could run away the old lady was standing there surprised as hell and a commotion erupted, with Doris holding out the heavy bag and the old man's face popping up behind the screen and the three of them saying things she was too upset to register.

Then the door swung open and she was drawn inside. She stood in their living room, which was smaller than hers and shocking, so modern and cheerful with its white walls and bright pillows. The first clear thing she noticed was the old man's hat on his bald head, a shapeless tan golf hat he usually wore outside. He was awfully tall; his head seemed to scrape the low ceiling. His wife had put on some slipper socks. She was so close, Doris had to look right into her wide blue eyes, with the wispy eyebrows raised high above them, which made Doris feel dizzy and like running away. "Sit down! Sit down!" the old lady was saying.

"I have supper in the oven and I have to get back in a minute," Doris said. Or that was what she meant to say, she wasn't sure how the words came out with the roaring in her ears.

"Well, we're . . ."

"I have a lemon tree and lots of lemons and I thought you might like some." She offered the bag.

They looked at each other. "We have a tree, too," the old man said. "Over by the side of the house. Boxes and boxes of 'em. Look!" He disappeared through a swinging door and came out a moment later with a wooden crate. Tenderly, he lifted out a lemon as large and deep-colored as her lemons and showed it to her.

The old lady had taken the paper bag and was holding it uncertainly. "But it's so nice to see you," she said. They were sitting down on the pretty pillows now, but what Doris wanted was to go. All she had to offer was the lemons and they didn't need them, and she had to get out before they started engulfing her

with pity, kindness, all sorts of sticky messy feelings. Just then the
phone rang in the kitchen, and the old man pushed through a
swinging door to answer it.

"I should have realized you had a couple of trees," Doris said.
"You can see them from the street, but I don't walk that way. I
have to go now." She pushed herself up and smoothed down her
skirt. The old man came in and both women looked at him. In
a very low and gentle voice he said to his wife, "It's your sister.
She's wondering if she can come over with a movie she just
recorded, so we can all watch it together."

"Oh, no! Thank you, but I really couldn't!" Doris said, interrupting in her panic, thinking, now they were starting; they were
trying to keep her, and she couldn't endure hours and hours with
them; it was too painful and too powerful to feel their closeness.
They looked at her, embarrassed.

"I only meant . . . you understand . . . just me and my wife and
her sister . . ." he said.

"Oh, of course!" she cried, her cheeks flaming, grinning idi-
otically, "What a great idea! You really must! And I'll be going . . ." With such tumult inside her, she could hardly keep track
of what she was saying. Her hands kept smoothing down her
clothes as if they wished they might somehow erase her horrible
gaffe. Including herself where she wasn't invited! She would
never forgive herself!

"Tell her no," the old lady said with surprising firmness to her
husband. "Maybe we could come see it tomorrow at her house.
Tell her I'm working on a project."

And now, realizing she had butted in and commanded them
to do something they didn't even want to do, Doris felt utter despair. She was hopeless. She had to get out of there quickly, and
then she would never see them again.

"You're always working on a project," the old man said.
"When could we go over tomorrow? We've got the laundry, and
that church deal in the afternoon."

"Just tell her," she said. He disappeared again, and the old lady turned back to her, saying, "We have such a small place. The TV's in the bedroom. We would all have to sit on the bed. It's real inconvenient."

The old man came back out, this time carrying a plastic sack with frozen muffins in it. "We freeze the juice in muffin tins," he said. "You should try it. It keeps forever that way. Only problem is, it's hard to pop them out. I tried a hair dryer but that melted them too fast, then after a couple years I tried setting the pan over the pilot light on the stove just for a minute or two. That worked fine."

"Then they all fell out of the pan onto the floor," his wife said.

"Got her floor spic-and-span for once. No complaints from the lady of the house that time. Ha, ha."

They didn't seem disgusted by her, or angry at her. In fact, they hardly seemed to be paying any attention to her. Timidly, she asked, "What do you do with the muffins?"

"Put one in a big glass of orange juice in the morning. Makes it taste better. Do you have a juicer?"

"No, but maybe I'll get one. That's what I'll do. I have so many lemons going to waste in my backyard. All that vitamin C. Since my husband died. Nobody to take care of the tree, and lemons lying on the ground..." A very big and long sigh flowed out of her.

"I know what we'll do with your lemons," said the old lady brightly. "We'll pass them on to Mrs. Floyd on the corner. She'd like them, wouldn't she, Gus? We'll tell her they're from..."

"Doris. I just couldn't stand seeing them go to waste."

"Sure," Gus said. "It was nice of you to drop by, Doris. We'll take good care of your lemons."

"Doris," she repeated. "Thirty-two years I was married. My husband's name was Gene. A mean man, through and through. And one day for no reason he says, 'That's it, I'm sick of that old thing, all that mess in the yard,' and he goes out there to the lemon tree and starts chopping away at the trunk."

Now she had their attention.

"I damn near took his head off," Doris said. "Luckily, they thought he fell on his axe."

Then she was free, running back to her house through a heavy shower down the slick street, past the garbage bags set out at the curb in front of each house that crouched in pools, water streaming off their deep black plastic, as thick and viscous-looking as blood. Well, her lemons wouldn't be out there. She lingered on the front porch a long time, even though she was shivering, thinking Gus sure could use a new hat. The lights at their house had gone out; the street was peaceful. She had gotten away with it, said what had to be said, and they hadn't believed her, or the police would be here by now.

At ten, Doris peeked out to the backyard through the curtains. She couldn't really see the lemon tree. But she could cry, so she did, standing at the kitchen sink, gripping the side, bawling about something or other for a long time, until she was all tired out and went to bed.

And out in the backyard, all that spring night long, the fragrance of lemons suffused the mist, and the leaves of the lemon tree trembled joyfully under the cool droplets of water.

A Grandmother's Tale

The world has gotten as hard-boiled as an egg forgotten on the stove, I'll grant you that, but magic still lurks in the corners, and sometimes even fairy tales come true. It happened to my grandmother, Jane Noonan, who told me this story of her life in Ireland long ago, and I tell it to you just as she told it to me.

He came to her on a night drifting with a fog that softened the brick of the old Irish seaside town where she grew up. Jane Kelly was her name then, plain Jane because she was tall and raw-boned, not the kind of girl the boys want to be seen with, a strong, angular woman as she grew older, with straight bangs and lank hair. Her parents were long dead; and who else would have guessed that behind that flat chest and those thin cheeks hid a mild and loving soul?

Her shoulders and back washing and ironing at the laundry paid her bills, and the years passed in good health, even if she lived a meager life centered in her rooms, filled with the green plants she tended. When she was forty, she gave up on the dream that had sustained her for so long, of a husband and children coming along for her to take care of. Gray appeared in her hair as she decided to leave her youth, and she spoke less and less. She didn't have to say it to herself, that she had nothing to live for anymore.

And it was soon after that he came to her, on a Friday night in April when she had gone to visit her sick employer, the old lady who owned the laundry, bringing flowers from the pots at home and a book or two. Her employer lived not three blocks away, so she walked down the cobbled streets of the town under the yellow lamps, carrying her packages. It was late, and she kept glancing around anxiously, because two fearsome murders of women had occurred in the town within the past year.

As she labored up the short hill with her packages, a man came toward her. He was hard to see in the fog; she had the impression of a long coat and a real man's hat, a fedora or something like that. He lifted it as he passed, and she thought, Why, I've never seen him here. Just then he said from behind her, Pardon me, and she hastened forward, as it was never a good idea to talk to strange men, but he said pardon me again in such a gentle voice that she couldn't help turning around and asking, What is it?

I'm lost, he said in a smiling self-effacing voice. I'm new in this place, and I'm looking for the Grant Hotel.

You walked right past it, Jane said. It's at the top of the hill. I'm going that way myself—and then she stopped. Thank you, ma'am, he said, very politely, and he went on, and she thought Oh well, it's only two hundred feet, am I going to trail along behind him like a ninny? You can walk with me, she said.

Under the lights of the hotel she had a good look at him. He was a short man with a bit of a potbelly, a large head furred with curly reddish hair, and a full beard of a somewhat darker shade. He would be fifty years along or even older, and an unkind person might call him bowlegged. Not a handsome man at all, but his brown eyes were kind, she could see that. Well then, many thanks for being my guide, he said, and she was about to go on

her way, when he said in a hesitating voice, I know you'll probably say no, but I can't help asking if you might come in and have
a cup of tea with me.

Through the carved wooden door he held open, a warm
breeze drifted, bringing savory dinner smells and the clinking of
dishes and the laughter of strangers. Human life seemed to have
retreated into the hotel, leaving only poor forsaken souls to wander outside. He was looking down bashfully, about to say good
night, when she answered with the same shyness, I suppose I
could spare five minutes.

In they went, up the carpeted stairs to the dining room,
where they sat down near the fireplace. A young waiter with big
ears under his clipped red hair, wearing an overstarched shirt,
brought them a heavy tray of tea and bread and jam, which was
all they asked for, the hour being late.

They began to talk, and it was as if they'd never stop. His
name was Francis Noonan and he had just moved from County
Armagh to work in the slaughterhouse down the road. His wife
had died the year before and the young ones were grown, so he
had closed his shoemaker's shop and left the sad memories.

Yet sadness was never a minute stamped on him. He had a
basic cheer which she liked very much, and a way of listening
like he was a priest with only one parishioner. No one had ever
listened so closely to her.

The warmth of the fire, the soothing tea, and his own kind
way worked on her like a spell; she felt a drowsy contentment she
hadn't felt since childhood and wondered where her nervousness
had flown.

After an hour she said good-bye, and he asked if he could
walk with her the next afternoon, to see more of the town. She
said yes and ran off to see the old lady, whom she had forgotten
about until then, dropping off her packages and leaving after five
minutes, then wandering home under the saffron lamps trying to
remember every single thing that had been said.

The next day they did walk. Sea-fog still ran along the streets, but it didn't steal her pleasure. Francis was fifty-five, he said, clearly a lonely man as she was a lonely woman. He did have a merry set of eyes, and though the rest of him reminded her a bit of a troll, she knew that she herself was no trophy, and all her old dreams came creeping up on her again.

And so they got into the habit of walking together after work. Jane bought herself a new plaid skirt and red sweater, and once he brought her flowers. It was all so old-fashioned, she knew, laughable to the young people who hung about the pier, a joke to the girls at the laundry. Jane and her troll! Jane in love!

Real life and real love didn't mix well, even then. The world was threatened then, as it is now, with war and poverty and hate and crime. Jane had believed that the stupid innocence she felt then could never survive. Yet it did survive; it flourished like a palm in the tropics.

Love it was, and she was sure Francis felt the same. She felt it in the touch of his hands on her and the cast of his face, and she herself was helpless to hide it. He was in love with her, and she with him, and damn the rest of them. In another month, he asked her to marry him.

Then they had a long serious talk. They were both poor, and he had no house to offer her; but they decided to rent a flat together and to try to save here and there for a house someday. Jane didn't care; the miracle was Francis, patient, peaceful, affectionate Francis. She felt womanly and alive. God had brought him to her!

They married and set up housekeeping. She cooked for Francis, washed his clothes, and tended to the place after she finished each day at the laundry. Francis brought home nice cuts from the slaughterhouse, made the fires, and fixed what went wrong. In the evenings they did little enough, sat by the fire and read, most likely. Most surprising was their lovemaking, when Francis turned out to be as passionate as he was hardworking.

Then one day, the last and most far-fetched of all her dreams came true when the doctor told Jane she was pregnant. He said she was old for a first baby but he thought it would be all right. And that night, what joy there was in the household!

So this went on for four or five months and everything was perfect. Francis had come to her on a night of fog and mist and brought all her life to her.

But as the baby grew inside her, she didn't sleep as heartily and had to get up in the night. And one night, she saw that Francis wasn't in bed with her.

Strange! He was nowhere in the apartment, nor was he right outside. She sat in the armchair shivering for a long time, until soon before dawn she smelled his pipe tobacco and in he came, looking very tired but at least not reeking of drink. She demanded to know where he'd been and he said many nights he couldn't sleep and went out walking, that it was an old habit, and she wasn't to worry, he hoped he had earned her trust. But she felt he was lying. The more questions she asked, the less he would say.

A worm began to burrow deep in her heart.

The next time it happened she pretended to be asleep. He was gone most of the night, and she thought to herself, he has another woman, dreams don't come true, I am a stupid fool, and like thoughts. She passed the night in a torture of doubt and worry, but when he came home all she showed him were her closed eyes and even breath.

The next day at the laundry they were all talking about it—about Alice McClary, who was stumbling home late the night before from a waterfront bar on Maiden Lane, only four blocks away, when she was brutally set upon, her throat cut and left in a doorway with no one hearing a thing—oh, it was awful, one of the girls at the laundry knew her sister. The police were always elsewhere, why couldn't they catch him and stop him, why do women always have to live in fear of men?

Jane listened with a such a chalky face that someone made her lie down on the leather couch in the owner's office.

She hardly spoke to Francis that night, and he might as well have saved himself the trouble of asking what was the matter. She turned her face away from him and brooded. And that night and every night after, she slept lightly, waiting.

Sure enough, a few nights after, he rose noiselessly from the bed and tiptoed out, carrying his shoes. She heard the click as the outer door closed and she, too, got up swiftly. Her coat hung by the door. In its pocket she put the largest knife from the kitchen. She was frightened but determined. She had to know, for the sake of the baby that was coming.

Francis stayed well ahead, walking with quick, preoccupied steps. The mists were moving in from the water and he was hard to keep in view. He went down a side road to the water, to a row of decrepit warehouses. While she peeked from around the corner, he drew out a key and went inside a boarded-up garage.

After five minutes he hadn't come out and curiosity overcame her. As quietly as she could, she went to the dirty window and peeked in. She saw a shape standing at a sort of table and heard muffled pounding sounds. And she felt quite certain—this was his own slaughterhouse, his lair, where he prepared to go out seeking his victims—the horror of it left her slumping against the wall, breathless, her eyes closed.

Then she smelled something familiar, a hand closed on her wrist, and she opened her eyes to see a masked face and the other hand with the knife raised high—

No time to scream—she took hold of the arm that held the knife and struggled bitterly in awful gasping silence. She thought, The baby! The baby! and she managed to knock the knife from his hand, but he had a firm hold on her coat as he scrabbled on the pavement for the knife, grunting—

But now she remembered her own knife and with her free right hand she drew it out and stabbed him in the back, leaving the knife which had gone in hard and clean. He fell to the pavement, groaning, and the life flowed out of him in gouts of blood.

Jane dropped to her knees beside him, moaning Francis, oh Francis. It seemed to her that she should pick up his knife at her feet and kill her own self in her misery—

The door to the garage opened and Francis looked out. When he saw her moaning beside the dead man, his jaw dropped and he ran out and picked her up, big as she was, and carried her inside and laid her trembling body down on the ground. Shouts and the pounding of feet sounded outside.

While he stroked her forehead and held water to her lips, she looked around the bright room in wonder. A workbench, tools lying on it, and shelves and shelves of shoes! Boots and ladies' shoes and little white leather baby shoes! And she looked at Francis, who wore a leather apron—he pointed at the rows of shoes on the walls, and he said, A little extra money for the baby.

Oh, it was one colossal whale of a shock, killing a murderer and becoming a heroine and finding her husband was a cobbler in the night just like an elf in a fairy tale—but she didn't lose the baby, who went full term and went to America and lived to be ninety—my own mother, and I believe every word!

And what, you may well ask, was the smell she smelled just as the malignant hand closed on her wrist?

Why starch, a smell she knew well from the laundry, the starched white shirt of the big-eared hotel waiter—a monster she sent where he deserved to go!

Permissions

"The Long Walk"—initially published in *Ellery Queen's Mystery Magazine,* June 1995; also appeared on FatBrain.com, 1999

"Success Without College"—initially published in *Ellery Queen's Mystery Magazine,* December 1998; also appeared on FatBrain.com, 1999

"Dead Money"—initially published in *Ellery Queen's Mystery Magazine,* September/October 1996; also appeared on FatBrain.com as "Soft Haze," 1999

"His Master's Hand"—initially appeared on FatBrain.com, 1999

"Gertrude Stein Solves a Mystery"—originally appeared on FatBrain.com, 1999

"The Furnace Man"—initially published in *Ellery Queen's Mystery Magazine,* May 1997; also appeared on FatBrain.com, 1999

"Chocolate Milkshake"—originally appeared on FatBrain.com, 1999

"Juggernaut"—initially published in *Women Before the Bench* anthology, ed. Carolyn Wheat, Berkley 2001

"Sandstorm"—originally appeared on FatBrain.com, 1999

"Lemons"—initially published in *Ellery Queen's Mystery Magazine,* July 1996; also appeared on FatBrain.com, 1999

"A Grandmother's Tale"—originally appeared on FatBrain.com